THE DARKEST MEMORIES

ALYSE N. STEVES

Alyse N. Steves

Paperback ISBN-13: 978-0-9979214-2-7
eBook ISBN-13: 978-0-9979214-5-8

ALSO BY ALYSE N. STEVES

Child of Humanity (2016)
Savannah the Kind (2020)

Alyse N. Steves

ACKNOWLEDGMENTS

This book would not have been possible without the help of:

Starr Baumann of Quiethouse Editing, who copyedited and proofread this manuscript.

Salt and Sage Books, whose editors performed sensitivity reads and developmental edits.

Faera Lane, who designed *The Darkest Memories'* cover.

The Penny Dreadfuls Writers Group (J'nae Rae Spano, Dawn Lyons, Steve Rodgers, Kevin Kilpatrick, Randal Doering, Kelly Flowers, Byron Earhart, Mark Barsotti, and Malini Iyer), whose members spent twenty-five months reading and providing feedback on this manuscript.

My wonderful beta reader, Stephanie Jones, who was the first to see this manuscript and provided invaluable feedback.

My partner, Debora Cartagena, who sparked the idea for this novel.

Alyse N. Steves

CONTENT WARNING

The Darkest Memories is a superhero serial killer thriller intended for mature audiences. This story contains content that might be unpleasant for some readers, including violence, blood, death, brief descriptions of physical child abuse, and mental health topics.

Alyse N. Steves

THE DARKEST MEMORIES

Alyse N. Steves

PROLOGUE

Most people arrive in the world in a squalling bundle, protective arms cradling them as they take life in for the first time with wide innocent eyes.

Not me.

Gray skies threatened a rare rain as dark, choppy waves crashed against the shore, hissing as they retreated back into a blue-gray abyss. A policewoman squinted against the harsh, whipping wind, stray strands of dark hair escaping a once-neat ponytail to lash her face. Frustrated, she futilely swiped at the wild strands pricking her eyes before resting her hands on her hips, sighing.

"Nick?" the woman asked, the two-way radio strapped to her dark-blue-clad chest beeping as she mashed a button on the side. "What exactly did the caller say?"

The radio crackled as a masculine voice answered. "What's the matter, Josie? I thought you of all people wouldn't mind tromping through the sand."

"Stop eavesdropping on my phone calls with my mother," the police officer muttered. "And I do not tromp through the sand. I carry my board from the parking lot to the water. I don't go hiking with it."

The officer cast a glance at the storm-tossed ocean and grimaced. There'd be no surfing today, not in those choleric waters. She resisted the urge to shiver, the biting wind finding purchase through her uniform now that she'd stopped moving.

"Someone's testy," Nick's staticky voice mocked.

"My shift ended fifteen minutes ago," the woman said. "Not even the seagulls are out in this."

"The caller said there's magic on the beach," Nick said.

The officer frowned at his barely suppressed chuckle. "Magic on the beach," she muttered, eyes scanning a gray horizon. "What does that mean? Am I looking for a parahuman? A traveling magician? There is absolutely nothing out here."

"That's all I've got," Nick replied. "There's magic on the beach."

"Exactly how slurred were the caller's words?"

This time, Nick couldn't contain his laughter.

The officer sighed, searching the beach for signs of life. To the left, waves crashed and hissed, a dark, murky sea nearly blending into the gray horizon. To the right, sand sloped upward into patchy, rugged shrubs eking out an existence in an environment where any consistent water supply was tainted by brine. Before her, sea cliffs rose high in the distance, veined after millennia of slow erosion. Behind her, a turquoise lifeguards' tower sat abandoned, a red flag flapping in the wind. She stood alone on the beach, the rhythmic crash of waves her only company.

"I'm at the location, but there's no one here," she repeated.

Her eyes drifted to the churning Pacific once more, and a twinge of sadness pulled at her.

"Did the divers find that girl?" she asked, already knowing the answer.

"Girl's dead," Nick said, response blunt after years of compartmentalizing life's worst moments. "With the way the currents are moving, they won't find her; she's probably miles out to sea by now. Damnedest thing though—they said the car's in pieces at the bottom of a *crater*. You ever hear of anything like that?"

"No," the officer said, sighing as she gazed forlornly at the unforgiving waves. "The poor parents."

"The mom's not taking it well from what I heard," Nick said. "Locked herself in the girl's room and won't come out."

"Damn," the policewoman sighed. It was always the parents who broke her heart, clinging to a false hope she knew they'd have to shatter, bringing their whole world down with it.

"Go ahead and call it," Nick said. "No use in chasing a prank call."

"Yeah," she said absentmindedly. Shaking her head, she turned away from the seething waves. She frowned as something brushed her shin with a gentle tap, almost imperceptible. Brows furrowed, she glanced down, then started at the sight of a tiny smooth pebble hovering just above the ground. She crouched down, eyeing the small floating rock with interest.

Whump!

She jerked as the ground rumbled, the pebble plummeting to the ground as if thrown. She waited, breath held. She gasped as it levitated again, rising a few inches before hovering in place. The officer raised her eyes, scanning the beach until she saw a larger rock hovering over the shrubs, then another just past it, yet another in the distance.

Whump!

The ground rumbled as the rocks came crashing down in unison. She waited patiently, her lips almost tugging into a grin when the rocks lifted and hovered yet again.

"Hey, Nick?" she said into the radio. She watched out of the corner of her eye as loose strands of hair rose, but it wasn't the wind that teased them now. "I might have something."

"Yeah?" Nick asked.

"Give me a minute," the officer said, rising. She regarded the bushes and the increasing number of rocks rising within them. It was almost as if they were ringing something . . .

"Hello?" she called. "SDPD. Is everything okay?"

Whump!

The rocks crashed to the ground once more. She waited, and sure enough, they rose again.

"What've you got, Jo?" Nick asked.

"Parahuman, I think," Jo said, slowly inching toward the bushes.

Whump!

"Shit," Nick muttered. "Leave it alone, Jo. I'll call the Agency. They'll send a containment team."

Jo rolled her eyes. "Don't bother them yet. He hasn't done anything."

"You need backup?"

"Calm down," Jo said. "It's probably just a kid fooling around."

"What kind of parahuman?" Nick asked.

Jo noted the hint of nervousness in his voice.

Whump!

She glanced at a rock to her right as it floated to hip-height.

"Telekinetic, I think," she said. "Hello? If you can hear me, please respond."

"*Shit,*" Nick hissed. "No. Jo, *no.* Do not fuck with a telekinetic. You know what happened in Cincinnati."

"Cincinnati was twenty-five years ago, and those officers were idiots," Jo muttered. She paused as she pressed into the bushes. Her hand brushed her weapon, and she unclasped the holster.

Whump!

Slowly, she pulled her gun from its holster. A breath passed, and resolution in place, she ejected the magazine and tossed both pieces away.

"Hello?" she called. "Respond if you can hear me. I'm here to help."

Whump!

"I'm unarmed." The silence made the hair on the back of her neck stand on end.

"Give me an update, Jo," Nick said, voice tense.

"I don't see—"

She gasped at the sight of a sneaker peeking out from under a bush, a damp, jean-clad leg disappearing behind the foliage. Breathless, she pressed forward, heart pounding as the greenery gave way to a supine figure on the ground.

"Nick, I need an ambulance," Jo said, dropping to the ground and pressing her fingers into the blonde girl's neck. She sighed in relief as the girl groaned at her touch. Her eyes fluttered but didn't open.

"I'm sending the Agency," Nick said.

"Dammit, Nick! Get me an ambulance! I've got a possible assault victim here!" Jo snapped. "Miss? Miss, can you hear me?"

Jo gasped as the girl levitated in time with the rocks around her, her lips parted and eyes wide as the girl and the rocks hovered, immobile. Jo cried out, leaping forward to catch the falling girl's head before it could hit the ground.

Whump!

"Nick, I've got a Caucasian female, blonde, early twenties, with multiple scrapes and bruises. What's the ETA on that ambulance?"

"I've got one a few minutes out."

"Hey," Jo said, holding the girl in her lap. "Hey, open your eyes. Can you look at me?"

The girl's eyes rolled, lids fluttering, but didn't open.

"Possible head trauma," Jo said into the radio. "I think she's been in the water. She's all w—"

The girl rose again, rocks levitating around them, and Jo threw her arms around her.

"Stop!" Jo pleaded. "Stop! You're hurting yourself!"

"Jo, what's going on?"

"I think she's trying to get up."

She pulled the damp girl to her chest and winced as she collapsed into her with force.

Whump!

"*Shh*," Jo soothed. "Stop. I've got you. You're okay. I've got you."

The girl's eyes rolled, whites showing, but again, they didn't open. The rocks began rising again, and Jo held the girl to her.

"It's okay," she said, brushing the girl's sandy, gnarled hair as she rocked her, willing her to be still.

The girl moaned, and Jo relaxed as she eased into her lap.

"Good," Jo said, sighing in relief. She stroked the girl's hair as the sound of sirens rang in the distance. The girl's eyes were closed now. Goosebumps rose on Jo's arms as her face slowly became slack, head slumping in her lap.

"Hey," Jo said, nudging the girl.

Nothing.

"No. No, no, no," Jo begged, pulse quickening. "Stay with me!"

Sirens screamed in the distance, but the girl remained still. Around them, the rocks sat, silent.

CHAPTER 1

Telepathy is a funny thing. At least, *my* telepathy is a funny thing. Some days, the world around me is nothing more than a din, a confusing cornucopia of thoughts that leaves individuals indistinguishable from one another. Some days, I don't hear anything at all. Then, there are the days where one thought stands out, resonating high above all the other confusing strings of cognitions and flashes of images that assault my mind. It works better on people I know—their magnetic pull, as it were, drawing me in. Sometimes, I can control it. Most of the time, it just does as it pleases. Today was the latter.

How kind of it to have chosen the day I faced a gunman.

I crouched on my hands and knees on a once-white linoleum floor, stained a dingy gray from years of foot traffic. I tried not to think about what my hands touched as sweat from my clammy palms mixed with . . . something.

There were more pressing matters to worry about.

I peered out at a man holding a gun. A display of potato chips and sugary snacks served as my untenable refuge. He hadn't seen me yet, his eyes—obscured from view by what could only be described as typical robbery attire: dark sunglasses and a nondescript black hat—were fixed on a gas station employee who backed against shelves lined with cigarette packs, hands up and trembling.

My palms practically dripped as I slipped back behind the display. Why did my palms always have to sweat? It didn't help that the floor was *really* sticky, and I was convinced the armed man at the counter could hear my heart assaulting my rib cage. It beat against my chest, forcing blood into my ears, which rang with an unbearable, high-pitched tinnitus. Even after five years, I still felt a cold shock when facing a bad guy.

Bad guy. Apparently, my vocabulary hadn't evolved much over the past five years either. My university classes called them criminals, felons, offenders, culprits—all the textbook words I should have known by now if I had any hope of passing my finals.

Why was I thinking about finals?

I steeled myself. I had to quiet my mind. I had to *focus*—forget about what was likely spilled soda on the floor. Why did this always happen? I was certain none of the other parahumans, the ones who served as highly trained, *competent* federal agents, had this problem.

Actually, I knew for sure they didn't have my problems.

I was a little different from the others.

I sneaked another peek from behind a bag of peach rings. The *criminal* was becoming more aggressive now. He waved his gun at the ashen gas station employee. The man with the gun wanted something—it was indistinguishable over the hum of refrigerators and my ringing ears. If I had to guess, it was the usual: the gun-wielding man wanted access to a safe or something, but the employee didn't know the password or combination. Or it was a dispute over payment. Gas prices in California were ridiculous.

Either way, I sensed the shelves were about to become decorated with more than just cigarettes.

Behind me, a breath expelled against my neck, hot and unmistakable. A chill raced down my spine. Craning my head to find the warm body behind me, I was surprised to find my haven empty. It was just me, the snacks, and the unsanitary linoleum.

Unnerved, I turned back to the gunman.

He was gone. I sat at a kitchen table, an older woman looking down at me. She looked kind, her warm brown eyes wrinkling deeply at their already lined edges as she smiled lovingly at me.

I smelled pancakes.

Hadley . . .

The sound of sizzling bacon caught my attention. I turned my head in the stove's direction, an old white appliance nestled among a sea of pastel-yellow cabinets and bubblegum-pink countertops. The delectable aroma of smoke and grease told me I'd get my bacon well-done today, and my mouth watered in anticipation.

Wait.

Where the hell had the gunman gone?

I caught my reflection in the kitchen window and lurched in my chair. When I had woken up this morning, I was a twenty-six-year-old woman. At the moment, a little boy clad in checkered pajamas stared back at me.

Shit . . . This wasn't real. Well, it was a long time ago and to someone else.

Like I said, telepathy was weird.

Hadley . . .

A hand grasped my shoulder. Startled, I swatted at the sensation but found nothing. The woman—Grammy, I called her Grammy—turned back to the stove, the bacon calling her attention.

Wait, no! That wasn't my Grammy. I didn't have a Grammy.

The room spun as my brain fought to keep me rooted in a situation that made sense. The smell of bacon became overwhelming.

It was okay if I stayed for breakfast, right?

"Hadley, get your ass out of there!"

I jumped, and suddenly, reality crumbled around me. Vertigo gripped me as my telepathic link to the other person was severed. The sensation of falling overtook me. And yet, a chair remained firmly beneath me as I found myself behind the one-way glass of the Agency for Parahuman Affairs' somber observation room. Nails digging into the armrests, I gripped my chair tightly, literally clinging to reality.

Glancing at the monitors in front of me, I blinked against the harsh light of the screens. Dim overhead lights cast everything outside of the monitors and the window before me in long shadows. The hum of equipment droned in the background. If I hadn't been able to see into the interrogation room in front of me, I might have felt claustrophobic in the small stark space.

On the other side of the glass, three men sat uncomfortably around a table, too-bright fluorescent lights making their features appear harsh and washed-out. An older man with a smooth, shaved head sat with his arms crossed, a distinctly pissed off yet anxious vibe emanating from him.

He was a stranger, though my intimate peek inside his mind revealed more about him than I ever cared to know. The two men opposite him could only be law enforcement based on their attire. From their haircuts, polished navy suits, and perfectly knotted neckties, at first glance, the only differences between Special Agents Tom Hartman and Glenn Rowlins might be Glenn's dark skin and sunglasses. The glasses likely appeared painfully cliché to anyone who didn't know their true purpose.

My nontelepathic colleagues also emitted a vibe that made me shift uncomfortably in my seat, yet the surrounding atmosphere was tinged with defeat as well.

"Jesus, Hadley," a woman's voice—Special Agent Brittany Whittaker, I remembered—said behind me. "It's been half an hour! I thought I was going to have to get Anna in here to get you back."

Glancing back, I noted her crossed arms. She was cast in shadows, her normally pin-straight blonde hair tousled from running her hands through it. Her blue eyes appeared harsh with a mix of concern, exasperation, and exhaustion, the light reflecting off the computer screens only amplifying her severe look.

"Sorry," I mumbled, still grappling with the disorientation resulting from my telepathic connection to the suspect being severed. It didn't help that we were doing this in the middle of the night.

And for the love of all things, why could I still smell bacon and pancakes?

"You got anything? This asshole's about to walk."

Squirming uncomfortably, I turned my frazzled attention to the file in my lap. A few sheets of paper had dropped to the floor during my time lost in the ether of our suspected criminal's memories. I stared at the top sheet, which outlined James Noack of Santee's impressive list of priors. Gang life had treated him well apparently.

Brooding in silence, Jimmy sat on the other side of the glass. One monitor revealed a close-up of his face, courtesy of a camera in the far corner of the interrogation room. The camera's pulsing red light indicated it was recording, though I doubted the realization would loosen Jimmy's lips. Suspected of either planning a hate crime against Mercy Rehab, the go-to rehabilitation center for parahumans struggling with their abilities in San Diego, or having knowledge of the intended crime, Jimmy had already expressed—quiet loudly—that he wouldn't be snitching on anyone tonight. Hence Counterterrorism's presence at this hour. The FBI tipped off the Agency, since it involved a potential hate crime against parahumans, and both the FBI and Homeland Security were waiting for an update to coordinate a response.

My ass was on the line. I absolutely could not shit the bed on this one.

I needed to go back in.

Too bad I couldn't remember what I was after. There might have been mention of a chat room and the Sons of Gaia, who sounded sweet but placed a bullseye on anyone they deemed to have "impure, unnatural genes." To put it simply, almost everyone made their shit list, and historically, they weren't afraid to air their grievances violently. I flipped through Jimmy's list of priors, but he might as well have been in every gang or hate group in Southern California, as if he had tasted almost everything on the gangster sampler plate.

I couldn't focus. My head throbbed. God, how I hated it when I ended up too deep in a stranger's mind. My brain had a bad habit of weaving me into the narrative, a process that was hardly flawless and might be comparable to an acid trip, much like what I just experienced. It was once explained to me as my mind trying to "rationalize an irrational experience," but nothing was rational about it, and the encounter usually left me with the desire to scrub myself clean with steel wool.

Telepathy was weird.

"Hadley?" Brittany asked, her voice a mixture of concern and impatience.

Dammit, I was all over the place! I didn't have the focus to go digging through this guy's brain again tonight, but I had to give her something. Letting down three federal agencies was not an option.

"You know that gas station robbery from a few weeks back? The one off Brant and Washington?"

"That's the guy?" Brittany asked incredulously, tipping her head toward the former gunman on the other side of the glass.

"I'd show him the surveillance images and see if it catches him off guard," I responded. I never made promises based on telepathy.

Brittany turned toward the door.

"Hey," I said before she could disappear. She craned her head toward me, eyebrows raised. I licked my lips as my mouth grew dry.

"If he still won't talk, they might be able to disarm him with his grandmother. Pretty sure she raised him."

My stomach twisted as her eyes flashed in understanding, and then I stared at empty space, the door hanging ajar. A high-pitched whistle faded as Brittany's inhumanly quick speed carried her away. Sitting back in the chair, the empty room pressed in on me. Using people's deep, personal thoughts against them left a foul taste in my mouth, but I had an obligation to do my job. Besides, the guy really was an asshole. A gang sign on the back of his neck was clearly visible, though I couldn't make out which group it was for. Not to mention the bigoted banter rattling around his brain.

At least, that's what I told myself as a knock on the interrogation room's door caught Tom and Glenn's attention. Tom stood, a wave of triumph emanating from him as he cast a glance at the interrogation room's dark glass. Brittany's blonde hair was visible on the other side of the door as he took a folder from her before returning to his seat.

I chewed my lip. It wasn't the information they wanted, but maybe they could use it to succeed where I failed.

I heard Brittany before I saw her, a sharp whistle signaling her swift return.

"You were right about the grandmother," Brittany said, closing the door behind her. "Court records show she was granted full custody when he was six."

I chewed my lip with greater enthusiasm but said nothing, focusing instead on the interrogation room. This guy *couldn't* get away because of me.

The former armed assailant glanced irritably at the door as Tom focused on the folder.

"When can I leave?" the surly interrogee asked, his crossed arms tightening across his chest. Jimmy Noack's back was to me, but his neck grew progressively redder as Tom made a point to slowly flip through the file. The camera caught Jimmy's expression, up-close and personal, as his scowl deepened. The camera inside the observation room caught mine, and I cringed. How wonderful that my incompetence would be catalogued as evidence . . .

Lowering his sunglasses, Glenn looked past the manila envelope, his otherworldly vision revealing the documents within. He finished reading before Tom, fighting a grin. Jimmy didn't notice.

To anyone who didn't know Counterterrorism's dynamic interrogating duo, Tom and Glenn's professional facade never dropped, but I had worked behind this pane of glass for years, and I could read their minute changes in expression as easily as I could read their minds.

My heart beat harder as Tom spread enlarged, grainy photos across the table. Images of a masked gunman and a terrified attendant were unmistakable.

Here we go . . . I thought as a chill spread across the room. The former gunman attempted to maintain composure, but his back straightened conspicuously. The camera caught a flicker of fear in his eyes. A trap was being laid, and he knew it.

"I understand your grandmother has some medical bills," Glenn said slowly. His eyes met Jimmy's—at least, they would have if not for his glasses. I felt a shot of panic run through Jimmy Noack as if it were my own. I imagined a deer might feel the same just after the crack of a rifle. My head swam for a moment. I blinked, trying to steady the room.

A feeble old woman, her hands curled in her lap, smiled at me. She had the same kind eyes as the woman from the distinctly 1950s-style kitchen.

I cringed inwardly. My job would be much easier if I could only see the criminal memories.

"Whittaker! Gordon!" a male voice—Tom's—called for Brittany and me, respectively, ripping me from the man's memories.

I looked up in time to see Jimmy's oversized fist sailing toward Tom. It passed through Tom's torso. Jimmy's eyes widened as his momentum carried the rest of his hulking body through Tom's now-transparent form. Jimmy crumpled under his own weight on the other side of Tom, but he wasn't going to stay down.

I leaped from my chair, knocking it over. Telekinetically reaching out, I grabbed hold of the belligerent man beyond the glass. By the time Brittany burst through the interrogation room door, Jimmy was subdued, dangling upside down from his ankles. Judging from the whites of his eyes, he never suspected a telekinetic was on the other side of the glass. Why would he? It's not like we were common.

"Huh," Brittany said, nodding in my direction in acknowledgment.

Beads of sweat forming on my brow, I tried to take satisfaction in a job well done as I lowered the enraged criminal to the ground. He flailed, and the effort it took to keep from unceremoniously dropping him was undoubtedly going to give me a headache. Well, a bigger headache.

"Freaks!" the man spat. "You're all goddamned abominations!"

17

Brittany fastened handcuffs around his wrists in a blink. Tom and Glenn dragged him from the room as he spewed profanity that would have made his grandmother blush.

Then, the drama was over. Brittany nodded in my direction as she closed the interrogation room door behind her. We were done, at least for the night. I stood there awkwardly for a moment, adrenaline slowly draining from my body.

Between the robbery and assaulting a federal agent, Jimmy wouldn't be released any time soon. He'd most likely be interviewed again in the morning after a long night in a cell, though I doubted he'd be any more cooperative after a night on a thin lumpy mattress. Maybe he'd be flustered enough to slip up, and the Agency and the FBI would get the information they needed?

I released my breath, the tension in my shoulders relaxing. I hadn't ruined our shot.

I wandered out of the observation room and down the still, quiet hall leading to a stairwell. On my way out, I passed a corral of cubicles. A dark sea of monitors, save for a handful of glowing screens scattered around the room, populated Counterterrorism's space. Brittany, Tom, and Glenn would likely work late, digging up more information to use against Jimmy, assuming he cooled off enough for round number two in the morning.

My desk, devoid of the stacks of papers and office supplies that cluttered the others, sat neglected in a distant corner. Desks were meant for field agents, not girls who read minds from the safety of an observation room.

I didn't pass anyone as I left. Pushing the stairwell door open, I descended the numerous stairs. Elevators weren't my thing.

Shoving my sweaty hands in my pockets, I kept my head down as I walked out the front door of the Agency's elegant seventeen-story fortress on the water. I descended the concrete stairs, the smell of salt and brine greeting me. Sprinklers had just gone off, and the scent of petrichor intermixed with the smell of the sea and the water park down the street. The smell of chlorine still lingered from the public park, though the fountains cut off after sunset. I would always associate the strange fusion of scents with the Agency.

Spotlights illuminated the front of the building, a hulking structure of enormous dark glass windows and polished steel. The glass caught the light, making the structure swell with iridescent importance. As I turned down the sidewalk, flags snapped in the wind: American, the State of California, and the Agency, all billowing high and proud. They, too, were lit up, a beacon to anyone within their line of sight.

Nothing about the Agency was subtle. Even the blindfolded could peg the building as a federal agency.

I walked down a sidewalk lined with palm trees. White streetlights, sets of two spiraling around each other in an artistic display, cast long shadows. Few people passed me, and those who did focused on the waterfront with its display of impressive boats and the occasional cruise ship. A handful of cars rushed by. No one so much as glanced my way.

When I first started the federal agent gig with its infrequent acts of bravery—from behind glass, of course—it had seemed so strange to walk outside the Agency's grand building and see the world continue apathetically around me. No one cheered. No one noticed my heart still raced, adrenaline from taking down a bad guy just starting to clear my system. The average person—the people I protected—really didn't give a damn who I was. I'd received a handful of curious glances over the years, but nothing that would inflate my ego. Granted, I wasn't supposed to be flaunting my association with the Agency. It was for my safety, they said, since I was a little . . . peculiar.

I didn't work for the Agency for the recognition though. I didn't expect people to rush up to me and beg for my autograph or ask to take a picture with me like they did with the city of San Diego's superheroes. It was selfish, but for me, being a federal agent wasn't even about protecting people. I mean, it was, and I liked making a difference, but I wasn't deluded enough to think it was the real reason I did it.

I just wanted a purpose. People didn't need to acknowledge me to have that.

Right now, I did need to study. I would have preferred settling my mind with music, but I dutifully put my earbuds in, a recording of Dr. Griffin's lecture on victims' rights filling my ears instead. How I could take only one class a semester and *still* fall behind was an art.

Well, maybe not. Most people majoring in criminal justice didn't work for the Agency for Parahuman Affairs. They weren't required to read criminals' minds, day or night. That didn't include the brutal physical training regime, among other things. As it was, I had been up since 5:00 a.m. for my gym routine with Courtney, and I felt it. Why a girl who sat on her backside and dug around people's brains for a living had to be in peak physical condition was lost on me.

I walked, listening to Dr. Griffin lecture on the law of restitution as the spiraling streetlights transformed into gas lamp–styled streetlights, the old Spanish-style Santa Fe Depot in the distance and the bus station just beyond. It was early May. While the days in San Diego were pleasant, I found the nights to be rather chilly, especially by the water. I rubbed my arms as the wind blew from the direction of the ocean, tossing my hair, and I berated myself for leaving my hoodie at home. I always forgot the stupid thing.

A warm glow emanated from the wide windows of the cute café on Lusk Boulevard. It was always open late. The people inside talked and laughed. My stomach growled as I eyed their late-night desserts and steaming coffees, but it was a short walk across the train tracks to the bus stop, and it wouldn't take long to get to my apartment. I could wait another half an hour until I got—

Home. Until I got home.

That's when it dawned on me.

Where was home?

Dammit.

CHAPTER 2

I sat in the empty diner with my eyes closed and arms crossed, sprawled across an uncomfortable booth, its old foam seats cracked and worn with age. With coffee that always tasted like a hint of dish soap and food that was consistently cold in the middle, the diner almost never saw a patron. And yet, without fail, the twenty-four-hour diner with peeling seafoam wallpaper and a water-stain-dappled, drop-down ceiling was miraculously still in business.

Of course, secret Agency-run meeting places had a funny way of doing that.

I came here when I forgot things. Sometimes, I forgot where the diner—which the Agency had spared no creative expense when they'd named it The Diner—was, but covert Agency meeting locations littered San Diego. I could usually remember the location of at least one.

The Diner was my usual haunt. It was close to home. I couldn't for the life of me remember where home was at the moment, but I knew it was nearby. The Diner's single employee, an austere woman named Gladys, was a mercurial individual—her gray hair wound in a bun about as tight as she was. Supposedly, Gladys wasn't a parahuman, but her inhuman characteristic of, apparently, never sleeping begged questions. No matter the hour, Gladys could be found fixed at the counter, looking like she was counting the minutes until her next cigarette break. She had a consciousness, so my initial cyborg theory was quickly debunked. Alien, however, was still a contender. I'd long suspected she lived at The Diner, though I had yet to figure out how or where.

Regardless, she was always at the counter, the same disgruntled expression fixed on her lined face, when the front door dinged and I stumbled in with my rehearsed sob story: "Excuse me, ma'am? My car broke down, and my phone is dead. Would it be possible for me to call my dad to come get me?"

After all, if there was a patron with a cast-iron stomach who wanted to test their mortality with The Diner's food, I had to keep up pretenses.

Assuming I remembered I had to keep up pretenses.

Gladys would sigh and begrudgingly shuffle away, her stooped form retreating to the back where she'd use the secure Agency phone to let someone know that Hadley had wandered in like some damned stray cat not knowing which way was up.

At least, I was pretty sure that's what she was thinking as she walked away. I wasn't always great at picking up narrative thought, but the mental image of a skin-and-bones, scraggy cat that popped into her head was pretty clear.

The Diner's front door dinged. The surrounding energy shifted as a consciousness approached. My lips twitched in a spontaneous smile as a familiar individual pressed closer, his soothing aura reminding me of an oak tree: strong, grounded, and sheltering. To anyone using their eyes, *boulder* would probably come to mind instead. The booth creaked in protest as the man sat down across from me, grunting as he squeezed in.

"Hey, Dad," I said without opening my eyes, my smile transforming into a mischievous smirk.

"Funny every time, Hadley," a gruff voice said.

My smirk dropped into a frown, and I opened my eyes. I cast a wary glance at the enormous man across from me. Muscular and hulking to the point of barely fitting into the booth, anyone in the vicinity would peg him as a parahuman. The distinctly military vibe he put out with his short-cropped hair, normally clean-shaven appearance, which was currently marred by a sea of stubble, and the disciplined way he carried himself usually made people give him a wide berth. Of course, anyone who knew him knew he was a teddy bear. An indestructible teddy bear, but a teddy bear nonetheless.

A look of concern crossed his face as he read my skeptical expression.

"You know who I am, right?" he asked.

I narrowed my eyes and pursed my lips, silent.

When he started squirming, I burst into laughter. "I'm so sorry, Mark. I'm an ass!"

"You *are* an ass," Supervisory Special Agent Mark Gilman grumbled.

"I'm sorry," I repeated. "This is the thanks you get for showing up at two o'clock in the morning to help me."

Mark grunted in reply, shrugging. "Can't remember the way home?"

"Nope," I said flippantly.

"You have your—?"

I pulled my wallet out of my pocket and set it down on the table. I couldn't remember where home was, but I could remember the string of questions people always asked me when I forgot where home was. The irony was not lost on me.

"Pretty sure I don't live with my parents anymore," I said.

Mark fished out a folded-up sticky note with my parents' address in Escondido hastily scribbled in my mother's anxious handwriting. Aside from the sticky note, there were no other documents to point me in the right direction. I'd failed my driver's exam five years ago, and everyone—me included—agreed it was best not to try again. I thought I had a state identification card, but the conspicuously empty slot in my wallet hinted it had either been misplaced or never existed in the first place. Lacking a document with my address, Mark was my best hope of getting home.

He sighed, handing the wallet back.

"How many times have I told you to fix this? I thought you replaced your ID," he said, running a hand across his buzz cut.

Ah, so I *had* lost it.

I animatedly placed a finger on my temple, rolling my eyes. "I have a condition."

"You try your—"

I offered him my phone before he finished asking the question.

"Forgot the passcode as Dr. Griffin was lecturing about . . . something."

Yeah, my final was going to go *really* well.

Mark tapped the phone's screen. It lit up; a message stated it was disabled for the next hour. He looked at me with defeat in his eyes—a lost cause he would never fix. "You locked yourself out of it again."

Mark's voice always took on a certain tone when he was exasperated with me. Not angry, just . . . disappointed. Somehow, that was worse.

"Sounds like a problem for tomorrow," I said.

"The Agency's number still should've worked."

"We have a number?"

Mark sighed deeply and attempted to rub the sleep from his bloodshot eyes. "Couldn't you get lost at a more decent hour?"

"I got called in for an interrogation."

"The Sons of Gaia guy the FBI is excited about?"

I nodded.

"I don't know why that couldn't wait until tomorrow," Mark grumbled. "You get him?"

I shrugged. "I'm sure there will be another interrogation," I said, suddenly feeling deflated. I wasn't looking forward to jumping back inside my new friend Jimmy's head.

"All right," Mark said, sighing again for good measure. "I'll take you home, but you need to make replacing your ID a priority. This can't keep happening, Hadley."

"I'd get my address tattooed on me, but . . ."

I grinned at Mark, trying to insert some levity into the situation, but he wasn't laughing.

"I know," I mumbled, dropping my eyes to my lap. "I'll write down my address tonight. Phone passcode too."

"And other safeguards," Mark added. "If you're going to use your telekinesis . . ." He trailed off, giving me a stern look.

Technically, only my telepathy was work approved since my telekinesis had . . . consequences. I grinned sheepishly, still hoping I could defuse the tension.

Mark was nothing but supportive of me. In fact, he was probably the most supportive of anyone in the Agency. I knew that, but I frequently wished he would leave the militant-dad thing for his own children.

Few people at the Agency could be described as Type B.

"We have to find ways to get around your memory loss and forgetfulness. This *can't* keep happening," Mark repeated.

He stood up, and thoroughly chided, I followed him from the booth.

"Thanks, Gladys!" Mark called over his shoulder.

Gladys's surly gaze bored holes into my back as I slunk through the front door, its irritating *ding!* chiming. I took a deep breath when the night air hit me, clearing my lungs of the smell of charred hash browns and grease.

A few steps in front of me, Mark stopped and sighed, keys in hand. "I don't mean to be short with you," he said, turning to me. "It's not your fault. I know you do the best you can. I just worry."

"It's a dad thing," I said with a small smile. "Jonah still keeping you up?" I added, attempting to shift the conversation to anything but my shortcomings.

"Every damned night," Mark said, but he grinned. A baby's face flashed in my mind, there and gone in a blink. "To be honest, if it weren't you keeping me up, it would be him."

Mark had once been a designated superhero—the chosen parahuman mascot for an entire city. He was known as Tank in Phoenix, Arizona. The name was a play on his veteran status and his extraordinary strength. Mark looked strong to begin with, hulking muscles bulging from his neck, arms, and thighs at least twice as thick as any normal human being's, but it went beyond that. Once, I had seen Mark lift a car over his head with the same effort I'd use to lift a foam pool noodle.

Mark had retired from superhero life after he remarried and his second child, a little boy named Logan, was born. He, along with his wife, Diane, son, and now sixteen-year-old daughter, Lilly, had moved to San Diego, where Mark could balance family life but still maintain the exhilarating—and yes, I mean that with irony—lifestyle of working for the Agency in a managerial position in San Diego's Counterterrorism unit. Logan was three now. Jonah was only six weeks old. I was his twenty-six-year-old colleague-turned-pseudo foster child that he definitely hadn't seen coming.

I knew Mark missed being Tank, the celebrated hero of a city. He missed the celebrity status and being in front of cameras as he took down criminals on a near-daily basis in the Phoenix branch of the Agency's Major Crimes division. I also knew he'd never go back. The way he talked about Jonah's first smile, Logan's successes with potty training, and Lilly's soccer practices as he drove me home—plus the flashes of thoughts I got from him—could convince anyone he would sacrifice anything for his family.

We passed a sign that read Hillcrest Est. 1907 and turned down an empty street lined with quaint houses and small condos. When Mark pulled up outside a taupe-painted apartment building lined with a row of jacarandas in full bloom, it was almost 2:30 a.m., and he would face a colicky newborn when he got home.

"Lilly has a soccer game on Saturday," Mark said as he put the car in park.

"Wouldn't miss it," I said, ignoring the fact I could and likely would if Mark didn't remind me sixty times between now and Saturday.

"Maybe leave Weasel at home this time," Mark said, cringing at the memory of my dog, Weasel, snatching a hot dog from a naïve Logan. I didn't remember it, but Mark—and likely Logan—clearly did.

"Poor Weasel," I said as I opened the car door. "He's probably had his legs crossed for hours."

"I'm sure Anna let him out," Mark reassured me.

I stopped, one leg hanging out of the car. I looked back at him, eyebrows raised.

"Anna," Mark said slowly, disbelief evident. "Your roommate? Best friend since middle school?"

As if I remembered middle school.

I shrugged. "I got nothin'. This'll be fun."

Mark sighed. "She's used to it," he said with resignation.

I didn't doubt it.

With a sigh that matched his, I closed the car door and waved bye to Mark. I watched his taillights disappear before shoving my hands into my pockets, resigned to my awkward fate. Then, I made my way to the apartment and roommate I couldn't remember.

I reached a boring beige door. A red-poppy-adorned mat reading Welcome and a wilting potted cyclamen—

an obvious attempt to bring life and color to the apartment's drab exterior—greeted me. I didn't recognize the door or décor, but Mark said this was the one, and who was I to know better? At least, who was I to know better in this condition?

I didn't have my keys. They, as well as my ID, were probably lost to some dark void forever.

It wasn't a problem.

I took a deep breath and steadied my mind. I felt the lock, a nucleus of cold, hard metal embedded in grainy wood. All I had to do was . . .

The deadbolt slid with a satisfying metallic scraping sound as I telekinetically turned the lock on the other side of the door. Not the smartest thing to do. Using my telekinesis when I was already experiencing memory problems tended to make things worse, but I prayed my roommate—Anna, that was her name—would be in bed, and I could possibly sleep off my memory lapse and avoid an awkward situation.

As I pushed the door open and smelled coffee brewing at 2:30 a.m., I knew that wouldn't be the case. Stepping into the apartment, my stomach growled at the tantalizing aroma emanating from the kitchen.

I might not have recognized the door, but I sighed in relief as I recognized my home. The apartment had an open layout with a narrow living room sprawled across the right half. A tiny kitchen resided in the back left corner of the apartment. Before the kitchen, a short hallway led to a single bathroom flanked by two bedrooms. Our—was it *our?*—style could probably be described as garage sale chic, with every piece of furniture coming secondhand. The wood end tables flanking the couch matched, though the coffee table was a darker wood. It sat in stark contrast to the dinged-up white TV stand opposite it. The TV was one of the few things we—Anna, maybe?—purchased new, and I was waiting for the day we—again, was it *we*?—regretted that choice. My favorite piece of furniture was our worn, lumpy obnoxiously red couch, which I'd found in a back alley with a FREE sign taped to it. Mark had carried it through the front door like it weighed no more than a pillowcase.

Yapping alerted me to a dog before I saw him. Weasel raced out of the bedroom closest to the kitchen, his tail wagging so fast it was a blur. The tan, possibly Chihuahua-Yorkie mix, with oversized, pointy ears and wisps of long fur around his eyes and mouth, dug his nails into my thighs and hopped up and down, begging to be picked up.

"Shh! Weasel!" I whispered, praying the neighbors couldn't hear him. His yapping turned into high-pitched whining as I scooped him into my arms, and I briefly feared the little guy would tinkle in his excitement.

It was a thing.

As I locked the door behind me, I caught sight of a skinny table awkwardly placed to my right against the wall, picture after picture crammed onto its surface. I stepped closer and leaned down, attempting to get a better look as Weasel licked my face.

"Buddy, contain yourself," I told the dog as I examined the two girls in the photos.

The vertically challenged girl with shoulder-length dark-brown hair and hazel eyes was me. Probably. An early-twenties version of me smiled back in some of the photographs, her blonde hair a distant memory. I glanced at a photo in which my arm was wrapped around the young woman who comprised half the other pictures. The significantly taller, paler girl with thick, somewhat unruly light-brown curls, gray eyes behind wire-framed glasses, and nose ring had to be Anna. It was not lost on me why the photos were placed right by the door.

A presence at the back of the apartment drew my attention, warm and comforting like a summer day. She enveloped me, her aura radiating like sunshine, bright like a sunflower in full bloom. I didn't remember Anna, but it only took a split second for us to become best friends all over again. She felt like home, and I smiled as her soothing energy moved closer.

With a burst of energy, Weasel leaped from my arms and ran to the girl emerging from the kitchen, a cup of coffee in her hands.

"Go bug your mother, pest," Anna said playfully as Weasel scratched her legs. She squatted down to pet the overzealous dog, attempting to keep her coffee from his tiny flailing paws.

"How'd the interrogation go?" Anna asked, turning her gray eyes to me.

I shrugged. I stared at the girl, trying to think of something to say. It was *really* awkward trying to act normal around a stranger, even one I immediately liked . . . and actually knew.

Her eyes met mine, a flash of understanding crossing them.

"You have no clue who I am, do you?" she asked, abruptly rising.

I pressed my tongue against my teeth and considered my reply. "I'm guessing you aren't the hooker I hired?"

Anna rolled her eyes. "Funny every time."

I sighed. "At least I'm predictable?"

"You're okay?" Anna asked, keeping a respectful distance, waiting to see if I'd go ballistic over the stranger in my home.

"We're good," I said. "Best friend since middle school?"

"Emo phase and all," Anna said, chuckling.

I cringed.

"What happened this time?" Anna asked.

Before I could respond, she shushed me. "Wait." She darted into the bedroom closest to the kitchen, the one Weasel had emerged from earlier.

I glanced at the dog. "Traitor," I said. *I* rescued Weasel from the pound two years ago. It was my room he should've been napping in.

Anna reemerged with a thick notebook.

"Okay," she said, opening the book, pen at the ready. "Continue."

I glanced down at the book, puzzled.

"You're part of my dissertation research," Anna explained. I could tell from her tone that we did this all the time.

"Is that all—?"

"Special permission. On track to work as a full-time profiler for the Agency after I defend," she said quickly, her brain practically buzzing with excitement.

"How does that—?" Never mind. It didn't matter. "The guy got out of hand. He went after Tom and Glenn."

"Did he fall through Tom?"

"Of course he did," I said, biting back a giggle.

"You dangle him by his ankles?" Anna asked.

I shot her a questioning look.

"It's kind of your signature move," she said, suppressing a laugh. "Was he a big guy? Heavy? Unusual in any way?"

"Just your average guy, I guess. Maybe a little overweight?" I answered.

"And that was it? You just telekinetically picked him up and dangled him in the air until someone got him?"

"I'd been reading his mind. Maybe half an hour? I went a little too deep."

Anna frowned, scribbling furiously in a notebook the Agency would certainly put under lock and key one day. "How so?"

"I wove myself into his memories. Brittany had a hard time getting me out."

Anna's frown deepened.

"What?" I asked as her brow creased.

She sighed, excitement draining from her as fast as her shoulders drooped.

"Just the usual. I don't see a pattern. Your amnesia is just as likely to set in moving the remote as lifting a suspect. A similar thing happened last week, and you were fine," Anna said, her face still scrunched in frustration.

"Lovely," I muttered. I slipped past her toward the kitchen, my stomach loudly voicing its desire for food. Exhaustion was setting in too, but I couldn't go to bed until I'd filled out a report on the interrogation.

"Did you use your telekinesis at any other time today?"

"No, but I could have forgotten."

Anna sighed again and closed the book. I was the world's most unreliable lab rat.

"There's peanut butter ice cream in the freezer," Anna said.

"Mark's right," I said. The freezer blasted cold air in my face, and I grabbed the frosty ice cream carton. "You must be my best friend. So what are you doing up so late?" I reemerged in the living room, shoving a spoonful of ice cream in my mouth. Anything peanut and anything ice cream were my comfort foods. It was a miracle I could still fit in my jeans. Of course, my Agency-mandated exercise routine probably had something to do with that.

"Same as you," Anna said, grimacing. "Finals tomorrow."

I paused, staring at her as if she just confessed to being an axe murderer with bodies stuffed in our flamboyant couch cushions. "Tomorrow?"

"Isn't your victimology final tomorrow?"

I blinked, inwardly screaming, mental red lights flashing as everything entered DEFCON 1.

"That's why your study group was today. Madison took you," Anna said slowly, probing my memory.

"Study group?" I squeaked, rushing to the calendar. It was *Wednesday*? *How was it Wednesday?* Anna was right. My victimology final was in roughly six hours.

I rushed to my room, ice cream carton still in hand, giving Anna an awkward, one-armed hug as I scrambled past her. "I'm sorry! I'm not ready! Gotta cram!"

Weasel barked excitedly and bounced on the bed as I abandoned the ice cream on a nightstand. I tossed my comforter aside in search of my class notes.

Nonchalantly, Anna wandered in and set my notebook down beside the ice cream. A neon sticky note with our address, my phone's PIN, and a note reading *Replace your ID!* was adhered to it, revealing Mark was a quick texter.

"Found it in the pantry this morning," Anna said.

Naturally.

CHAPTER 3

I t was pitch-black and icy cold. A deafening roar engulfed me. I
couldn't see, but I felt water rising higher and higher around me,
rumbling as it worked its way into the car with blinding speed. It
was up to my chest now.

I was going to drown.

Frantically, I beat on the window. Nothing happened. I felt my
way to the handle. I pulled it and pushed against the car door as
hard as I could, but it wouldn't budge. My numb hand slipped,
and I fell forward against the steering wheel, biting my tongue. The
taste of blood welled in my mouth. I sobbed, screaming and

pounding against the steering wheel. I prayed someone—anyone—was coming to save me.

Water was to my shoulders now, the frigid temperature biting at me, my body screaming in shock from the icy water gnawing at my flesh. The roar boomed in my ears; the smell of the sea—salt and sulfur—assaulted my nose. If someone was coming, it was almost too late.

My heart hammered harder. I panted, trying to catch my breath from my hysterical sobbing. My mind raced, but only one concrete thought ran through it now . . .

I am going to die.

I am going to die. I am going to die. I AM GOING TO DIE.

I startled awake from Weasel's agitated barking. Light flooded the room as Anna threw my bedroom door open, the hall glowing golden behind her. I hissed, shielding my burning retinas from the light.

"Are you okay?" Anna asked breathlessly.

"What'd I break this time?" I asked with resignation, knowing she'd only rush in if something went boom.

The most-expensive items we owned flashed through my mind. I started doing the mental math on how much it would cost to replace it all; fortunately, we had been wise and hadn't purchased expensive furniture to begin with.

Okay, so the decision to go garage sale chic came after I broke our first items. Small details.

"No casualties to repor—" Anna stepped toward my bed.

Crunch!

She paused, midstep. Thankfully, experience from the months after I'd first moved in had taught her to put shoes on at the sound of things exploding into oblivion. *That* had been a trying time for both of us, and Anna still jumped any time something went boom in an action movie. So did I, actually.

It had been a while since my last incident—a marked improvement from when I was first released from Mercy Rehab—but Anna was smart not to let old habits die.

The ceiling fan's lights flipped on. At least, the one functional bulb did. Glass littered the floor and foot of my bed, a sea of dangerous shards gleaming in the light.

"Well, shit," I muttered, observing what was left of the ceiling fan's three shattered bulbs. At least it was still attached to the ceiling. I didn't want to explain to the property managers why we needed *another* ceiling fan replaced. They had barely bought my excuse for the last one.

Carefully, I picked Weasel up and handed him to Anna. He wriggled excitedly as I passed him to her, making the process that much more difficult.

With the overzealous canine clear of the bed, I focused on the mess. The comforter lifted off the bed, seemingly of its own accord. The glass surrounding me scooted away from me as if someone passed a broom over the bed. Thankfully, most of the glass was localized at the foot of the bed.

With a sigh, I stood up, making sure I had telekinetically pushed most of the glass out of the way and contained it to a corner. I'd probably pay for the use of my telekinesis later, but it was better than a trip to the ER after I forgot—and I *would* forget—where I was stepping and ultimately lanced my foot open.

I glanced at the alarm clock beside my bed. How was it 6:00 a.m. already? I managed to get an hour and a half of sleep after rushing through my interrogation report and exposing myself to my class notes just long enough to realize I was a lost cause.

"Are you okay?" I asked Anna as she clutched a much-too-hyper Weasel to her chest.

"Yeah," she said quickly, flashing a smile.

Never lie to a telepath. I sensed the adrenaline still coursing through Anna's veins, but if she wanted to pretend she was fine, I'd let her.

"Test anxiety?" Anna asked.

"You could say that," I muttered, deciding not to go into detail about the nightmare. I had them all the time. I looked Anna up and down.

"How are you dressed already?" I mumbled, noting her gray dress pants and blazer combo.

She'd straightened her wavy hair and started her makeup. She looked every bit like an Agency profiler. I looked down at the oversized, ratty T-shirt I pretended was pajamas and bit back a cringe. Begrudgingly, I yanked a pair of pajama bottoms from my nightstand and slipped them on.

"I got up early to read your report," Anna answered.

The smell of fresh coffee crept past the doorway. The girl had a serious caffeine dependency issue.

"Of course you did," I said with a yawn. Somewhat properly dressed, I took my wriggling dog back and headed for the front door, tiptoeing out of my room to avoid any glass shards that might have escaped my poor attempt at cleaning up. I was exhausted. It could wait.

No, I was not a high-functioning adult.

I cast a glance at the TV as we entered the living room and was relieved to see it in one piece. Slipping a leash on Weasel, I opened the front door. He bounded out, and I leaned against the wall as he ran to a patch of grass a few feet from our apartment. He knew the drill. Silently, I thanked the powers that be that we had a first-floor apartment with a conveniently located public bathroom for Weasel.

"So . . . Jo was the arresting officer?" Anna asked from the other side of the apartment.

The sound of pouring liquid followed, and I took it as a sign I hadn't murdered our coffeepot. Thank God.

I flinched and cast a guilty look in the kitchen's direction, though Anna couldn't see it.

"She made the arrest. She wasn't there," I said.

Anna stepped out of the kitchen, attempting to hide a grin behind her mug. It wasn't effective.

"It's too early for you to be meddling in my nonexistent love life," I grumbled.

"Oh, come on," Anna said, grinning openly. "You said you caught some of her thoughts. She *likes* you, Hadley. Jo's great. I don't see what the problem is."

"We've had this conversation," I whined. "What people think and how people act aren't necessarily the same thing, and it isn't my business to act on things that are kept private. She hasn't said anything."

"Yet. Is that why you're avoid—"

Anna's eyes widened as realization dawned on her.

"I need my notebook!" she cried breathlessly. She scrambled away, nearly spilling her coffee as she hurried past me. "When did you remember me?" she asked, giddy, as she rushed back. God, she had too much energy in the morning.

"About the same time I started redecorating my room with glass shards," I muttered.

She scribbled furiously.

I was not meant to function on this little sleep. How was Anna this . . . this . . . *How was she being typical Anna?* Caffeine addiction aside, she never seemed to get tired. Maybe it was because she never gave her body enough time to switch her caffeine-to-blood ratio back toward the biological.

I shuffled toward the kitchen, my nose leading me to the coffee that would make me human again.

Or parahuman. Whatever. I just wanted to come back to the land of the living. I grabbed a mug and filled it almost to the top, leaving just enough room for milk and sugar but wasting no space for the life-giving, caffeine-enriched liquid. Anna drank hers black like the psychopath she truly was.

"How many hours was that?" Anna asked from directly behind me. Any closer, and I'd feel her breath on my neck. "This has to be a record."

"No math!" I whined.

From behind me, the sound of notebook pages flying signaled Anna was rifling through her entries.

"Hadley, you remembered me in under six hours!"

"I will be so excited when I'm actually awake," I mumbled into my caffeine. The hot beverage touched my lips, and the world suddenly seemed a little brighter. I sighed in relief.

Anna's face hovered inches from mine when I lowered the mug.

"We *have* to discuss last night in detail. Hadley, this could be *huge!*"

"Okay," I said. "But after my final. I need to go fail it."

Anna swatted my arm with her notebook. "Fine," she said. "After you *pass* your final. Promise?"

"Promise," I said with a sizeable yawn.

Groggily, I shuffled to my bedroom to get dressed, giving the glass shards a wide berth instead of dealing with the mess like a responsible, well-adjusted adult. I threw open the closet. What was the best outfit for the academic ass kicking I would most assuredly endure in a mere two hours?

"Hadley?" Anna called after me.

I popped my head around the corner, my top two T-shirt options in hand.

"Weasel would appreciate it if you opened the door," she said, trying her hardest not to laugh.

Scratching and whining emanated from the closed front door. Weasel's leash was stuck between the door and the doorframe.

I shot Anna a look. "You let me do that."

My morning didn't get much better after that. I rushed out the door, only to realize I'd missed the bus to campus. Madison, my usual ride to campus when I missed the bus, didn't pick up. Anna, who had her own finals and a meeting at the Agency to deal with, had to drop what she was doing to get me to class on time. Not enough thank-yous would suffice as I scrambled out of the car, only to take two steps and turn around.

"I forgot my bag!" I cried, throwing the door back open in a frenzy. "Do you have a—"

Anna already held a pencil out to me. She was a beautiful saint of a woman.

"*Thank you!*" I said for the ten thousandth time while Anna continued to insist it wasn't a big deal.

When I arrived ten minutes after my final officially started, Dr. Griffin shot me a glare intense enough to boil water. He continued to hold his glowering gaze on me as he thrust a test on my desk without a word. The *slap!* of paper said enough. I shrank in my seat, whispering an apology as my neck and cheeks flushed. Briefly, I wondered if he and Gladys would make a lovely couple. They could bond over their contempt for my shortcomings.

I glanced at the other students. Some cast irritated glances at me; others ignored me. Most were younger than me by at least a few years. At twenty-six, I was among the oldest students in the class. I guess that's what happens when you're forced to abandon your previous schooling and completely start over. Once, I had been on track to study nursing . . . not that I remembered any of that. That path had come to an abrupt halt on my twenty-first birthday, and there was no going back.

I closed my eyes and took a deep breath. I *would* focus. I *would* steel my mind against distractions, and I *would* pass this test. Opening my eyes, I scribbled Hadley Gordon at the top of the page. It was a good start if I could get my name right.

I was wrong. It all went downhill from there. Forty minutes later, half the test remained blank, and at least a quarter of the answered questions had question marks next to them.

This was what happened when I had one of my "episodes." I usually forgot big things, such as where I lived and who I lived with, and my ability to focus was shot while I recovered. Doors were left open, lights left on, I forgot where I was going, I forgot what someone told me thirty seconds ago, and so forth. Actually, most of that was normal, but having an episode took everything to the next level. If I forgot a long-term memory, like my relationship with Anna, it would eventually come back. If a short-term memory was the victim of an episode, it was usually gone for good. "Space cadet" was a more than apt description and a moniker I had been called more than once, mostly by Mark. My telepathy also ran amuck. While I could never completely control it, a big memory loss event always left me more sensitive to other people's thoughts. I had no

43

explanation why, and at that moment, I was trying *so hard* not to cheat and see the answers to the test in twenty-three other brains focused exclusively on it.

Well, make that all but one.

Something was . . . not right with someone. I squirmed in my seat, a surge of adrenaline making me nauseous. Someone was taking this exam *way* too seriously. Sweat beaded my brow. I focused on my breathing as my heart began to race and my hands trembled. I looked around. Everyone *seemed* fine. Sure, they were anxious, but no one appeared to be on the verge of a panic attack.

"Eyes on your own test, Ms. Gordon," Dr. Griffin said.

I jumped as he loomed over me, arms crossed and a scowl spread across his face.

"S—" I choked out.

My throat constricted. I shuddered, dropping my pencil. It rolled off the desk, hitting the floor with a *crack!* that caught a few students' attention. My vision faded at the edges, the center much too bright, and my ears rang. My heart was going to beat its way out of my chest.

This wasn't test anxiety. Someone near me was scared to death.

I wheezed, drowning in the other terrified psyche. I couldn't untangle the person from my mind. I needed to get away from the classroom. Explosive things tended to happen when I felt fear, and right now, I couldn't disentangle the unknown person's terror from my own emotions.

Cars flanked me as I ran. I caught my reflection in a side mirror, auburn ringlets dancing around my head as I raced past, eyes focused on the exit before me, the sidewalk visible just beyond it.

No, not me: someone else. Auburn ringlets melted into straight brown hair, and the scene dissolved around me.

I stood too forcefully, panting as I fought for control of my mind. My chair skittered across the floor before tumbling over, catching the remaining students' attention. I failed to notice the stares as a high-pitched shriek lanced my brain. It wasn't a normal scream. It was almost ultrasonic—the type of ear-piercing noise that could shatter glass.

I knew of only one parahuman capable of making that sound.

I wasn't worried about myself anymore. I understood what was happening, and I was the only one who knew.

Madison. I had to save her.

"Ms. Gordon?" Dr. Griffin asked.

I rushed toward the door, clamping my hands over my ears in a futile attempt to silence the psychic scream rattling my brain. I bumped into desks, and exams flew to the floor. The room swam around me.

"Hadley!" Dr. Griffin shouted.

I threw the door open with a *bang!* and ran.

A knife flashed before my eyes, the edges of the thought stained red with unbridled panic.

I dialed 1-1-1 on my phone, thankful the Agency's emergency code worked even when I was locked out of my phone.

"Miss Gordon?" a female voice asked.

"It's Madison!" I shrieked. "She needs help!"

I burst out of the building, and the bright sunlight briefly stunned me. Heads turned as I nearly tripped down the steps, almost losing my grip on my phone. I pushed through it, racing toward the parking garage where Madison needed me.

I stumbled when a thought tore through my mind: I saw concrete. I was looking at the side of a building. The pavement was wet.

The pavement was red.

There was another feeling too: guilt. I couldn't see the other person's thoughts, but I felt his emotions, strong enough to permeate across campus—past all the other minds clouded by anxiety over impending finals.

Someone had done something awful, and the guilt was eating him alive.

I raced into the parking garage, darting among the cars, searching in every direction. It was empty.

I clenched my jaw in frustration. Doubt crept up my spine in a chill. Was my stupid brain still too addled from yesterday? I *knew* she was here—she had to be—but Madison was nowhere to be seen. Mind racing, I tried to call back the flashes of thoughts I'd witnessed. Where had I seen her? Where had I—

Something crunched under my feet. Startled, I stepped back, revealing a crushed hearing aid. For a moment, my brain was too panicked to make the connection.

Madison wore hearing aids. She was in here . . . somewhere.

I felt him, then—the man near me. The man was near Madison.

I couldn't feel her.

The stairwell.

I sprinted across the parking garage. I slammed into the door and forced it open, breathing in gasps. I nearly fell on her as I barreled into the stairwell.

Madison lay alone in a pool of blood; it smelled hot and metallic, permeating the air. It soaked her yellow blouse. Tears in the fabric revealed ragged flesh beneath.

"Madison!" I cried, dropping beside her.

Her closed eyelids were smudged with red. She didn't respond. Everything had happened so fast; now, everything was happening in slow motion. My heart thundered in my chest as the situation suddenly became much too real.

One beat . . .

Two beats . . .

"Madison, it's Hadley! Can you hear me?" I choked, a hard lump in my throat.

She didn't respond.

I reached for her, moving out of time.

Three beats . . .

My fingers brushed her shoulder, but I recoiled when I touched her skin.

She was too still.

Hands trembling, I dialed 1-1-1 on my phone again.

"*Please!*" I screamed into it. "Please get someone here! Madison is really hurt!"

"Can you describe her condition, Hadley? Help is on the way," the woman responded.

"Someone stabbed her," I sobbed. "There's blood everywhere."

My hands were red with it. It soaked into my jeans. The sickly warm sensation spread across my legs, and I steeled my mind, forcing myself to ignore it.

"Keep her awake, Hadley. Help is coming. I'm on the line with you," the dispatcher said.

"She's not awake," I wept.

What should I do? What had the Agency taught us?

I sat there on my knees, staring at the pretty girl with curly auburn hair, so much like Anna's. Her eyes were blue when they were open. She was only three years older than me—thirty next month. I had been helping plan her birthday party. This couldn't happen to her—not to Madison. Everyone loved Madison.

I put the woman on speakerphone and tossed my phone down. I threw my trembling hands on a wound, red oozing between my fingers as I applied pressure. There were too many of them . . .

"Is she breathing?" the woman asked.

My eyes frantically raked Madison's body, trying to figure out which wound was the worst. She wouldn't die. I wouldn't let her!

I didn't get the chance to respond. Scuffling sounded on the stairs at my back. I sensed a man behind me, realizing too late I never made sure the stairwell was empty.

He was going to hurt me.

Arms reached around my chest. A blast rocked the ground as I telekinetically wrenched myself from his grip. I tumbled across the grass, and he flew back and landed hard.

Grass? A sickly sweet, earthy smell flooded my nostrils.

My head spun as I tried to make sense of my new surroundings. What happened?

I sat up. I was alone. A persistent racket screamed in the background, making the situation that much more jarring. I stared down at my red hands. Dread rose in my throat, harsh and acidic. Where was Madison?

I'd lost time. Goddammit, I didn't know how much. Madison didn't have time to waste!

"Hadley!" someone shouted.

I jumped as Mark collapsed next to me, eyes wild.

"Hadley!" he panted. "Thank God!"

He reached out to me, then froze, his hand hovering inches away before he jerked it back. Blood drained from his face, turning him a color I didn't realize was humanly possible.

"Is Madison okay?" I whispered, voice pleading for the answer I knew I wouldn't get.

I looked to my left. An ambulance was parked at the side of the garage, lights flashing. The EMTs who stood at the back of it hardly seemed to feel a sense of urgency. Their attention was toward me, but I wasn't the one who needed help. Madison needed their help.

Half a dozen police cars and black SUVs, AGENCY displayed prominently on their sides, added to the display of strobing lights, red and blue flashes I couldn't bring myself to make sense of. The medical examiner's van pulled up.

Mark's voice cracked as he struggled to say what I already knew. "Hadley . . ."

He looked into my eyes, truly sorrowful. I stared down at my red hands and felt grief welling in my throat.

"No!" Wracking sobs erupted from me, and I curled into myself, clutching my bloodstained hands to my chest.

Mark let me cry for what felt like forever before gently edging closer.

"Hadley," he said, compassion heavy in his voice. "You understand this is a crime scene, okay?"

I choked and nodded, still slumped over on the ground. I inhaled the smell of dirt and grass. *Anything* but the smell of blood that blanketed me.

"We need to collect evidence, okay?" Mark said, talking to me in a tone he might use on his toddler.

"No," I said, sniffling.

The words *evidence* and *crime scene* made it too real. I couldn't accept that Madison was gone.

"We need to do it for Madison."

"I can't," I whispered.

I bit my lip and shuddered. Nothing made sense. Madison was fine. Her birthday was next month. She was defending soon. She was getting married.

Mark sighed heavily. "I'm sorry, Hadley, but I need you to calm down, okay? What did Mercy have you do? Where's your music?"

I shook my head. My phone was in the stairwell.

With Madison. Madison was dead. She was *dead*. I hiccupped, breathing coming faster as sobs threatened to return.

"Okay, okay," Mark shushed.

His shushing turned to humming, and I clenched my eyes shut, focusing on the rhythm. It was a lullaby, but I didn't remember my childhood, so it took me a moment to recognize the melody to "Twinkle, Twinkle, Little Star."

The third time Mark started over, I lifted my head, eyes still closed as I focused on taking deep, steadying breaths. I opened my eyes after the fourth time.

"Are you okay to be near people?" Mark asked.

It dawned on me why Mark had made the EMTs wait. If anyone could handle being blown up trying to talk down an out-of-control telekinetic, it was the former Tank. I looked around, bleary eyes searching for . . . something. No, someone. Someone was missing.

"I think I hurt someone," I whispered, scanning the scene.

The grass was torn up around me. There was a hole just up the hill; something metallic gleamed in the grass beside it. Drawn toward it, I started to rise.

"Let's let Forensics deal with that," Mark said, snapping my attention back to him. "The person you hurt, did he hurt Madison?"

I nodded, unable to form words.

"Okay, we'll get a BOLO out. He might need a hospital."

"Sorry," I whispered. I wasn't sure what I was apologizing for.

"You did good, Hadley. You did nothing wrong," Mark said, voice still calm and low, trying to talk the neurotic telekinetic off the proverbial cliff. "Now," he continued. "Can we go collect evidence for Madison?"

Slowly, I nodded. Mark rose to his feet. Like a zombie, I stood and followed him. He led me to the back of the ambulance, and I sat down heavily.

Mark caught the attention of one of the forensic examiners as he walked toward the stairwell. The tech rushed over. I stared at the sterile white gown covering everything but his face. He stared out at me from the tightly drawn circular opening, his eyes calculating.

"I have this covered," Mark said, taking a bag from the man. He dug around until he found a pair of gloves. I wasn't sure they'd fit.

"I need a few guys up on that hill," Mark added, nodding toward where he'd found me.

"You remember your forensic training?" Mark asked me.

I nodded, though I probably didn't. Mark forced the gloves onto his oversized fingers. The purple nitrile stretched taut, appearing almost flesh colored at their tightest points, but didn't tear. Dazed, I held my red-stained hands out for him.

The persistent racket of honking and beeping assaulted my eardrums.

"What's that sound?" I asked.

"I think you set off the car alarms," Mark said. "You fought the guy?"

"I think so. I forgot," I said, remembering the feeling of someone's arms wrapped around my chest.

"Where are you hurt?" Mark asked.

I felt his disappointment as he realized I was having a memory lapse. My heart sank, comprehension dawning on me as well: I wasn't going to remember who hurt Madison.

"I'm fine," I whispered, focusing on my sticky red hands. It wasn't real, right? My brain was just . . . I just needed a minute for my broken brain to settle. It would settle.

A small crowd of stunned onlookers had formed not far from us, and their thoughts seeped in, buzzing in my brain like a cloud of flies circling carrion. I shook my head, trying to clear them. It was too much. It was all too much.

"Where are you hurt?" Mark repeated.

I flinched as nail clippers clicked, a nail falling off into a plastic evidence bag. I had to stop myself from jerking my hand away as he dug under my nail bed for more blood. More evidence.

There was so much of it.

"He barely touched me," I said.

Mark sighed. He reached up and gently pressed a cotton swab against my forehead.

"Ow!" I cried as throbbing pain shot above my eye. I reached up and felt the gash that started precariously close to my right eye and extended halfway up my forehead. Stunned, I pulled my hand away, staring at the fresh, glistening red. Or was that blood still Madison's?

The need to wretch became overwhelming. My stomach twisted, and my saliva suddenly felt too thick to swallow as adrenaline began wearing off.

Mark eyed me warily, passing a cotton swab over my cheek. Was he going to run out of cotton swabs? The idea left me with the urge to burst into hysterics. I knew I was in shock, but I didn't know how to stop it.

"What do you remember?" Mark asked.

"I was taking my final," I said. "I felt something weird and—"

Oh, God, I couldn't.

Madison's face, frozen, growing paler by the second and smudged with blood, flashed through my mind. I tried to choke back sobs, but they erupted from my throat in a fit of hysterics once again.

"Someone killed her, Mark!" I wailed.

Mark remained quiet as I cried. Another ambulance pulled up while I lost my composure. Then, more police cars and Agency SUVs—what appeared to be at least half a dozen of them. How had Mark beat them there?

"We can talk about it later," Mark said gently, sliding another red-tipped cotton swab into a transport tube. The smell of the marker he used to label it made my stomach churn.

"Your clothes are evidence," Mark said. "I have some of Lilly's clothes in my car. Will they fit?"

I nodded, but to be honest, I didn't process the question.

By the time Mark sealed my clothes in evidence bags, the scene had exploded into even worse chaos, with lights and voices everywhere, car alarms shrieking in the background, and yellow tape sealing off multiple areas.

Suddenly, a man—a paramedic?—was in my face, asking me where I was hurt. I stared at him dazedly as he examined my bloodstained skin.

"It isn't mine," I heard myself say, but it sounded like the voice of a stranger.

The sharp sting of antiseptic on my face snapped me back to reality with a painful jolt.

"This needs stitches," the paramedic said, applying butterfly closures to my wound.

I winced as he tugged at my skin. "Is Dr. Patterson here?" I asked numbly. How long had it been since Mark found me? Five minutes? An hour?

"He and Art are with Madison," Mark said gently. "Are you hanging in there?"

If Art, the Agency's medical examiner, was here, they didn't need Dr. Patterson.

I nodded and took a shaky breath. The cops were trying to push back onlookers, and there I was, sobbing my eyes out, covered in blood and dirt, as they snapped pictures like it was a day at the zoo.

A familiar presence edged into my awareness, soft like a candle flame flickering in the dark.

"Hadley?" a woman asked.

I blinked, confused. I recognized the voice from somewhere. A police officer with tawny skin and black hair pulled into a sleek ponytail rushed toward us, movements controlled and professional yet distinctly urgent, barely suppressing her alarm.

"Hadley!" the woman called again, panic at the edge of her voice as she threw her arms around me. "We heard there was an attack on a parahuman. I didn't know it was you!"

She pulled back, and I studied her face—angular, feminine features and warm brown eyes. I knew her. I glanced at her name tag: Ramirez.

Jo.

The remaining blood drained from my face when another person stepped behind her, the sensation of hornets buzzing in my brain the only forewarning I got that he was coming.

"What happened?" Assistant Director William Ryker, my boss and the most terrifying human being in San Diego, if not the country, asked matter-of-factly, brushing the others out of his way and standing firmly in front of me.

Mark, who easily had six inches and one hundred pounds on the formidable man, jumped to attention.

"It appears to have been a knife attack, sir," he responded, rigid, as his military training and years with the Agency kicked in.

Ryker narrowed his eyes. "I want to hear it from her."

I choked as his ice-blue eyes bored into me.

"You were the first one on the scene?" he asked.

"Yes, sir," I whispered. I couldn't maintain eye contact.

"And the victim was deceased when you arrived?"

My mind blanked. The victim? Deceased?

"Madison?" I blurted out.

Ryker gritted his teeth.

Mark gently inserted himself. "Sir, she needs a minute."

"She can have a minute when I get all the damned facts!" Ryker seethed. "I have a dead agent and a killer on the loose! You can cry about it once I've caught the bastard!"

Everyone's eyes were on me. My surroundings shifted in and out, like they had in the classroom. I really needed a minute.

Madison was—but Madison couldn't be . . .

The ambulance bucked and rocked beneath me. I leaped up, startled. On the other side of the crime scene tape, the crowd exclaimed in excitement.

Mark stepped toward Ryker. "Push her any harder," he said firmly. "And she won't remember anything."

Ryker turned a startling shade of red, but when he spoke, it was with forced calm. "You have until I'm done examining the body to regain your composure and behave like someone employed by the Agency."

He disappeared into the parking garage. Where grief had been, rage bloomed, bubbling up from the pit of my stomach.

If there was one thing I remembered from rehab, it was that nothing was more dangerous than a scared or angry telekinetic. I needed to get away from people. Not caring that everyone was watching, I turned on my heel and rushed away.

Jo surprised me by following me, the unstable telekinetic, but then, she'd never been afraid of me.

"Hadley?" she said, keeping a respectful distance behind me. Her footsteps paused every step or two as if she was watching where she—

I stopped and groaned. Had I just stormed over evidence? Jesus, I was the one who made the evidence, and I couldn't even remember where it was! I'd just add it to the list of things I could blame myself for.

"Five minutes," I hissed, clenched fists trembling. "Five minutes faster, and Madison would be alive."

"You can't know that," Jo said.

"I felt her. She was alive and crying for help, but I was too goddamn slow!"

"Hey," Jo said, gingerly laying a hand on my shoulder. "This isn't your fault."

I jerked away. I wasn't sure why. The flash of hurt reflecting in Jo's eyes only fueled the self-loathing boiling within me.

"I let him get away," I growled under my breath.

"Hadley, you did the best you could."

"He was standing right over there! I literally touched him!" I said, suddenly shouting, gesturing toward the white-clad technicians as they placed numbers on the ground and snapped pictures. "If I was a better telepath, I would have him, and Madison would be alive! She's dead, and I can't even remember what the bastard looks like!"

I shook. Tears burned at my eyes again. God, I would never stop crying. I just wanted to go home. I didn't want to deal with Ryker. I didn't want Madison to be dead in some dirty stairwell with forensic examiners clad in white, snapping pictures of her and dipping swabs in her blood. She deserved better.

I rubbed my face, only to feel searing pain. It sent me over the edge again. I collapsed on the ground, evidence be damned, and tears fell again as I pressed my hand against the stinging farewell present Madison's butcher left me. Jo was beside me in a second, shushing me like a child.

"All right," she murmured, taking my free hand. "Let's calm down." She pressed her thumb into my palm and massaged—a tactile coping mechanism for ungrounded telepaths the nurses at Mercy had once taught her. I hadn't needed it in a long time.

This wasn't the Jo most people saw, and it was something I had once taken for granted. At least, I did until her feelings toward me changed, and I became acutely aware that we'd always been different with each other—bonded, though I'd always assumed it was nothing more than friendship. I wasn't sure if she was even aware of how she felt yet. Officer Jocelyn Ramirez probably came off as introverted and composed. She could probably eat the bad guys for breakfast, though I'd

Alyse N. Steves

never seen that side of her. I met Jo, the off-duty officer, first. She was gentle and soft-spoken the first time she sat with me at Mercy Rehab, a burned CD in one hand and a peanut butter cookie in the other. Outside of family, Anna, and Dr. Patterson, I'd known Jo the longest of anyone.

And yet, I had avoided her for weeks, completely and utterly at a loss for how to handle the shift between us.

My emotional bullshit didn't matter. At that moment, only Madison and how I'd utterly failed her mattered. Spent, I propped my head against my knees, wincing at the gash I kept forgetting about. I pulled my hand away and wrapped my arms around my face, hiding from the world. Hiding from Jo, Mark, Ryker, and Madison's cold, empty shell in the stairwell.

Arms circled me.

"Five minutes earlier," Jo said, lips beside my ear. "And I might be standing over your body, too."

Jo couldn't hide her mind. The thought terrified her, but I didn't have it in me to process what that meant to me. The only person I could think about was Madison.

I pulled away from Jo as footsteps approached. Dr. Ian Patterson shambled toward us, a haunted, shell-shocked shroud blanketing him. He was still wearing a white gown, though he had pulled the hood down, giving him a more-human appearance in stark contrast to the grim reapers floating in and out of the stairwell.

"I hear you got a nasty cut," Dr. Patterson said in a tone he likely used to soothe ER patients in the past. He kneeled down to my level, warm brown eyes glistening with emotion.

The Agency's on-staff doctor was in his early forties—probably only a year or two older than Mark. Like me, he was a parahuman. A propensity for quick

58

healing—both himself and others—didn't make him much of a crime fighter, but he was one hell of a doctor. How the gentle, soft-spoken man had handled the chaos and anguish of an emergency room for so many years was beyond me.

Right now, he probably missed it.

Dr. Patterson laid a gloved hand on my shoulder. "There was nothing you could do."

"Did she suffer?" I whispered.

"It was brutal," Dr. Patterson said. "But it was over quickly."

He knew he couldn't lie to me, so he never did. Dr. Patterson—he insisted I call him Ian, but I couldn't—had been one of the first people I met when I woke up after my accident. He'd attempted to heal the traumatic brain injury that had nearly killed me, but some things couldn't be repaired. Not completely. Dr. Patterson couldn't save my first twenty-one years of memories—the things that made up the identity of who I once was. I'd always have the lesion that was left behind. I suffered amnesia if I did anything to inflame it. And by anything, I meant using my telekinesis too much. Or too little. Or if I thought about using my telekinesis.

But I was awake, walking, talking, and breathing on my own because of Dr. Patterson, and for that, I was grateful.

"Let's focus on easing your suffering, why don't we?" Dr. Patterson said gently. He pulled a glove off, placing his hand on my forehead. He cringed, breathing in with a sharp gasp.

"Could I have—"

"No," Dr. Patterson said through clenched teeth. "She was gone before you found her."

It was no secret that parahuman abilities weren't always rainbows and sunshine. They sometimes—frequently—came with drawbacks: Dr. Patterson's was feeling the pain of his patients as he healed them . . . or really anything else if he touched someone. Hence, the gloves. It was a downside that made it even more remarkable he'd been willing to help a girl on life support whose brain was bleeding. He had to be given a week-long leave of absence after he saved my life—he nearly needed a hospital himself as a reward for his efforts.

A hot, stinging sensation bloomed across my face, but a warm sensation also washed over me. After a few minutes, Dr. Patterson dropped his hand and exhaled heavily. He sniffed, fighting back tears.

"Thank you," I said gently, relishing the relief and numbness flooding my system. The emotional leeching was temporary, but at least everyone could stop wondering if I was going to blow the entire scene to hell.

"I'm here if you need me," Dr. Patterson said.

Then, I felt *him* coming. William Ryker marched across the grass, his face pinched and red in stark contrast to the sterile white gown covering him from head to toe. Steeling myself, I stood up and brushed the grass off my hands.

I left Jo and Dr. Patterson behind and went to face my boss, knowing the nightmare had only just begun.

CHAPTER 4

I trudged to the start of the trail where Mark waited for me, my calves already protesting the hike up the uneven terrain. To my right, a cloudless sky stretched across the ocean. To my left, an equally impressive view of a sandstone canyon populated by coastal chaparral, sagebrush, and cacti greeted me. A sea breeze caught my hair as I reached the apex of a hill. In the distance, craggy sandstone precipices abruptly dropped into crashing, roaring waves below, the occasional surfer or boat speckling the ocean's deep-blue surface farther out. The Torrey Pines trails were stunning, with miles of sand trails and breathtaking views that could distract anyone from their troubles.

Well, maybe not my troubles.

Mark grinned as I slumped beside him against the fence, already breathing hard.

"I hate cardio," I panted. "If you're trying to distract me, a movie would be better."

"Didn't you blow something up once?"

"It was *one* time, and Jo forgave me. Just don't watch action movies with me," I muttered. "Or horror. Or romance. Just avoid things that make people feel strong emotions, and we're good."

"Uh-huh," Mark said skeptically, relaxing against the railing.

With his chiseled jawline and rippling muscles, he bore an uncanny resemblance to one of those white marble statues that graced museum pamphlets. He probably didn't need to run to keep his godlike physique. Damn him.

"Think you can keep up today?"

"We're running? On these trails?" I asked. "I thought you wanted me alive."

Mark's eyes flicked toward me, and I inwardly winced at my choice of words. In the two weeks since Madison's death, Mark had become my shadow. He never said why, and if it weren't for the gift of telepathy, I'd assume his support was in regard to the normal grief and healing process. In truth, the fact an escaped murderer could stand right in front of me and I'd be none the wiser haunted his waking moments.

I tried not to think about that too often myself. I enjoyed sleeping through the night, though I'd been plagued with more nightmares than usual lately. Besides, no one was getting to me while a Tank guarded me.

At least, that's what I told myself.

"You know I'm never going to keep up with you," I said, groaning. "Even if my legs weren't half as long as yours, you could outrun an Olympic athlete if you wanted to."

Not that parahumans could participate in the Olympics. Mark merely laughed at my whining.

"I appreciate you slowing it down for me," I said glumly.

"It keeps me humble."

"Clearly." I rolled my eyes.

I looked down the trail with its elevation changes, uneven ground, and winding path and groaned again.

"Explain why we can't run on pavement? Or, you know, inside? Anywhere level would be great."

My lungs were already quite unhappy. Mark chuckled at my suffering. Then, without warning—which I should have been embarrassed about as a telepath—he took off.

"Not cool!" I shouted at him. I stood rooted in place, petulantly denying the fact I had to move.

"Two miles, space cadet! Let's go!" Mark shouted back at me.

"*Two?*" I shrilled as he vanished around a bend. "I'm going to slip on pine needles, Mark! I'm going to eat cactus!"

My protests were met with the sound of Mark's footfalls growing fainter in the distance.

Begrudgingly, I pulled my phone out of my pocket and put my earbuds in. I pressed play and closed my eyes, inhaling deeply as I focused on blissfully insentient words and rhythms. My legs would hate me for this, but I wouldn't miss the opportunity to give my mind a break on the sparsely populated trail.

I dug my feet into the ground and scurried after Mark.

"You know I hate that nickname, you ass!" I yelled as Mark's backside appeared ahead of me.

"Catch up and do something about it!" Mark shouted above my music.

But no matter what, there was no passing him. The best I could do was jog beside him when I wasn't scrambling over rocks or running up stairs, and only because he let me.

At the halfway point, we stopped. I drained an entire water bottle and slumped over with my hands on my knees, panting.

"Oh, God. I hate running. How are you not dying?" I gasped.

"If you want a real workout, I have a toddler you can borrow."

My laughter turned into coughing as my lungs protested our chosen activity. When I stopped, I found myself staring into the distance, watching waves crash against cliffs in explosions of white and blue, foam hissing as they receded before repeating the pattern. A seagull cried overhead, and I watched it ride the currents above us.

A seagull cried from above as footsteps crunched in the sand. The hum of cars—

"You going to invite me to the pity party?" Mark asked, dragging me back to reality with a jolt.

"It's not a . . . I'm sorry," I said with a sigh, shaking my head to clear the cobwebs from my brain. "It's just that everything reminds me of Madison."

Mark nodded sympathetically.

"She really wanted kids," I explained, crumpling the empty water bottle in my hands as I avoided eye contact. "She and David were talking about it, you know, after they got married and she defended her dissertation."

"We'll catch the bastard. He'll pay for what he did," Mark said. The confidence in his voice was convincing, even if I knew the truth: crimes like this didn't always end in an arrest.

"Did the forensics team finish running the DNA samples?" I asked hopefully.

Mark sighed, effectively stamping out my optimism. "Yeah. Bastard knew what he was doing. That stairwell has to be one of the most trafficked scenes I've ever encountered. The only DNA Forensics could link back to the scene with any confidence was yours and Madison's. Asshole was careful. Didn't even give us the courtesy of leaving a bloody shoe print."

"What about my clothes? I swear to God, Mark, he touched me."

"I believe you," Mark said, "but all the blood was yours or Madison's."

I leaned my head back, staring up at the sky as if I could appeal to a higher power. "At least we have the knife."

At least we have the knife? I thought petulantly as a breeze tossed my hair.

The knife in question was an eight-inch chef's knife. More than overkill for the occasion. Madison's killer might as well have brought a sword. Presumably, I had gotten a good look at it when it was slicing my face open. Poor Madison had gotten to know it pretty well too, if the fourteen stab wounds in her body were indicator enough. Dropping it had been his only mistake—one he likely wouldn't have made if I hadn't tried to blow him to kingdom come.

Mark shook his head, running a hand across his short hair.

"No blood but yours and Madison's," he said, sighing. "You know I'm proud of you for maintaining control in . . . in that situation, but if there was ever a time to lose it . . ."

Despite a BOLO that sent every law enforcement officer and hospital searching for an individual with severe contusions, no one had turned up with injuries consistent with being blown up by an out-of-control telekinetic. It was a bittersweet victory for me: on one hand, I somehow maintained enough self-control not to injure someone. On the other hand, if I hadn't, this would be over.

"Guess Mercy trained me better than I thought," I mumbled.

"What do you think of Anna's profile?" Mark asked.

Despite my uselessness, Anna did her best, and coordinating with profilers from the Agency's other branches and the Behavioral Analysis Unit at the FBI, they determined we were looking for an older Caucasian male prone to violent outbursts. He was likely highly intelligent and disciplined, perhaps with a military background. The FBI and DoD were helping the Agency look into dishonorable discharges and any active-duty service members stationed in San Diego who might fit the profile, though something about it didn't sit right with me. Not that an amnesiac telepath's opinion mattered much.

Unfortunately, the profile didn't stop there.

"Which part? That he's done this before? That he knew her? That he's been practicing, waiting to go after Madison?" I asked.

According to Anna, the meticulous planning involved to lure Madison into the parking garage, then apparently leave no evidence—suggested he'd killed before. The

Agency and the FBI were running themselves ragged trying to tie cold cases to Madison with no luck. Then, there was Anna's belief that the level of aggression suggested a personal connection. That and the fact he closed her eyes, an intimate act Anna assumed meant there was an emotional connection.

Thinking too hard about that part risked me making things go boom. The only thing that made the morbid reenactments haunting my mind worse was imagining the look on Madison's face as she realized she'd been betrayed by a friend.

"What do you think?" Mark asked. "You remember feeling him, even if you don't remember his face."

"If it's a him," I muttered.

It pissed me off that I couldn't even give them that much with certainty, though my initial impression remained that a man had ambushed me.

Anna had sat down with me for three days, pushing her education in abnormal psychology (which she would never admit she had gotten because of what happened to me) and her training as a profiler (which was also tied to my decision to join the Agency) to the brink attempting to extract information from the black pit that was my brain. We gave up on the third day, much to Ryker's displeasure. He brought in others, of course. Other profilers—even the Agency's on-staff psychologists—also came up empty-handed. We all knew I wouldn't remember.

"I mean, he felt guilty. What sort of practiced murderer feels that much guilt and keeps stabbing anyway?"

"Maybe he felt called to do it? Plenty of people use their beliefs as excuses to do some terrible things."

"Yeah, well, I hate to break it to him, but God was not in that stairwell," I mumbled, my water bottle crinkling as I twisted it sharply in my hands. "Just me, for all the good that did Maddy."

"Look," Mark said. "I'm not going to tell you it's going to be okay, but you've *got* to stop blaming yourself."

"Why?" I blurted out. "If I were a better telepath, I could have found her faster. She'd still be alive."

"Hadley," Mark said, sighing in exasperation. "Of all the stupid things . . . Ian said—"

"I know Dr. Patterson said she was gone. *I know*," I snapped, then winced, glancing at Mark apologetically. "Let's not forget that I *forgot what the murderer looks like*. Tell me the truth, Mark. If it had been anyone else, would we have him?"

"You want the truth, Hadley? Fine. Sure," Mark said matter-of-factly. "Maybe someone else would have gotten a good look at his face. Maybe they would've stopped him even. You want to know what I think would have actually happened if you hadn't been there? I think Madison would have lain in that stairwell until some stranger tripped over her after who knows how long. I think you're the one person who could've felt her, and if you hadn't been there, no one would have run to her. It wouldn't have been a friend who found her and fought for her. And I think *that* would have been a damned tragedy."

I sniffed, blinking back bitter tears. I hadn't thought of that.

"Are you seeing the therapist?" Mark asked.

Ah, that. The whole being suspended from duty until they cleared me thing. Apparently, crying over the death of one of your best friends with cameras around—

though not the useful kind, like, oh, say, a security camera that could have recorded Madison's murder— was frowned upon. Well, to be fair, it might have had something to do with a telekinetic agent losing her shit at a crime scene. Thankfully, no one had linked the "freak incident," where two dozen car alarms went off at the time of the murder, half of them with their windshields blown out, to a rampaging telekinetic. I was certain more than a few students with cell phones were bribed. The Agency's reputation remained unblemished. Still, Ryker wouldn't have me digging through suspects' minds until he was certain I was in control of myself.

Besides regular visits from Dr. Patterson to make sure my grief didn't blow anyone up—well, besides the knife-wielding murderer—I had to see the Agency's shrink to make sure I was fit to return to duty. I hadn't told anyone yet, but I didn't think my psych eval at the end of the month was going to meet her standards.

I shifted uncomfortably and dropped my gaze, cheeks burning. "Yeah, I've been going."

"Good," Mark said bluntly. Much to my appreciation, he didn't push it. "I think we've done enough for one day," he added as I tried to regain my composure.

"I can keep going," I said, dropping my gaze, even though I *really* didn't want to.

"Nah. You're grumpy," Mark said, glancing down at his phone. "Besides, Anna texted. You know you have class?"

"Oh, *Je*-sus!" I moaned, throwing my hands up in exasperation.

Retaking Victimology—a class that appealed significantly less considering what happened—was, perhaps, not high on my list of smart life choices. I justified the decision thinking it might make for a good

69

distraction or help me regain a sense of normalcy, but it was still syllabus week, and things were already circling the drain.

If I was late again, Dr. Griffin would do what a knife-wielding murderer could not, I just knew it.

I scurried into the library forty-five minutes later, still sweating, though I was wearing another one of Lilly's outfits, so maybe I wouldn't gag the person in the desk beside me.

I tapped my wallet against the sensor on the wall and nearly pranced in impatience as the system recognized my ID tucked within it. The fancy Plexiglas doors whirred open to allow me through. I rushed inside and turned right, nearly running toward the computer station.

Dr. Griffin's class started in fifteen minutes, and I'd forgotten to print out . . .

I stopped. What was I here for?

PowerPoint slides! I'd left my computer and notebook in my room this morning, and my phone was dead. Again. I shouldn't have used it to listen to music on my run. Now I had no way to record Dr. Griffin. I didn't know why I bothered. Auditory information and I weren't friends. Trying to listen to Dr. Griffin speak *and* take notes never went well, but I had to do *something* to help me remember later.

It was a losing battle. I knew it. The universe knew it, but *no one* could say I didn't try.

I *tap tap tapped!* on a keyboard to wake up the computer in front of me.

"Come *on*," I muttered as the machine took its sweet time.

"Oh, God! That's sick!" a male voice said from the other side of the computers.

"Shh!" his friend hissed.

They glanced up, realizing they'd drawn my attention. My eyes met theirs.

Madison looked back at me through their minds, bloody and screaming.

I wasn't going to make it to class.

"Show me that!" I snapped.

Their eyes grew wide, fingers scrambling to *click! click! click!* out of the window as I rushed around the corner, but I was faster. I telekinetically ripped their mouse away, and they yelped, lurching back from the computer, their faces pale. I shoved them aside, grabbing the mouse and pressing play on the video they had attempted to close.

The video had been shared anonymously on social media and already had thousands of views.

It was Madison's murder.

Blood drained from my face as the scene played out, bile rising in my throat. The video was taken from behind the parking garage, exactly where I had seen her two weeks ago. She trembled on the ground, crying and crawling, trying to get away. She was already bleeding badly, red streaking the pavement as her strength failed and her arms gave out beneath her. The man—he must have had the camera strapped to his chest from the angle—grabbed her by the ankle. She cried out as he wrenched her leg with a sickening pop and flipped her to face him. Her wide blue eyes stared up at the camera.

An inhuman shriek erupted from the speakers, so loud that every patron in the library turned to look at us.

The hidden figure didn't hesitate. He raised his knife. Her scream cut off.

The psychic scream I'd heard lasted much longer.

I nearly threw up at what followed.

Then they were in the stairwell, the man dragging Madison in by her feet. He tossed Madison's legs down and forced her over with his boot, casting her aside like she was trash. He slammed the door closed. Madison was still. The figure leaned down and took her hand. A black sharpie appeared. Slowly, and in full view of the camera, Madison's murderer spelled out three words in an unmistakably masculine scrawl:

KILL THE FREAKS

The screen cut to black and words filled the void:

THEY WILL ALL FALL

My breath came out in short, hiccupping gasps. I stared at the screen, now blurred by tears.

The sick bastard had recorded one of my best friends being murdered, and then he put it online for everyone to see!

Madison's mom—her poor fiancé!

Voices raised in alarm around me. My head shot up, though too late to realize what I was doing. The chairs the two boys had been sitting in hurtled across the computer station, slamming into the opposite wall as a student leaped out of the way. Dents remained in the wall as they clattered to the ground.

People backed away from me, staring with wide eyes.

"I-I'm sorry," I stammered, heart hammering. Angry, grief-stricken tears slid down my cheeks as I rushed for the exit.

When Mark approached me half an hour later, I was sitting in the grass, staring at the godforsaken parking garage and a half-dozen cars with their windows blown out. Glass was scattered everywhere. Again. Car alarms blared. Again. I sat there, shaking, reliving *that day* all over again. I stared at my hands, half expecting them to be soaked in blood.

"Ryker is going to kill me," I said, sniffing, as Mark sat down beside me, the only person willing to come within twenty yards of an upset telekinetic.

"What happened?" Mark asked.

Agents and tow truck operators scuttled around, trying to remove the cars before too many onlookers showed up. How many times could they spin the story as vandalism? I was so, *so* dead if this drew attention to the Agency.

"I saw the video, and then glass was everywhere. I don't remember what happened in between."

If only the memory lapse had taken the memory of the video with it . . .

Mark placed his hand on my shoulder and sighed. He had already seen the video. He had been trying to get to me before I saw it.

Everyone knew what could happen when I got upset.

"I called Anna," he said. "She's coming to get you."

I nodded in numb acknowledgment.

"Why would he record it?" I asked. It came out as a whisper. "What did Madison do to deserve that?"

"We'll never understand someone like him," Mark said.

"It's on the news," I said. It was a statement, not a question.

Chaos was buzzing in Mark's head like a bunch of disoriented moths around a floodlight. Ryker was livid. The only reason he wasn't standing in front of me, chewing my dumb ass out, was because he was attempting to control a mob of reporters.

Unfortunately, the only thing that didn't cower in the presence of Ryker's temper was a reporter with a viral murder video that drew in viewers like flies to a corpse.

The media erupted that day—locally, first, but it didn't take long before the national news stations also had a censored video of Madison's death playing on a loop. The headlines were abuzz with shocking attention-grabbers like: "Superhero Murdered. Government Cover-up?" "Why Was She Targeted? Who Was Madison Crawford?" "Parahuman Killer? Who's Next?" "Agency Claims 'Situation Under Control.'"

Madison's face haunted every screen. They used a beautiful headshot with a bright smile that made everything feel all the more tragic. Her name was on everyone's lips. People couldn't stop talking about the murdered parahuman and the freakish warning her butcher had left behind.

Never mind her life. Never mind the fact she had been going for her doctorate or that she'd never made it to her birthday or that the wedding dress that had brought her mom to tears was hanging unworn in her closet. No one talked about any of that, but the public still rallied behind her as if she meant something to them, calling for her to posthumously be honored as a superhero.

They didn't care before the video, when Agent Madison Crawford died in a "tragic accident." She made the local news and was an old story by morning.

The journalists had no trouble clearing their schedules to be at her memorial.

"Madison looked like her mom," Lilly, Mark's teenage daughter, said somberly beside me, rocking her infant brother, Jonah, in her arms. We stood in a crowd at Liberty Station, watching San Diego's twin superheroes, Livewire and Wildfire, give moving speeches about what an honor it was to have known Madison and how they would work tirelessly to hunt down and bring her murderer to justice.

Not that they'd done anything close to that yet. Good luck getting Ryker to give Major Crimes the case.

Cameras flashed and reporters asked them a barrage of questions about viable leads and motives.

"Stephanie's nice," I said absently.

Reporters shouted questions over each other, and no one seemed to care that Stephanie Crawford stood in the background as they asked invasive questions regarding her daughter's personal life.

Madison's fiancé, David, stood at her side, his head bowed. I didn't need telepathy to see the toll this was taking on him. Hell, the dark circles and haunted expression on his face were probably courtesy of the Agency. The home he shared with Madison—*had* shared with Madison—had practically been ransacked looking for evidence. David himself was initially a suspect under the assumption that it's always the significant other, but the theory didn't survive the afternoon. He had swiped his badge at work half an hour before Madison's time of death. Security cameras recorded him sitting blissfully unaware at his desk until the fateful moment his phone rang.

"Do you know what they're going to name Madison?" Lilly asked, referring to the city's poll for Madison's superhero alias.

Each city boasted representative parahumans— superheroes, as everyone liked to refer to them, though the national Superhero Superlative Program had officially ended decades ago as parahuman acceptance became mainstream. Well, more mainstream. Few could argue that *everyone* accepted parahumans being out in the open.

Damani and Janelle Aluko in the Agency's Major Crimes division were known to everyone as Livewire and Wildfire, respectively. Mark had been Tank. I doubted anyone knew their real names, even though they weren't kept from the public. Only designated superheroes had aliases, but with so much public pressure, the city chose to posthumously name Madison and induct her into San Diego's Parahuman Hall of Fame.

"They're naming her Banshee," I whispered to Lilly.

Her face scrunched in disgust. I rolled my eyes in silent agreement. Madison would have hated her alias too. I could see it now, Maddy griping about being named after some hellish she-demon who shrieked upon the arrival of death. Frankly, I found the choice repulsive, but the city hadn't thought further than how badass it sounded.

Maybe Madison would have liked that part.

"I voted for Siren," Lilly whispered sheepishly, as if I'd disapprove of her taking part in the dog-and-pony show.

"So did I," I whispered back. "A creature with a beautiful voice fits Maddy much better."

Jonah fussed in Lilly's arms as the crowd erupted into applause over something I'd missed. Mark's wife, Diane, did her best to clap with her oldest son, Logan, propped on her hip.

Mark patrolled by the stage where Livewire and Wildfire spoke. I'd seen him a few times and waved, but if he spotted us, he didn't acknowledge us. It was probably for the best. Mark moved to San Diego to get out of the spotlight and keep his family safe. He probably wasn't too thrilled that my behavior might call attention to them.

Stephanie Crawford stepped forward. I turned away when she started crying, recent memories of fresh-cut lilies and a preacher's somber voice flooding my mind. Funerals were hell on telepaths. Madison's mother's grief still shrieked in my brain like the godforsaken Banshee they'd named her daughter after. I didn't need the real thing again.

I focused on Jonah, too young and innocent to understand what was going on. His naïve, simple thoughts—more emotions and urges than anything—were blessings to my exhausted brain. He reached for Lilly's shoulder-length hair, which she somehow masterfully kept away from him. Logan began fussing, squirming in Diane's arms in an attempt to get down.

"I'll take him," I told Diane. I'd had enough of empty speeches. With a relieved sigh, she passed me her toddler.

"Let's go find something fun," I told Logan with cartoonish excitement.

I should have felt guilty for abandoning Madison's memorial, but between the feigned grief and fake sympathy from at least half the crowd and the genuine grief of too many others, my head was going to explode . . . or worse: something else would.

"I'm coming with you," Lilly said, turning on her heel.

I'd figured as much, though part of me had hoped she would stay. Her anxiety was half the reason I needed to get away.

As we walked out of earshot of her stepmom, Lilly leaned in close and half whispered, "My dad is safe, right? Diane promises me he is, but I don't know if she'd tell me the truth. I know you will."

Lilly and I had a close relationship, much like Mark and I did. In a sense, I considered her to be a little sister the way Mark viewed me like a daughter. I glanced back at the stage but couldn't see Mark.

"Nothing suggests he's going to go through with his threat, but the Agency has all parahumans dressed like SDPD, just in case. Everybody's on edge thanks to that damned video," I said in a hushed tone, so others wouldn't overhear as we pushed through the crowd to the sidewalk. "As far as anyone knows, the only parahumans here are Livewire and Wildfire."

Lilly sighed in relief. "This is bullshit," she muttered under her breath. "Dad said it would be different here, but the Agency still puts him right in the middle of anything dangerous!"

"Your dad's skin is basically steel. Besides, there are a lot of other parahumans up there with him," I said reassuringly.

"You're not," she said, her voice full of teenage petulance.

"I'm not a field agent," I offered as an explanation. Not to mention I was still on probation for at least two more weeks, assuming the Agency's therapist would allow me back.

Lilly was quiet for a minute before she spoke again. "I'm really sorry about Madison."

Outside the throngs of people, I found a bench by a fountain and dropped onto it, holding Logan in my lap. He didn't want to be still but quickly changed his tune when a leaf began magically dancing in the air.

I was good with kids . . . so long as I remembered I was watching them. While it was only a small fraction of the reason Lilly had left the memorial, someone had to make sure I didn't lose the baby.

"Madison was amazing," I said quietly. "She was one of my first friends after . . ."

"The accident?"

"Yeah," I said bluntly.

"You still don't remember it?" Lilly asked.

I stared at the fountain in front of us, trying to imagine what it must have been like for my car to be underwater five years ago.

"Nope," I said. "I never will."

"You're sure? Like, nothing has ever come back?"

I shook my head. "I have dreams—nightmares, but I don't know what's real and what isn't."

It was Madison who had explained why I sometimes remembered things and sometimes didn't.

"Think of your memories as if they're being stored in a warehouse," she had said over lunch in the Agency's lackluster cafeteria.

I was twenty-one and had recently joined the Agency after six months at Mercy Rehab, adjusting to my newly manifested abilities and the episodes of memory loss that would forever be a part of my life. Madison had just started the neuroscience program at City of San Diego University—CSDU—and was working on a PhD. Still a novice agent with only three years of experience, she had taken me, the awkward new hire, under her wing and bought me lunch frequently as an excuse to check on me.

"When something new happens, like a lecture for a class, that information gets put on a truck to go to the memory warehouse," she had said, separating her food into neat little piles so nothing touched. It was one of her odd habits.

"Now," she had continued, "imagine the inflammation from using your telekinesis is like an EMP pulse. It knocks out the power to the warehouse and the truck. The warehouse can get the power back on, so your established memories come back.

"But," she finished, poking some mushy corn casserole into its designated place. "The truck gets stranded. Its information is lost. That's why you can get your established memories back, but you can't always recover the ones you just made."

"Then why can't I remember anything about who I am yet?" I asked.

There was a warmth in her eyes as she thought it over.

"Because that wasn't an EMP," she finally said. "That was an atomic bomb. The old warehouse is gone."

She was right. The memories from the first twenty-one years of my life were gone forever.

Around Logan's head, two more leaves joined in, jumping in the air as the little boy giggled and grabbed at them. Technically, I was advised against using my powers until my memory problems settled back to their base levels, but . . .

"More! More!" Logan squealed.

A smile tugged at my lips. Worth it.

"I didn't see Anna," Lilly said.

"Her advisor needed to see her, and the Agency wanted her to retake her firearms test. She got stuck in traffic," I answered while trying to keep Logan from jumping out of my lap after the dancing leaves.

The boy had *way* too much energy, much like my overcaffeinated best friend.

I didn't add that Anna was about as impressed with the city's newfound grief over Madison's death as I was.

Lilly's face scrunched as she shot me a look: "Anna carries a gun? I've never seen it."

I sighed. "She's supposed to, but . . ." Heat rose in my cheeks.

Lilly's brain was buzzing for an answer.

"The Fischer Law," I explained. "You can't carry a gun around certain kinds of parahumans—like telekinetics or speedsters."

Some trigger-happy cops in Cincinnati learned real quick that pulling a gun on a telekinetic violating his wife's restraining order was a one-way ticket to a Darwin Award.

"I also blow things up in my sleep sometimes," I added in a rush. Sometimes, even when I was awake, I remembered, thinking back to my recent "incident" on campus.

Lilly laughed so hard that Jonah startled in her arms. She quickly quieted down and made calming "*Shh, shh . . .*" sounds at him when he whimpered.

"Sorry," she said. "It was rude to laugh."

"It is what it is," I said, shrugging.

"It sucks that they made her do it today. She loved Madison too," Lilly continued as she bounced the baby on her knee.

He still didn't have the best head control, but Lilly was a pro at being a big sister and knew exactly how to hold him. I thought hard, but I couldn't remember ever holding a baby that small. I must have. My brother, Collin, was six years younger.

I shrugged off the thought. My earliest memories were of teenage Collin. I wouldn't let myself touch anything as fragile as an infant. God forbid I find a way to drop them or forget to hold their heads right.

"Yeah, well, that's the government for you," I said, shrugging again.

I blinked hard as my head swam, suddenly regretting my choice to use my powers. I knew better, and I still—

"Stop!" a woman's pleading voice shrieked. He loomed over her, silent.

"Please," she begged as he held up the knife. He stepped closer, numb to her cries.

A shriek filled the air, muffled by industrial strength earplugs he had worn for just this occasion.

"Do you think—" Lilly began, oblivious to my moment.

I sat perfectly upright on the bench, my sudden movement cutting her off midsentence. Leaves fluttered to the ground. I held the toddler to my chest and stood, turning on my heel in a flash.

"Hadley?" Lilly asked, alarmed.

"I need to get you back to Diane," I said abruptly.

"Why?" she asked, bewildered.

Because I felt *him*. In the distance, a murderer weaved through the crowd. That sick bastard was watching Madison's memorial, remembering how he stabbed her over and over. I could see it as clear as a movie. He was *obsessing* over it, playing the scene out in his head, delighting over every gory detail.

I couldn't let him escape this time.

"He's here, isn't he?" Lilly asked, color draining from her face.

I didn't respond. I focused what little attention span I had on Madison's murderer's mind. If I slipped for even a second, he might be gone.

Diane was bewildered when I unceremoniously ran up to her and dumped her child into her arms without a word, her teenage stepdaughter rushing up behind me with tears on her cheeks.

A brief flash stole my breath and stopped me in my tracks—Mark. A dagger sank into his chest as a faceless man loomed over him. No, wait. A dagger couldn't break Mark's skin. Not real. Lilly! Lilly was panicking. I shook my head, trying to clear the sudden jolt that had knocked me off course.

"Hey!" I called behind me. "Your dad is bulletproof, remember?"

The teenage girl's relief swept over my body, and I disengaged from her mind.

I had only one focus now.

He was by the stage.

Stephanie joined Wildfire and Livewire as the center of attention. Livewire stepped forward to hand Stephanie a plaque from the city. The Parahuman Hall of Fame ceremony was coming to a close. Livewire's twin sister, Wildfire, leaned forward to give the woman a tight embrace.

It was endearing, yet Madison's murderer hardly seemed moved. It was an odd change for a man who'd felt guilt as he plunged a knife into a young woman's chest. It was weird, but it felt like he was there to do more than watch the damage he had caused play out. He was looking for . . . something.

Kill the freaks!

It was the message he had written on Madison's hand. He didn't want to stop with her.

He was hunting. He was hunting *us*.

"Mark!" I shouted. I pushed through the crowd, bewildered attendees stumbling aside as I barreled forward. "Mark, where are you?"

"Hadley!" someone yelled.

I nearly slid to a halt as a petite woman with black hair pulled into a ponytail and dark, angular eyes ran toward me. She wore a uniform that read SDPD, but I recognized her as a parahuman.

"Alice!" I gasped.

Special Agent Alice Cho met me, her brown eyes glistening in panic. "Hadley, wh—"

"He's at the stage!"

Then, waves roared in my ears. I stumbled, the world cartwheeling around me. I blinked rapidly, willing the vertigo to stop.

Jesus. What the hell happened?

When my vision steadied, I was alone on the other side of the park, a calming breeze and the warm kiss of sunlight from a cloudless day completely at odds with the situation. Absolutely nothing was out of place.

Bewildered, I spun around in every direction. I was by the water on a dirt path near the playground. Small watercraft were tied to the dock, but it was deserted otherwise. The crowd of people was far away in the distance. Faint applause sounded as Madison's memorial came to a close, but I could no longer feel anyone around me.

Where was Alice? Where was Madison's killer?

"Gordon!" an unmistakable voice boomed in the distance. "Cho!" the voice continued, roaring like a lion.

At that moment, I feared William Ryker far more than any murderer. Alice was gone, the unsub was gone, and I had absolutely no idea what had just happened.

I was so fired.

If Ryker didn't kill me himself first.

My hair fluttered as Brittany slid to a halt beside me, whistling wind alerting me to her arrival only a split second in advance.

"Here! They're here!" she called. "You okay? You're pale. What happened?" she asked in a rush, surveying the area.

"I—um . . ."

As Ryker rounded the hilltop with half a dozen personnel in police uniforms, a splash caught my attention. I turned as Alice clambered onto the soggy shore. She struggled to walk in the thick mud, slurping sounds announcing every step. She coughed, water streaming from her mouth. She continued to spit mouthfuls of water as she wrung her hair and clothes dry. Switching from gills back to lungs was always an uncomfortable experience for her, and I attempted not to stare as the slits on the sides of her neck lay back down, leaving only faint lines on her skin to betray her genetic anomaly.

"Alice!" I ran toward her as she crawled up the embankment.

Perhaps most important, it was the direction away from Ryker. I offered her my hand. Brittany's joined mine a split second later.

"He got away," Alice croaked. She closed the gap between us and reached out a damp hand.

Brittany and I pulled as she scrambled up the slippery hill. She breathed deep and spat out another mouthful of water as she stumbled to the top.

"Jesus," Alice grumbled. "This water tastes *awful*."

"Are you hurt?" Brittany asked her.

"No," she said, her breathing returning to normal. "Just pissed. I *almost* had him."

I blinked, and Ryker towered over us. He was an average-sized man with no extraordinary abilities, but with a presence like his, he might as well have been ten feet tall.

"Where is he?" Ryker demanded.

"He left the park," Alice said.

Ryker cursed. "I need a description."

Alice shook her head. "I never saw him. He wore a hood; his face was hidden underneath."

"Then how did you identify him as our suspect?" Ryker demanded.

"I just called it in, sir. Hadley identified him."

And just like that, Ryker's ice-blue eyes, so pale they almost appeared white, stared daggers in my direction.

I was definitely going to die.

CHAPTER 5

This was *not* where I wanted to be.

Fluorescent lights cooked my eyeballs as a cold metal table bit into my elbows. Equally inviting was the rigid metal chair that creaked as I attempted to find a more relaxed position. There were few rooms within the Agency's San Diego branch I considered cuddly, but the interrogation room probably topped the list of the least welcoming with its stark walls, lack of windows, and Big Brother blinking over Anna's shoulder in the corner. Even with Dr. Patterson and Anna seated across from me, I still squirmed in place, palms sweating.

Ryker was taking no chances with the Agency's overly emotional telekinetic.

Dr. Patterson clasped my wrist, his abilities throwing my central nervous system into overdrive. A soothing rush of serotonin surged through me with every heartbeat. While he kept me calm and kept anything from going boom, Anna had been dragged in as the resident Hadley expert and the person most likely to coax information out of my skull. Small wonders the Agency allowed her to do a dissertation the public would never be aware of.

I couldn't see Ryker, though I sensed him in the observation room on the other side of the glass with at least three other people. Probably Tom, Glenn, and Mark based on the bits and pieces of thoughts I could discern. Staying out of sight was futile when the person you were observing could see your mind.

Well, sort of. Telepaths had existed for centuries. Back when there was parahuman hysteria, people had fixated on how to neutralize us. Several hundred years of fear in mostly Western nations had resulted in more than one witch hunt and more brutal executions than I cared to think about, but some of the knowledge gained during that time was still applicable.

For example, Ryker was particularly adept at blocking telepaths from reading his thoughts. It was rigorous and frustrating training that few people succeeded in mastering. Therefore, few ever bothered with it. It's not like there were many telepaths—we had been particularly hunted in the past. Most of our ancestors had been eliminated, to put it politely. Inheriting the combination of recessive genes that conferred telepathy was about as rare as getting hit by lightning on your way to cash your winning lottery ticket.

Well, maybe not that rare, but numbers aside, most known telepaths were employed by the Agency or some other institution that served the greater good. The chance of some rogue telepath sneaking into the president's office and getting the nuclear codes out of his brain essentially did not exist. In the off chance one decided to attempt nuclear winter, President Ogden had a telepath on the Secret Service's payroll. Nothing defeated a telepath quite like another telepath.

Anyway, tangents.

Ryker underwent anti-telepath training, and it was mostly successful. The man's brain sounded like a buzzing, angry hornet's nest about 99 percent of the time. For the other 1 percent, I was too terrified to listen anyway.

"Hadley?" Dr. Patterson said, gently squeezing my wrist. I lurched in my chair, eyes flitting away from the dark, mirrorlike surface separating me from Ryker to focus on Anna.

"What was the question?" I asked, mouth dry.

A nauseating wave of anxiety subsided as Dr. Patterson's grip tightened, a rush of serotonin leaving me nearly giddy. I was high as a kite on feelings, and I wasn't sure if I would burst into laughter, start screaming, or vomit.

I glanced at the camera mounted in the room's corner, red light flashing. Nice to know my substandard performance was being recorded. It was a theme lately. Maybe they'd put them all in a montage and roll the video out during the next office party.

"How did you know the suspect was in the crowd?" Anna asked, voice irritatingly steady.

I focused on Anna. Her legs crossed and uncrossed beneath the table. Even without sensing her energy, I recognized her nervous habit of repeatedly tucking and untucking a curl behind her ear. She'd worked with me for a number of cases, but Ryker himself rarely supervised, and we were never on this side of the glass. Oh, and I was never the subject of interrogation. At least I wasn't suffering alone.

I took a deep breath, willing myself to channel my inner Anna. "He was thinking about Madison. I saw him stabbing her."

"Most of the crowd saw the video of what happened to Madison. How can you be sure it was him?"

I squirmed in my chair.

Dr. Patterson's hand squeezed tighter. My eyes darted toward the glass again. Ryker probably already thought I was a liability. The suspect had escaped me twice. I didn't remember either incident. It was a miracle I hadn't been fired already, but I knew it was coming.

And why shouldn't it? I'd done nothing right. My condition screwed things up every time, and it was a miracle I wasn't dead myself.

I leaned back, trying to force myself to relax. If there was any chance of saving my job, Ryker couldn't think I was a basket case. I needed to be able to function without Dr. Patterson acting as a human happy pill.

Easier said than done.

"What set the man's version of events apart so you could identify him as unique?" Anna asked.

Her voice trembled slightly; I found it oddly comforting.

Just pretend we're having a conversation at home. I tried not to jump as Anna's voice infiltrated my mind as intimately as if she'd spoken into my ear.

That always creeped me out. Just as Ryker had learned how to block me, Anna knew how to project her thoughts. She'd become increasingly skilled at it, though her voice still hit me like a cymbal's peal.

As if we're home and Ryker is chilling on our couch, I thought. She didn't hear me. It didn't work in both directions.

"He knew more than the video showed. He remembered following her from class. He hit her from behind in the parking garage. That's how her hearing aid fell out. He was reliving the thrill of chasing her outside. He remembered the moment she realized she was in trouble."

Bile churned in my stomach. I swallowed hard, willing myself to forget Madison's ragged pants as she crawled on the ground or how her skin was slick with sweat when he grabbed her.

"How do you know it was a man?" Anna asked.

Ryker still wasn't ready to assume gender, but it was the *one* small thing I was actually certain of. Well, now I was. Anna had pressed the issue earlier, insisting that, statistically speaking, men committed most violent crimes, but Ryker didn't want numbers. Ryker wanted the real version of events.

I closed my eyes, feeling the heat of Madison's body as his hand wrenched her ankle and his sleeve slipped, revealing his wrist.

"His arm hair was visible."

"That's not enough to conclusively say anything," Anna said.

I breathed deep, willing the memories to surface. I had never seen his face, but I knew I was right. When I closed my eyes again, Madison was running, but she wasn't fast enough. Strong arms wrapped around her. He covered her mouth before—

I didn't want to remember the rest.

"His hair is short. When his hoodie was up, I couldn't feel hair against his neck. It's longer in the front than on the sides. It didn't touch his ears, but it touched his forehead. He shaved, but he had enough stubble for his hood to brush against it. When he grabbed Madison, he reached down. He was taller than her. He's fit. His muscles flexed when he grabbed her. He was strong enough to restrain her and throw her down. His pants were looser. His hoodie fit across his stomach and chest the same. He had a watch. It was big. His wrist was big. He's probably fit but with a big-boned frame."

Now, if only I could catch a memory of him looking at himself in a mirror . . .

I opened my eyes. Anna scribbled on a notepad, fighting the urge to grin.

You're doing great!

I made eye contact to show I understood.

Still. So. Weird.

We nearly leaped from our seats when the door flew open and slammed into the wall.

"Where was this information weeks ago?" Ryker yelled, slamming his hands on the desk.

I froze. Thanks to the human happy pill, nothing blew up.

"I don't remember engaging with the suspect in the parking garage, sir."

Oh, thank God. I did not say *bad guy*.

"But you remember now?"

"No," I nearly whispered.

Ryker's cold, rage-filled eyes held mine. I wanted to look away, but I was too scared to move.

"I remember what he saw. I remember what he felt. He thought about it at the stage."

"You remember him at the stage?"

I nodded.

"I can't remember anything after Alice found me, but I remember him at the stage. He was watching Madison's mom."

What little blood I had left drained from my face. I hadn't admitted yet that I'd had another memory lapse. Dr. Patterson sensed my panic and cast a glance toward Anna.

"Don't worry about that," Anna said, her voice shaky as she attempted to distract me. "Alice is filling us in on when you engaged the suspect. Tell us more about how you identified him. Why was he there?"

I settled back in my chair, my stomach churning. I saw and felt the innermost thoughts of a murderer. It wasn't the first time. My job involved sitting in on interrogations and immersing myself in ugly memories. This time was different though. He killed Madison, and he . . .

"He was reliving the moment," I said.

"What does that mean?" Ryker asked, biting out each word as if exerting patience might kill him.

"He's wanted this for a while," I said, closing my eyes and allowing myself to feel *him*. "He's dreamed of what it would be like to kill a parahuman for so long, and now he's realized he can do it. It's . . . I think this is deeply personal for him."

"Does he plan to do it again?"

It was the question that kept us up at night. Was he merely posturing with his threatening messages and videos? Was he satisfied with just Madison? Was she his one and only intended target, and he was just trying to disarm us? His mind confirmed our worst fears. I nodded.

"He's hunting us. Parahumans, that is," I said. "He was picking his next target at the memorial."

"Did he seem interested in anyone in particular?" Anna asked.

"I don't think so," I said. "I don't think he expected to be identified."

Why would he? Three weeks had passed without a single lead until today. As far as he knew, he had gotten away with it.

"You never saw his face?" Anna asked.

I shook my head.

"We can still update the profile," Anna said quickly, before Ryker could jump in. "What kind of person is he? What was he thinking?"

"He was different from when I first engaged him," I said. "I felt him before I found Madison. He felt guilty for killing her. But this time . . ."

I scrunched my face, concentrating hard on what I had felt. "It was like he was a different person, almost. He didn't feel guilt. He's moved past the initial shock of taking a life—I think Madison *was* his first . . . his first victim. He feels proud now, like he's done the impossible and has the power to do it again."

Ryker stood up, straight and rigid. I licked my chapped lips, wondering if I should mention the last thing. It would make Ryker go nuclear, but Anna's profile was the only thing we had right now, and she needed to know.

"He's emboldened because he knows we aren't close to catching him," I choked out.

Ryker went eerily still, his eyes boring into me.

"I want everything you know, and I want it today. *Right now,*" he said quietly.

I'd thought the loud, angry version of Ryker was scary. The steely, quiet version was downright terrifying.

Four hours and one miracle later, Ryker did the opposite of firing me, proving that I could not, in fact, read my boss's mind. Dr. Patterson and Anna pulled as many miracles as possible and extracted what they could from my broken brain. They brought in a sketch artist, and the result was the roughest sketch of a suspect I'd ever seen. I glanced at the drawing in my hands as the world rushed by outside the bus's window. The brown-eyed, neutral-colored male with faint stubble and ambiguous features stared back at me, completely unfamiliar. Most of his features were nothing more than educated guesses based on snippets I gleaned from his mind. Beyond that, everything was based on statistics, numbers, and profiling. Less than 20 percent of the population had blue eyes, so he probably had brown eyes. He was taller than Madison, and she wasn't short, so he was probably at least six feet tall. He was fit and muscular, so he was probably two hundred pounds or more. The only things I knew for certain were that he was male and Caucasian. Every detail put him in line with maybe 5 percent of San Diego's population of four million.

Somehow, narrowing things down to a mere two hundred thousand people did not make me feel better, regardless of all the encouraging lines Anna threw at me.

I couldn't guess at age or education, despite the repeated push for what felt like the suspect's entire medical history. No, I didn't know if he had a large vocabulary. I didn't get narrative thought from him. No, I didn't know if any of his body parts ached. No, I wasn't sure if he felt winded when he ran. Was he thinking about his outfit? Did he interact with anyone while he was there? Did he seem more at ease around younger members of the crowd, or did he appear drawn to older individuals? Did anyone invite him to join them? Was it possible someone there might have known and recognized him?

I didn't know, and I didn't know the answers to the thousands of questions that followed.

Anna had been correct in her assumption that, because most white victims had white killers, Madison's murderer was white. I had seen his skin clearly this time. At least we could nail that one down.

Yay Anna. Yay me.

Everything else about him was still nebulous. I didn't get the sense that Madison's killer was psychotic, and his self-control, meticulous planning, and desire to, theoretically, target only parahumans specifically put him in the category of a "mission-oriented killer." In other words, if we didn't find him quickly, he would definitely kill again. Anna acted as if understanding that about him was some sort of victory, but I didn't understand why.

Anna disagreed with me about Madison being his first victim, and who was I to argue? It was all crap based on my fragmented memories. The Agency sent forensic scientists out to find a shoe print—really anything that might nail down more specific details—in the memorial's vicinity and by the water where we had pursued him, but they had come up just as empty-handed as they had at the stairwell. At Madison's memorial, he could have been one of hundreds of sets of prints in the dirt.

He was as bold as he was clever. He ventured into public places in broad daylight, both to kill and to hunt for his next victim. What should have increased the risk to him only hampered our efforts.

Anna thought it would be to his detriment in the future. What she didn't say out loud is that we might not find out until he killed again, and she was certain he would try.

Despite everything, Ryker ordered Madison's murderer's presumed description posted on every door, hall, and elevator within the Agency, and they sent the description to the police department and every other federal agency that had an office in San Diego County. Anna was now attached at the hip to her contacts at the Behavioral Analysis Unit in the FBI as they combed over every detail I had given them, desperate for some sort of break that would narrow the suspect pool. I tried not to think about how some of the nation's top agents were currently watching me stumble through an interview, but I reminded myself I should be comfortable with humiliation by now.

Suddenly, I had been repurposed as a telepathic bloodhound. Much to the consternation of the Agency's therapist, my psych eval was waived, and moving forward, I lived and breathed for the Agency, working *in the field* full-time for the first time in my five years as an agent. That meant walking the streets and listening to every stray thought that crossed my path, hunting for the mind of the person who had killed Madison. Tips had been coming in nonstop since they had sensationalized her death on the news, and it was now my job to chase them.

It was for Madison, so I would do whatever they needed. I started tomorrow.

When I stepped off the bus, my legs felt too heavy to move, my body imitating a deflated balloon after hours of happy feelings surging through my brain. Dr. Patterson warned me I might be even more confused than usual and have trouble sleeping for a night or two. I couldn't wait.

Sarcasm, of course.

I trudged the half mile to the apartment I shared with Anna. Using the last bit of energy I had, I slid the key into the lock, turned the deadbolt, and dragged myself through the door.

Loud, excited yapping and the sweet aroma of cake greeted me.

Cake?

"Down, buddy," I mumbled as Weasel danced around my knees, clawing at my jeans in excitement.

"Anna?" a male voice called.

"It's Hadley, Elliott," I called back to Anna's boyfriend. "The Agency has taken her hostage."

A curly mop of light-brown hair popped out of the kitchen.

"Lord Almighty," Elliott said empathetically. "Anna warned me, but you look like hell."

"Thanks. Ryker has that effect on people," I mumbled.

"But you nearly got the guy?"

"I mean, he was there," I said emptily. "We chased him. He got away. Again."

I stepped into the kitchen and laid eyes on the fresh tray of cake on the stove. It must have just come out of the oven. The kitchen was sweltering, a common side effect from it being the size of a shoebox.

"Oh," I said, what little energy I had left getting sucked out of me in a rush.

Elliott shifted uncomfortably as I stared down at Madison's birthday cake. He hovered over what looked to be the start of his famous buffalo chicken dip.

"Anna said we were still on," he said.

"Yeah," I said. "We are. I just . . . forgot."

Elliott and I stood there for a minute before he gave a one-shouldered shrug and looked over at the fresh confection. "Want to frost it for me?"

Stepping up to the stove, I grabbed a tub of white frosting, glancing at the sprinkles and candles on the counter. Everything was purple—Madison's favorite color.

Moving forward with Madison's birthday party to honor her memory among friends had seemed like a great idea at first, but after her memorial, a showdown with her killer, and Ryker having me in a proverbial chokehold all day, I was at my emotional limit.

I didn't say that though. Instead, I grabbed a knife out of a drawer and started frosting. Behind me, Elliott's brain was buzzing, and it wasn't about the cake or the dip. I bit my lip and tried to hold back.

Oh, what the hell. Today couldn't get any more messed up.

"Can I break the rules for a minute?" I asked without looking back.

"You mean about something in my head?" Elliott asked as he cracked open a can of diced chicken.

"Yeah."

"Yeah," Elliott said with a laugh. "You can break the rules."

The corner of my mouth tugged upward. Elliott, Anna's boyfriend of six years, was a source of stability for all of us. I was told it was me and my ex, Emily, who had set them up in college.

My smile dropped at the thought of Emily. We had been together for two years before my accident. So everyone told me. She was still no more than a stranger to me. She tried to stick around after I'd woken up without a single memory of who I had been, but ultimately, we hadn't been able to rekindle what we had. She was gone after only a few weeks, and I couldn't blame her.

Her Hadley—Old Hadley, as I liked to call her—had never come back.

I briefly wondered if this was what it felt like for her: as if I died. In a sense, I had. Anna and Elliott were the only ones who had been able to rebuild their relationship with me. I wasn't even close with my family the way Old Hadley was, but Anna and Elliott pulled a miracle.

"I know you've had that ring for six months," I said, pushing thoughts of loss and my own desolate love life from my brain for a moment.

Elliott released his breath in a rush.

"Ah, that," he said, chuckling nervously.

"Why haven't you asked yet?"

"It's just, umm . . ."

"Me," I said. For someone who was emotionally drained, I sure was adding to the emotional abuse tonight.

Life was already hell. Might as well get all the drama over with at once.

"I mean, it's not—"

"Anna is afraid to leave me," I said matter-of-factly.

"She's never said it," Elliott said. "But . . . yeah."

He knew he couldn't lie, so he didn't try to. While hearing him say it out loud stung, I respected him for it.

"You need to live with someone, Hadley," Elliott said as I globbed frosting onto the cake and messily spread it across its surface. The cake was still too hot. I pursed my lips as little pieces broke off and crumbled in the now-lumpy frosting.

"It doesn't have to be Anna," I said. "I'm sure someone else from the Agency would be willing to live with me."

No, they probably wouldn't.

There was a long pause behind me. I reached for the purple sprinkles while Elliott picked his words.

"She's barely left your side in five years," he said. "I can hardly get her to go on vacation with me."

I shook sprinkles onto the poorly frosted, torn-up cake and pretended we weren't talking about me as if I were the incontinent family pet.

"Ask her anyway," I said. "You don't know what she'll say."

Elliott's mind buzzed in sudden alarm.

"Hadley, do you know what she'll say?" he nearly squeaked.

I finally turned to face him. I crossed my arms and kept my eyes on the floor.

"You know I won't tell you that," I said, trying to keep my face expressionless.

The truth was that Anna found the ring in a drawer in Elliott's bedroom five months ago and had been waiting ever since. I wasn't about to let that cat out of the bag. As far as even Anna knew, I hadn't picked up on the ring.

"You and Anna deserve to be *happy*, Elliot," I said, finally meeting his eyes. "Not everyone gets a happy ending."

He winced.

"I'm not sure it's the right time," he said softly.

"Why? Because Ryker's crawled up my ass and built a nest, and there's a murderer on the loose? What if it's never the right time?"

The door flew open then, and I heard Anna stagger in. Elliott nearly leaped out of his skin. Voices carried behind Anna, prompting Weasel to burst into excited yipping.

"Hadley!" Anna called. "Tell me you're here."

"Ask her," I hissed under my breath to Elliott.

"Present and accounted for!" I called, my voice surprisingly even. I couldn't remember what had happened five minutes ago to save my life, but damn, I'd make a fantastic actress.

So long as the audience wasn't Ryker.

"Oh, thank God," Anna said as she rushed around the corner, looking haggard. "I was almost convinced Ryker was going to keep you stashed away at the Agency under lock and key."

"He is absolutely foaming at the mouth right now," Special Agent Christine Chhoeun, a fellow parahuman, said from behind her.

Special Agent Benson Pierce's onyx-colored face popped up behind her, sniffing. The parahumans now officially outnumbered the humans.

"The cake smells good," Ben said.

"It was all Elliott," I said, casting him a grateful look.

Christine stepped into the kitchen and wrapped her arms around me. "You did good," she said. "You did really, really good today."

I blinked rapidly as tears sprang to my eyes. "Thanks," I said, sniffing.

"I hear Alice nearly caught the bastard! Leaped out of the water like a freaking great white and nearly had him by the ankles!" Ben said, clapping me on the shoulder.

"Nearly," I said somberly.

"Hey!" he said. "You guys were close, and now we know you can get him!"

I swallowed the self-doubt rising in my throat like bile. "Where's Alice? I thought she was supposed to ride back with you guys?"

"Ryker," Anna said with a roll of her framed eyes.

"He sent her back to the park with the forensics team, and then she got a call about something near the Scripps Pier in La Jolla," Christine added.

"Oh."

"She'll be here."

Stray thoughts tickled my mind like strands of hair tossed by a breeze, cementing into clearer words and images as the minds that contained them drew closer.

"How many people did you fit into your car?" I asked as I squeezed past the crowd hovering around the matchbox-sized kitchen and poked my head around the corner.

Weasel danced in the living room as yet more parahumans arrived.

I narrowed my eyes.

"Invisibility off, Navin. Someone's going to sit on you," I said, my attention turning to our worn, hand-me-down red couch.

A young man with spiky black hair and tanned skin materialized in our living room, grinning.

"Took her thirty seconds!" Ben said.

"You're damn near on fire today!" Brittany said as she crossed the threshold carrying a cheese platter.

My lips curled upward slightly as a smile tried to materialize. She passed the snacks to Anna and pulled me close, giving me a tight hug.

"Alice is right behind me," she said, releasing me.

As if on cue, Alice appeared at the door. Her black hair was wet and a damp shirt clung to her.

"All right!" Ben shouted. "All of today's heroes are here!"

Alice grinned sheepishly as a crowd formed around her, clapping her on the shoulders.

"Sorry, guys," she said, motioning to her soggy clothes and still-dripping hair. "I changed, but . . . I didn't want to miss it."

"It's fine," Brittany said. "After what you did today, you can do whatever you want."

"I hope to God Ryker doesn't send me back into that damn water," Alice said, laughing. "Do I smell?"

I shook my head, somehow managing a small laugh at her expense. Alice was the Agency's newest hire. Though she had only been part of the team for six months, the transition had been nearly seamless. I didn't know her well yet, but I'd liked her from the start.

"Did you find anything?" I asked.

She shook her head.

"What was going on at the pier?" Anna moved past me to give Alice a careful hug.

"Not a thing," Alice said, doing her best to keep Anna at a distance from her damp clothes. "Got a call that some guy might have jumped or something, but I swam around for an hour and came up with nothing but a couple of startled seals."

"How many are coming tonight?" Elliot asked as he poked his head out from the kitchen. "I hope one cake is enough."

"This is it," Brittany said, settling onto the couch with Navin. "We would've had more, but Ryker's got everybody working in shifts pursuing leads. Hadley and Alice are going to have quite a day tomorrow."

I turned to Alice and raised an eyebrow.

"I volunteered to be your partner for your first day. It's my fault he got away today. Figured I'd take a shot at redemption."

I gave her a weak smile. I knew that feeling.

"Thank you," I said. "For jumping in today. That was impressive."

"You're pretty impressive yourself," Alice replied.

For a brief moment, the park materialized in her mind. She ran behind me, the hooded figure only feet in front of me. He took a hard left near the water, and Alice saw her opening. She went straight and leaped into the water. She lost sight of us, but the trail looped around, and she could cut him off on the other side if she swam fast enough . . .

I'd almost had him, I realized. He had been just within my grasp. Is that what had caused the memory lapse? In my desperation, had I tried to use my abilities to close the gap and snatch him?

If I hadn't, would Madison's murderer be behind bars?

"Should we get started, then?" Elliott asked, and I blinked with a jolt, coming back to reality with a start.

The mood in the room immediately darkened.

"Yeah," Ben said finally. "I guess we should get this over with."

We had one small round table tucked into the back of the living room. It was an ugly piece, the dark wood outdated and dotted with nicks and gouges. We'd picked it up at a garage sale when we first moved in, intending to replace it with something better eventually, but eventually had never come, not when pieces of furniture were frequently victims of my nightmares. The table only sat four people, so we all crowded around as Elliott set the cake down.

He finished decorating it while our guests arrived. HAPPY BIRTHDAY, MADISON was scrawled across the top in purple frosting, some of the lines broken or overlapping as Elliott had struggled to find his inner baker. He managed to shove thirty of the purple candles into the confection to the point where everything was one big abstract hellscape of purple.

I swallowed the lump in my throat as Elliott struggled to light each one. I glanced around to make sure no objects were floating or threatening to implode, and it gave me a moment to force back tears again.

Finally, the last candle was lit. We all stood there awkwardly, staring at the cake.

"Should we sing?" Navin asked.

There was a heavy pause.

"I think a moment of silence is fine," Anna finally said.

After what felt like an eternity, we all agreed to blow out the candles together. On the count of three, the candles blinked out in a rush, and we all stood there, watching wisps of smoke drift up in a somber silence.

"Well, I need a drink," Christine mumbled as she drifted into the kitchen and opened the cooler on the floor. A can hissed as she popped the tab.

"Right behind you," Ben said.

The group drifted toward the emotion-numbing beverages we had stashed in the kitchen.

Anna slipped beside me and grabbed my arm, pulling me away from the table into a corner. I raised an eyebrow at her, concerned.

"Elliott slipped some cream sodas in there for you," she said.

I didn't touch alcohol, partly because it exacerbated my memory problems, but mostly because it had caused my condition in the first place.

Drunk driving didn't always kill.

"I'll tell him thanks," I said, waiting patiently.

Anna didn't want to talk about soda. "Jo stopped by the Agency," she said.

Both eyebrows shot up at once. "Wha—Why?" I sputtered.

"I'm pretty sure she's been hitting Control F and searching for police reports with your name in them since the . . . well, since the stairwell," Anna said. "She wanted to make sure you weren't hurt. She was going to give you a ride home, but you already left."

Mention of the stairwell made me wince. In the right light, I could still see the faint scar that ran down my forehead.

"She wants to know if you lost your phone again," Anna said pointedly, face pinched in an expression of disapproval. "You haven't called in a while. She's really worried about you."

My cheeks burned. I dropped my eyes, avoiding Anna's critical expression.

"She—you—yeah. Yeah, I'll call," I sputtered, my tongue suddenly fat and clumsy in my mouth.

Anna's eyes narrowed. "Will you? If you don't like her that way, that's fine, but don't screw up your friendship just because she thought some things that made you uncomfortable. She's been your friend for five years, Hadley."

I stood there, dumbfounded, as she shoved a piece of paper with Jo Ramirez's number into my sweaty palm.

"Life can be really, really short, Hadley. Don't do something you're going to regret."

I cast a nervous glance at Elliott as he placed a bowl of chicken dip on the table, wondering how my own advice had been lobbed back at me.

The rest of the night was about like that. Everyone was a rollercoaster of emotions, and when they left, I retreated to my room to nurse a migraine and cry into my pillow.

No one touched the cake.

CHAPTER 6

"Quit stalling," Courtney said.

He hovered over me, appearing upside down from where I lay. A smug smirk spread across his face, quashing any hope he wasn't going to make me finish the set despite my repeated objections. A squeak of protest escaped my lips as I forced a set of dumbbells above my head and back down again.

"I'm just saying," I panted from my undignified supine position on a weight bench. "It's better for business if you keep your clients alive."

I forced the dumbbells back up again, my muscles burning and my shoulder joints giving a creak of protest.

What number was I on?

"You don't pay me," Courtney said with a laugh that confirmed he had no sympathy for my situation. "The Agency pays me to keep you in shape, and frankly, I'm not sure they care if I kill you."

"Most days, I think I agree with you," I choked as I finished the set. At least, I hoped I finished the set. I'd lost count halfway through and prayed Courtney wouldn't notice.

The dumbbells hit the mats with muted thuds as I set them down on either side of me. I lay on the bench and sweated, arms crossed over my middle as I willed my heart and lungs to stop being crybabies. It was this or cardio, and I *hated* cardio.

This was the price I paid to keep my job. Classes willing, I got my ass up several days a week and endured some form of torture: usually weight training with Courtney or running with Mark. No amount of whining would spare me from my fate. Both men had military backgrounds, making them nothing short of brutal hard-asses when it came to my fitness. The only upside to five years of torture was that I could eat my weight in peanut butter ice cream and keep my figure, but I still wasn't convinced it was worth it.

"Is this really necessary?" I whined, waving my aching arms in the air dramatically. "I'm not a field agent. Bad guys can't get me behind the observation room's glass, and even if they could, I can fight bad guys with my brain, not my limbs."

"Uh-huh," Courtney quipped. "You know they *love* it when you use your telekinesis on the job. Unless it's a matter of life or death, I suggest using those arms."

"I'm not banned from using telekinesis at work," I mumbled. "They just don't like it."

Courtney raised his eyebrows, lips tugging into another amused smirk.

"I've only broken a few things," I muttered. I usually broke myself first—and frequently—but I left that part out.

I glanced at the clock placed tauntingly close to the door that led to freedom, its seconds ticking by much too slowly, and groaned. Ten minutes until Alice came to my rescue. I never thought I'd feel excited about potentially running into Madison's murderer again, but I'd do anything if it meant getting to catch my breath. I sat up, grimacing as my sweaty backside peeled off the bench, the sound like wet Velcro separating, and took a greedy gulp of water from the water bottle at my feet.

"Rowing machine until Alice gets here," Courtney said, seeming to read *my* thoughts. "Give it all you've got."

"Are you really going to make me sweat up a storm and then dump me on Alice? That's cruel," I said, begrudgingly hobbling past the weight machines to the rowing machine tucked against the wall as requested.

"Alice missed her training session," Courtney replied, smirking. "I have to get my torture in where I can today."

"Lucky Alice," I muttered under my breath as I strapped my feet into the machine and grabbed the bar.

Thirty minutes later, Alice still hadn't arrived, and if I had to spend one more second on the rowing machine, I would throw up. Courtney only seemed amused, hovering beside me with that damn smirk plastered across his face.

Damn him and his perfectly toned ebony body.

"Looks like Alice thought you needed more cardio today," he said, grinning as he leaned against the wall.

"I. Hate. Cardio. Aren't you supposed to torture someone else soon?" I managed to say between pulls.

"Oh, I've been here," Navin said, appearing out of nowhere. His spiky black hair erupted into existence as he let go of the light waves around him and seemed to melt back into reality from the top down, like he'd been poured from a bucket.

I slid to a halt and stared at him, chest heaving, my "squatting frog" position as I scrunched up on the machine completely ruining the murderous vibe I was trying to project. The droning white noise of the rowing machine softened in the background as the flywheel slowed.

"One point for me!" Navin said, laughing.

"If my arms weren't about to fall off," I said, "I might be inclined to hurt you."

"That's my job," Courtney said.

I slumped over and groaned. "Al-*lice*," I whined like a petulant toddler.

"Mark caught me in the hall," Navin said. "She had to check out the Scripps Pier again. He'll give you a ride there."

I threw my hands up and hopped off the machine. "Now they tell me!"

I felt no shame as I fled to the locker room.

Twenty minutes and one quick shower later, I was sitting in the passenger seat of Mark's SUV. A black behemoth with AGENCY sprawled across the sides in obnoxious yellow print, the SUV dropped precipitously on one side as Mark squeezed into the driver's seat. I sank back into the passenger seat gratefully, wincing at the fire raging between my shoulder blades.

"Another jumper?" I asked Mark as we made our way to the pier.

Jumpers at the Scripps Pier were not a common call; thankfully, the pier wasn't high. Most people who jumped off were teenagers on a dare, and while water searches rarely fell within the Agency's duties of defending parahumans against crime—or containing a parahuman raising hell—deploying Alice in times of need proved quicker and cheaper for the city. Her abilities were frequently requested to support Search and Rescue.

Christine was the parahuman of choice prior to Alice's arrival on the team, but being able to breathe underwater proved more useful than hydrokinesis in search and recovery missions, at least early on. The county's fire department, however, was more than happy to keep Christine and her ability to manipulate water busy, especially during wildfire season.

"It was a water call," Mark said, shrugging nonchalantly. "Not sure exactly what, but you know Alice is their go-to for anything water."

"The perks of having gills and webbed toes," I said. I rolled my shoulders and attempted to force the soreness out of my neck. Damn Courtney and his sadistic streak.

The ride to the pier took twenty minutes. I tried not to nod off as my body attempted to slide into a coma to protest the morning's activities. Conveniently, the pier wasn't too far from CSDU. Ryker wanted us to patrol campus first, since that was where Madison's killer had struck. Based on the profile Anna had put together with the help of the FBI, the murderous prick was likely older. Chances were he wasn't an undergraduate, so at least I knew which population didn't deserve as much attention. CSDU still had plenty of graduate students and employed people from all walks of life, so while we had narrowed my suspect pool, there were still plenty of individuals to search through. The thought made my stomach do flip-flops. For all I knew, I could've seen this guy hundreds of times. What if it was the librarian? Or one of my professors? Admittedly, Dr. Griffin had given me a few looks that might kill, but I didn't think anyone I'd taken classes from was capable of such a thing.

Ryker suspected he'd seek others who shared his ideology and could be a member of the Anti-Parahuman Association, or the APA, as they liked to call themselves. Their acronym was a blatant bastardization of the Agency for Parahuman Affair's, and it was a source of great pride for them that they won that identifier back in the 1950s, when the Agency began pushing for the normalization of parahumans in society. Hence, the Agency had been the Agency for the past seventy years, and the APA had taken every chance it could to gloat over their appropriation.

Thanks to the First Amendment, which I normally held in high regard, the assholes had plenty of opportunity for free speech and could hold regular meetings. How lucky for me that San Diego County's chapter met this week, and Ryker wanted me to sit in. I would be sure not to eat beforehand, lest I risk puking on someone in disgust. I hoped they weren't the first on a list of hate groups that, unfortunately, operated within the city. The APA was relatively tame, all things considered. Their MO was to scream at protests with large angry signs or spout off their propaganda on the news. The more organized APA branches in other locations were more likely to be involved in policy and liked to whisper in politicians' ears. They had amassed a rather large platform over the years, and news agencies loved to give them airtime. The drama brought views and good ratings.

Other hate groups that weren't as mainstream, like the Sons of Gaia, were more likely to engage in militancy to get their point across. I did not enjoy the thought of being in proximity to them.

My eyes drifted closed, and thoughts of bigots faded from my mind for a split second. My head snapped up as I fought the urge to pass out in the passenger's seat. Though it was still early, the marine layer wasn't burning off today, the gray pall muting the colors of the world. That was the June Gloom for you. Chances of clear skies were virtually nonexistent, much to my energy level's dismay. I leaned forward and turned on the radio, hoping the noise would keep me alert.

"Thanks for driving me," I told Mark.

"I'll be joining you on campus too," he replied.

I blinked, poking at my memory for the conversation I must have forgotten. Wasn't I with Alice today?

"Did I forget something?" I asked.

"I made my case to Ryker this morning. If you two are going after a lunatic, you're going to have a bulletproof Tank shadowing you wherever you go."

I grinned at the reference to his former life.

"And he actually agreed? I thought he'd want you out there smashing skulls, not babysitting the liability."

"You need to stop being so hard on yourself," Mark said. "Ryker will never admit it because he's Ryker, and God forbid he behaves like he's not carved from an unfeeling hunk of marble, but you're our top asset right now. As far as Ryker's concerned, he's protecting the most valuable thing in all of San Diego."

My eyes bugged out of my head, and I made a strangled sound.

"So stop being dramatic," Mark said firmly.

As if on cue, I looked up and realized we were in the Scripps parking lot. The pier, gated off and deserted, was in view. It was a surprisingly desolate structure considering a very busy beach was only a half mile away. It wasn't exactly in a beautiful location, though, with concrete research structures surrounding it, and it had an uninviting fence erected to keep nosy people out.

I opened the car door, and the pungent smell of brine immediately assailed my nose. Wind whipped my hair as I stepped out, and I could already feel the salty spray clinging to my skin. The roar of the waves echoed in my ears, completing the assault on my senses. I paused for a moment, overwhelmed, and squeezed my eyes shut.

"Miss, can you hear me?"

Please, don't die!

I counted to five before I opened my eyes. I didn't remember the accident that had nearly killed me and robbed me of my memories, but sometimes, I thought the lingering ghost of trauma might haunt my physical body. It was as if the sudden rush of stimuli associated with the worst moment of my life might awaken some sort of subconscious self-preservation instinct that had been instilled in my cells.

With a slow, drawn-out stretch, I forced away the desire to flee. I reached for the car door hanging ajar, and I paused.

I frowned. "You're sure Alice said she was coming here?"

"Caught her this morning as she was leaving," Mark replied, pulling himself from the car. It bucked as he stepped out. "Why?"

My face twisted in confusion as I concentrated, eyes squinched closed and eyebrows knotted together. I'm sure I looked real attractive with my wilted, damp hair clinging to me.

"I think she left. I don't feel her."

"There's an Agency vehicle in the parking lot." Mark nodded toward the more than obvious SUV across from me. "She's probably in the water."

I shrugged. He had a point, and I was oblivious.

I'd remembered my hoodie for once, thank goodness. It was always colder by the ocean, and the overcast skies, whipping wind, and hair I hadn't bothered to dry didn't help keep me warm. I pulled my hood over my head, strands of hair already snarling in the wind, and shoved both hands into the front pocket. I glanced at the cold waves and shivered. How Alice could handle jumping in without a wet suit was beyond me.

"Alice!" I called as we approached the fence blocking access to the pier.

Mark and I glanced at each other when she didn't immediately respond, and with a groan, I marched down the sidewalk to the stairs. Without the buildings to shield us, the wind picked up. The salty spray coming off the ocean only made things that much chillier. I grumbled as I descended the stairs, my legs protesting with every step, and then I grumbled some more when I reached the sand. Waddling through it, I wished Courtney could have left well enough alone with the strenuous arm exercises.

No one passed me as I plodded through the sand, though a lone man walked a dog in the distance. Most everyone seemed to have the good sense to wait for the sun to come out. Well, that and it wasn't even 9:00 a.m. yet.

I stopped near a turquoise lifeguard tower and scanned the choppy horizon.

"Alice!" I shouted at waves that roared back.

It was pointless. Alice was practically part fish, but she was no dolphin. Her hearing was crap when she was underwater. I scanned the waves, hoping to see her pop up, but that was pointless as well. The girl had a perfectly functioning set of gills. Even in this salty, icy-cold mess, she didn't need to come up for air.

I planted my feet in the sand, pulled my hood tighter around my head, and pouted.

"Well," I mumbled. "I guess we wait."

I turned to Mark, who had fallen behind.

Everything happens in slow motion the moment you realize something is irrevocably, horribly wrong in a way that's going to destroy life as you know it—something so unnatural it takes your brain a moment to comprehend it actually exists. That moment where your stomach drops but your heart leaps, and a cold shot of adrenaline makes your spine feel like ice while your quickening blood makes you feel like you're on fire.

I hate that moment.

My face fell at the sight of Mark, standing rigid in the sand, not even his chest rising and falling with breath as he stared down at something with wide eyes wild with panic. His fear slammed into me like a rogue tidal wave, nearly knocking me off my feet.

"Hadley, get over here! *Now!*"

I didn't argue.

Mark frantically searched in all directions. He grabbed me by the arm when I reached his side. I nearly yelped from surprise as he practically dragged me through the sand. I stumbled in my shock, simultaneously trying to follow him and not fall over into the sand. I glanced over my shoulder as Mark led me from the beach, trying to figure out what could have sent the human equivalent of an armored vehicle into a blind panic.

There was something in the sand . . .

"What are we—?" I asked, shock and the beginnings of panic—maybe mine, probably Mark's—impacting my ability to form a sentence.

"We're calling the Agency, and you're staying in the car until backup arrives."

That's when I saw it. A serrated knife glinted on the beach as Mark dragged me toward the stairs. The surrounding sand was red.

A group of surfers found Alice floating in the ocean two hours later. She had seven stab wounds, the medical examiner eventually told us, and I wasn't sure if it was a mercy that she had half as many as Madison. Divers struggled to drag her body through the surf, waves threatening to reclaim her, while I slumped in the sand, my red-rimmed eyes unfocused on seagulls that shrieked from above.

"Christine!" Mark called.

A wave nearly drove one black-clad man into water that hissed and foamed as it crashed to shore.

Christine rushed past me, shoulder-length black hair twisting in the wind as her hand rose and her face contorted in concentration. The ocean withdrew at her approach as if sucked back by a building tsunami, and finally, Alice was brought to shore. Art, the Agency's medical examiner, was waiting, and the forensics team went to work snapping pictures before the divers finished laying her out. Hot tears stung my eyes and rolled down my cheeks as amorphous humans in white suits swabbed wounds and checked under Alice's nails for DNA we all knew wouldn't be there.

We all knew who had done this, and he wouldn't be sloppier this time. Whatever battle we had stepped into—whatever war against parahumans San Diego's resident psychopath had declared, he was winning.

Technicians roped off the beach with yellow crime scene tape that fluttered and snapped in the wind. Numbered evidence identification markers lay in the sand, marking the knife and blood spatter.

Well, half a knife. Art found the other half during the autopsy.

I sat there, thumb massaging my palm and eyes trained on the flurry of movement and the too-still body at the center of it all. I had to give the technicians credit; on the outside, their faces were masks. Calm, expressionless professionalism didn't betray their internal shock and thoughts—thoughts that were all too easy to see, and I saw it all.

Alice's unblinking eyes stared up at a cloudless sky, the color of which matched her bloodless lips; her hair was snarled with seaweed. A technician lifted her blouse to reveal the carnage beneath, and my breath hitched, ears ringing as my vision narrowed to a dark cone. Seagulls cried overhead. Waves roared, and the wind kicked sand into my eyes. The smell of brine and salt saturated my nose.

"Miss, can you hear me?"

"Miss—"

A seagull cried from above. Footsteps—

"Hadley?"

I blinked. Christine squatted in front of me, angular brown eyes creased in concern.

"You okay?" she asked.

No, and neither was she, but at least she wouldn't blow the scene up if she went over her emotional edge. I wished I could compartmentalize like a real agent—like all the experts told me I had to, but any attempt to suppress a part of myself just left room for other minds to infiltrate the void.

Telepathy and traumatic brain injuries were real gifts.

"She should've been dragged out alive too," I whispered.

Christine nodded, clenching her jaw as she blinked rapidly. A wave of raw heartache washed over me, and I swallowed hard, willing her emotions to remain with her. Someone behind me caught her attention, and she inclined her head toward me. Mark's shadow fell over me a split second later. I stared up at him, sniffing and wiping tears off my cheeks.

"Why'd she go alone?" I whispered. "We aren't supposed to be alone."

"Why don't we find Ian?" Mark asked.

He offered a hand, and I nodded, allowing him to pull me to my feet. He tucked me under one arm, shielding me from the wind—and others from me. I felt frozen, but no longer from the temperature. When Ryker marched past, casting us a glance, I realized what else Mark was shielding me from.

That was my strongest memory from that day. That and the blue and red lights lighting up the medical examiner's van as they took Alice away in a black bag. What followed was nothing short of media frenzy. News of Alice Cho's death broke immediately and spread like wildfire. Tensions in the Agency rose a thousandfold, with pressure to catch San Diego's "superhero serial killer" swamping the halls.

Then there was the video.

It broke a week after Alice died as the city paid homage to another fallen agent. I lingered at the back of the crowd again, watching the stage, waiting for the madman to reappear as he had for Madison as the city honored Tempest and welcomed her to the Parahuman Hall of Fame. It was an odd name for Alice but more appropriate than the name they picked for Madison. Not that my opinion mattered in the slightest.

Ripples—like wind on the surface of a pond that only I could feel—crawled through the crowd as Alice's parents were handed a medal meant to honor their daughter. Onlookers suddenly turned to their phones as social media spread Alice's last moments like a disease at the most insensitive moment possible. Alice's parents' pride would turn to horror once they realized a madman had carved his mantra into their daughter's body:

KILL THE FREAKS!

CHAPTER 7

"I don't think I can do it," I whispered to Mark.

I stared at the hotel in the distance, ominously looming five stories above Mark's minivan like some sort of monster. Any other day, the beige building with its perfectly manicured landscape of deep-pink bougainvillea wouldn't stand out, but I knew what went on within its walls today. The Anti-Parahuman Association rented a conference room on the first floor twice a month. Some members were visible through large open windows.

The APA's first June meeting started in twenty minutes, and—never mind the fact I wasn't meant to leave my observation room—I was the Agency's mole. I kept telling myself it wasn't much different from my usual day-to-day. I just had to think of the meeting as one big interrogation room. With me right in the middle with the suspects.

What could go wrong?

Thanks to his former life as Tank, Mark was too high-profile to attend. The meeting would have devolved into chaos the moment he stepped into the hotel, and we probably would have lost our suspect in the ensuing hysteria. We were already subjected to looks and whispers while patrolling on campus, and I sensed Ryker would change his mind about my oversized bodyguard any day now. Mark refused to be left behind though, parking Diane's minivan, which he reluctantly agreed to bring instead of his black SUV that literally shrieked AGENCY, where he could watch me through the windows.

That being said, I wasn't going in alone . . .

"Personally, I find this all very exciting. I've always wanted to do this," Navin said from the backseat, chewing loudly. His spicy breath caught my attention as he leaned between our seats to get a better look at the hotel.

"All you do is undercover work," Mark responded. "How many times have you been to one of these meetings?"

"Yeah," Navin said, popping another chip into his mouth. "But not with Hadley! Those bozos are going to have a telepath sitting *right there*, and they'll have no idea. None!"

"If you don't stop eating those, they're going to smell you," Mark said, casting a disapproving glance at Navin's Flamin' Hot chips.

How Navin hadn't burned a hole in his stomach from his love-affair with spicy food was beyond me.

"Says you," Navin replied. "You wouldn't believe how oblivious people are."

Mark stared at him with a flat expression, then rolled his eyes.

"Hadley gets to eat snacks at the meeting! You can't expect me to stand there and be hungry!"

"It's an hour," Mark said dryly, snatching the bag from him and shoving it between the seat and the console.

"I really don't want to go in," I said, sniffing.

I blinked hard as tears formed at the corners of my eyes. It had only been three days since Alice's memorial; three days of a heavily censored version of that goddamned video of her screaming and running through the surf being paraded across every news station at all hours. Anna made me promise not to turn on the TV for a few days, but I could still see what others watched thanks to my never-failing gift of telepathy.

"Whoa!" Navin said dramatically, throwing his hands up. "I'm not that useless! It'll be fine!"

"It's not that," I said through clenched teeth, swiping hard at my eyes. It felt like all I'd done for weeks was cry. I was only beginning to process Madison's death. Now I had Alice on my conscience too.

If she hadn't gone alone, she might still be alive. That's all there was to it.

I wouldn't be back to work if it weren't for the fact that the APA only met twice a month. I had already blown up a lamp and cracked a window in our apartment.

Anna was ready to march into Ryker's office and demand I be put on leave again. I wouldn't let her. In another two weeks, someone else could be dead, and another horrific video could be circulating. I owed it to my friends to end this.

"I know I have to do it," I said, my voice only barely remaining even. "I'm just gonna lose it if he's in there. I'm really not prepared to see him gloating over Madison and Alice."

Mark clapped a hand on my shoulder. "I won't lie to you and tell you we can find a better way. This guy has left behind no forensic evidence. There's nothing we can link him to. You're our best chance. I know it's a lot to ask, but if he is in there, you can end this today," Mark said. "I know you want this to be over," he added, softer.

He was right. Forensically, despite the additional evidence left on the beach the day Alice died, absolutely no progress had been made. Only Alice's DNA was present at the crime scene. Forensics found no fingerprints, and forget about any shoe prints in the soft sand.

From her perspective as a profiler, Anna had made some headway, which was impressive considering she only had two crimes to build a profile from: he targeted not just parahumans, but those who differed from him as well. At least, based on our original profile, we assumed he viewed Madison and Alice as "different." Madison's hearing aids were visible for anyone to see, as was Alice's race. Both were women. Not only did this asshole hate parahumans, but there might also be white supremacist and misogynistic angles. Everything we learned about Madison and Alice's murderer made my stomach twist.

Of course, that also begged the question of whether or not we were chasing the right leads. The APA hated parahumans, no doubt, but the Sons of Gaia, for example, hated *everyone*.

I wasn't sure I could bring myself within fifty yards of a Sons of Gaia meeting, and I silently prayed they fell exclusively into Organized Crimes' purview.

"I really hope he's in there," Navin drawled. "I hope he sees Hadley and shits himself. These meetings are so boring."

I couldn't help it; I laughed, the subsequent endorphins lifting my spirits just enough that I might not have a complete meltdown in Mark's passenger seat.

"Let's get him for our friends, yeah?" Mark said, giving my shoulder a comforting squeeze.

I straightened in my seat, fighting to strengthen my resolve. I nodded. Brusquely, I brushed away the lone tear that had fallen onto my cheek, embarrassed with myself. I was crying because a man might be thinking mean thoughts. Madison and Alice had been stabbed to death, their murders put on display for the world.

I looked down at my button-up blouse, an odd choice of attire for me, but on this particular day, I wore a shirt from what we—and by that, I meant the field agents who typically wore this stuff—lovingly referred to as the "Agency fashion line." I felt beneath my shirt's top "button" until I rubbed my thumb over the hidden camera's power button. Holding it down, I felt a satisfying vibration as my button camera powered on. I slid my thumb across the surface of the device until I felt the record button and held it down. There was another *buzz,* and for good measure, I checked under my shirt for the pinprick red light to make sure I hadn't clumsily turned it back off.

"Light's on," I told Mark.

I knew he also wanted to make sure I operated the darned thing correctly. His relief that he wasn't going to have to fiddle with it and possibly end up on HR's hit list was palpable.

"Is my face puffy?" I asked sheepishly.

He shook his head.

"Go get 'em," Mark said, patting me on the shoulder.

His reservations about sending me in boomeranged in his brainpan, but he was nice enough not to voice them aloud, so I pretended not to pick up on them. Ignorance really was bliss sometimes.

I threw the car door open and all but leaped out. The minivan's side door slid open, seemingly of its own accord. When it closed, I couldn't see Navin, but I knew he was there. If sunlight hit him just right, I might see a distortion, almost like a heat haze just above the surface of hot asphalt, but I had to pay incredibly close attention to notice.

"I've got your back," Navin whispered.

I glanced nervously at the hotel, biting my lip.

"The APA's not so bad," he added. "Kind of boring, actually. Much better than the Sons of Gaia."

"Yeah?" I asked.

"Pretty sure those assholes can't even do a milk run without an AR-something within arm's reach. Talk about paranoid. You know some lunatic told them UV lights work against invisibility, and those idiots actually installed them?"

"They don't?" I asked.

Navin's laughter seemed to echo across the pavement. "No. Idiots gave themselves a wicked sunburn."

A smile tugged at the corner of my mouth. "Thanks, Navin. Let's get this over with." Taking a steadying breath, I turned on my heel and marched toward the APA meeting.

I pushed through a glass door into the hotel's lobby, my cheeks burning as the girl at the counter caught sight of me.

"How can I help you?" she asked. Her smile looked like it'd been glued on.

How did she get her teeth so white?

Inwardly, I groaned. Not the sort of thing I needed to focus on.

"I'm just here for the . . ."

I pointed toward the conference room door, a single table with a sign-in sheet and a serious-looking woman restricting my access to the meeting within.

"Of course," the young woman at the counter said, smile never faltering.

Bigot! she thought, professional facade still in place as I turned and stepped toward the table. I winced and hoped my cheeks weren't as red as they felt. Heat crawled up my neck, and I pulled my hair forward, hoping to hide any outward signs of discomfort. On the bright side, if things went sideways, not everyone in the building would want to see me dead.

Minor victories.

The serious-looking woman with a highlighted pixie cut and too much mascara looked me up and down as I approached. In truth, she looked a bit like my mother with an extra splash of narrow-mindedness and maybe a touch less neuroticism thrown into the mix. "Heather" was scrawled hastily across a name tag on her shirt in red marker.

"How can I help you?" Heather asked without cracking a grin on her blush-colored lips.

"I'm here for the—" My voice squeaked and broke; I had to clear my throat before speaking again. "I'm here for the meeting."

"Sign in. All new members need to include their email address," she said, slapping a pen on a clipboard and shoving it in my direction, looking as bored as ever.

I was Bethany today, and the Agency gave me a phony license, student ID, email address, and phone number to go with my new name, just in case.

Assuming I remembered it all.

I scribbled my details, doing my best to position my "button" to get a clear image of the list, and pushed the sign-in sheet back toward the woman. Breath held, I stepped around the table.

"Wait," the woman said.

Oh, shit!

I froze, beads of sweat forming across my brow. Could she see the camera? I never believed the Agency when they said it wasn't visible beneath the shirt! I managed not to reflexively look down to check.

Shit, shit, *shit!* Caught in thirty seconds! This was why I wasn't a field agent. Did nobody remember the proverbial F slapped on my initial Agency assessment, the phrase "STRONGLY RECOMMEND AGAINST FIELD PLACEMENT" written literally at the top of my file? There was a reason I hadn't been out of the observation room in five years. Who the hell—

"Don't forget your name tag," the woman said, pointing to the "Hello, my name is . . ." stickers and assorted pens.

Hands trembling, I hastily scribbled my fake name on one and slapped it on my shirt, away from my button. I practically ran past Heather on shaky legs as she stared at her phone, oblivious to my moment of panic.

When I stepped through the door into the conference room, I was both overwhelmed and underwhelmed by the number of people in attendance. The meeting started in five minutes, and twenty people were scattered before me, sitting in foldable chairs or hovering over snacks laid across a table against the wall. An old oak podium was positioned on the opposite side of the room, matching the out-of-date forest-green walls and patterned, musty-smelling carpet I wrinkled my nose against.

The out-of-date vibe of the room certainly matches the mindset of those inside it, I thought smugly. It was a minor comfort knowing the APA didn't hold its meetings in luxury.

That being said, everyone seemed . . . normal. Somehow, I thought hate would look different.

The APA was on the news fairly regularly. They firmly opposed the Agency, claiming parahumans were being "weaponized" against the average person—or that the federal government was the only thing keeping us from going rogue and burning the country to the ground. It seemed like they couldn't decide what to be angry about most of the time. Most of their interviews involved raised voices and sensationalized behaviors. It was hard to picture these people doing that. Still, a lump formed in my throat as I chose a seat firmly in the middle of the crowd—a location of neutrality, I hoped—and sat down, wondering when I'd be made and chased from the room with pitchforks.

As discreetly as possible, I glanced down to make sure the outline of my recording device wasn't visible through my shirt. The hard plastic pressed against my chest, but on the outside, my shirt remained a normal-looking pink blouse. I telepathically sensed Navin as he silently circled the room. With any luck, he was also recording the meeting and had gotten a clearer picture of the sign-in sheet.

"I've been saying something needs to be done about the Agency for years," a male voice said behind me. He sounded older. "Personally, I'm glad someone is finally doing something."

Ah, there was the expected hatred. I squirmed in my seat as I focused on the man's thoughts. Other than his unnerving excitement over the videos of Alice and Madison circulating on the internet—not to mention the rise in anti-parahuman sentiment unleashed in his bubble of the web—he was guilty of being nothing more than an asshole.

"When do you think the next one will pop up?" another older man asked the first. His thoughts revealed him to be another prime example of humanity, but he hadn't killed anyone either.

They didn't fit the profile, anyway. Based on the amount of rage behind the stabbings, I was probably looking for someone with a personal vendetta against parahumans, not just general disdain. As far as I knew, the two men never had so much as a negative interaction with a parahuman—hell, I wasn't sure they had even met one—which only helped rub me the wrong way.

Looking around, about half the guys in the room *might* make the list based on appearance alone. Most of the meeting's attendees were male with a few women scattered among them.

A chair creaked. I jumped as someone sat down beside me.

"Whoa! Didn't mean to scare you," a man said, extending his hand. He was older, Caucasian, and looked like he belonged in a 1960s sitcom with his combed hair, white button-up, and tie.

I took his hand, forcing a smile, and tried not to be obvious as I glanced down at his arm. Thoughts aside, the man had a thinner wrist and darker arm hair than the murderer I hunted.

At least, I thought so. I never trusted my telepathy.

"S-sorry," I said, my voice nearly breaking. I licked my lips, my mouth suddenly dry. "It's my first time at one of these. I'm pretty nervous."

The man flashed a set of perfectly straight white teeth and laughed. "Nothing to be nervous about. These meetings are all pretty boring."

"Are there always so many people?" I probed, casting a glance around the room.

"More or less," he said. "I see a few new faces. It usually depends on who can find the time. Babysitters, you know?"

Ah, a family man. Inwardly, I groaned. That meant not everyone was here, which meant either more meetings in my future or some other fieldwork I'd be required to do. Great.

"I'm Jeff," the guy said.

Jeff seemed perfectly friendly, but boy did he have a strong opinion about parahumans. I winced as I rifled through his thoughts, avoiding the memories of him watching certain stabbing videos a few times, and withdrew from that dumpster fire. Definitely not a murderer though.

"Bethany," I replied hastily.

"What brings you to your first APA meeting, Bethany?" Jeff asked.

I glanced at the podium. The last thing I wanted was to make small talk with this guy, but it didn't look like the meeting would start on time.

"It's just . . . you know?" I sputtered. "With everything going on, I got curious."

"Yeah, we've been getting *a lot* of interest lately," Jeff said. "It's terrible, of course. They're all sick. They deserve treatment, you know—medical intervention. Not this. Breaks my heart, really."

"Oh?" I said, *praying* someone would step behind the damned podium soon.

"It's all just genetic mutation," Jeff continued as I focused on not blowing anything up. "Like cancer or Alzheimer's. It's terrible for sick people to be exploited by our own government instead of cured. They won't fund the studies, of course—political correctness and the social-justice warriors will make sure of that! It's just such a shame; we could be one simple blood test away from catching it early, before they have a chance to hurt themselves or others, and maybe only a few years away from clinical therapies if they'd just look into it."

"Uh-huh," I squeaked, knowing full well how early my new friend Jeff would like to catch it and what sort of treatment he *really* thought was necessary. I felt nauseous. Thoughts about eugenics tended to do that to me though.

"I was reading a study," Jeff continued while I willed a giant meteor to drop on both of us. "That environment plays a role. Studies are coming out that you need some sort of toxic environment—a bad family life, for example—to activate the genes. That's why you see it so much more nowadays: family values just aren't what they were."

Oh, dear God. I would give anything for a serial killer to find me just then.

My head throbbed. Being stuck in a room full of people with toxic thoughts was the last thing I needed, and Jeff continued to prattle on while I nodded and made encouraging sounds to pretend I was engaged. As it stood, I had checked three people off my list and had at least fifteen to go, and the distraction did not help. I would need painkillers and the hottest shower in existence by the time I got out of the room.

"All right," a man said, stepping behind the podium. "I guess we'll get started."

Jet-black hair, a perfectly trimmed beard, and a strong jawline . . . I recognized the man: Kenny Nolan. While he wasn't prominent nationally, Kenny had made quite the name for himself in Southern California, appearing on television and radio interviews to debate his views and defend his organization. I despised the man. He was loud, vulgar, and factually correct maybe 10 percent of the time. He pandered to fear and hate and seemed to have an allergy to logic.

Of course, I *was* biased, but that didn't mean it wasn't true.

With the APA meeting starting, everyone took their seats. Blessedly, Jeff stopped talking.

Back to work.

I started with Kenny, but much to my disappointment, he was clean of any murderous thoughts. Oh, sure, his fantasies were within that realm, but he didn't seem twisted enough to carry them out. From there, I systematically went from seat to seat, scanning each mind as the group discussed letters to senators, their yearly protest outside the Agency, which always proved to be a headache for us and SDPD, and a few more demonstrations I really couldn't care less about.

"Can we discuss a plea to our representatives for more of our research dollars to go toward parahuman research?" Jeff asked. I resisted the urge to cringe. "It seems worth our while to bring it to their attention. Clinical trials for cures will never be within reach if the public doesn't demand it."

I tried not to roll my eyes. Shut up, Jeffrey.

"I want to know where the legislation keeping parahumans away from our children is!" a woman demanded. "They're everywhere. If they aren't in our schools, they're on our TV every night. My husband and I are exhausted trying to raise our boys on wholesome family material!"

Right. Because being a fraction of a fraction of a percent of the population meant parahumans were coming out the ears of society.

"I hear they're going to let them adopt in some states," another voice chimed in.

"How unconscionable!" the woman squealed, aghast.

"We need to make changes where it counts," a man interjected. "Too much of our taxpayer dollars go toward funding the Agency! Cut their funding, and we won't have these parahumans showing up on TV, being paraded around as if they're heroes."

"If this guy running around with his knives keeps up, we won't have parahumans to fund!" someone else said.

They laughed. They actually laughed. Madison and Alice's faces flashed before my eyes, and I squeezed them shut, willing away tears.

I couldn't believe it when nothing blew up.

Forty-five minutes into the meeting, and I'd seen enough dark thoughts and heard enough hurtful words for one evening. I rose from my chair.

"You okay?" Jeff asked.

"Bathroom," I whispered hurriedly.

He nodded, convinced.

I rushed out the door and nearly ran across the parking lot to Mark's minivan. I stopped my button camera from recording and turned it off before I started venting.

"Never again," I muttered as I slid into the passenger's seat. I rummaged through my book bag angrily, searching for my painkillers. I'd probably need the entire bottle to numb the migraine taking hold, and what I wouldn't give for a memory lapse to wipe clean the last hour of my life.

"How'd it go . . . Brittany?" Mark asked, eyebrows pinched in confusion as he looked at the name tag on my shirt.

"Oh, damn it!" I snapped, reaching down and ripping the sticker off. I had written the wrong name! So much for a successful undercover operation. It would be a miracle if no one had noticed the blunder.

"I'm sure no one noticed," Mark said reassuringly, as if reading *my* thoughts.

"Oh, God," I muttered. "What if I filled out the wrong information and they catch on? Ryker will dangle me out a window if the APA sues."

"We'll check the footage," Mark said. "It's not anything that can't be dealt with. Did you pick up on anything?"

"They're all disgusting," I grumbled, feeling sorry for myself. As if I wasn't already in a bad enough mood . . .

"We knew that."

"He's not in there," I said. "If he's been bragging about what he's doing, it's not to those people. No one there has any idea who it is."

"Damn," Mark said, slumping in his seat.

I understood his frustration. How convenient it would have been to generate a lead. I was not looking forward to our next steps. What would it take to infiltrate the Sons of Gaia? A hate symbol tattooed across my forehead? Would they have to strap an AK-47 to my hip to make me blend in? My mother would be aghast.

"Can we get out of here?" I asked. I forced the pill bottle open, threw two painkillers in my mouth, and swallowed them with what little saliva I could produce. They went down like pebbles. I could still catch glimpses of thoughts from the passenger's seat and considered taking another one.

"Well, we should probably rescue Navin," Mark said.

"Navin?" I asked.

"That explains why you didn't wait for him," Mark said with a laugh. "He can't very well open the door and see himself out right now."

It felt like my eyes would pop out of my skull.

"Oh, God. He's going to hate me! He's really in there?"

Mark burst into laughter, the minivan rocking as he threw his head back. I slumped down and put my face in my hands.

"I forgot Navin and the damn name! What if the murderer's in there too? What if I forgot him?" I said through my fingers.

"Remember what I told you about establishing routines and identifying what's a recognizable behavior for you?" Mark asked, still chuckling.

"Yeah," I said, my palms making my words come out mumbled.

"What would you have done if you *had* found him?"

"I sure as hell wouldn't have sat through any more of that meeting," I grumbled, dropping my hands. I kept my eyes focused on my lap.

"What else?" Mark asked.

I shrugged, lifting one shoulder and dropping it like a limp noodle.

"How upset would you be if he was there?"

"Ah," I said. "Probably would have blown something up."

"Nothing blew up. Ergo, he wasn't in there."

"Nobody says *ergo* anymore," a muted voice said from outside my window.

I jumped as Navin materialized beside me, spiky hair erupting into existence, followed quickly by the rest of him as he released his hold over the light around him.

"Another point for me!" Navin shouted triumphantly.

"I didn't leave you?" I asked, rolling the window down.

"Nah," he said, grinning mischievously. "I was waiting by the door. Couldn't wait to get out of that place. I just wanted to see what you'd do if you thought you left me."

He continued to beam at us, quite pleased with himself. The car door kept me from smacking him.

"I grabbed this though," he said as he pulled a handful of pigs in blankets from his pocket.

"Well, at least someone got something good out of that," Mark said with a shake of his head.

"I have absolutely nothing to tell Ryker," I told Navin as he slid the minivan's door open and climbed into the backseat.

"I heard," he said, shoving one of the pork snacks into his mouth, his smacking lips setting my teeth on edge. "Honestly, I was really hoping it would be one of those guys."

"Yeah," I said, leaning back in the passenger's seat.

The next few days were just as unproductive. The profile indicated we were looking for the perpetrator of a hate crime, but none of the hate groups panned out, physical or electronic, local or national. There was nothing online—at least, nothing we could find.

The knives the killer had used were part of a set. I was told the set was expensive, which further suggested we were looking for an older, financially stable male. Still, they could be purchased at a number of stores, so not even the weapons were traceable—at least, not practically—if he had even purchased them recently. Anna suggested he picked the knives from the set on purpose—the biggest and most brutal options. Knives were likely chosen for the intimacy they'd allow during the murders, but whether they held any special significance to him was unclear.

I hoped the loss of his kitchen knives was an inconvenience. It was petty, but the thought that his crimes had caused him some disruption to his daily life helped me find a tiny bit of peace. It would have to do until we tracked him down.

Any and every lead led to a dead end, and every day I picked up nothing led to another night where I lay in bed and wondered how I had messed everything up so badly.

That's how I ended up lying on the couch in the dark, Weasel tucked under one arm. My earbuds would have been blasting music in a vain attempt to focus on *anything* other than the neighbors' thoughts if I could find them. Instead, a lumpy throw pillow was shoved over my head, as if that could block telepathy.

. . . pick up Sasha from practice . . .
. . . need to confirm with Rob about . . .
. . . hasn't called back. Maybe she's . . .

I half screamed/half groaned as I clenched the pillow to my head, trying to force the intruding thoughts from my mind. I couldn't turn them off! After days and days of seeing and hearing a rainbow of human experiences, good and bad, I just wanted peace, but my brain was in overdrive. It was like an on switch had been taped in place.

"Oh, God, buddy," I muttered to my dog. "Is it you who has to pee that bad, me, or the neighbor's kid?"

I laughed hysterically as Weasel cocked his head, his tail thumping against me. I patted his head, bottom lip quivering as laughter turned into tears. Anna kept sleeping aids in one of the bathroom cabinets. I wasn't supposed to mess with anything that could alter my brain chemistry, but I was becoming desperate for an off button.

Keys scraped in the front door's lock, and Anna and Elliott walked in. The lights flipped on, briefly blinding me as I pulled the pillow away from my face.

"Oh . . ." Elliot said. "Bad day?"

"I can't find him," I muttered, my words punctuated by a wet sniff. I angrily brushed tears from my puffy cheeks.

Anna sat down by my feet, picking them up and putting them in her lap. Elliott went to the kitchen, coming back thirty seconds later with a spoon and a tub of peanut butter ice cream.

141

"It won't fix it, but it helps," he said, forcing the cold tub into my hands.

"Thanks," I said, sitting up and pulling the top off. Thanks to my condition, I couldn't drink my sorrows away. Considering it's what led to my car accident, I wouldn't even if I could. That didn't mean I couldn't drown my sorrows in sugar and saturated fat though.

"It's only been three weeks," Anna said.

"And I have been to an APA meeting *and* patrolled the entire campus a thousand times, the area by the pier, and every other area the asshole could be lurking. I can't find any sign of him!"

"It's not your fault if he's not there," Elliott said.

"It is if he *is* there and my stupid brain can't find him."

"He has to know the Agency is looking for him. He's probably lying low," Anna said.

It was probably also why we weren't being more direct and dragging members of the APA or Sons of Gaia in by their hair for interrogation. God forbid we send this guy further underground and miss our chance to get him, but *my God*, I couldn't keep this tediousness up. Something had to give!

"Or he's deciding which of us to kill next," I muttered miserably. "If he kills someone else, it's my fault."

"No," Anna said, her inner therapist getting riled up. "It's *his* fault."

I glared at her petulantly.

"Obsessing over something you can't control isn't healthy. You need boundaries between work and home," Anna continued. "I know it seems impossible because Alice and Madison were friends, but you *need* to find a sense of normalcy. Go out with friends, binge-watch a show, go on—"

"Go on a date?" I asked her, eyebrows raised.

"Cheater," Anna replied. "But, yes. Have you even thought about calling Jo? You can't keep ghosting her, Hadley. She's been your friend for years. You can't keep punishing her for *a thought*. She's going to realize something's wrong soon, and she won't have any idea what she did."

"No, I haven't called her," I said miserably.

Anna sighed.

"I'm on Anna's side," Elliott chimed in with a voice that would be excellent for deep talks with his future children. "It's been *five years*. You're doing pretty good with your powers. You've held down the Agency job, and I know you're frustrated with school, but that's progressing too. You've known Jo for forever. You'd be good for each other. Why not give it a go?"

"Okay, first, you really think starting a relationship in *all this*," I said, waving my hand, spoon and all, dramatically in the air, "is a good idea? Second, Anna's right. She had *one* thought, during a movie, late at night after a long day at work, and there was alcohol involved. It probably hasn't occurred to her since, and I never should've told Anna."

Pursing my lips, I glared at Anna, making clear my displeasure that she'd told Elliott too. Damn the lovebirds and their healthy communication.

"You're very pointedly not talking about what you want," Anna said. "Do you want a relationship?"

"I don't know. I thought we were just friends. I was *fine* with being just friends."

"Life is *always* messy, Hadley," she said. "That's the way it is. If you don't feel ready right now or—"

"It's not fair," I said bluntly.

"What isn't?" Anna asked.

"To J—to whoever ends up with me," I mumbled.

Anna was utterly aghast. "Why would you say that?"

"Think about it," I said miserably. "Do I feel more like your roommate or more like your child?"

Anna looked even more taken aback. "You can't be serious."

"I am!" I bit back, then cringed. I hadn't meant for it to come out quite that forcefully. "I'm sorry," I mumbled. "But I can't be trusted enough to cook, I can't drive, I forget to set my alarm most of the time, so you have to wake me up most mornings. I don't always know what day it is or what I was doing when I walked into a room. You're constantly cleaning up after me—hell, you even take care of my finances! How much *does* the Agency actually pay me? The list is a mile long. I'm a barely functioning adult who needs help every single freaking day."

"Okay," Elliott said gently, trying to defuse the tension. "So . . . you're quirky. Plenty of people in this world have far less lovable quirks, and they still get married and have families."

I groaned. "Let's pretend I go on a date with someone—with *Jo*. Let's pretend we eventually get married and have kids. How many times do you think I can forget to pick the kids up from school before they call CPS on us? Hell, that assumes I don't forget the baby in the bathtub and drown it before it reaches grade-school age. That sort of future with me doesn't end well."

"It's not like Jo doesn't know . . . about your quirks," Elliott said.

"You literally almost died in her lap," Anna added. "She practically went through rehab with you. There isn't a woman alive who understands what you've gone through more than Jo, and she's still here. Stop treating her like shit and call her."

"I'm not treating her like shit. It's just . . . being my friend is one thing. She can send me home at the end of the day. Tying herself to me—tying her life to me—that's asking too much. I don't want her . . . I don't want her to resent me. I don't want to lose her," I said, practically whispering the last part.

"Is this really coming from you, or is this your mother?" Anna asked.

"Does it matter?"

She wasn't wrong though. In the five years since my accident, my mother had never stopped wishing I'd wake up one morning and suddenly be the daughter she lost again.

"Hadley, your mother is an absolute piece of work, and I don't know if I'd rather send her to a shrink for her issues or smack her, but most people aren't like her. *Jo* isn't like her," Anna said.

"Best not to find out," I grumbled, stabbing my spoon into the tub full of ice cream.

"So, what? You just don't try? You used to talk about having a family all the—"

Anna snapped her mouth closed midsentence, and her eyes grew wide. She got emotional and slipped up. The rational part of me knew I shouldn't hold it against her, but the comment brought stinging tears to my eyes.

"I'm not that Hadley anymore!" I snapped.

"It doesn't mean you deserve to be alone!" Anna shot back.

The lamp next to me began wobbling at its base. I sighed and slumped deeper into the couch.

"And then there's that," I grumbled. "I can't even have a fight like a normal person. Can we please just drop it before we have to go furniture shopping? Again."

Mercy Rehab has a Golden Rule when it comes to telekinetics: Avoid scaring them or pissing them off at all costs. In fact, avoiding any strong emotion in our presence is a smart idea. It was a rule Anna very much wanted to violate at that moment. Instead, she looked at Elliott and threw her hands up in exasperation. She dutifully got up and marched herself—and more importantly, her anger—to her room.

"She means it with love," Elliott said, deflated.

"That's what makes it hard," I replied.

My phone rang. Anna's went off in her bedroom a split second later. I scooped mine up, grateful for an opening to escape.

"Hello?"

"Have you seen the TV?" Mark asked.

His tone made my heart jolt.

Dammit, never mind! I wanted to fight with Anna!

"What happened?"

I couldn't handle anyone else dying. My heart hammered against my rib cage as I waited for Mark's reply.

"He sent letters to all the news agencies in town."

Anna rushed from her room and grabbed the remote. She turned the TV on and flipped through the channels until she landed on a news station. A bird's-eye view of a building evacuation played out on screen, people scattering in all directions as bomb squads moved in.

"This looks like more than just letters," I said.

"He's threatening anyone with 'pro-parahuman sentiment.' He planted a bomb, and unless every news agency stops covering the—and I'm quoting him here—

'disgusting parahuman menaces as undeserving martyrs,' someone's going to get blown up."

"You really think he planted a bomb?" I asked, dumbfounded.

"They've already found one."

I looked at Anna and Elliott, eyes wide. Elliott's mind raced. Anna was . . . confused.

"Did you suspect he'd do this?" I asked her. "Mark, I'm putting you on speakerphone."

"I mean, walking into a public place with a bomb is certainly bold," Anna said slowly. "But he's an angry, egotistical maniac. He likes to be in control when damage is dealt. He chose a knife so he can experience the devastation he causes in the moment. A bomb is . . . impersonal."

"A bomb does a lot of damage," I said. "Maybe he got tired of taking out one person at a time."

"But he didn't even go after parahumans."

"The letter seems like him," Elliot said. "He seems like the kind of guy to release a manifesto. Besides, doesn't changing public perception of parahumans fit with his mission to eliminate them?"

Anna bit her lip. "He's not the kind of person to give a warning. He's always been silent when he hunts. It would have been more like him to bomb first and then release the manifesto."

"Maybe he wants to cause more fear?" Elliot said. "Maybe the novelty is wearing off, and he needs something to make it exciting again."

"I'm not sure he gets that kind of satisfaction from it. He's mission oriented. That alone seems to drive him."

"So, what?" I asked. "You're saying this wasn't him?"

"To go from a knife to a bomb . . . that's a huge escalation," Anna said. "I don't know that I've ever seen that before."

"It fits with the profile if he has a military background," Mark chimed in.

Anna grimaced.

"Anna's making a face," I told Mark.

"It's more likely the unsub has emboldened someone, and they're taking advantage of the situation to live out their own fantasies. It's not uncommon, particularly after events that receive a lot of news coverage," Anna said.

"You do not want to be the person to tell Ryker we're looking for another individual," Mark said.

"Someone must have seen him," I said, addressing Mark. "You don't just walk into a place with a bomb and go unnoticed."

My hopes were up. If someone had seen him, I was off the hook. I wasn't the Agency's best option anymore.

"That I don't know," Mark said. "Ryker wants everyone back at the Agency for a briefing. He's about to speak to the press."

My heart sank. If no one had seen him, Ryker would be out for blood. Probably mine if I didn't produce results soon. Well, Anna was fair game if she mentioned her theory.

As if on cue, Ryker appeared on screen. He looked cool and collected in a black suit that brought out his menacing eyes and stark white hair. On screen, he appeared collected and professional, but I knew we'd have our asses handed to us as soon as he stepped from behind the podium. We'd gotten nowhere with our investigations, and now the situation had developed into an entirely new beast. Ryker's ego and reputation likely felt more than a little bruised, and we would all pay for it.

Anna was already reaching for her purse.

"Can I go with you?" Elliott asked, barely containing his panic. According to our madman, she was as fair of game as me now.

"No one will get anywhere near her," I said, tapping my temple. It helped, but it hardly appeased him. I probably shouldn't have gone on that rant about being defective if I wanted to be convincing.

"Stay here," Anna said, pressing her lips to his cheek. "We'll talk about it when I get home."

Elliott and I exchanged a look as I followed his girlfriend out of the apartment.

Ryker was waiting for us when we got there, his face red and eyes reflecting a barely contained wild rage. God help our stabber if Ryker got his hands on him. And that assumed there was only one criminal out there.

I was beginning to doubt we would ever make any progress. No one had seen the bomber that day. If it was the same person as the stabber, he'd also killed two parahumans in broad daylight. He had snuck a bomb in during working hours. If it was Alice and Madison's killer, it was clear he was becoming emboldened. He was leaving his stomping grounds behind him and expanding his hunting grounds and tactics.

We had no idea how much.

CHAPTER 8

I withdrew from Dr. Griffin's class, probably much to his relief. With my new, demanding life as Ryker's telepathic bloodhound showing no signs of changing and the utter hopelessness of me actually passing the class, I marched back from the registrar's office defeated. Anna was also taking a leave of absence from school, so I shouldn't have been hard on myself but . . .

I sighed deeply as I began patrolling today's route, scrutinizing the courtyard and throngs of summer students scurrying to class. The June Gloom was ending, the marine layer that had blanketed the city for a month giving way to cloudless, blue sky. Those who weren't in class sat at tables, coffee cups in hand as they chatted with classmates. One guy pulled out a guitar and started playing while another wove through pedestrians on a skateboard, the wheels grinding against the sidewalk as he glided past.

I'd never had a carefree life like that—at least, not one I remembered. After my accident, I'd been subjected to six months of rehabilitation at Mercy Rehab under the Winefield-Drummer Act, a clause of which was designed to help newly identified parahumans control their abilities if they first activated negatively. Considering that parahuman abilities usually manifested in children undergoing puberty, most abilities activated undesirably. A twenty-one-year-old late bloomer imploding a car and causing a self-inflicted permanent brain lesion certainly fell under the act. The first six months of existence as I knew it started in an institution, which thankfully, employed some of the nicest experts in the field. I still kept in touch with some of them . . . when I remembered.

I jumped straight from rehabilitation to the Agency. The Agency's San Diego branch couldn't pass up the opportunity to recruit a coveted telepath . . . once Mercy Rehab worked out most of my quirks, of course. It's not like I knew what else to do with my life. Being a telepath, a career in healthcare suddenly seemed ill-considered, and so many other career paths came with parahuman safety restrictions that it made my head swim—at least, until I was five years out of rehab and a specialist deemed me stable, which would never happen. I leaped at any opportunity for stability and purpose. In hindsight, life might have been different if I'd waited to know myself first.

"You okay?" Navin whispered.

I glanced at the seemingly empty space next to me, careful not to be too obvious.

Mark wasn't with us today. His tactical bomb training proved useful on the bomb side of things. I had taken a Bomb-Making Materials Awareness course once upon a time and might have remembered it. Probably not. It all sounded like gibberish to me. Mark claimed the bombs might help narrow our suspect pool, since bombers usually had a signature. He hoped whoever left the bomb at the news station might already be in the system, but with the way the past few weeks had gone, optimism was in short supply. Counterterrorism chased leads with a renewed sense of vigor, hoping the bomb and stabbings might be connected, but the more we learned, the less convinced I became there was any connection. No additional bombs had been discovered, which I should have been happy about, but I knew better.

Much like the stabbings, it was only a matter of time.

"Hadley?" Navin prodded.

Normally, I'd turn toward Mark and speak at him to talk to Navin. Today, I had to be a bit cleverer. Thankfully, most people assumed you were on the phone if you wore earbuds.

"I guess," I said, brushing my hair away from an ear to make my earbuds more obvious.

My phone rang, and I groaned.

"Ryker?" Navin asked, voice pinched with worry.

Thankfully, it was too early for Ryker's mood to have soured enough to send someone to check on us. By my guess, we had two more hours to fail to produce results before Tom or Glenn was sent to handle us.

"Worse. Family," I muttered, answering my little brother's call.

"Hey, Collin," I said hesitantly. My brother and I tried our hardest to have a relationship, but between our age gap, my lack of memories, and my tense relationship with my mother, things always felt strained—more so for me than for Collin. Collin had resigned himself to living a laid-back life and had a frustrating habit of taking things in stride.

"I think I moved something with my mind today" was my brother's way of saying hello.

"What?" I asked, stopping in my tracks.

"Not really. I'm hopelessly normal. As a sibling courtesy, I'm letting you know that Mom and Dad are flipping out. I just figured I'd start with something else," Collin said jovially. "Of course, by Mom and Dad, I mean Mom. She's finally quit seeing reason. I'm actually kind of impressed with us. I think we contained her for quite a while."

"What?" I asked again, wondering if it was possible for me to wring his neck through the phone.

"Oh, good! I beat Mom's call," Collin said. "I wasn't sure."

"*What* are you talking about?"

"Bombs. Murdered parahumans. Mom and Dad have decided you have to come home," he said. "But I really mean Mom."

"Oh," I replied.

"*Yeah*," he responded. "I mean, I don't blame them, but I told them—her—they're overreacting. You wouldn't stay if you were really in danger. The news is making this out to be a lot worse than it actually is."

"Yeah," I said bluntly.

I had a lot of guilt about my family. *A lot.* After they released me from Mercy Rehab, I'd gone to live with a mother, father, and brother I had no memories of—total strangers, as far as I was concerned. I went back to my old room, with all of my old clothes and belongings, and I prayed every day that *something* would jog my memory and that everything would come flooding back like the optimistic nurses kept saying it might. For every hope and dream I had, it was tenfold for my parents.

We went through a year of inside family jokes at the dinner table, my parents holding their breath every time, just knowing that *this time* something would come back to me. I wore Old Hadley's clothes. I listened to Her music and let Mom make all of Her favorite foods. There was visit after visit to the salon to maintain Old Hadley's trademark long highlighted hair. We recreated old family vacations, and there were so many "Do you remember whens?" that my head swam. Their desperation nearly tore me to shreds. I could see, feel, and hear it all, unspoken or not.

After a year, I gave up. Old Hadley was never coming back, and as much as I tried to like her clothes, her hairstyle, and her favorite foods, I couldn't. Living someone else's identity was exhausting.

I got rid of the blonde highlights Old Hadley loved so much and cut her long locks to my shoulders. Mom cried. When I came home wearing a new, foreign style of clothes—and by that, I mean I have absolutely no style, and I didn't feel right in Old Hadley's chic wardrobe—Dad stared and pursed his lips, but he didn't say anything. Mom had more to say.

When I finally turned down "my favorite" mint chocolate chip ice cream after dinner one night, finally admitting it wasn't really my thing, Mom suffered a complete breakdown. I spent another six months listening to my family's inward grief about their daughter being gone and replaced with a stranger before I finally lost it. The end result was a hysterical screaming and crying match as my mother and I had it out in the living room, both of us venting our grief and frustration, before I practically fled my parents' house and moved in with Anna. Things got better after that, and I also learned, with a bit more time, that I couldn't hold people's private thoughts against them. My relationship with my family was better now, though Collin ended up being the middleman and conciliator between me and my parents when emotionally charged topics came up.

"Mom and Dad were wondering if you're taking summer classes?" Collin asked, ripping me from the past. "They said it's been a while since we've had a family vacation."

I pressed my lips into a thin line. I shouldn't be ungrateful. I was fortunate to be alive and have a family to angst over, but we didn't do family vacations because they never went well.

"Oh," I said, trying to sound sincere, though the forthcoming lie was already stuck in my throat like a lump. "I'm retaking Victimology this summer."

I cringed, the lie hanging in the air with an oppressive fog of guilt, but even if I wanted to trade a parahuman-obsessed killer and a fear-mongering bomber for a Gordon family vacation, Ryker was likely to track me through the ski slopes of Colorado or wherever they wanted to go and drag me right back to the Agency to interrogate suspects.

"Oh," Collin said glumly.

"Yeah," I said, standing there awkwardly, unsure of what to say.

"Well, give Mom a call or something. I'll calm her down as much as I can," Collin said.

"Thanks, Col—"

My phone nearly tumbled from my hand as someone bumped my shoulder, earbuds flying with it. The thumps of heavy books hitting the ground and the rustle of papers as someone's class notes went sprawling across the pavement only added to my confusion.

"Hadley?" my brother asked, his voice rising an octave.

"It's nothing. I'm a klutz. Sorry, Collin, I need to go for a minute!" I said hastily, grasping the situation and hanging up.

I turned to the twentysomething-year-old man kneeling on the ground, reaching for pieces of paper that had exploded out of a binder. The man looked up at me, blue eyes meeting mine beneath blond hair tastefully held in place with just the right amount of hair gel. The scents of his aftershave and body spray hit me as I rushed to help.

"I'm so sorry!" he said. "I have an exam, and I wasn't paying attention to where I was going."

"Anatomy?" I asked as I crouched down and picked up a ridiculously thick textbook with a translucent human and tastefully colored organs on the cover.

"The one and only," he said.

I reached for a piece of paper and froze when my hand brushed an APA pamphlet. I managed to regain my composure before the man noticed and handed the pamphlet back, a fake smile plastered across my face. I was suddenly very uncomfortable.

We both stood—me a little faster. His eyes flashed to me, lingering on my forehead for a moment before darting away just as quickly to focus on his textbooks.

Suddenly self-conscious, I resisted the urge to pull my hair in front of my face and cover the "gift" Madison and Alice's murderer had given me.

"Well, I hope the exam goes okay," I said, hoping he would rush off. He didn't disappoint.

"Thanks," he called over his shoulder as he power-walked toward his exam.

"Jocks," Navin muttered under his breath. It was a miracle he hadn't bumped into my invisible chaperone instead.

"You think so?" I asked. For some reason, I couldn't take my eyes off the student's back.

"Oh, he's definitely played football," Navin said indignantly. "Guy was built like a—Hadley?"

My unwavering focus hadn't broken. There was something . . .

I reached out telepathically, but the sidewalks still bustled with buzzing minds, and the young man . . . I clenched my eyes shut in concentration. He was hard to read, but perhaps because I expected him to be thinking about his exam.

Instead, the memory of my face lingered in his mind, churning in a dark recess—a strangely still void in the world I hadn't expected to be there. Black whispers brushed my mind, and I recoiled.

"I think he knows who I am," I said breathlessly.

"Like . . . from a class?"

"Maybe," I said.

Once, I had been a pre-nursing student and took science classes in nearby buildings, but that was years ago. Wouldn't he have been in high school? Or perhaps he was older than he looked?

"It's just . . . I'm too clear in his mind," I said. "Visions of strangers are usually blurry and amorphous—details are usually missing, but I'm clear. It's like he's seen me more than once."

157

It was more than that, but I couldn't find words to describe what I telepathically felt. I watched the pre-med student disappear around a corner. My hair practically stood on end.

"Follow him," I said, making up my mind. "I'm calling Mark."

"Seriously?" Navin asked, so startled that a flash of his dark hair materialized as he briefly lost his hold over the light waves around him. "But doesn't the profile say—"

"*Quickly*," I said, pulling my phone out.

I wonder if I still would have made that phone call if I'd known what would happen.

An hour later, I stood behind one-way glass, analyzing the student as he reclined under fluorescent lights in the Agency's interrogation room, raw human psyche rolling off him in waves—no concrete thoughts, no images or feelings, just . . . cold.

I held my breath as Tom and Glenn entered the room, Mark trailing behind them. While the dynamic interrogating duo took the two seats across from the blond, muscular young man, Mark opted to loom in the background, propped against the wall with his bulbous arms crossed.

Surprisingly, our interrogee never flinched, his energy never shifting. Mark, at the very least, was one of the scariest men alive. Well, until you got to know him and realized he was just a marshmallow with abs.

This guy—Preston Weiss, they said his name was—hardly gave Mark a cursory glance. I sensed the three parahumans' disappointment immediately. They'd anticipated a reaction from their suspect.

"Care to tell me why I got pulled out of an exam?" Preston Weiss asked, leaning back in the chair, one leg across his lap.

"Because we can use telepathic evidence under the Smith Act," Anna mumbled beside me.

She was attempting to be witty and distract me from chewing my nails to nubs. Maybe I would have found it amusing if I weren't sweating bullets.

Preston Weiss, on the other hand, looked oddly unconcerned for someone who had just been dragged into an interrogation room inside a government facility I assumed he felt no fuzzy feelings for. I glanced at Anna, whose brow furrowed in thought. I wondered if she could sense the leaching void in the interrogation room or if Preston Weiss's unusual energy was apparent only to me.

Tom and Glenn ignored Preston's comment. Tom glanced over his shoulder to check the status of the camera in the corner. Content that the interview was being recorded, he opened the thinnest file I had ever seen. Clearly, this guy had no priors. That already didn't fit. Didn't Anna mention bombers usually have a history of crimes? Even if he wasn't the bomber, would someone who killed with so much rage look this put together? Preston Weiss looked like a picture-perfect frat boy jock. Immaculate blond hair, vibrant blue eyes, and a square jaw with faint stubble—girls must have fawned over him. He was nothing like what I pictured Madison and Alice's murderer would look like.

"You're aware that this interview is completely voluntary?" Tom asked as I clung to every word. "You can stop the interview at any time."

"Yeah, I got it," Preston said bluntly. He tapped his fingers on the table, a clear signal he had more important places to be.

Glenn's eyebrows raised behind his glasses, and Tom suddenly began scanning through the file slower, seconds ticking by.

"Cocky guy," Anna mumbled as we waited to see if Preston would start squirming.

"He was polite enough when he bumped into me," I said, my mouth strangely dry.

"But something about him felt off to you?" Anna asked.

"I really don't know," I said. "I'm too familiar to him, and energetically . . ."

I had been around a number of strange individuals, but what I felt in the interrogation room was . . . inhuman, like a specter made real.

"You sure you didn't share a class with him?"

I tried not to wince. I had only wondered the exact same thing the entire hour it took to bring Preston in.

"He . . . uh . . . He seemed interested in my scar," I said. It was hardly damning evidence. In the right light, my scar was pretty prominent. Still, most of the time, you had to really look . . .

I doubted myself more and more by the second. The room was becoming stifling despite the fact the AC was blasting and Preston's icy energy tickled my mind.

Ryker would blow a fuse if we came back and said we'd—I'd—made a mistake. Maybe I shouldn't have said anything. A stranger knowing me was hardly a crime—a kid, no less. His driver's license indicated he was twenty-two—younger than Navin. No way he had the life experience to be a serial killer mastermind, even if his mind felt like a bucket of wriggling eels.

"Huh" was Anna's response as she stepped closer to the glass, eyeing our suspect thoroughly. Her curiosity was piqued, but her tone only made the room feel hotter.

Damn it, I shouldn't have said anything. There was too much pressure to produce results for Ryker. It was making me desperate. *This* was desperate. I clenched my jaw. It was too late to reverse course now.

I tapped my foot on the ground, eager for the questions to start. Anna glanced at me but said nothing. My heart skipped a beat as Tom closed the file and turned his attention to my suspect.

"For our records, can I confirm your name is Preston Weiss?" Tom began.

Preston nodded. I noted his haircut. His hair was longer in the front. Not so long as to look rebellious or unkept—on the contrary, everything about him appeared put together. I assumed he came from money or that his family was well enough off that he hadn't struggled. Everything he wore—from his shoes to his wristwatch—looked like more than your average college student could afford, and they were all brand new or close to it.

"And you would like to waive your right to counsel, Mr. Weiss? We can do this at another time if you'd like a lawyer to be present," Tom said.

Preston shrugged. "It's fine. I've got nothing to hide."

Anna made a noise. "Definitely sure of himself, isn't he?"

"You said he'd get bolder as he grew more confident," I said, my voice hushed despite the fact Preston couldn't hear us through the thick glass. "You mean like this?"

"Perhaps," Anna said. "An inflated sense of superiority could push him to confirm an imagined advantage over our investigators."

I felt my hopes rising. What if I had identified the killer, and he just slipped up and landed himself in our interrogation room? I swallowed my excitement, fearful of having my optimism crushed.

"I'm sure this comes as no surprise, but with two parahumans murdered in what certainly appears to be hate crimes, we're looking into anyone with anti-parahuman sentiment. You're a member of the APA?" Glenn said.

"No," Preston responded.

Glenn pulled out the pamphlet I had seen earlier. Though his eyes remained obscured behind dark glasses, his face encouraged an explanation.

"This isn't yours?" Glenn asked.

"They were handing them out on campus. I took one in case I wanted to hear more later and signed up for some emails. Forgot I even had it. Is that a crime?"

A mischievous look crossed Preston's face, like this was all very amusing to him. It was strangely at odds with the waves of ice that pulsed from him.

"No," Glenn said, though his tone gave the impression he wished it were.

"Explain what you'd like to hear more about?" Tom asked.

Preston eyed him, the look of amusement never faltering. Unlike Mark, it was less than obvious that Tom and Glenn were parahumans, which was one of the many reasons they were the go-to guys for interrogations. It helped that Tom couldn't be touched unless he wanted to be, which was fantastic if a suspect became unruly. I wondered if Preston's smirk would falter if he realized just how many parahumans occupied the room with him.

"I'm not a fan of the Agency having their own elite military squad," Preston said, sweeping one arm at the white room. "It all feels a little too authoritarian to me, you know?"

I winced as I tried to probe Preston's mind. He was lying. I knew that much. The anti-parahuman sentiment went deeper than that, but I couldn't see what it was beyond twisting tendrils of blackness.

"You getting anything?" Anna asked.

I cringed. "His brain is . . . weird. It's as if his thoughts are under a current, and there are black patches where I get lost. Every time I try to go deeper, it's like putting on a blindfold and digging through a bucket of cold seaweed."

Anna grimaced, though her eyes glinted with academic curiosity. Having sat behind this wall more than once, I had been exposed to all manner of warped minds. Certain types of people exhibited very distinct thought patterns.

"You think he's a psychopath?" Anna asked.

"He could be," I said, trying to figure out how to navigate the black void that was Preston Weiss. "Or he found a darker part of the internet that details anti-telepath training."

"I wonder why he'd need that?" Anna muttered.

"You're a student at CSDU?" Tom continued, unaware of my telepathic impediment.

"Pre-med."

"Sports scholarship? That's impressive," Tom said. He didn't sound impressed.

"Wrestling," Preston responded. "Been doing it since middle school."

The hair on the back of my neck stood on end. He would certainly know how to subdue two petite women like Madison and Alice. Anna glanced in my direction, eyebrows raised.

"Have you ever seen these two women on campus?" Tom asked, sliding two pictures across the table. My throat tightened as he looked at Madison and Alice's headshots, his face revealing nothing.

"I've never seen the Asian chick," he finally said. "But the other girl was a TA for my neuro class."

Madison.

A chill raced down my spine. What had Anna said to me all those weeks ago? That the killer might've known Madison, and that's why I felt the killer's guilt during her murder?

"I thought we cleared all of Madison's students?" I asked in a rush.

"We did," Anna said, equally surprised. "No one had a record or fit the profile. Almost all of her students were in class or had other alibis."

Almost all . . . perhaps Preston Weiss fell into the category of students with weak alibis? Anna stepped closer to the glass, eyebrows knitted together as she observed our suspect with increased interest.

"You ever see anyone bother her?" Glenn asked from the other room.

Preston shrugged. "Not really, but it's not like I knew her outside of class."

"Anyone in class ever have a problem with her being a parahuman?"

"I don't think anyone knew," Preston said. If the line of questioning had any effect on him, he didn't show it.

"Did you?" Mark asked tersely.

Preston shook his head. "Not until the video came out."

Briefly, a flash of memory emerged from under the black ocean that was Preston's mind: hands fumbling with a camera. It was there and gone in a blink. I tried to hold on to it—to get more detail—but it slithered away. I tensed my jaw and tried to lower my blood pressure with a deep breath. This guy felt all sorts of wrong, but I was getting absolutely nothing concrete.

"And if you had?" Tom asked.

Preston shrugged noncommittally. His lack of anxiety was infuriating.

"Madison was a cool TA," he said. "I'm more of an anti-Agency guy. I don't care if a parahuman grades my exams."

He said it with a grin, and I felt fire in my stomach.

"Anything?" Anna asked, turning toward me.

"*No*," I snapped. I didn't mean to, but the guy was seriously pissing me off.

There were too many coincidences. He didn't exactly match Anna's profile. He was too young. He couldn't have enough experience to become the proficient killer we hunted.

And yet . . .

"I'm sorry," I said hastily. "No, everything is too deep and slippery. If he's done anything or feels anything more than what he's saying, he's amazing at internalizing. I don't know how to read him."

Anna sighed. "His outward behavior is a little odd, but it's hardly a crime."

"He knows we have nothing," I said miserably.

Just like the murderer does, I thought bitterly.

"You really think he should be a suspect?" Anna asked.

165

"I don't know," I groaned. "He doesn't feel right. You don't?"

"He's certainly interesting," Anna said. "I'll have to review the video footage later."

I blinked. Video?

"What if we showed him one of the videos? Of Madison and Alice? Caught him off guard?" I asked.

Anna shook her head. "If the only evidence we get is telepathic information and we only get it after he sees the video, any decent defense lawyer will write it off as a coerced reverie and try to toss anything else that falls under the Smith Act."

"Including how I found him," I muttered.

"And where were you on May fifth at approximately 8:45 a.m. and June third at approximately 7:15 a.m.?" Mark continued beyond the glass.

"I'd have to check. Class? My girlfriend and I get coffee beforehand sometimes. I'd have to ask her."

"This girlfriend have a name?" Tom asked.

"Carlie Newsom."

Glenn pulled a notepad and a pen from his jacket. He pushed them toward Preston and nodded pointedly. Preston leaned forward, scribbled on the notepad, and pushed it back with a matched haughtiness.

"You ask all the APA guys these questions? I didn't hear anything about the Agency looking at them," Preston asked.

Mark leaned forward, his mass casting a shadow across the table, and took the notepad. He lumbered out the door without another word.

"I thought you said you weren't a member of the APA?" Glenn asked, eyebrows raised behind his glasses.

"I follow the news," Preston said. "And I hear things on social media, you know? I wonder how they'd feel if they knew you're taking a special interest in them? I mean, you haven't presented me with any evidence to implicate them."

His teeth flashed as his grin widened, making him appear wolfish. He was *enjoying* this. And yet, he was cold inside, a different person only I got to know.

"Is there any pertinent information you may have? From the internet, of course, since you have no direct involvement with the APA," Tom said through clenched teeth. "Have any APA members said or done anything you find suspicious?"

"As I told you, I mostly signed up for the emails," Preston said slowly. "I haven't really spoken with anyone. More of a loner, you know?"

I struggled to swallow my disappointment as Tom and Glenn collected their papers and stood.

"Do you need a ride back to campus?" Glenn asked.

"I've got it covered."

"Thank you for your time, Mr. Weiss. Give us a few minutes to make sure everything is settled," Tom said.

When Tom and Glenn entered the room ten seconds later, their slumped shoulders and shuffling gaits matched the tone of the room.

"Little shit," Tom muttered under his breath.

"Is he our guy?" Glenn asked, taking off his glasses and pinching the bridge of his nose.

"It's possible," I said. I couldn't look at them.

"Possible doesn't keep him from walking," Tom said. "I'd love to have an excuse for a forty-eight-hour hold—wipe that smug smile right off his pretty face, but he knows we've got nothing."

"There's no point in spooking him if there's nothing we can do," Glenn added.

I wanted to scream.

"His mind suggests he may have psychopathic tendencies," Anna said. "It's hardly damning; more people are identifiable as psychopaths or sociopaths than you'd think, and it doesn't always correlate with—"

"That or he's using some sort of self-trained anti-telepathy tactics—certainly nothing formal. It makes him hard to read," I said, cutting Anna off before we lost her down the psychologist black hole.

"He's weird, I'll give you that, but we've got no reason to keep him here. He has no record. As far as I can tell, he's a model student. We'll check his alibi, but that's all we can do for now. Unless you give me something to work with, any further poking and prodding is just going to delight his future lawyer. You know how those bloodsuckers hate telepaths."

"His mind is wired differently," I said, sighing. "It will take me a while to figure him out."

Tom was sympathetic, but personal feelings aside, we all had to abide by the law.

"I wish I could give you the time, but I have no choice but to let him go."

"Do you think it could be him?" Anna asked Tom and Glenn, glancing at the man in the interrogation room. Preston Weiss leaned back in his chair, drumming his fingers on the table as if he was waiting for us to bring him a coffee.

"I'd bet money on something being wrong with him," Mark grumbled from the doorway, looking deflated. "But whether it's some sort of affluenza or he's just a young jackass, I don't know."

"Did you call the girlfriend?" I asked, though I already knew.

"She says they were getting coffee," Mark said. "But forgive me if I don't just take her word for it."

"There are a few obvious pieces missing," Tom added.

"He's too young. He doesn't have the life experience to be a proficient killer, and there's no evidence he has the knowledge to build a bomb," I said, drooping at the thought that I just wasted everyone's time. "Does he even have a military background?"

"The bomb they found wasn't that sophisticated. With the right amount of research, your average Joe could build one in his garage," Mark said. "It was on a pressure sensor—designed to go off if someone picked up the box and tilted it. Honestly, it was a miracle whoever built it didn't blow themselves up delivering it. It's still possible he could have done it."

"We'll have Navin tail him," Tom said. "It's an odd coincidence that a possible psychopath with resentment toward parahumans knew the first victim."

"No," I sighed. "Don't waste Navin's time just because I jumped on the first person who felt a little funny. Ryker will be pissed if he finds out we're chasing empty leads."

"Even if it's just your jerk radar on its highest setting, it won't cost us anything to have Navin follow him for an afternoon," Mark said, jesting on my behalf.

"And I can pop by for some bird-watching after work," Glenn said with a smirk. "I hear there are some interesting things in . . ." He paused to read some papers through the folder. "La Jolla."

Tom whistled. "He can afford an apartment in La Jolla?"

"Says here Mommy and Daddy are both plastic surgeons. I don't think our friend Preston knows what the rent bill looks like."

"Affluenza indeed. I hate this guy even more," Glenn said, laughing.

They were trying to make me feel better for crying wolf. The corner of my mouth tugged, but I found it hard to lift my eyes from my feet.

"In all seriousness, Hadley, if there's something to this, there's a chance he didn't stumble into you by accident," Mark said. "If you want to lie low until we check this guy out, I can talk to Ryker. You could leave town for the time being."

"It's not a bad idea," Anna said. She suddenly looked scared for me.

My eyes nearly popped out of my head. The thought hadn't even occurred to me. Preston Weiss didn't seem to feel any animosity toward me, and I felt certain I was all sorts of wrong, but then, would I be able to tell if I was going to be his next victim? Was it possible he *was* dangerous, and he was playing cat and mouse with us? I hadn't seen myself as the potential mouse until right then.

"Wait, what?" I asked in a rush.

"It unnerves me you identified a possible suspect with a connection to Madison. I think we should proceed as if Preston Weiss's a suspect until we officially rule him out. What if he's been watching you, Hadley? What if he bumped into you on purpose?" Anna asked. "You're the only person who could know who the killer is. If he is the guy, he may have been trying to figure out if you could identify him."

"But I don't—I can't—"

"Well, he might've just figured that out," Mark said, a dark shadow crossing his face. "But he also may not be willing to leave things to chance. I'll talk to Ryker," he added, as he and Anna both exchanged looks. "We'll see what he thinks."

He was going to think Preston Weiss was just a pompous jerk, wasn't he? What the hell had I missed, besides everything in Preston's head?

Mark, Tom, and Glenn left in a defeated shuffle. Anna wanted me clear of the building before they released Preston, citing concerns of him following me. My head spun, so I agreed. I didn't understand what had just happened. Had I screwed up or not? Was Preston Weiss a threat or not? I walked slowly as we made our way across the parking lot toward Anna's car, unsure of what to feel.

My phone rang. I glanced at my caller ID and groaned. I wasn't sure why I was surprised. Collin had warned me, and ignoring the call would only come back to bite me.

"Hey, Ka—Mom," I said, trying to sound like absolutely nothing of consequence happened today. My mother was easily agitated.

"Hadley!" my mom said. Her high-pitched tone screeched at me through the phone. By the sound of her voice, she was clearly beaming. She always got a little excitable when she was up to something.

"You sound chipper," I said. It was best to get right to the point. I wasn't in the mood to dance around it.

"Well, your dad and I were wondering if you can take some time off? We haven't taken a family vacation in the longest time, and my friend Tracy—you remember, Tracy?—she told me we absolutely need to take a trip to Sedona."

She knew I didn't remember Tracy, and I resented her for asking.

Still . . . Sedona. I wondered if she picked the little hippie town in a desperate attempt to pique my interest. Well, it was Old Hadley's interest, which made my blood boil for the second time in just as many seconds, but . . .

I glanced at Anna. She leaned against her black Mazda, waiting patiently. At least, she appeared to be. Internally, she replayed the interview with Preston Weiss, reflecting on every movement, the inflection of his tone, facial expressions . . . everything.

She was truly worried. It made my hair stand on end.

"I've always wanted to see Sedona," I said. I guess Mark would have to have that conversation with Ryker after all.

My mom made a noise somewhere between choking and a yip.

"Would it be okay if I invited Anna? I think she could use some time off," I asked.

Like hell I was leaving Anna behind if a psychopath might be after me. Mark still had to pull off the miracle of getting Ryker to remove his claws from me, but my mom didn't need to know that.

"Of course!" my mom said in a breathy rush. "Tell her to bring Elliott. When can you get time off?"

Mom had a thing about boys being in the same room as girls on family trips. She must have *really* wanted me to get out of town.

"It's actually been pretty slow for me. Whenever."

"How about—"

My mother's voice drifted away for a moment, and for a split second, I saw it clear as day.

"The watch!" I blurted out.

"Watch?" my mom asked.

"I remember the watch!" I said breathlessly. I glanced back at the building behind me, where Preston Weiss wore a watch I had seen before.

"N-no, sweetie. We're not talking about a watch; we're talking about Sedona," my mom said nervously, though I hardly heard her. "Are you a little confused today?" she asked, though the real question was quite clear.

I ignored her patronizing tone. "Anna!" I called, heart pounding.

I don't remember what happened after that. I hope we ended the conversation without my mom hearing what happened next. As for me, I blinked, and suddenly the world around me was dark with smoke. Anna lay at my feet, her arms wrapped around her head as car alarms blared around us. The air was thick and smelled nauseating: acrid, like burning plastic and hot wires.

I never found my cell phone, but Forensics found a few lumps of plastic that might have once been it later.

Something felt weird—wrong. I glanced down and nearly fell backward at the sight of the nail sticking out of my upper arm.

"Anna?" I asked hysterically. My voice sounded miles away. "Anna, what happened? Are you okay?"

Anna's arms slowly dropped to reveal wide eyes. She looked around frantically as the surrounding cars continued to screech.

"You're bleeding," Anna whispered. Or maybe I just couldn't hear her.

"We need to move," I said, glancing around. The smoke began to clear. Through the haze, an overturned Agency SUV was visible, flames licking its underbelly.

In that moment, I knew what happened.

There was no guarantee there wasn't another bomb.

Adrenaline driving me, I ignored the odd pressure and ache in my arm as I dragged Anna to her feet. We ran back toward headquarters, just in time to nearly get barreled over by Brittany as she sped past in a whistling blur.

I blinked, and Brittany stood beside me again, her body appearing to vibrate as she trembled at inhuman speed.

"Hadley?" she asked, wide eyes staring at the nail in my arm.

"I think it was a bomb," I choked out.

Anna stared out at the scene, eyes glazing over. I felt shock seeping into her brain. The color drained from her face, and she looked like she needed a chair.

"Is there anyone else——?" Brittany began, turning toward the parking lot, but by some miracle, I reacted faster. I saw her thoughts and reached out, grabbing her wrist to keep her in place.

"There might be another one!" I yelled in a nearly incoherent rush.

Brittany might have been the fastest person in San Diego, but I was skeptical she could outrun bomb shrapnel.

"How did you know?" Anna asked, eyes fixed on me.

"Know what?"

"I was by the car. You called my name, and then you dragged me across the parking lot. You knew it was going to happen. You blocked all the . . ." Her eyes locked on my arm. She drew a sharp breath and tears started rolling down her cheeks. She sat on the ground, head between her knees, taking deep, rhythmic breaths.

Mark, Ryker, and a herd of other people burst out the Agency's back door as the wail of sirens rose in the distance.

Brittany urged Anna up and tugged us in their direction.

"Bomb!" Brittany called. "Get everyone back inside!"

By some miracle, there was only one bomb. The only injuries were the nail in my arm and Anna's skinned arms and legs. I whined like a small child as Dr. Patterson pulled the piece of metal from my arm and nearly threw up on him as shock made the room spin, but it could have been much, much worse. He closed the wound in under a minute. Anna's injuries didn't take long either.

When we reviewed the surveillance video later, I felt a twinge of guilt as I watched an unsuspecting Anna telekinetically yanked across the parking lot, only to skid the last few feet to stop at my feet in a heap. The bomb went off as she hit the pavement. I still wasn't sure how I'd been able to block all the packed nails and glass.

Someone had planted the bomb under an Agency SUV. It had pulled into the parking lot half an hour earlier. The driver had just come back from lunch and remembered nothing suspicious. We interviewed everyone, but no one saw a thing.

And Preston Weiss, who was still sitting in our interrogation room as the parking lot turned into a war zone, suddenly had the best alibi of anyone in San Diego.

He smiled when we let him go.

CHAPTER 9

kept my eyes on the orb. Luminous tendrils drifted off it, distorted through the wall of water separating me from it. It was familiar to me, but the memory of what it was remained just out of reach. The burning in my lungs grew worse; a deep pressure at the base of my throat grew ever more painful. I knew if I didn't reach the orb soon, what it was or was not would cease to matter. My vision grew dark around the edges, the cone of blackness tightening, but I knew I couldn't take my eyes off the orb. Reaching it meant life.

With a gasp, I broke the surface of the water, the moon hanging high above me in the night sky. I stole one quick breath before a wave hit. I tumbled in the dark water, top and bottom interchanging so rapidly in the dark that the only indicator of direction was air bubbles escaping my lungs as the wind was knocked from me.

I didn't get to come up for air before the next wave hit. It hit hard. Stars danced before my eyes as my skull collided with something—was I at the bottom again?—and I inadvertently took in a lungful of water, burning seawater rushing down my throat.

By some mercy, I felt something solid beneath me. I clawed at it frantically, desperate to escape what was surely about to become a watery grave. When my head broke the water, I vomited, salt and brine burning my esophagus and nose as what felt like half the ocean came up. I choked and coughed as the surf hissed around me, the waves that had threatened to pull me under now breaking harmlessly against the shore.

I crawled on the floor, taking deep breaths as life returned to my body, but I choked on smoke as fire raged around me. The stinging in my eyes grew worse as I traded salt from the ocean for the smoke billowing from the burning home.

"Mommy!" a little boy cried.

He wept, down the hall, curled up in the corner of his bedroom as flames crawled ever closer.

"I'm coming!" I tried to tell him, but I only coughed up more water. It flowed from my mouth in an endless torrent, hissing as it hit the flames around me and vanished into steam.

"Mom!" the little boy wailed as flames licked at the curtains only a few feet from him. They caught, the fire crawling up them with amazing speed.

"Hello?" a woman called behind me.

I turned to see her silhouette in the house's doorway. Hesitantly, she entered, shining a flashlight in my direction.

"The boy," I whispered. I turned back to him, but he was lost to the shrubs.

177

Cars sped past in a blur on the road above, a steep incline separating me from the guardrail.

"Miss, are you okay?" the woman called. "Can you hear me?"

I lay on my back, the light flashing in my eyes.

"No, no, no, no!" the woman chanted, though her lips never moved. "You can't die!"

"I won't," I tried to say, but I was paralyzed. The words never came.

"Goddammit! Please! Please, don't die!" the woman sobbed, audible only to me.

I startled awake, Jo's voice echoing in my ears. At least, I thought it might be Jo. I rolled over and grabbed my new cell phone. The screen lit up and read 6:57 a.m. I groaned.

Weasel wiggled out from under the comforter. I groggily attempted to shield my face as his tongue went for my nose.

"No," I moaned. "Be a good boy and go find what I broke."

He didn't care. Mama was up whether or not Mama wanted to be up. Grudgingly, I dragged myself out of bed, and we performed Weasel's morning bathroom routine. He burst back in the door after five minutes, dancing and whining in excitement.

If his bladder hadn't been empty, he would have piddled the floor as I dropped kibble into his bowl.

"I wish I could feel that way about mornings," I told the overzealous dog as he did his best imitation of a vacuum, his bowl's harsh clanging jarring to my ears.

I turned to the fridge in search of my own breakfast.

Fingerlike tendrils of tension tickled my mind before my roommate's muffled footsteps announced her approach.

"You're up early," Anna said as she entered the kitchen and went for the coffee maker like a targeted missile, dark circles ringing her eyes.

"Heads up," I said as I grabbed a cardboard box full of leftover pizza from the fridge. "I had a nightmare. Not sure if I broke anything."

Anna held one foot up and waved a slipper in the air. "Figured as much when I heard you. I'll tell Elliot. Drowning again?"

"Drowning," I said as I threw a slice of pizza on a plate and stuck it in the microwave. "Fire. The works, you know? Elliot's here?"

I didn't ask what her nightmares were. She'd already unwittingly shared.

"Elliott came over for dinner," Anna said, taking my memory lapse in stride.

I shrugged at no one in particular. I didn't remember dinner. Typical. Elliott had been here every night since the bomb went off at the Agency, making my forgetfulness even more ridiculous.

"It's wildfire season." Anna took a heaping scoop of coffee out of the can. "You should probably avoid Christine if you don't want burning to be your nightmares' theme."

"I guess that won't be a problem," I muttered as the microwave beeped and I eyed the coffeepot enviously. Bless her, Anna was making enough for all of us.

It was a surreal moment of forced normalcy in a time that felt anything but, willfully imposed by two roommates who needed to not talk about *the thing* to maintain some sanity. We were both a bundle of nerves, counting down to the moment of escape.

It had been three days since the bomb went off at the Agency and Preston Weiss, the only person to set off my telepathic alarms, practically laughed off our attempts at an interrogation and walked free. That was Thursday.

I fully expected any semblance of normalcy to vanish again promptly at 9:00 a.m. the next morning when the investigating team was due to turn in their report on the bombing to Ryker.

Not that we'd be there for it. Anna already had suitcases lining the living room wall, packed and repacked in the night when nightmares had woken her and sleep had never returned. She had woken me up too, and I spent my sleepless moments cataloguing what items I'd failed to account for.

Thanks, Anna. Thanks, telepathy and your lack of boundaries.

We would trade killers for my mother in twenty-four hours, and I wasn't sure I was trading up.

In hindsight, I don't know why I ever thought we could escape. I never saw disaster coming as Anna and I stood in the kitchen with bedheads and frumpy pajamas, Weasel noisily turning over his bowl in search of more kibble.

As a telepath, I take offense to that.

My phone rang. Shoving my less than nutritious breakfast in my mouth, I ran to my bedroom and dove for my brand-new phone without checking caller ID.

"You need to come home!" my mother sobbed hysterically.

I stood bewildered with a slice of lukewarm pizza hanging from my mouth at 7:30 a.m.

"What?" I asked, swallowing a hard lump of cheese. "We'll be there tom—"

"I can't think straight knowing some madman is trying to blow up my daughter!" my mother wailed.

I hadn't told her about the bomb.

The cameras outside the Agency showed I had hung up on my mom only seconds before the bomb went off, dropping the phone and yanking Anna away from her car just as fire erupted and the video turned to static. The Agency had kept the bomb quiet. There was only one way Kathy—Mom—knew. I rushed to the TV and found a news station.

I nearly dropped the phone.

The angle was different and clearly farther away than the Agency's security footage. Wherever the camera had been hidden, it captured me perfectly as I telekinetically ripped Anna across the parking lot, windshields exploding outward and the earth rocking beneath us. The vantage point was ideally located to capture the SUV as it lifted off its wheels, the bomb erupting under it in a flash of blinding light, scattering packed nails and glass in all directions. But not around us. The concussive blast lifted my hair only briefly before weaponized hardware began bouncing in opposite directions as if encountering a wall. I finally caught the moment the one stray nail hit my arm as my telekinetic shield went up. It barely broke my concentration then, but it made me cringe now. I unconsciously grabbed my arm—the open wound healed by Dr. Patterson but still deeply bruised—and felt the dull ache that was the foremost reminder of how I briefly became a human pincushion. If I hadn't been there, I wouldn't believe it was me. The person on TV looked confident, put together, and honestly, like a total badass.

Which was probably why the video already had thousands of views and the media had my name.

"No," I muttered. *"No, no, no, no."*

My head swam as the commentator extolled the "heroic efforts of Hadley Gordon" and praised "the new face exemplifying San Diego's heroes in this wave of tragic hate crimes" in a way that hardly made me seem human—parahuman, whatever.

"Oh . . . *shit*," I mumbled numbly as the foremost, but certainly not last, consequence of the previous week's events reared its ugly, high-profile head.

We weren't going to Sedona.

"Who is that? What's on the TV?" Anna asked shakily, frozen at the entryway of the kitchen with white knuckles clutching her mug. She'd heard the TV just fine. The look on her face begged me to tell her she was wrong.

A knock on the door made me jump. Weasel sounded the alarm and bolted across the living room, paws hardly touching the ground as he practically flew to be the first at the door. I sensed Mark on the other side, his agitation palpable.

"Mom, I'm so sorry, but I really need to go. I promise I'll call you!"

A wail of protest assaulted my ears as I hurriedly hung up and reached for the doorknob, encouraging Weasel back with a gently placed foot.

"Elliott! *Wake up!*" I called. We needed all hands on deck.

"What's going on?" Elliott asked, stumbling into the living room in boxers and a shirt, hair sticking out at ridiculous angles and a groggy cloud of panic befuddling his brain. Anna finally stepped from the kitchen and faced the TV.

"Oh . . . my . . . *God*," she said slowly.

Elliott's face drained of color as my fifteen minutes of fame repeated on the screen, his girlfriend sliding across a parking lot as fire and glass rained around her. They had her name, too.

I threw the door open, and Mark's face fell as he surveyed the eerily still living room.

"I guess you already know," he said as he stepped inside, twisting his broad shoulders to squeeze past the doorframe. I nodded numbly as I held the door open, balancing awkwardly on one leg as Weasel failed to read the room and hopped excitedly on his hind legs, my foot still against his chest.

"Ryker's trying to get ahead of it, but this thing has taken off. It's only been two hours!"

What the hell was the internet doing up at 5:00 a.m.?

"What do we do?" I asked breathlessly, closing the door and releasing my dog.

"Ryker sent me over to make sure the media wasn't already here. SDPD should be right behind me. They'll set up a perimeter until we can figure this out."

My eyes nearly bugged out of my head.

"Wait, what?" Elliott asked.

"It's just a precaution. It's probably unnecessary," Mark said.

"Probably?" I asked, glancing at Anna. Her eyes were still trained on the TV.

"Do we need to leave?" Elliott asked, stepping protectively closer to Anna.

She was wearing pajama shorts, and I resisted flinching when I saw the angry red flesh of her legs. She'd kept her legs covered for the past few days, probably for both of our benefit, and the sight of them was a stark reminder of how we had both almost been blown to pieces—the video playing on a loop on the damned TV notwithstanding. Dr. Patterson had healed Anna's road rash from when I dragged her across the parking lot, but she still had some inflammation, and it had left faint scars.

I dropped my gaze to the floor. A better telekinetic wouldn't have flayed her.

"Ryker's going to call once he's put out a few fires at the Agency. We'll see what he advises, but yeah, I think you should be prepared to leave now and stay in Sedona for a few extra days," Mark said, noting the suitcases as he settled on the couch. He patted the space beside him, and Weasel leaped up, tail wagging as fast as he could make it go. I wished I could be that oblivious.

As it was, I could sense Mark's mood much too clearly.

"What else?" I asked hesitantly, though I already knew.

Mark sighed and gave me an apologetic look.

"We finished analyzing the bomb. Someone detonated it remotely. They waited until you were in the parking lot and called it from what we presume was a burner phone."

"Someone targeted Anna and Hadley specifically?" Elliott squeaked.

"No idea," Mark said. He sounded like he'd already been up working on this for hours. "Could be they were just the first two to walk by."

"They were close, weren't they? That's why I knew it was going to go off; I caught their thoughts?" I asked somberly.

Mark nodded. "Had to have been. Bastard got close enough to see the parking lot but knew where the damned cameras were. We have no idea where he was."

I slumped down on the couch beside him. "So there was no way Preston Weiss was behind the bomb. He was still inside the Agency when it went off."

"That's not all," Mark said, absently stroking Weasel's head. "It's not like the one we found at the *Tribune*."

"What? No," Elliott blurted out. "How can you even tell?"

"Completely unique signature," Mark said. "This one was far more sophisticated. We're not looking at someone who tried to copy plans off the internet. Whoever set off the bomb at the Agency knew what he was doing."

"Couldn't he have just gotten better between the bombs?" Elliott asked hopefully.

Anna finally tore her gaze away from the TV and cast him an apologetic look. She shook her head.

"What does that tell you?" I asked Anna.

"First guess?" she said, rubbing her temple as if that would clear her mind. "Someone is trying to use the first bomb to their advantage. Someone inspired by the first bomber's message is trying to pursue his own cause and hopes we won't look for two suspects."

"Doesn't it make sense just to have one person get better at making bombs?" Elliott insisted, internal hysteria growing exponentially worse as he attempted to reconcile the number of unsubs who might be after his girlfriend.

"Bombs have pretty distinct fingerprints," Mark said. "Bombers rarely change their MO that much. It's pretty easy to tell if different people made them."

"If the second one was more sophisticated, wouldn't the second bomber know that?" I asked.

"He may not care," Anna said.

Elliot shook his head. "But you just said—"

"It could be a number of things," Anna said briskly, rubbing her temple harder. "It'll take me more than five minutes to develop a profile."

Elliott closed his mouth and shifted uncomfortably. I dropped my eyes. Talking about bombs so soon was not what Anna needed. In her mind, she relived the parking lot all over again, as if she hadn't already done so twice last night in vivid nightmares. I winced, trying to extricate myself from her mind.

Not that my other options were much better.

"So, I was completely wrong about Preston," I said, hanging my head.

"Navin tailed Preston all weekend. He went to some event with his fraternity Friday night but has otherwise stayed home and studied for an exam. Glenn still has his apartment staked out. Aside from having a place no undergraduate should be able to afford, he hasn't seen anything suspicious."

"Hang on," Anna said, sitting down beside Mark, looking at us earnestly. "That doesn't mean Preston isn't our guy. We can't stop looking into him just because he behaved himself for a few days."

"How do you figure?" I asked glumly.

I appreciated her desire to support me, but that was it: I was wrong. We were back at square one, and we had to move on and do it all over again from scratch.

Meanwhile, the media had my name. How was I supposed to patrol now? How was I supposed to get justice for Madison and Alice?

No, wait. Wasn't I about to give up and run away?

"C'mon," Anna said. "How many freshmen do you know who'd make a phone call for beer money? All he'd have to do is persuade someone, tell them a time, and we'd be convinced we were after the wrong guy."

"He thought he was going to be in an exam at the time. There's no way he could have planned me siccing the Agency on him, not even if he was telepathic," I said, tapping my temple for emphasis.

"It took an hour to bring him in," Anna said. "Did he make any calls?"

Mark shook his head, either indicating Preston didn't or that he wasn't sure.

"Did Glenn get a look at his knives?" Anna asked. "Was he missing any?"

"He's a frat boy," Mark said. "He ordered pizza and drank beer all weekend. Glenn never saw his knife collection, if he even owns utensils."

Something tickled the back of my mind: some detail that was important. Darkness greeted me in place of a memory. Whatever it was, it was lost to the void. Pressing it was futile.

"It doesn't matter," I muttered. "There's nothing to suggest Preston even knows how to build a bomb. We don't have proof he's a killer of any kind."

Anna pursed her lips and locked eyes with me. A whisper of a thought floated in her mind, still forming and light like gossamer.

"No," I said, sitting up straight. My heart was suddenly pounding. "You really think so?"

"Think what?" Elliott asked. He paced in circles, trying to keep himself from rushing for Anna's suitcases and bolting to the car.

"You think Preston has a partner," I said. "You think the second bomber is helping Preston?"

"It could fit," Anna said. "Unless it's a complete coincidence the bomb went off while we locked Preston Weiss in an interrogation room with a camera recording his every move. Not to mention they could have meant it for you, the *only* person who could identify him."

"Or it could be someone who wants to protect the killer. Maybe not a partner, but just someone who doesn't want the guy caught yet," Mark proposed.

"That's suggesting some random person knows the identity of the killer before we do and knew we picked up a suspect. How would they know?" I asked.

"Maybe we didn't dig deep enough," Mark said, slumping deeper into the couch as if the thought was dragging him down. "Maybe he's connected with a group, and he's telling them everything."

"I just . . ." I sighed, running my hands over my face. "I didn't get that from the guy at Madison's memorial. Or Preston Weiss. Both are very much lone wolves—he even admitted as much, for whatever that's worth."

"What do you think?" Elliott asked Anna. She glanced at me, defeat in her eyes.

"I mean . . . Hadley has a point. The murders were unannounced. The killer made no threats beforehand. He had no manifesto. There was no trail to forewarn what he was about to do. He merely acted. Now, think about the bombs—the first one, at least. We got a warning. In that instance, he was practically shouting at us to look at what he was doing."

"It could still be one person," Elliott said. "What if all the positive press parahumans were getting kind of sent him over the edge? What if he felt like he *had* to escalate things?"

"Our guy always acted and *then* sent the message," Anna replied. "We get a video after the fact, not a warning that someone is about to get killed."

"I mean, he sort of did. 'Kill the freaks. They will all fall.' From the video? Oh! But the murderer only went after parahumans before," I said, doing my best to rationalize the convoluted information we had. "Maybe Anna's right? He's only ever hurt parahumans until Anna nearly got caught up in the bomb."

Elliott flinched when I said the words.

"*But*," I added, trying to backpedal. "I was the closest person to the SUV when it blew up. He waited until Anna passed by."

"Which also points to the idea that he already knew exactly who and what you are," Elliott said, paling. "Do you think he knows where you live?"

"It's likely. Like Anna said, someone may have figured out Hadley can identify the suspect," Mark said, somewhat defeated.

"But I can't," I said, frustrated. "If I could, wouldn't I have done it by now?"

"What if it just looks like two people because he has a different MO regarding parahumans and non-powered people?" I continued, trying to ignore the sudden urge to finish packing a bag and flee myself . . . and also really proud of myself for correctly using a term from class.

"Did they even find a bomb at any of those news stations?" I asked. I suddenly couldn't remember, which was annoying.

"The *Tribune* had one under the sink in one of the break rooms," Mark said, taking my memory lapse in stride.

"Wait, really?" I asked, suddenly deflating as my theory lost credibility.

Mark, Anna, and Elliott all nodded.

"Okay, so . . . does my theory hold, then?" I asked.

"Going from stabbing to bombs is an enormous change," Anna said. "It's a stretch."

I groaned.

"Madison and Alice's murderer is a hunter. He waits until he has complete control; every move is calculated. He has a weapon that's nearly impossible to track. He only kills when he's certain that he controls the situation and is guaranteed success, and he does it in public places

189

to project his aptitude. A bomb is chaos. It's messy and nonspecific. It could miss the target . . . like it might have with you. It just doesn't seem to fit our stabber's personality. He's a control freak," Anna said.

"When you felt the murderer at the park, it definitely felt like he was working alone?" Elliott asked me.

"Honestly, yeah," I said. "Guy felt isolated. It didn't feel like a strong human connection like a partner was a thing for him."

"So, for all we know, this is just another completely separate lunatic who was inspired to act after the murders. It could all be a random coincidence," Mark said, sighing. He looked exhausted.

"Or worse," Anna said somberly. "It could be an entire group organizing themselves. A hate group could take advantage of the murders to orchestrate their own hate crimes and hope it gets blamed on someone else. It's been known to happen, and I think we all know at least one group with a history of violence."

I resisted the urge to groan. I was going to end up tailing the Sons of Gaia. I just knew it. A member of the Sons of Gaia had shot someone outside the Agency headquarters in DC only a few years ago during an APA protest. Years before that, someone had driven a car into a crowd in New York during another protest. Nearly a decade before that, the FBI and the Agency had apprehended a small group attempting to send pipe bombs through the mail. If memory served, and I didn't trust that it did, they'd addressed one package to Ryker.

"*Great*," I said, hysteria on the edge of my voice. "So, Preston could be the guy, or maybe he isn't the guy. We could be looking at one guy, or it could be a team, or the whole damn city could be losing its mind. Glad we worked it all out."

"Yeah," Mark said glumly. "I think that's about where we are."

"You said the guy could have a military background," Elliot said. "Is it possible that he knows how this all works, and he's intentionally doing things to throw you off?"

"Honestly," Mark said, "it could be a number of scenarios, and we aren't any closer to narrowing them down or coming up with a concrete subject right now. We're stuck."

There was a heavy pause as we all sat there, miserable.

"I'm going to call my mom," Elliott finally said. "We'll stay with her in Portland."

"We can't go to Portland!" Anna exclaimed, her eyes frantic. "We can't leave Had—"

"Portland's perfect," I said, cutting her off.

She wouldn't leave me behind. Not unless I made her. Elliott gave me an apologetic yet thankful look. We both knew the truth: without knowing exactly what we were up against, it was too dangerous for anyone to get near me.

"If the media is going to be following me and this guy—or *guys*—knows who I am, you should get far away from me until it's over," I said before Anna had time to argue.

"And what are you supposed to do?" Anna asked, hysteria rising.

"Relax," Mark said tiredly. "I'm sure Ryker has already found which desolate region in the Canadian wilderness he's going to airlift you to."

I raised an eyebrow.

"You can think whatever you want about Ryker," Mark said. "But if he thinks this guy is targeting either of you, he won't risk it. You guys are his job, and in case you hadn't noticed, Ryker is *very* serious about his job."

I gave a weak half shrug. "You make a valid point."

It was quiet for a minute. Outwardly, at least. I counted down the seconds until Anna burst.

"*No*," she finally said, marching toward her bedroom. "I'm not speculating about this from the couch, and we're not going anywhere. I'm getting dressed and going in. I need to see the newest evidence."

Elliott stared at me, eyes pleading, but I didn't know what to say. Anna was a mule if you caught her in a mood, *especially* about me.

Mark's phone rang. Wearily, he pulled it out of his pocket and checked caller ID.

"Speak of the devil," he muttered before answering. I heard Ryker's voice—sharp and angry—from the other side.

"That shouldn't be a problem," Mark said. "We'll be there soon." He hung up and sighed. "He needs you both to come in."

"And you," he added, casting a glance at Elliott. "You can't stay here until he smooths this out with the media . . . maybe not even then."

"I thought you said the police were setting up a perimeter?" Anna asked.

"You really want to risk it?" Mark asked pointedly. "I wouldn't plan on coming back."

"I'll start packing Weasel's things," Elliott said.

I nodded glumly as he headed toward the kitchen and began shoveling kibble into a bag. Weasel's ears perked, and he leaped from the couch, convinced some poor sucker was giving him a second breakfast.

"That didn't sound great," I said anxiously.

"You know how Ryker hates dealing with the media," Mark offered as an explanation, but I knew something else was coming.

Chaos ensued the moment we arrived at the Agency. Much to my annoyance, Mark dragged me up the dreaded elevator. I was ready to gratefully rush back into the claustrophobic death trap as soon as the doors opened. Ryker's pinched face materialized the moment the bell chirped its sharp *ding!* and the doors slid open to reveal my new reality. Surprisingly, his eyes locked on Anna first.

"You're consulting on this case remotely from now on," he said abruptly, shoving a thick manila envelope into her arms. "Consider it a working vacation. The address for your safe house is in there. I have transport waiting. You do not speak to anyone about this case—not your mother, not your best friend from college, not your favorite teacher from preschool. No one. I want your opinion once you get settled."

Anna turned and looked at me, eyes wide. "Hadley?" she nearly whispered.

"Ms. Gordon is not your concern," Ryker said through gritted teeth.

I thought the vein in his forehead bulged at the mention of my name.

This was . . . not good.

Anna's eyes stayed fixed on me, her head swimming.

. . . can't leave . . .

. . . stove . . . are we low on dog food? . . .

. . . shit, how much cash does she have? . . .

. . . when did I see her phone last? Did she lose it? . . .

I took a deep breath and tried to push back against Anna's hysteria. Jesus, I'd make Ryker call a babysitter if it meant calming her down.

"Where's the boyfriend?" Ryker asked Mark.

Ryker knew Anna was in a relationship? What?

"Leaving their apartment," Mark replied.

"Both of you should enjoy your vacation," Ryker said, giving Anna a pointed look.

"Why?" Anna squeaked.

"Because the goddamn media has your name and will circle your apartment like vultures, and I'll be damned if another one of my agents ends up a target of an attack," Ryker finally snapped.

This time, I was fairly certain an aneurysm occurred. Anna flinched.

"Enjoy your trip, Ms. Kinney," Ryker said, fuming, and that was the end of the conversation.

Anna stepped into the elevator and pressed the down button. Her eyes were wide and pleading as the doors closed.

The elevator took her away, and I suddenly felt like a rock was sitting in my stomach.

That left me as the sole focus of Ryker's intense gaze.

Please, don't blow something up, I begged myself.

"With me, Gordon," Ryker said through clenched teeth.

His angry hornet brain gave me no answers as he turned on his heel, and it took me half a second to realize he meant for me to follow. I trailed him into a conference room. As my foot crossed the threshold, I realized my life as I knew it was about to change forever.

I wasn't sure it was in a good way.

A man in a dark-blue suit stood and faced me. His head was shaved smooth, and his dark eyes reflected the confidence of a man in a position of immense power.

He was familiar, but I couldn't place him. He reached a hand out, a politician's fake grin plastered across his face. Like Ryker, he was trained against telepaths, and I shied away from his energy, his bee-brain buzzing as his psyche pressed into me. Unlike Ryker's angry-hornet buzzing with its churning ebb and flow, this man's brain was an all-consuming white noise, constant, stifling the other energies in the room as he took over my personal space. I took his hand, wincing a smile as his aura wrapped around me like a wet blanket. His grip was powerful, much like his gaze . . . and everything else about him.

"Marshall Kelley," the man said.

My breath left me in a strangled squeak. Marshall Kelley was *Ryker's boss.* The man was a mythic beast in the Agency—the boogeyman meant to scare parahumans into being good boys and girls. If this man could control *Ryker* . . .

A chair tipped on its side and Kelley jumped. Mortification flashed through me, and what dignity I had tucked tail and abandoned the room. I imagined I looked like I was about to wet myself. It certainly felt that way. Suddenly sweating profusely, I tried to nonchalantly wipe my palms on my jeans.

I glanced down, self-conscious. Jesus, what was I wearing?

"I've heard that happens around you telekinetics!" Marshall Kelley exclaimed. He hid his unease behind nervous laughter, though the white noise in his brain faltered at his surprise. An oppressive energy, like heat from an oven, sucked the air from my lungs.

I didn't get the sense that Kelley actually liked parahumans, which I found both odd and unnerving considering his position and that the number of parahumans in the room outnumbered the non-powered people.

That and I was pretty sure the next five minutes with him were about to change the course of my future.

Marshall Kelley's presence wasn't the only one putting me on edge. Three other energies swelled within the room, each of them stifling in their own right. The polished woman with large artificial strawberry-blonde hair held in place by what I assumed was an entire can of hair spray and a semipermanent smile with too-white teeth was the mayor, Donna Handler. Donna didn't have anti-telepath training, and her thoughts and energy oozed from her, slippery and cold like a fish—no, a shark. The large hair and flashing teeth were meant to hide the predatory intelligence of a politician that glinted just behind the bright-blue eyes of a supposed superficial diva.

The two other individuals were Damani and Janelle Aluko—Livewire and Wildfire, respectively.

Wildfire's amber eyes complemented flawless, sepia skin and wavy black hair that flowed past her shoulders. She surveyed the room, hands I had seen hurdle fireballs on news reruns clasped before her. Her energy smoldered like an ember, warm and glowing, but I knew the right fuel could turn a smoldering ember into a raging inferno. She was the least daunting of the newcomers, but I knew she could play their game just as well as they did.

Whereas Wildfire's body language projected a serious, professional air, her twin brother was more relaxed— almost flippant compared to his sister. He leaned back in his chair with one leg over a knee and arms folded against his chest. He was as striking as his sister: his head of tight curls and deep, walnut-colored eyes had graced many a magazine, but behind the charm, I sensed the lightning he was named for crackling and racing under his skin, always just below the surface.

"I think Impulse will fit you nicely!" Donna Handler exclaimed.

"What?" I squeaked, even though I already knew.

Donna's thoughts leaked from her like a cracked dam. My head began throbbing, a migraine rushing to make my situation even more uncomfortable.

"Isn't it lovely?" Donna asked. "It won the city in a landslide! No other alias would do for San Diego's newest, most loved superhero!"

I stared at her, dumbstruck. It had barely been three hours since the news had plucked me from obscurity and the city had first seen my face. Now I had an alias? What was this about *most loved*?

I cast an anxious glance at Livewire and Wildfire. They were perfect actors. No one in the room knew how ridiculous they found the situation, and I felt a sense of relief in knowing that the number of people in the room who found this ludicrous outnumbered the people who didn't. That being said, the people with sense weren't the ones with power.

Thoroughly cowed, I resisted the urge to curl into Ryker, for once the least terrifying face in the room.

"I would like to state once again that Ms. Gordon has proven instrumental in generating leads, and any interference on the city's part only delays bringing Madison Crawford and Alice Cho's murderer to justice," Ryker said through clenched teeth.

I thought he was maintaining calm fairly well, considering that he was an alarming shade of red under his collar . . . and everywhere else.

Wait, was that a compliment? Did Ryker pay *me* a compliment? My head throbbed harder.

"Yes," Kelley said, his interest in me increasing. "All reports indicate that Ms. Gordon is the only individual to identify the suspect. At Madison Crawford's memorial, if memory serves. It's certainly impressive that she's survived his attempts on her life on two occasions. She is also the only one to do so, correct? As I see it, it would be a disservice to the Agency to fail to take advantage of Ms. Gordon's many successes and have her speak out against the man terrorizing the city of San Diego. After all, that is what you want, isn't it, Bill? To catch this man and calm the city?" Kelley's smile was the toothy snarl of a predator—there was nothing warm about it.

Speak out . . . oh, God. It wasn't just Donna. They were out of their minds.

Heat radiated off Ryker, and I turned wide eyes up at him, pleading for him to say something. Bite their heads off, put them in their places like they were his agents. They had to know what a bad idea this was. Instead, he bit back a retort, though I knew what he was going to say. Ryker, for all his crassness, had a set of moral standards he abided by. Though he wanted to shout my shortcomings to the room, he wouldn't.

He preferred to do it in private and to my face. I, on the other hand, was more than happy to shout my problems from the roof of the Agency if it meant getting me out of this.

"S-sir," I stammered, a flush creeping into my cheeks. "If you've read the reports, you know that I . . . I have a condition. I am not the best candidate to be a public face."

"It says here you have a near-perfect record subduing suspects," Mayor Handler said as she flipped through pages of an employee file. *My* employee file.

Again, I resisted the urge to hide behind Ryker.

"With respect, ma'am," I choked out. "I think I've assisted with less than ten unruly suspects, and all have been controlled situations with supervision from other agents—usually from behind a wall."

Donna grinned at me, and I realized I'd stepped right into her trap. Ryker sighed almost imperceptibly behind me. He knew from the start there was no arguing, but now Donna had the opening she needed.

"Which is why you'll be working with Damani and Janelle. No two parahumans have more experience with both the press and criminals."

"The press?" I squeaked, hoping rolling over and playing stupid would disarm her.

No such chance. Mayor Handler's sharklike eyes only glinted as she wrested more control of the situation. I was outclassed, and everyone knew it.

"Ms. Gordon," she said saccharinely, her smile growing impossibly wider to reveal white teeth that practically glowed in the fluorescent lighting of the conference room. "The people of San Diego are frightened. Young parahumans are watching the news and wondering 'Am I next?' You've given people a sense of hope. It seems only fitting that you should say a few words to calm their fears and assure them that this matter is being handled."

I cast a pleading glance at Livewire and Wildfire, who were completely at ease. They could talk sense into the politicians, though they wouldn't, I realized with a sinking sensation.

"Look," Livewire—Damani—said, finally speaking now that the talking heads had vomited their overly rehearsed lines at me. "The guy can't touch us. Any knife-wielding lunatic grabs ahold of us, and he's coming away with a nasty burn or one hell of a shock."

"And bombs are just fire," Wildfire said. She snapped her fingers, and a flame danced on her thumb. In a blink, it was gone, crushed in her fist. "I can handle fire."

I wasn't sure if she was naïve or simply trying to sate my likely obvious anxiety. Both siblings had already accepted their assignment, and I knew they'd been encouraged to get me on board before I walked into the room. As almost twenty-year veterans of the Agency, this had been their life since they were eighteen. They could give a speech to the press in their sleep.

"And I'm bulletproof," Mark said, stepping into the room. Nearly trembling from the deluge of thoughts and emotions saturating the air—confidence, smugness, greed, and Ryker's smoldering anger at the forefront—I hadn't noticed his paternal ambiance lurking in the doorway.

A tense edge tightened his voice. "It stands to reason you'll want to bring me in on this too."

It wasn't a question, but he was met with startled looks from most of the room.

"I imagine it will add to the headlines," Mark continued slowly, clearly unamused at having to play the game. "To have Phoenix's former hero reemerge."

"Well . . ." Donna said, gaudy red-stained lips pursing. "Isn't that delightful? I expect we have your cooperation, Ms. Gordon?"

My mouth had turned to cotton, much like my numb, throbbing brain. Reading the room, I realized no one thought I had another option. I was playing a convoluted game against experts. I didn't stand a chance.

"I think it's Impulse now," I nearly croaked, my eyes falling to focus on a spot on the floor.

Donna Handler's eyes glittered. One corner of Marshall Kelley's mouth tugged into an almost grin.

Donna stood and made her way from the room, placing one hand on my shoulder and flashing me yet another glimpse of her red-framed, perfect teeth as she left. I had never met the mayor. She'd never given me a reason to not like her, but now, I'd give anything to never be in a room with her again. Power-hungry thoughts and urges projected from her like a movie in a theater, replaying phone calls from angry voters and half-veiled threats from the governor if she couldn't get the city's hysteria under control soon.

Kelley's motives were harder to understand, his mind that steady, smothering roar of white noise, but I imagined it also had more to do with public perception and funding and less to do with catching a parahuman murderer. He stepped before me, his oppressive energy seeming to suck the oxygen from around me. Once again, I got the eeriest feeling that he enjoyed the power of his role more than the individuals under his command. A newfound appreciation for Ryker and his god-awful temper bloomed.

"I'll start working on that press conference," Kelley said in his smooth politician's voice, eyes meeting Ryker's in a show of dominance.

"Not until she's set up elsewhere. I won't have the press hounding my agent at her home and making her a target," Ryker snapped, allowing some of his professionalism to drop now that Donna was absent. "You too, Gilman."

Mark nodded, silent as Ryker's angry gaze drifted to him. Ryker appeared more than irate at having to find a fourth individual and his entire family protective housing. He did not like being out of control.

"Of course," Kelley said coolly, though his eyes reflected a sharp edge. He was not a man who appreciated being challenged any more than Ryker. I resisted the urge to step closer to Ryker's protective shadow and away from Kelley, wishing he'd leave too.

I breathed a sigh of relief when he departed, Livewire and Wildfire trailing behind him.

"A pleasure to meet you," Wildfire said, smiling.

I could have sworn the air warmed by a degree as she walked by.

"Welcome to the team!" Livewire said, louder and more boisterous than his sister. He cast me a glance up and down, his face a combination of curiosity and skepticism, before shoving his hands into his pockets and nonchalantly strolling from the room.

With the bigger personalities gone, Ryker let out a frustrated sigh. I eyed him warily, not sure what to make of the deep, tired lines that creased his eyes or how a sudden fatigue made him seem tired—older.

"Ms. Gordon," he intoned. "I hope this is nothing more than a knee-jerk publicity stunt in response to a social media–induced craze that will pass just as quickly as it started."

"If it isn't?" I nearly whispered.

"Let's address that situation if it comes to it. Gilman," Ryker said, back straightening in resolve as an angry edge returned to his voice, the Ryker I knew back in charge. "Get her to her apartment. Get in. Get what she needs. Get out. If the media is there, you have two lines: 'The press will be updated on the situation shortly. No other comments.' Do you understand me?"

Mark nodded and took me by the shoulder, sheltering me with his bulk as I slunk from the room like a skittish cat. My senses returned like a roaring wave as we crossed the threshold, and a suffocating panic seized me.

"I can't do this," I whispered in a frenetic rush as Mark dragged me back toward the claustrophobic elevator I detested so much. "I can't go in front of the media. They're going to find out what's wrong with me!"

"Ryker knows how to handle the media," Mark said.

"*Mark*," I hissed. "I *can't* do this! Don't they know about . . ."

I glanced around as we stepped into the elevator. I waited until the doors closed around us, ensuring no one could hear the rest of our conversation.

"Everyone's going to know about the DUI," I whispered. I resisted the urge to grab my middle as the elevator lurched and began its descent of seventeen floors. "Heroes aren't supposed to have DUIs. How is that going to reflect on the Agency? Ryker will murder me!"

"Ryker knew when he hired you."

"He hired me to sit in a chair and read minds. Not this!"

"Look," Mark said, running a gigantic hand over his weary face. "The newspapers only reported your crash. They only speculated about drinking; they never said anything conclusive."

"It's not hard to figure out," I whined.

The circumstances around the manifestation of my powers were protected by the Winefield-Drummer Act, which was the only reason the worst mistake of my life—or was it Old Hadley's life?—had been withheld from the media. It wouldn't take a tenacious reporter much snooping to dig up the rest of the story.

"Hadley," Mark said, sighing. "I won't make you do anything you don't want to do, but be careful with the politicians."

"*Me* be careful? What about *you*? They only wanted me," I asked.

"I'm making sure those idiots don't kill you," Mark grumbled.

"You don't have to do this. I'll have Wildfire and Livewire. It sounds like I won't be much more than an ineffective celebrity. Maybe it'll just be one quick thing, and then it's done? Everyone will lose interest?"

A sudden hope blossomed. People had short attention spans. Maybe it wasn't as bad as I thought?

Mark's derisive scoff doused my optimism like a bucket of ice water.

"Livewire and Wildfire?" he said skeptically. "Major Crimes exists solely to kiss their celebrity asses. It's just the Superhero Superlative Program hiding within the Agency's legitimacy."

"What's that supposed to mean? Major Crimes has a great solve rate."

"It's an umbrella program designed to give city mascots an excuse to show up in front of media cameras at crimes that'll get the most attention: burning buildings, robberies, car chases. It may exist within the Agency, but it's a political machine. Did you see Livewire and Wildfire's agent in charge? No. He's either perfecting his golf game or cashing his checks from a beach in Mexico."

"You were a superhero," I argued. "You're one of the best agents we have."

"I'm not saying Wildfire and Livewire aren't trained agents. Either of them could send me on a long vacation to a burn ward, but they're also egotistical celebrities, and fame makes you stupid," Mark said, his voice low.

"I thought Wildfire has a reputation for being by the book?"

"It's Livewire I worry about," Mark begrudgingly admitted. "He has a reputation for being a hothead. Twenty years of having his backside kissed has made him fast and loose with the rules."

"Maybe we need that," I muttered. "By the book hasn't caught us a killer."

"You notice it hasn't been them chasing after Madison and Alice's killer? The mayor didn't want them anywhere near this," Mark admitted. "She didn't want any more attention on 'San Diego's Superhero Killer.' It's bad for her image, but her hand's been forced, and she's more worried about saving face than results."

"So, this won't do anything but get in the Agency's way?" I asked bitterly.

"It's going to make you a target. They don't understand your vulnerability," Mark continued, mood darkening. "If a tense situation occurs, I don't trust them to protect you."

"Wait . . . they just want me to do a press conference," I said. "What could happen at a press conference?"

Mark shot me a look, and I swallowed hard. I didn't want to know. Not today. I already had too much to process.

The elevator jolted to a halt, and the doors slid open with a *ding!* I rushed for open space, needing air for more than one reason. I practically ran toward the ill-fated parking lot, wanting distance between me and the building.

"What are you going to tell Diane?" I asked as Mark effortlessly kept pace with me.

What are you going to tell Lilly? is what I really wanted to ask. She was going to lose her mind.

"She'll understand. You really think my family would let you get turned into a shish kebab if I could stop it?"

"You think I'm going to be a shish kebab?" I asked.

Mark rolled his eyes. "They aren't ignorant about how politicians work."

"I picked up on Donna's thoughts," I said, keeping my voice low. "She's taking a lot of heat for this. Do you think she threatened Kelley's job? Can she even do that?"

"Wouldn't be surprising. Kelley responded by putting Ryker on a leash, otherwise he'd never go along with this."

"None of them care about Alice or Madison," I said, the anger in my voice surprising me.

"Nobody ever said politicians were smart or altruistic."

I hesitated as we pushed past the double doors into the parking lot, a gentle, familiar pull and the promise of solace drawing my eyes up. The black pavement spread before me, bleak and ominous. The Agency performed routine bomb sweeps, but few brave souls dared park here anymore, and the parking lot was desolate. Well, almost.

One brave soul was a policewoman leaning against a SDPD cruiser, dark hair pulled into its customary ponytail. She uncrossed her arms as we approached, her lips quirking while I stared at her as if she'd grown a second head.

"Jocelyn?" Mark asked.

"Jo?" I blurted.

"Anna called," she said, poorly suppressing a grin at my expense. She shrugged one shoulder. "She thought you could use some help."

I was the very essence of grace and dignity as I stood there dumbstruck and gaping like an idiot. Mark had to nudge me forward. It was an excuse, of course. Jo knew my life was turning upside down the moment the police started putting up a boundary around my address. Anna might have called, but Jo had texted her first.

"You know—you realize—what if someone's there?" I said, stumbling over my tongue.

"Sounds like you might need some backup, then," she said calmly.

Mark grinned. "I do like her. I've told you that, right?" he whispered, though it was still too loud for my comfort. I flushed with the warmth of embarrassment, both for the situation and the fact that Anna and Mark conspired like schoolgirls.

"My God," I muttered low enough that Jo couldn't hear. "You and Anna."

"Are you really surprised she's here?" Mark asked pointedly.

No. Jo was a constant in my life, though I don't think she intended to be the day she showed up with a burned CD and a gas station peanut butter cookie. She just wanted to check on the girl whose life she had saved. One visit turned into a dozen, and somehow, supervised visits at one of Mercy's uncomfortable visitor's tables, Nurse Joyce hovering in the background, transformed into friendship.

Jo pushed off her cruiser and approached us. I searched her face, wondering if she realized yet that her feelings for me were developing beyond friendship.

"I've checked the vehicle," Jo said. "I'm clean."

"You take Hadley," Mark said. "I'll follow behind."

He winked at me, and I stared at him in paralyzed confusion, trying to figure out what the hell was happening to my life. How could *anyone* think about the wasteland that was my love life right now? I glanced at Jo, hoping she hadn't noticed the exchange, but if she read anything into it, it didn't reflect in her face or her mind.

I approached the police cruiser and opened the back door. Jo raised an eyebrow.

"Nobody wants to ride in the back," she said, biting back laughter. She opened the passenger door, leaning against it as if driving an accident-prone telekinetic into a possible media frenzy was something she did every Sunday.

My face warm, I stepped past her and climbed inside. The cruiser always felt eerily familiar, and I wondered if she'd had the same one for the past five years.

I was twenty-one years old when my car had gone into the Pacific. According to all sources, I had been driving after my twenty-first birthday party and was plastered. To this day, Anna disagrees, but from what I understand, Old Hadley was a party girl even before she could legally drink. My reaction time was too slow when I came to a sharp curve at 2:00 a.m., and my car went over a cliff. They found it in pieces under the waves the next morning, thanks to my overly cautious mother and the tracking app she'd forced me to install on my phone. It was a quirk that Anna now adopted. According to the report, SDPD found my car—rather, what pieces of it they could identify as a car—in a crater on the bottom. I wasn't there. Everyone assumed I'd died and been swept away by the current, so my family spent several painstaking hours convinced I was gone forever. Jo found me unconscious in some bushes about half a mile from where my car was found. People had driven past me all morning without realizing I was there, and no one could understand how I made it that far with so much brain damage.

Jo slid into the driver's seat as I buckled myself in. I sat rigidly, biting my lip as guilt ate at me. She had attributed the fact I "forgot" about movie night for weeks to my memory. After all, it wasn't the first time. Then, San Diego's resident serial killer reared his ugly head. Eventually, she'd realize I was avoiding her, and a double helping of guilt washed over me at the thought that she wouldn't know what she did wrong—because she hadn't done anything wrong.

Jo remained oblivious to my internal struggle as she started the cruiser. The sleeve of her uniform slipped, revealing a handmade hemp bracelet with a beach pebble tied to its center. Had she always worn that? As I glanced at it, something in the back of my mind sparked.

"So, what's going on? Anna didn't really say," Jo asked.

Oh, right. *That.* I tore my eyes off the bracelet.

"Anna doesn't know yet," I said, sighing, as she pulled out of the cursed parking lot.

Anna was going to freak the hell out.

Jo kept her eyes on the road, but one eyebrow rose.

"They're making me a superhero," I blurted in a rush.

She glanced at me, eyebrows pinched as if to say *seriously?* She turned her eyes back to the road, corners of her mouth drooping into a disapproving frown.

"I think I'm working with Wildfire and Livewire to catch the parahuman killer—I guess he's the bomber too. We don't know. I have to say something to the media."

209

It all came out in a rush. When I finished, I bit my lip and kept my eyes on my hands. I felt something boiling under my skin, and it took me a minute to realize it was Jo. She was pissed.

"Miss? Can you hear me? Are you okay?"

"And you're okay with this?" she asked. She sounded calm, but I knew she wasn't.

"Miss? Hello?"

"I didn't get the feeling I have options."

She cursed under her breath—or maybe she thought it?—and changed lanes a bit too quickly, causing me to jolt in my seat.

"Wake up!"

I flinched away from her suddenly vulnerable mind. I didn't need to see that day again. Jo glanced at me, a flash of guilt flickering in her eyes. Her energy retracted, and I straightened, breathing a little easier. Most people would consider Jo introverted—and she was . . . on the outside. Mercy Rehab had taught her how to contain what she felt on the inside, but she was prone to slip on things concerning . . . well, me.

"Those idiots wouldn't know the way to their own ass if you gave them a map," Jo growled. I blinked at her in stunned surprise. "All they care about is public perception, and they know people will start clawing at their doors soon."

"You think this is a bad idea too?" I asked quietly.

She glanced over at me and sighed. "I think it's a good way to piss this guy off and make you an even bigger target."

"Mark said something like that," I said. I paused for a moment. "He says he's doing this with me."

"Good guy," Jo said. She spoke only a few words, but in her mind, she was having a conniption. Her mind reminded me of the ocean, and at the moment, a storm was raging, waves pummeling the shore.

"When's this press thing?"

"Some time tomorrow. I have to go to a safe house first."

"At least they're doing one thing right."

I nodded and tried to focus on my hands for the rest of the drive, though in my mind, I heard the faraway cry of seagulls and the distant sound of waves. I didn't know how to tell Jo it would be fine, that Mark wouldn't let anything happen to me, so I didn't.

We passed the Hillcrest sign and pulled up to the apartment complex a minute later. I breathed a sigh of relief when an army of reporters failed to ambush us. I was suddenly grateful that I hadn't remembered to replace my ID with my current address. I felt a pang of guilt as I wondered if that meant the media was swarming my parents' house. The guilt was briefly swept away by the image of the media having to survive my crazy mother and her theatrics. God help them. I had to bite back a laugh.

An upset Weasel erupted from my room, barking angrily, when I walked through the door. He sensed something was going on. Took him long enough.

My heart sank: Weasel.

"Can I take him?" I asked Mark, my eyes stinging at the realization of how this would affect him.

"Anna already asked me to watch him. She said Elliott put some things together," Jo said before Mark could answer. "Molly loves Weasel. It's not a problem."

I hesitated, looking at my fuzzy brown companion— he was essentially nothing more than a loud, blurred tail and flailing paws as he danced around my feet—but the mental picture of a bomb going off as I walked Weasel to a patch of grass, blowing him off the face of the planet in an instant, made me reconsider. The thought of having to tell Anna what happened to him made me feel sick.

"You really don't mind?" I asked, tears springing to my eyes.

"Molly will literally pee herself," Jo said, grinning. "You're doing her a favor."

Jo bent down and called to Weasel. He bounded to her, tongue lolling, and she scooped him up, searching for his belongings while I focused on remembering what items I needed to bring.

My phone chimed, and I pulled it out of my pocket. It was a text message from Anna.

What happened? she asked.

Honestly? I had no freaking idea.

CHAPTER 10

"Look," I said quietly, peering out from behind the stage curtain, phone pressed against one ear. "Tell Mom and Dad everything is fine. I'm surrounded by Mark, Livewire, and Wildfire, plus every available police officer and federal agent in the city. Nothing's going to happen."

According to Collin, our mother was "losing her damn mind." Despite an invitation to attend my first ever press conference—as a superhero, no less—my family remained holed up in their house in Escondido. I was fine with it—sort of. I'd probably dodged a bullet.

My mother's anxiety would have found its way through the crowd to me no matter what. My telepathy didn't work over major distances, but even now, I could've sworn I felt my mother's energy seeping through the phone.

"Are they cool?" Collin asked, excitement evident.

He wanted to be here, but Kathy had nearly broken down when he suggested coming by himself. That stung. Collin called or texted fairly often, but I hadn't seen my little brother since the last time my mother and I engaged in a battle of wills.

"Livewire and Wildfire? I guess. I haven't really talked to them. Major Crimes and Counterterrorism don't interact much. I guess I'll get to know them better after this."

"Your life is so cool!" Collin said enviously. "Do you like your superhero alias? Impulse sounds so awesome! Everyone has been blowing me up about it. I'm getting serious benefits from being a superhero's brother! I have, like, three dates next weekend—don't tell Mom!"

I laughed, my nerves momentarily replaced by my growing ego. "Don't let it go to your head!"

Mark approached, and a brief glimpse of his mind told me it was time to go.

"I think we're about to start," I told my brother. "Tell Mom to chill out."

"That'll never happen," Collin muttered.

"Hey, before I go, do me a favor?" I added.

"Yeah?"

"If my hair looks weird or if I have something on my face, don't tell me later, okay?"

Collin laughed. "Hey . . . um . . . If you get a chance, I know Mom is a pain and your job really needs you, but can we try the family vacation thing again some time? It would be cool to see you."

"I miss you too."

The call ended with a definitive beep, and I turned to Mark.

"How are you doing?" he asked.

I shrugged. "Last night was okay. I watched TV. Brittany brought me dinner. Anna asked her to. You?"

"Logan and Jonah had a hard time getting to sleep in the new place, but honestly, I think everyone's a little relieved. Lilly's been having horrible nightmares of this guy showing up at our house. I think last night was the best she's slept in weeks."

I knew a thing or two about nightmares.

"I'm glad the kids are okay."

"How are you doing about *this*?" Mark said, gesturing over my shoulder to the stage.

"I am absolutely not thinking about it. I'm going to look for the teleprompter, avoid looking at the crowd, say what I have to say, and survive this. I never thought I would look forward to hunting a serial killer so much. I would so much rather be patrolling than on that stage."

"You and me both," Mark muttered.

"I don't think I properly thanked you for doing this with me."

The crowd erupted in applause only a few feet from us, and I jumped a little. It took me a moment to realize Donna Handler had taken the stage, Livewire and Wildfire flanking her. Livewire and Wildfire looked every bit the superheroes they were, with glowing smiles and friendly waves. They even made the Agency-issued tactical gear look inspiring. My own gear was swallowing me whole; I looked like a kid in a Halloween costume. I took some comfort in the fact that Mark also looked ridiculous. Despite wearing the largest tactical vest available, Mark's pecs still threatened to bust through with one wrong flex.

Swallowing a lump forming in my throat, I examined the superheroes on stage. They were silent yet resolute, projecting nothing but confidence and poise.

A sobering clarity seized me as my plan to keep my head down and escape as soon as humanly possible all but vaporized. More was expected of me—much more. As soon as I stepped on that stage, I would become a symbol. There were expectations. I leaned forward, desperately watching Livewire and Wildfire's body language. If only I could see how they—

Mark clapped a hand on my shoulder, and I nearly leaped out of my skin. He gave me an encouraging smile. "There's nothing to thank. You're going to do great. Besides," he added. "I think this is getting you points with someone."

He nodded toward the crowd. Confused, I tore my eyes away from Livewire and Wildfire. A dark head of hair in a police officer's uniform patrolled near the press. Oh, lord: Jo. Worse: the press. Mark shouldn't have said anything.

"That doesn't help," I muttered, my stomach roiling.

Acid crawling up my throat, I prayed I wouldn't throw up the moment I opened my mouth to speak. Actually, if I threw up now, would that get me out of it?

We were supposed to wait behind the scenes until the twin heroes of the town introduced us. San Diego naming a third superhero and a fourth coming out of retirement was a monumental occasion. That much was clear by the number of local *and* national news station logos in the crowd. Of course, the serial killer and bombs probably factored into their interest. Every big city flaunted a christened superhero or two handpicked from its scant population of parahumans. Having a small herd of heroes was incredibly unusual. Whether it was tradition or because keeping superheroes rare—well, *rarer*—kept them novel, it just didn't happen. With their flashy abilities and celebrity looks, Wildfire and Livewire had been San Diego's mascots for nearly two decades.

I had been told in the highest-stakes pep talk I had ever received that this needed to work, Ryker glowering at Kelley and Mayor Handler as they lectured me on how much the city needed me to give them hope.

It hadn't hit me then. Now, reality slapped me across the face: it was my turn. *I* was going to be a superhero. My dissociation from and denial of the situation had been working fantastically until that point. A splitting headache blossomed in my skull to complement my queasy stomach. Fantastic. I shifted uncomfortably, turning away from the stage's bright lights. A cold sweat broke out across my brow. The bulletproof vest they'd slapped on me chafed under my perspiring arms.

I couldn't be a symbol for the city, I realized with chilling clarity. No matter how hard I tried, I'd never be good enough. This could only end in disappointment.

Maybe they were right. Maybe the city needed an Impulse.

It just couldn't be me.

"I don't think I can—" I started, nausea clawing at my insides.

I never got the chance to finish.

Maybe if I hadn't been focused on everyone's expectations, I would have felt what was coming.

As it was, I was experiencing an existential crisis when Livewire and Wildfire grew rigid. Their eyes locked, expressions severe.

217

Donna Handler obliviously continued her speech.

I blinked, and before I could register what was happening, the city's heroes were responding.

In one swift moment of perfect coordination, Livewire seized the mayor and Wildfire turned in my direction.

I'll never forget the look on her face.

They were quicker than I was, but it was still too late.

The horror hidden below the stage erupted into life between us. A deafening boom roared, and the ground rocked, nearly knocking me off my feet.

The stage caved inward as the bomb went off, a disorienting flare of light blinding me. Wooden beams shattered into splinters, and claws of flame reached for the sky.

One heartbeat. Wildfire fell in slow motion, the inferno engulfing her and pulling her under. Thick black acrid smoke belched toward the sky. She vanished, the chasm consuming her. Livewire and Donna Handler leaped in the opposite direction of the blast into the stunned crowd, Livewire acting as a human shield and pulling Handler away.

Two heartbeats. Screams rang in the air. The panicked crowd pushed in all directions, desperately attempting to escape the smoke and raining debris.

Mark was already responding while my brain struggled to process the scene. He ran to the crater in the stage, thunderous footfalls making the unstable stage sway, and leaped into it.

He fell for what seemed like years instead of a second, vanishing as the smoke parted around his gigantic form and then enveloped him.

The world moved in slow motion until he disappeared into blackness. Losing him to the unknown snapped me back. My ears rang—maybe from the blast, maybe from shock—but I forced myself forward.

"Mark!" I called.

"*Dad!*" someone shrieked from the crowd.

Lilly. Of course, Mark's family had come.

"Mark!" I shouted on my hands and knees into the abyss. I didn't remember closing the gap to the crater. "Wildfire! Are you okay?"

A support beam the size of a small tree sailed up from the chasm, landing feet from me with a *crack*. I recoiled, scooting away from it.

The compromised stage sank, weakened by what I presumed was the loss of what lay at my feet, buckling beneath the weight and threatening to collapse.

"I think she's buried!" Mark shouted.

I breathed a sigh of relief at the sound of his voice and pivoted toward the fleeing crowd, searching for the Gilmans, hoping to give some sort of reassuring sign. I couldn't see past the smoke.

Another deafening boom. Light from within the chasm before me blinded me. The stage beneath me lurched with such force that I felt it in my bones. My arms gave way, and I crumpled onto the stage as it bucked beneath me. A sharp pain pierced my skull, causing me to cry out. Silence, save for a high-pitched ringing in my ears, followed. I threw my arms over my head, curling into myself and choking as something acrid clawed its way down my throat.

Another belch of smoke erupted from the crater toward what had been a clear blue sky moments before. I fixated on a beam of light that winked in and out of the haze as the world twisted and tumbled, vertigo turning everything upside down.

I'm not dead. I'm not dead. I clung to the thought like a lifeline. Heat kissed my face as fire burned in the dark chasm before me, reaching for me with angry orange flames.

I registered the fact I'd survived the second bomb as the stage buckled across from me, but unlike the first bomb, it didn't cave. Curled up on the ground, I didn't dare move. My heart hammered in my chest as I waited to be swallowed up like Wildfire.

"*Daddy!*" a shrill voice shrieked what felt like years later, snapping me back to reality.

"*Mark!*" I screamed.

The pungent smell of smoke and fire filled my nose. Smoke clawed at my throat, making me cough.

Clutching an ear that throbbed with every movement, I scrambled back toward the edge of the gaping hole, trying to see past the smoke.

A hand erupted from the murky void, and I gasped. Rushing forward, I grabbed hold of Mark's wrist and pulled as he hefted himself up. He rolled onto his back, coughing and wheezing.

"Are you okay?" I asked, voice raspy. It sounded like I was speaking through water. Talking made my ear hurt. "Did you find her?"

"I can't see past the smoke," Mark said in between coughs. His outsides were invincible, but his insides weren't. He was as helpless as the rest of us when it came to smoke inhalation.

A blur shot past, a whistle in its wake.

"Shit! Brittany!" I called after my colleague.

The smoke began moving of its own accord, lifting up and out, and I turned to find Ben behind me. He moved his arms in slow, careful movements, commanding the mass of contaminated air up and away.

Blonde hair materialized beside me.

"Everything's on fire. There's debris everywhere," Brittany gasped, her sides heaving as she coughed beside me. "The stage isn't stable. I didn't see her."

As if on cue, water began precipitating from directly above, raining down on the crater in the middle of the stage. Christine stood at the edge of the stage, arms outstretched, struggling to get a good view.

I had a bad idea.

"Christine!" I called out. "Brace yourself!"

It wasn't sure if she heard me or if I could even do what I was planning, but I reached out, telepathically feeling Christine in the distance, and gave a swift telekinetic yank. Despite being ripped from the ground like a fish on a line, she more or less gracefully catapulted into the air and on stage. She managed to stick the landing and gave me an appreciative tilt of her head, never breaking her focus, never letting the rain fail.

Brittany braced herself to jump back down the hole as water tempered the flames and Ben parted the haze, Mark right behind her.

I grabbed her arm. "Ryker's coming."

Ryker marched toward us from behind the stage but stopped a safe distance away, face ashen and eyes severe.

"Get off the stage! Clear the area until the bomb squad says it's safe!" he barked.

"Sir," Mark protested. "Janelle—"

Ryker shot him a look. "I will not put any more of my agents at risk! Get off the stage and let the bomb squad do its job!"

With heavy, defeated movements, we cleared the area, leaving Wildfire to the abyss.

They found Wildfire half an hour later. They couldn't tell if it was the fall or the bombs that had killed her, but it didn't matter. We couldn't have saved her.

At least, that's what I told myself as they carried her away toward the medical examiner's van—just like they had Madison and Alice—wondering how I managed to sense the bomb meant for me but somehow missed the two bombs under the stage meant for all of us. When the stretcher emerged, Mark bowed his head and sighed heavily. I clenched my eyes against a strangled cry as Ryker told Livewire they found his sister, and I hated myself even more.

Adrenaline wearing off, I trembled as the stretcher disappeared within the van. The back doors closed with definitive thuds, and I winced, clutching the side of my head where my blown eardrum pulsed with pain. Hiccups punctuated sniffs as I fought back tears, making everything hurt all the worse.

Ryker was nearby, as were the press and their cameras, but I finally couldn't fight it anymore. Hot tears slid down my cheeks, and I choked back sobs.

Mark placed a gentle hand on my shoulder, encouraging me to step away. "Let's see if we can find Ian. He'll make you feel better."

I nodded and leaned into him, letting him shield me as we slipped away from the scene.

"Where did the kids go?" I asked.

"They're back at the safe house."

"I'm sorry they saw that," I said, sniffing.

Mark nodded but was otherwise silent, his expression haunted.

"They're winning," I said tearfully, my voice breaking.

"Yeah," Mark said. "They are."

We convened at the Agency, and I silenced my phone as "Mom," "Dad," "Collin," "Anna," "Elliott," and "Jo" lit up the screen repeatedly. The news had broadcasted the event live. They had seen every horrible minute.

I sent a text: *I'm okay* and turned my phone off. I knew they were panicking, and I was being selfish, but I needed time to collect my thoughts before I talked to them.

Everyone sat in stunned silence. I stayed in the back of the briefing room, as far from the others as I could. Of course, my colleagues found me anyway as we waited for Ryker to step into the room and give us the horrible details.

"It's not your fault," Christine told me.

That's what she said, but Ben, Navin, Brittany, and other eyes looked on from their seats. I could see everyone's thoughts drifting around the room: *How did Hadley miss the bombs?* Some of them wondered if Ryker blamed me. A few wondered why I hadn't been fired yet. I wondered the same things myself. I kept my eyes focused on my feet and nodded when she spoke to me, but I didn't have the words to respond.

"Hey," Christine whispered to Brittany, who sat down beside me. "Where are Tom and Glenn?"

"They had eyes on Weiss," she whispered back.

My heart skipped a beat. Brittany caught my expression, and she shook her head.

"He was in class."

I sank lower in my chair and exhaled with a heavy sigh. I had messed up tremendously. Glenn was the one parahuman who might have seen the danger hidden under the stage. He hadn't been there, doing his job, because I had given him a wild goose to chase.

I had done nothing but provide false leads and distractions. It was all my fault.

"Gordon!" Ryker suddenly snapped from the doorway.

I leaped from my seat. He jerked his head and vanished, and I all but ran out of the room after him.

Every set of eyes bored holes in my back as I left.

Ryker's office reflected his personality—rather, his lack of personality—perfectly. There was absolutely nothing personal on his desk: no pictures of family—not that I knew if he even had one—and no evidence of any hobbies or anything that resembled décor. Not even a neglected houseplant existed to suggest there was some human element to the man. Ryker lived and breathed the Agency, and the only items adorning the walls were various plaques and awards pertaining to military service and accomplishments at work.

I sat in the uncomfortable black leather chair across from his desk. Sweat broke out across my forehead, heat rising in my cheeks. Ryker's attention remained fixed on me, and I squirmed under the scrutiny, fully aware I hadn't washed all the soot off my face and still reeked of burning stage.

"The call that triggered the bombs came from a cell phone. We have no reason to believe the caller was at the scene yet. As far as we know, there was no physical presence there for you to feel, so whatever guilt trip you've sent yourself on needs to end now."

I blinked, startled.

"S-sir?" I stammered.

"None of this is on you, Gordon. I need you out of your own head because whether or not we like it, we need it. I need you to be up to the challenge."

"I'm not sure I understand," I said slowly. "Wildfire . . ."

His eyes held mine, and I suddenly felt very small.

"I'm going to be frank, Gordon, because agents are dying and I am out of patience with the situation. You are not a good agent. You should not be in the field, but I need you out there. Can I rely on you to hunt this man, or men, or should I focus my efforts elsewhere?"

"I . . ." My throat tightened. Wildfire flashed in my mind, her body flailing as the stage beneath her opened up, greedily swallowing her.

She was the city's hero, and she was gone forever.

"I don't know."

There was a long tense pause while Ryker held my eyes. No expression gave away his innermost thoughts.

"Then perhaps you're better suited to a safe house until this matter is resolved," he finally said. Not even his tone gave away how he felt. He was all business, nothing but cold, calculating logic as he battled disaster head-on.

The words stung, but he was right.

"I think that might be best," I said so softly that it almost came out a whisper. For a moment, I could have sworn I saw a flicker of disappointment in Ryker's eyes.

"Very well," he said, the cold facade never once dropping.

I stood with my head bowed.

Ryker held out his hand. "We're not done."

I sat back down so quickly I thought the chair might tumble over. My cheeks burned, and tears stung my eyes.

"What happened on the stage?"

I was momentarily confused.

"Do you remember the stage?" he asked me, what remained of his patience thinning. Still, he held his temper in check, something I was eternally grateful for.

"Yes," I said slowly.

"All of it?"

"I think so," I said, brows furrowing as I probed my mind for the customary dark holes that usually filled the space of an absent memory.

"Okay. Walk me through it. The bomb went off. You didn't sense it?"

"Livewire and Wildfire did."

"But you sensed nothing until it went off?"

My cheeks burned even hotter, and I bit my lip.

"I'm not accusing you of anything, Gordon. Someone slipped past security and planted two bombs. I'm trying to discern who and how."

"I didn't sense anything, but I . . . I was distracted."

Ryker raised an eyebrow at me.

"Stage fright," I clarified shamefully.

"How did Damani and Janelle know the bombs were about to go off?"

"I don't know. I think they could feel the fire and electricity as it went off. I didn't see or hear anything. I wouldn't have known it was going to happen if they hadn't responded."

"What happened after Janelle fell?"

"Mark went after her."

"Why? Did she call for help?"

"He just . . . he went after her."

"Was there any sign she was still alive?"

I shook my head. "I don't know. If she was . . . wouldn't she have stopped the fire?"

Ryker was quiet. The entire situation was wrong. Wildfire was pyrokinetic. Fire shouldn't have been able to touch her.

"What about before the bomb went off? Anything unusual?"

For a moment, I caught a blip—a brief breakdown in Ryker's mental armor. Whether from stress, exhaustion, or some other human attribute I didn't think he possessed, I saw my boss's thoughts for the first time in five years.

He saw it in my eyes as I cast a panicked, guilty glance in his direction. He folded his hands across his desk and held my gaze, sighing.

"Ms. Gordon, Ms. Aluko's autopsy is still ongoing, but I just received a disturbing phone call. Janelle was not well. Her brain was bleeding before she got on that stage. That's what made her too slow to react. The second bomb was packed with glass, much like the one that went off in our parking lot. I'm confident the medical examiner will list it as her official cause of death, but I need to know why one of the city's most prominent parahumans was rendered ineffective just before those bombs went off. Did you sense *anything*?"

I sat frozen in place.

"A brain bleed?" I choked. As if a damn bomb wasn't enough.

"A slow one," Ryker said. "She may not have noticed."

"Would it . . ." I licked my suddenly dry lips, a sense of foreboding blooming deep within. "Would it have hurt?"

"I imagine it could have," Ryker said, eyes fixed on me.

Sometimes, I had a hard time discerning my feelings and emotions from someone else's. Thanks to my condition, I got headaches frequently. I didn't always pick up on the fact that the pain wasn't mine.

"I got a headache both times she got near me. I thought it was me."

"Did you get a sense of what could have caused them? Did she feel distressed? We have no record of her getting into an altercation that could have resulted in a head injury."

"I—I'm sorry. I thought it was me. I didn't think about it," I stammered. "What could cause a brain bleed if she hadn't been in a fight?"

Ryker stared at me for a long moment, his mental shields fortified and his mind a tumultuous din of angry buzzing once more. Then he sat up straighter, adjusting his jacket in a manner that made it obvious we were done.

"We'll bring you in if we have more questions. Gilman is waiting for you. Go home and rest."

"Sir?"

"As you said, Ms. Gordon, you need time to think about whether or not you want to be a part of this. You have until the end of the week to get back to me. No need to attend the briefing."

"What about Marshall Kelley and Donna Handler?" I asked.

"Donna Handler is in the hospital with minor injuries," Ryker said. "As are you."

I blinked.

"Do not answer your phone unless it's someone you recognize. Do not speak to anyone about what we discussed. As far as the press and politicians are concerned, you sustained injuries from the blast. Impulse won't be expected to make an appearance."

I sat there, unsure of what to say.

"*Go*, Ms. Gordon," Ryker said slowly, his anger rising to the surface.

I nearly ran out of the room. I stepped out just in time for Livewire to turn down the hall, approaching Ryker's office. He looked up, and I froze.

His red-rimmed eyes held mine. A burst of anger erupted in my direction.

Above me, a lightbulb shattered. I took off at a sprint, heading for the exit in the opposite direction. My sides heaved as I fought back tears. I bolted past Mark, who followed me past the elevator and to the stairwell in a panic.

"Hadley?" he called. "Hadley! What in the hell happened?"

I raced down more than a dozen flights of stairs and slammed into the door leading outside. I kept running. I nearly collapsed at the edge of the eucalyptus grove lining the parking lot, tears streaming down my face.

"I'm useless!" I sobbed. "Ryker knows it. Livewire knows it. I know it. You know it. She'd be alive if I wasn't fucked up, and now the entire world knows it too!"

"Hadley," Mark said sympathetically, his face falling. "There was nothing anyone could do. He wasn't sitting nearby in the bushes this time. He wasn't even there. You couldn't have sensed him."

"When did the bombs get there? Didn't security perform a sweep this morning? He had to be under us at some point."

"Or they missed them."

"Because Ryker sent Tom and Glenn to another location because I'm an absolute shitshow and shouldn't be trusted with anything! Glenn would have seen under the stage!" I shouted, then hiccupped against a sob. "Three people are dead because I'm broken. I have been within feet of him—touching him, no less—on multiple occasions, and I couldn't stop him. I put the wrong person in our interrogation room, and we wasted time and resources that cost Wildfire her life! People keep looking at me like I have answers, but the only thing I've contributed to is the body count!"

"Hadley . . ." Mark said gently. "We've put too much on you, and I'm sorry, but we've all failed. This isn't your problem alone. There are half a dozen other parahumans in Counterterrorism with all the resources of the Agency at their disposal, plus the support of SDPD and other federal agencies, and we still haven't found him."

"That's kind of you to say, but we all know if I remembered his face from the first time, we wouldn't be here."

"You're assuming you saw his face."

I shook my head and clenched my jaw, whimpering.

"Just take me back to the safe house," I said, weeping. "I'm done."

CHAPTER 11

I startled awake at 2:00 a.m. to dreams of drowning and fire. Insomnia and anxiety lingered in place of sleep. Sunlight bled through the blinds what felt like minutes later. I stared at the ceiling of the scarcely adorned, plain white room. It contained one twin bed with a mattress that had probably been there in the '90s, a single nightstand with a dusty lamp that had probably been there longer, and a desk in the corner with the hardest chair I had ever sat on.

The safe house itself was on the edge of town, though safe "house" was a misnomer. The Agency had stuffed me away in an apartment building nestled amongst a street of rundown or abandoned houses, the quiet area forgotten and slowly succumbing to decay. Well, mostly quiet. At night, after I finally found a comfortable position to sleep in, a train's shrill whistle pierced the quiet.

The area didn't see many visitors, but I guessed that was the point.

Rolling over with a groan, I grabbed my phone. It mocked me as 8:04 a.m. lit up the screen, and I unlocked it. I had watched the video of Weasel and Molly fighting over a rope toy at least a dozen times since Jo sent it last night. Still, I laughed as the German shepherd, Molly, who had at least fifty pounds on my dog, humored Weasel into thinking he could win a game of tug-of-war. Ultimately, she snatched the rope toy from him and bounded off, leaving Weasel to stand in the middle of the living room with a dumbfounded look on his face.

"Weasel? What are you doing?" Jo asked in another video, rounding a corner just in time for Weasel to skitter from behind the kitchen island, a stuffed duck in his mouth.

"Is that Molly's *favorite* toy?" Jo asked as the little dog wiggled at her feet, Jo laughing off screen.

The camera zoomed in on Molly, passed out on a dog bed, oblivious to the theft.

My phone chimed as a text message came in.

Are you okay? Anna's message read.

I groaned and set the phone down, staring up at the ceiling once more. I didn't know how to answer.

I missed Anna and Weasel. I missed our neighbors. Waking up to foreign minds and their thoughts each morning was disconcerting. I'd get used to their ebb and flow in time, but at the moment, it had only been four days since I'd moved into the safe house, and the neighbor's stress dream about work was hammering at my skull, a headache blooming at either temple. At least I remembered where I was. I'd shattered a lightbulb yesterday when I'd woken up and couldn't remember where I was or how I'd gotten there. A slightly hysterical phone call to Anna kept me from calling the police to report a kidnapping.

My phone chimed again.

Did you think about what I said? Anna asked.

Anna wanted me to see a therapist, as any former psychology major would. She wasn't wrong. Dead bodies greeted me every time I closed my eyes, and I blamed myself for each one. Survivor's guilt and post-traumatic stress disorder, Anna had repeatedly said. She was probably right, but I didn't have it in me to air all my shortcomings to a stranger right now. The Agency shrink was out of the question if I wanted to keep my job.

But then, I wasn't sure I deserved it, so what was the point?

Sighing, I forced myself out of bed and went to the window, peeking between the blinds. The same unmarked police car was parked in the same place it had been every other time I'd looked. The officer inside saw me and waved. I waved back. It was a little game I played with my guardians to keep the boredom down. The dated TV in the living room only got about twenty channels, and most of them were sports. I'd probably die of boredom before a serial killer, mad bomber, or mob of reporters ever got to me.

A knock at the door startled me.

Maybe not.

I glanced back at the officer. If I was in trouble, he didn't seem concerned as he intently texted on his phone. The knocking continued, and I waved furiously at the officer. Finally, he looked up. I gestured toward the door and gave a questioning thumbs-up. Texting Officer smiled and held up his thumb.

Livewire was the last person I expected when I opened the door wearing nothing but pajama shorts and a tank top.

I stared at him, stunned. Something cracked behind me, and we both jumped. Livewire started to say something but closed his mouth, averting his eyes in an awkward attempt to pretend he didn't notice me telekinetically pull the fan loose from the ceiling. My cheeks burned as I wondered how much that would cost the Agency.

"I . . . um . . . that happens," I mumbled, fixing my eyes on my bare feet.

"Sorry it's so early," Livewire said quietly.

It took me a moment to remember I was supposed to be a functional human being and respond.

"It's . . . um . . . it's fine. I wasn't asleep. Do you want to . . . ?" I gestured over my shoulder to the dingy apartment.

"Uh . . . yeah," he said uncertainly.

He cast a glance in my direction as he crossed the threshold. I closed the door behind him.

I sensed the agitation slithering under his skin. It made me itch; I had to resist scratching. "Is everything—"

"Why'd you give up?" he asked.

His voice was louder now that we didn't have to worry about disturbing the neighbors. A manila folder in his hand caught my attention for the first time as he nervously crumpled it. He stopped himself and flattened it back out again.

"I—um—I-I didn't," I stammered. I realized that wasn't the case as soon as the words left my mouth. "I just, um, I'm not a field agent. I should go back to the observation room. I-I belong there."

"Why?"

His dark-brown eyes stared down at me, and I suddenly realized how tall he was. Not only was he tall, he was incredibly muscular. I wasn't exactly a large person, so most people were taller, but Livewire had to be well over six feet. An equally intense personality matched his overwhelming size, I discovered as Livewire focused intently on me.

I shifted uncomfortably, feeling like the victim of an ambush. It had only been three short days since he lost his sister, and I felt everything he was attempting to bury. His inside looked nothing like his outside.

"Why?" I blurted out in an inarticulate, bewildered response.

Livewire didn't respond, holding my gaze with a stare that had probably disarmed a few criminals.

At the moment, I certainly felt like one.

"I got your sister killed," I blurted out in a rush.

Still no response.

"I'm sorry," I whispered.

Livewire rubbed his neck, and his face softened, his eyes like a wounded dog. "I thought that at first. I'm sorry to just say it, but it's probably pointless to lie around a telepath. So, yeah, I blamed you for a minute there."

"But you don't now? Why not? I do."

"I needed someone to be angry at. Ryker took the brunt of it that day. Got me in a bit of trouble."

My eyebrows shot up. He had taken on Ryker and lived?

"You can't sense someone who wasn't there," Livewire said. "Someone remotely detonated the bomb with a cell phone. Ryker was adamant about that."

"Have you considered I was his target? I sensed him during the first bombing, so maybe he thought I knew who he was? Everyone else became a casualty of him going after the one person he thinks can identify him? Maybe your sister died because he missed."

"I considered it, yeah. I tried to stay mad at you, so at least I'd have someone to blame, but the only person I blame is the person who killed her. I don't think you were his target at all. At least, not the only one."

"Why? It makes as much sense as anything else."

Livewire pulled a photocopy of a handwritten note from the manila folder and handed it to me.

"Donna Handler got that in her mailbox the morning of the press conference."

I stared down at the piece of paper.

THE FALSE GODS WILL FALL WHILE THE WORLD WATCHES.

"*Seriously?*" I asked, blood suddenly boiling. "She got a threat in the mail, and she still went through with it?"

"Politicians aren't credited for their intelligence," Livewire said. He meant it as a joke to lighten the atmosphere, but his attempt at a smile never reached his eyes.

"Wait . . ." I eyed the note closer. "Have they done handwriting analysis yet?"

"I don't know, but read the first few words: false *gods*," Livewire said. "This might be my ego talking, but if you had to pick the two most powerful superheroes in

San Diego and call them gods, who do you think the city would pick?"

"Or he's just referring to how he's already picking us all off one by one. He has an aptitude for calling us names."

I handed the note back to Livewire. The familiarity of the handwriting made my stomach twist. Did that mean the bomber who killed Wildfire and Madison and Alice's murderer were the same? Or was it a coincidence that the note appeared the day Wildfire died? Or was my brain confused and remembering things incorrectly?

Probably the latter.

"Why don't we go ask him what he meant?" Livewire said abruptly.

When I looked up, startled, his eyes met mine and held them.

"*What?*" I blurted. "Who?"

"You've got a suspect, so let's follow him. Let's see what you get."

"You want to stalk a potential superhero serial killer?" I intoned.

"You're damn right I do."

"And you want to do it with me?"

"Look," Livewire said. "They're bringing in a telepath from Atlanta. He may be good, but I don't trust him. I trust you."

"Why on earth would you trust me?" I asked, voice raising an octave.

"Because . . . when that bomb went off, you ran toward it. When the second one went off, you didn't leave. You stayed by my sister. You stayed by Mark and Brittany. That's the type of person I want working with me to bring my sister's killer down."

I hesitated and bit my lip. It was a well-rehearsed, flattering speech, but I didn't for a second believe it was the complete story. I *knew* it wasn't. Livewire's mind was an open, emotional book.

Livewire waited, his eyes a mix of haunted and hopeful. I pursed my lips and looked away.

"Look," he said. "I know I didn't do enough. Some sick bastard killed Madison and Alice, and all I did was get in front of a camera and give a speech. I shook hands with their parents, looked them in the eye and told them how sorry I was, but I didn't do a damn thing. It was wrong of me to assume it wasn't my problem, that Counterterrorism would handle it, and now *my sister* is dead. I'm trying to do the right thing too late, I know, but *please*, I need your help."

"It's not my help you want," I muttered, avoiding his gaze.

Livewire sighed and pinched the bridge of his nose. "Look. I'm not doing this right. I haven't slept in three nights, and I came in here ready to fight. I don't want to fight you. I'm sorry. Can I start over?"

"Just . . . tell me the truth," I said, sighing. "You aren't here because you trust me. *Nobody* trusts me."

I tapped my temple for emphasis.

"That's the memory thing?" Livewire asked.

"Seems like you've been looking into me," I said, face flushed. "What do you think?"

"I've made you mad," Livewire said, shoulders drooping.

"All I want is the truth."

"All right, the truth," he said. "I meant what I said. But you've also been *right there* in the middle of every shitshow since this started, so a part of me is hoping that, if I just keep you next to me, the next time shit goes down, I'll be there."

"It's selfish," he added when I didn't respond.

"The next time shit goes down?" I said, seething. "Someone tried to kill me *twice*. That shit? My friends *died*."

"So did my sister!" Livewire snapped.

I stepped back at the sound of a pop, an arc of electricity snapping off his fingers.

Jaw clenched, he looked away. "I'm sorry," he said, struggling to regain his composure. "Did you know that 40 percent of serial killers are never caught?" His voice was quavering. "They keep saying it on the news—over and *over* again. Some of them kill for decades before they're stopped. If this guy goes underground, we'll never catch him. I know you don't want that for Madison or Alice either."

I sighed heavily and leaned against the wall. "I have done nothing but fail—"

"I'm not asking you to catch him," Livewire said quickly. "The Agency is giving up. They pulled Tom, Glenn, and Navin off Preston Weiss. We don't have any more suspects. If something doesn't happen soon, they're just going to do what they need to do to cover their ass and save face. The media and public will grow numb and then bored, and it'll all be forgotten."

"Preston Weiss has concrete alibis for both bombings *and* Madison's murder," I said. "He was under Agency surveillance both times the bombs went off. I screwed up when I identified him. *I told you*. I am not someone you want to rely on."

"I dug up some stuff about the day Madison died," Livewire said, raising the envelope. "It's nothing damning, but I don't think we can exclude him yet. At least, not for Madison. Just, please, don't give up yet. Give me an hour or two. Absolutely nothing dangerous, I swear. If you still feel the same in a few hours, you can go back to the observation room. I'll leave you alone. *I swear.*"

It was a bad idea . . . but he was desperate. I thought about the weeks I'd spent patrolling campus, *praying* I'd pick something up so we could avenge Madison and Alice—prayers that were met with disappointment and heartbreak day after day after day. How could I do that to him when the most recent victim was his only sister?

"Okay," I said slowly. "I'll meet you at the Agency."

"I'll wait for you to get dressed," Livewire said. "We can leave from here."

I raised an eyebrow.

"I—uh, I failed my psych eval yesterday. Technically, I'm on leave indefinitely. Ryker's still pissed at me, so who knows how long he'll make me sweat," Damani said.

So, I wasn't his top option . . . just his only option. I squirmed uncomfortably and opened my mouth to protest.

"I know evidence gleaned from telepathy isn't admissible if gathered outside the legal mumbo jumbo, and this is far from that. It won't ruin anything. I'm not worried about red tape; I just need to know if I'm chasing the wrong guy."

His choice of words wasn't lost on me.

"This doesn't seem safe. Or smart," I said. "Ryker will kill us."

"It's worth it." Livewire's eyes held mine, begging.

I groaned inwardly. Ryker *was* going to kill me.

"I'll get dressed," I said. "But if I don't like this, I'm leaving."

"Okay, *yes*." His breath released in a rush. "Thank you."

Fifteen minutes later, I waved to Texting Officer as I exited the building, but he never looked up.

My hero, I thought grumpily as I slid into the passenger's seat with an unhinged superhero I barely knew.

Livewire started the car. Texting Officer was still focused on his phone as we pulled away from the curb. My stomach dropped as the unmarked patrol car disappeared in the rearview mirror.

"Where are we going?" I asked.

"The university," Livewire said. "That's where you found him the first time, right?"

"Preston?"

"Yeah."

"We can check him out if you really want to, but like I said, he has alibis, and they found nothing incriminating on him. As far as anyone knows, he has no suspicious contacts or even evidence of a criminal record—hell, not even a speeding ticket. He's a Boy Scout."

"They never definitively confirmed the alibis, and I heard they connected him with the APA," Livewire said.

"It's all circumstantial. He says he just signed up to be on their mailing list."

"Bullshit. His mommy and daddy are loaded. Maybe they paid people off?"

I shot Livewire a skeptical look.

"Bombs started going off the day you found him. Seems like a weird coincidence, doesn't it?"

"Yeah, but we brought him in. I got nothing off him."

"From what I heard, you couldn't decide one way or another. That's not nothing. That's cause to double-check."

Livewire dropped the manila envelope in my lap. "I had some contacts look into him."

"Contacts?"

"Despite what people say," Livewire said. "I've been doing this for a while. I'm not just a pretty face for the cameras."

I withdrew the sheets of paper and raised an eyebrow at the numbers on the first page. The Agency didn't have enough for a warrant to search Preston's phone or computer, yet I was pretty sure I was looking at bank statements and Preston's phone calls dating back several weeks.

"These contacts?" I asked. "They got all this legally?"

"I just need to know if I should invest my energy elsewhere," Livewire said. "I'm not looking to arrest the guy . . . yet."

"What's highlighted?"

"Someone used his credit card right around the time of Madison and Alice's murders."

I set the paper down and shot him a look. "That's his alibi. His girlfriend said they were getting coffee together."

Livewire cast me a disapproving glance. "Why are you so determined to be wrong? Look at the image."

I flipped through the pages until I came across the security footage of a girl picking up a cup of coffee. The image was from May fifth.

"Okay, that's not Preston Weiss," I admitted. "Who am I looking at?"

"That's his now ex-girlfriend, Carlie," Livewire said. "Chatty thing."

I arched an eyebrow at him. "I'm very glad Carlie has an alibi."

"It means *he* doesn't," Livewire said. "The credit cards weren't him, he wasn't with Carlie, and no one can remember if he went to class or not."

I flipped through the rest of the documents. "So, he was standing outside or waiting in the car. She said he was there."

"She says she can't remember now."

"I don't want this to come off the wrong way, but you realize you're a bit intimidating, right? And you're a celebrity. She'd probably admit to the murders herself if she thought it would make you happy."

"She seemed genuine," Livewire said. "And the barista didn't remember him coming in either."

"The barista probably sees about a thousand frat boys a day. What's the rest of it?" I held up a missing dog flyer, eyebrows raised.

"There are a bunch of those in the area where Preston lives. Didn't the profile indicate he probably had experience? What if it wasn't with people? There's a ton of research showing that some serial killers start on animals before progressing to people."

"Over the course of years," I said, channeling my inner Anna. "And isn't that usually when they're kids? Preston Weiss is in his twenties."

"The ex says he's turned into a total ass too," Livewire continued, ignoring my criticism. "She said he's had a complete personality change this summer. They got into a fight, and she thought he was going to hit her. That's why she dumped him."

"Good for her."

My phone rang. I glanced down as the screen flashed "Anna," and silenced it. I'd call her back.

We sat in silence for a few minutes, Livewire clenching the steering wheel. I grappled with the prospect of continued exposure to Preston Weiss's warped brain.

I flipped through a few more pages. "You certainly did your homework."

"He grew up in New York until his parents moved their practice to Los Angeles when he was fifteen. He moved to San Diego for college on a scholarship, though he is every bit the stereotypical spoiled, rich jock you'd expect him to be. His parents are loaded."

"Which means they will have plenty of money to sue you for harassment if anyone finds out about this," I said, nodding toward the papers. "Damn, you even looked into the parents' records. They're saints."

"Dad does free reconstructive surgery on burn victims."

I winced. I'd had way too many nightmares featuring flames lately.

"His dad has a registered firearm. You'd think that would be easier?" he continued.

"Anna says he's a control freak. He enjoys the thrill way too much. He wouldn't do that."

Livewire's jaw clenched, and a wave of guilt crashed over me. They hadn't even had Wildfire's funeral yet. He rigidly turned another corner toward the university.

"Are you okay?" I asked.

"Don't you already know?" He eyed me curiously.

"That's against the rules," I said.

"What rules?"

"I don't get to make assumptions about how you perceive yourself or your world around you based on anything I've picked up."

"So, like, what? I could think about jumping off a bridge tonight, and you wouldn't say a thing?"

"Depends on if you really intended to."

"So you can break the rules. Besides, I'm pretty sure you broke them back at the apartment."

"I didn't have to be a telepath to know you weren't being completely honest," I said, face growing warm.

He shot me a skeptical look.

"I didn't break the rules exactly," I admitted petulantly. "The rules are more like . . . say there is something personal about you. Maybe you're a different person behind closed doors—something you keep private from the rest of the world. You can't hide it from me, and that's not fair, so I don't bring it up."

Like Jo.

"So you already know I'm a wreck about my sister, but you're not coming out and saying it because I might perceive it as a violation of privacy? How do you know it's a violation? Because I'm not openly weeping? Maybe this is just how I grieve."

"It's not," I said bluntly. "At least, not completely. Look, not very many people are comfortable around telepaths. If I keep my mouth shut long enough, they relax and stop worrying about it."

"So, it's a trust thing too? It's not just about respect?"

"I just want to have normal interactions with people," I said, exasperated.

Livewire opened his mouth but closed it again, pensive.

"Hmm," he said, eyes focused on the road.

"What?"

"I bet you know what kind of porn literally everyone watches. Would you tell me if Ryker was into anything weird?"

My eyes nearly popped out of my head. I slapped my hands over my mouth as an unexpected, hysterical laugh escaped.

"How did you not see that coming?" Livewire asked.

"I don't see everything," I said, fighting an amused grin. "It's not like reading a book or watching a movie."

"Are you trying not to laugh? Did I make you laugh?"

My cheeks grew warm again, and I struggled not to smile. I was still irritated with him and wasn't ready to be done just yet.

"Ah, so maybe you don't hate me," Livewire said with a grin.

"I don't hate you. It's just . . . it's been hard."

"Sounds like it's always hard. You're over there worrying about offending everyone. Seems like an anxious way to live."

"You get used to it. You didn't answer," I said. "Are you okay?"

Livewire's face hardened. "Janelle responded to a fire about a week ago."

"Did she do the fire tornado thing?"

"Of course. Media eats it up every time," Damani said, grinning. His smile didn't last long. "It wasn't bad when she got there, so she didn't think twice about getting too close. She was never afraid of fire obviously. The fire hit a gas line, and the windows blew out. She stopped the flames, but a piece of the window frame hit her. She said she was fine, but . . . I guess it was a slow bleed. She started getting headaches a few days ago. I didn't notice it was making her slow until . . . I should have noticed."

"I'm really sorry," I said.

Livewire said nothing.

"Why didn't she see Dr. Patterson?"

He shrugged. "She said she felt fine. She never even reported it. I wish . . ." Livewire shook his head.

I didn't push. That explained why Ryker couldn't account for her brain bleed. It was nothing nefarious, just bad luck and poor timing. It didn't make it any less tragic.

The university came into view, and my stomach twisted.

"Preston might not be here," I said.

"He will be." He gave me a quick look.

I had to resist the urge to once again remind him he was going to get charged with harassment if he kept stalking our pseudo-suspect.

"Maintaining a rigid schedule seems like a bad idea. Won't someone notice when he misses class?"

"None of his professors take attendance, and he sits in the back by himself. The classes are large. He has no friends. I doubt anyone would miss him if he disappeared for the rest of the semester."

"You really know a lot about this guy," I said.

Livewire parked the car. "His calculus class started at nine." He ignored my disapproving scowl as we stepped out of the car. "How does this work for you?" he asked.

"I just need to get close."

"There's a window at the back of the room."

"Lead on."

We threw our hoodies up and put on sunglasses. It had only been three days since the infamous press conference where Livewire had saved the mayor on live television, and more than one reporter managed to snap photos that somehow made me look heroic as I ran for the burning pit under the stage. The images were circulating on every news station. The chances of walking across campus without getting mobbed were slim unless we blended in.

Thankfully, college students everywhere had come to an unconscious consensus that baggy hoodies and sunglasses were the unofficial dress code. We were perfectly camouflaged as we slipped our hands in our pockets, ducked our heads, and vanished into obscurity.

I trailed after Livewire as he marched across the school, his long legs making it so I had to walk/jog to keep up.

I heard the whispers long before we got there.

I stopped in my tracks. Black waves lapped against my mind, alien yet familiar. I recoiled, my mind naturally resistant to the poisoned tendrils as they sensually caressed my consciousness, encouraging me to welcome them back like a friend. I shuddered, the hair on the back of my neck standing on end.

"Hadley?" Livewire called from a few yards away.

Slowly, I turned my head, following the siren's call as it lured me in a direction I wasn't sure I wanted to go.

"Hey?" Livewire said, suddenly in front of me. "Is this because of your . . ." He looked around and dropped his voice. "Is this your memory thing? Do I have to, like, help you somehow?"

I held up a hand to silence him.

It was always easier connecting with a mind if I'd encountered it before, and now I felt a magnetic pull from across campus.

"He dropped his guard," I murmured. I wasn't sure if I was speaking to myself or Livewire.

"What?" he asked.

Angry waves lashed at me, crashing against my skull. I didn't want to let them in, but I had to. With a reluctant sigh, I relaxed, and the dark thoughts seeped in like icy water oozing from a crack in a dam. Resolve in place, I marched forward, following the tendrils like bread crumbs, waiting to see where they led.

Startled, Livewire scurried behind.

When we finally approached a tall cement building with large windows, I was panting. I slipped around the back of the building, Livewire on my heels. I craned my head, staring up at the second-story window where the calculus class was visible.

"How did you know where Preston Weiss's class was?" Livewire asked.

I wasn't sure if it was his pounding heart I felt in my chest or my own.

"Is he in there?" I asked, mouth dry.

"I see him. His head is just visible to the left."

I stood on my toes to get a look, but I was too short. It didn't matter. I knew whose mind I followed.

"You felt him? Does that mean it's him?"

"It just means I recognize his mind. I'm not getting concrete thoughts yet."

"What do we do?"

"Take a seat." I slid down the wall and settled on the concrete. At least it wasn't linoleum. My phone buzzed again from my pocket, and I quickly silenced it.

"Seriously?" Livewire asked, staring down at me.

I made myself comfortable on the ground. "Yes, now sit down and try to calm down. Your thoughts are all over the place. It's distracting."

He planted himself beside me, though his buzzing brain never quit.

Closing my eyes, I let the world melt into a sea of images, sounds, smells, sensations, and emotions.

They crashed against me like waves against a shore. They ebbed at my feet, caressing me, and I fought to let go of the minds I wasn't looking for.

It wasn't hard. The black waves beat against my skull like a jackhammer, distinct from the other whispers that floated by. I let them go, focusing instead on the sensations that demanded my attention.

"Are you getting anything?" Livewire asked.

I shot him a look. He threw his hands up, embarrassed, and made a lock and key motion against his lips. He thought about it for a second and made the same motion on his forehead. I tried not to roll my eyes before closing them again.

"He's angry. Not just angry, enraged. Something has absolutely pissed him off, and . . . he's envious. Someone's done something to make him jealous," I said after about five minutes of Livewire squirming beside me.

"What?" Livewire asked.

"Not sure yet," I said. "This guy has always been hard to read. I don't get concrete thoughts."

"It's Preston though, right?" he said, almost breathless.

"It's most likely his mind," I said, attempting to maintain concentration while talking. "The thoughts are familiar, but there are a lot of people around me."

Livewire groaned in frustration.

"You're more than welcome to take over," I grumbled. A hammering sensation started in my temples, and I winced.

"I hope you brought ibuprofen," I said. "This guy is going to leave me with one hell of a head—"

I caught a flash of something and paused, afraid to breathe lest I lose it.

"The news," I said.

"What?"

"He's watching the news on his phone. I think it's the press conference."

Of course it was. Fireballs and screaming were the only material worthy of the media's attention right now.

A wave of anger and grief washed over me, and I turned, startled.

"Sorry," I said. "I didn't mean to dig it up."

Livewire shrugged. "It was never buried."

I closed my eyes . . . and my phone buzzed again. Sighing, I fished it out of my pocket. The display revealed five missed calls from Anna and three from Mark. Jo had even called once.

Anna was trying again.

"Anna?" I answered on speakerphone. "How pissed would the serial killer be to be out of the spotlight? What if he thought his mission was being hijacked by the bombers?"

"What the hell, Hadley? What are you doing out of the safe house?"

My cheeks burned. Anna could track my phone. I had forgotten.

"I'm okay," I said quickly. "I'm with . . . um—Livewire's with me."

There was a pregnant pause. I cast Livewire a quick glance. He raised his eyebrows, a smirk on his face.

What? I mouthed at him.

He broke into a wide smile.

"What are you doing with Livewire? Why are you asking me about the serial killer?" Anna asked slowly. Damn her. She didn't miss much.

"I might be, um, sitting under Preston Weiss's classroom trying to read his mind," I said, blurting out the words as quickly as humanly possible. I bit my lip and waited.

"And the Agency knows this? *Ryker* knows this? Hadley, the law forbids you from using anything you get as evidence," Anna stammered.

"I mean, Ryker probably knows?" I said, remembering Texting Officer. He probably reported straight to Ryker . . . assuming he noticed my absence.

Anna sighed on the other end of the phone. "You should know I sent Mark after you. He's not happy."

"Oh," I said slowly.

"I thought you weren't doing fieldwork anymore."

"Maybe, but . . ."

"Look, if you still want to be in the field, that's fine, but don't go rogue. We all thought you were being abducted and killed. Call Mark or Navin next time. Livewire seems nice, but I don't know if I trust him."

Livewire looked theatrically taken aback. I cast an apologetic glance in his direction.

"And, yes," Anna added. "The suspect might feel like his toes have been stepped on. It might cause him to spiral."

"Spiral how?" I asked, glancing up at the window.

"If he's smart, he'll stop and take time to regroup until he can take the narrative back."

"What if he's not smart?" I asked.

"Then he might do something desperate to be in control again."

"Of course," I said, pinching the bridge of my nose. I really hoped Livewire had painkillers in his car. My head was throbbing. I sighed. "How mad did Mark sound?"

"Worried. Don't go out alone."

We said our goodbyes, and I glanced over at Livewire.

"My name's Damani," he said, laughing. "You can use it. Only the media calls me Livewire."

My cheeks burned.

"We're about to have company," I said.

His face fell. As if on cue, a dark shadow loomed over us. I'd felt Mark coming as I hung up with Anna. He crouched down next to us and shot us both a look.

"Ryker's going to blow a gasket if he finds out you left the safe house and are trailing a suspect without his knowledge. If that's the guy, do you really want to risk blowing the entire case?"

"Do you think he'd buy Damani and me grabbing coffee?" I asked.

Damani snickered beside me, and I knew it wasn't because of the joke.

"Oh, shit." Mark grabbed his vibrating phone out of his pocket. "Speak of the devil. We'll try the coffee story," he said with a disapproving scowl.

He answered the phone with a grimace.

A barking voice erupted from the phone. Mark's expression fell. A face flashed across his mind, and he looked at me, praying I hadn't picked up on it.

I had.

"*No!*" I shouted, tears filling my eyes. I couldn't stop the sobs as they clawed their way up my throat.

Navin was dead.

CHAPTER 12

I hovered outside a pair of doors, staring at the metal tables beyond them through two rectangular windows. Humming fluorescent lights cast a yellowish hue on an otherwise windowless, concrete corridor that made me claustrophobic even on better days. The distinct scents of decay, bleach, and alcohol increased the urge to retch from my already churning stomach. I couldn't remember how I'd come to stand outside the Agency's morgue— whether because of grief or just due to my broken brain—but I could remember my intention.

I took a deep, steadying breath and knocked. I stepped back as Art, an elderly, stooped man with delicate white hair ringing a large bald patch, opened the door.

Dr. Arthur Faber had been the Agency's medical examiner for decades. While non-parahuman bodies typically ended up with the county's medical examiner, parahumans and non-parahumans suspected of dying from parahuman-inflicted injuries were sent to the Agency. Some parahumans were dangerous after death, like Janelle Aluko, who was combustible if not treated carefully. Victims of parahumans, of which there were a regretful few, could be toxic to the touch or hazardous in other ways depending on the parahuman's ability.

Art always performed parahuman autopsies with delicacy and deference, probably out of respect for the fact that his brother was a parahuman who had died in the line of duty over twenty years ago—certainly before I was even born. His parents' recessive parahuman genes hadn't been passed to Art, which—as I stood outside the morgue and waited to see what remained of my friend— I thought was probably a blessing.

"Ms. Gordon, as lovely as it is to see you, I wish we would stop meeting each other under such somber circumstances," Art said with a weak smile. "This isn't the best time."

"I know," I whispered, staring down at my feet.

"He just arrived." Art placed a comforting hand on my shoulder. "I don't have much information yet."

"Can I . . . do you think . . . can I say goodbye? I'll only be a minute."

"It might be best to come back after I'm through," Art said gently. "He might not be as you remember him."

Madison's bloody body flashed through my mind; I could still feel her warm blood seeping through my jeans. I relived them pulling Alice and Wildfire—Janelle—out of their respective abysses. What was one more trauma? It's not like Art could keep me from seeing the carnage in his mind anyway.

"I know. It's okay," I said.

Art hesitated, a flicker of concern in his eyes, and then nodded. He held the door open with a veined, liver-spotted hand. I took a deep breath, crossing the threshold.

The morgue was colder and even less inviting than the hall. Windowless, gray, and devoid of anything resembling comfort, I wondered how sweet Art handled being trapped in such a sullen workspace day in and day out. To the right, the wall encapsulated a nine-body morgue refrigerator, the three rows of three pristine, stainless-steel doors making the hair on the back of my neck stand on end. White identification cards adorned with Art's messy scrawl indicated two were occupied.

I briefly wondered if Janelle still lay in one or if the Agency had released her body to her family.

The opposite wall was taken up by deep stainless-steel sinks and shelving with various objects and binders. To the back of the room was a wooden door. A rectangular glass pane granted a view of Art's messy office with his antique-looking desk decorated with papers and an assortment of coffee mugs.

The center of the room was home to two metal tables, scales hanging from the ceiling above them. My pulse quickened at the sight of a black body bag on the table to the right. Maybe I didn't want to do this . . .

Art approached the black bag, taking the zipper in a gloved hand. He looked at me for confirmation. I clenched my jaw, bracing myself, and nodded.

I choked back an involuntary cry.

Art's warning was warranted: Navin didn't look like himself. His dark skin was ashen; his spiky black hair in disarray and full of sand. Warm brown eyes that usually crinkled in mischief were closed forever. Navin was always a bundle of life and energy, and now he was just . . . empty—a shell.

I stepped closer, then stood frozen, staring at his rigid body. There were so many things I would say if he could hear me. That I was sorry I didn't call him—didn't let him know Damani and I were pursuing a suspect on campus. Would he have come? Would he still be alive? What the hell was he doing by the goddamn pier in the first place? Alice had died under it. Now, Navin. The godforsaken thing was cursed.

I didn't intend to look, but I glimpsed Navin's partially exposed torso. For a moment, confusion replaced grief.

I hesitated for a moment—what I could see was horrific enough, but . . . as if on its own, the black bag shifted just enough for me to see Navin's entire chest, red stains bleeding across the torn fabric of his shirt.

Art cleared his throat, voicing a polite disapproval.

"Sorry," I said, realizing what I'd unconsciously done and releasing my telekinetic grip on the bag.

"No harm done, Ms. Gordon," Art said.

"Those look . . . different," I said, swallowing back the bile worming its way up my throat.

My voice trembled, but Art was kind enough to pretend not to notice.

"A smaller blade, I suspect," Art said, choosing his words carefully.

My mind flashed back to Madison and Alice. Their wounds were large gaping holes, and there were so many. I noted the ruddy patches on Navin. Only three wounds? At least, only three that I could see.

As if three wounds aren't bad enough, I thought bitterly. I was becoming so desensitized to violence that three wounds seemed like a blessing.

"Was it bad?" I asked, thinking about the videos and how Madison and Alice had fought for their lives before they succumbed to their killer's knife.

How long before a video of Navin circulated the internet and the world knew every detail of his final, horrible moments? The inevitable horror would be a stain on my memories for the rest of my life. Bitter anger welled in my chest. I didn't want to remember Navin like that, but then, seeing him laid out, still and pale, on a metal table wasn't any better.

"I'll know more after the autopsy," Art said. "But based on my inspection at the scene, the killer's first blow landed between the second and third rib. The unsub didn't have the strength to push past the rib cage. The knife might've caught on a rib and broken. The next strike severed the femoral artery. I suspect he didn't last long after that. The two subsequent wounds were superficial."

"It was quick?" I asked.

"Over in minutes," Art assured me.

It didn't help.

I stared down at my friend, tears pricking at the corners of my already red-rimmed eyes.

"Was it—?" I asked, voice breaking. I swallowed hard and clenched my fists, reminding myself that Art would not thank me for blowing up the morgue. "Do you think it was the same person who killed Madison and Alice?"

The clock on the wall counted the seconds with a jarring *tick! tick! tick!* as Art considered my question.

"Ms. Kinney's insight is likely of more value here, but the wounds Madison and Alice sustained were deep. Several went through the rib cage. Their killer had substantial upper body strength."

"And this killer did not," I said flatly.

"No, Ms. Gordon. It wouldn't appear so, but he could have been rushed. There were witnesses to the attack from what I understand."

"You don't think it was the same person," I said.

It wasn't a question. Art had been doing this long enough to know. Hell, I didn't think it was the same person. No one had seen Madison and Alice's killer. Navin's killer was reckless, attacking on the beach like that; his death didn't fit their killer's MO.

"I can't make any assumptions. I'll know more after the autopsy, and like I said, Ms. Kinney might be able to shed more light on the killer's state of mind," Art said, but he couldn't hide his thoughts. He'd already drawn his conclusions.

The scale beside my head began swinging subtly, a gentle rocking that, thankfully, Art didn't notice. I sucked in a breath as my ears began ringing, my pulse quickening. I already couldn't find one killer. If Art was right, there's no way I could track two—I simply couldn't—but what else could explain the differences in the wounds?

"Can I stay while you perform the autopsy?" I asked. I needed to know the truth.

"You are welcome to wait outside until I'm through," Art offered sympathetically.

I nodded. "Thanks, Art."

He placed a hand on my shoulder and smiled weakly. "I'm sorry about your friend."

I reached up and grabbed the scale beside my head, halting its swaying. Though I was long out of tears, my eyes stung. I gave Art another weak nod and turned, marching toward the doors. Once outside, I slid down the wall, deflating like a balloon.

Crunch!

Confused, I reached into the front pocket of my hoodie. Hysterical laughter bubbled up like an overflowing pot as I pulled out a bag of Flamin' Hot cheese puffs, probably pilfered from one of the Agency's vending machines before I came downstairs. What the hell had I intended to do with *cheese puffs?*

Trembling, I huddled on the floor, clutching the bag like a lifeline.

Damani slid down next to me two hours later. I lifted my head from my knees and stared at him with puffy, tired eyes.

"Hungry?" he asked, nodding toward the bag of what was now likely powdered puffs.

"No." I removed my fingernails from the bag and slipped it back inside my pocket.

"You missed the briefing," he said.

I tapped my temple. "I have a condition."

We sat in silence for a while. Damani examined the morgue's doors warily, and I attempted to distance myself from his most recent memories of the morgue and Wildfire's lifeless, charred form. I breathed a sigh of relief when I realized she wasn't in there anymore.

"I'm sorry," Damani finally said, tearing his eyes away from the morgue. "I was wrong. I shouldn't have pushed Preston on you. I should've listened to you."

I didn't have it in me to tell him Preston could still be Madison and Alice's killer, that there could be two. Or maybe I was wrong all along, and there was only one serial killer who happened to be rushed this time? Or maybe he hated women, and Alice and Madison's murders were fits of passion whereas Navin's was just business? There was too much to consider. Art was right; we needed Anna.

"I wanted it to be him too," I said, keeping my rambling thoughts to myself. I sniffed, my sinuses still swollen and irritated, and ran a hand over my face. "I want it to stop."

"What are you going to do?" Damani asked.

"I don't know. It's hard to think right now. Why was he alone?" I asked, my voice breaking. "What was he doing on the beach?"

"He wasn't," Damani said, sighing heavily. "He and Brittany were investigating the beach near the pier. Brittany was only half a mile away when Navin was jumped. She just wasn't fast enough."

"Oh, God," I whispered. "Brittany must be so messed up."

"I think Ryker's grilling her now."

Having been on the receiving end of one of Ryker's inquisitions, I felt even more sympathy for Brittany. That being said, if she had been with Navin, maybe Art was right. Maybe the killer was rushed. Maybe there *was* just one, but it couldn't be Preston. He was twenty feet from us when Navin died. I pressed my palms into my eyes until I saw stars. I couldn't handle the uncertainty. Either I was pulled toward an innocent, albeit repugnant, person and was hopelessly wrong, or there were ten thousand other plausible scenarios that were just as confusing and horrible.

"You know," Damani said slowly. "I won't blame you if you march upstairs after this and tell Ryker you're out, that you don't want to be in the field anymore but . . ."

Drained, I resisted the urge to roll my eyes at him. All I wanted was for this to be over, and I wasn't in the mood to hear otherwise. Damani clenched his jaw, Adam's apple bobbing.

"We're all going through this too. You lost your friends; I lost my sister," he said, surprising me by blinking rapidly. He turned his head away. "I don't know if it's easier if we stick together, but it can't be worse than isolating yourself and going through it alone."

I silently stared down at my knees tucked against my chest, pulling at a loose thread in my jeans, and swallowed hard.

"It's so selfish," I whispered. "But, sometimes, I wonder what the point of surviving that damn car crash and waking up with no memories was if everything good was just going to get replaced with *this*."

"That's not selfish. That's a pretty shitty situation."

"You're supposed to scold me for making this about me," I muttered.

"If we're being honest with each other, I'm simultaneously wishing it was me who went through the stage and being grateful I was four feet to the left when that bomb went off. How selfish is that?" Damani said. "You really like putting yourself down. What does it hurt to believe in yourself? You can read minds. You can move things *with your mind*. I would give anything to have your abilities right now."

"They haven't helped."

"Maybe because you don't want them to," he said. "I think you blame them for what happened to you."

"Of course I do," I said bitterly. "I had a life before this that didn't involve my friends getting stabbed to death. Who I was—she was strong, confident, smart. I was studying to be a nurse. I was going to save lives and help people. I don't help anyone now."

I practically spat the last line. My skin crawled with agitation, but I couldn't tell if the emotion was mine or Damani's. If I could have scraped my skin off and replaced it with someone else's—be anyone else but the broken telepath who couldn't save her friends—I would have done it in a heartbeat.

"I don't know a lot," Damani said slowly, exuding patience that seemed uncharacteristic. "I didn't know you before, but I read your file. From what I read—those powers that you hate—they saved your life. The girl you envy so much was drunk. She drove. She fucked up. If your powers hadn't manifested when they did, Christine would have fished you out of your car the next morning. I don't want to be offensive or insensitive, but someone who put themselves and others at risk doesn't sound like someone I'd envy. Maybe she wasn't the better Hadley."

"So, you're judging me on the worst mistake of my life?" I asked bitterly, blood boiling. "Based on one moment, you assume I used to be a bad person? You know, you're being really invasive at a really inappropriate time."

I jerked my head toward the morgue doors.

"No, I—I—" he stammered. "Dammit, I'm sorry. I keep saying the wrong things."

"Maybe you should quit while you're ahead," I snapped.

Damani's face fell. He nodded somberly, avoiding my gaze.

"Has the telepath from Atlanta arrived yet?" I asked, also making it a point not to look at him.

"Yeah. His name is Graham. He was at the briefing."

"He'll do a better job than I have," I said matter-of-factly. "You should ask him to find you a real suspect."

"Are you going to meet him?"

I shook my head.

"He might be able to help with . . ." Damani tapped his temple.

"They tried that. In the beginning. It was a shitshow."

"But not since?"

"No," I said. "And I don't need to try again. Nothing helps. I've accepted that. Are you done being judgmental?"

"Says the girl who wanted to be scolded five seconds ago. You want to know what I think?" he asked, voice rising.

I met his gaze and raised my eyebrows. "Really?"

He realized the joke and rolled his eyes.

"Go ahead," I muttered, attempting to dial back my agitation before our raised voices distracted Art.

"You know how when you first start working out, your muscles are really, really sore?"

I humored him and nodded. I'd felt like I had the flu for two days after I started training with Courtney.

"It eventually goes away, right?" Damani continued. "But then you go on vacation or something for a few weeks, and when you come back, your muscles hurt all over again."

"I have a brain lesion," I said bluntly. "I can't exercise it away."

"But it's the inflammation that causes the memory loss, right? You always have the brain lesion, but you only forget things—really forget things—after you've used your telekinesis. In a sense, after you've worked out."

I pursed my lips, expression remaining skeptical. "No," I sighed, remembering Anna's dissertation and her pages upon pages of notes. If she couldn't figure it out, how could Damani? "I mean, maybe? No one really knows what triggers my memory loss."

"So, it could be inflammation?"

"I don't know," I admitted grudgingly.

"I know you said you tried training in the beginning, when your injury was new, but nothing since? How do you know it won't work?"

"It's been five years."

"Would it hurt anything to just try?" he asked.

"Just my ego," I said. Sighing in exasperation, I held my hand out toward him.

"You knew I was going to do this the whole time?"

"Yes. Give me the stupid penny." I wiggled my fingers for emphasis.

He fished a penny from his pocket and placed it in my palm. "That's just weird."

Slowly, the penny levitated. It rose roughly six inches. Then, it turned on its axis, heads to tails and back again, before slowly descending back into my palm.

"I'll play with the penny if you'll stop pushing," I muttered. "But it won't change anything."

"You know, I heard you were fun. No one mentioned you being so grumpy."

"I'll be fun when my friends aren't dead," I said.

Damani snapped his mouth closed and nodded, averting his eyes.

"Isn't working with the new telepath a better use of your time?"

Damani sighed and rose to his feet. "I'm an ass. Janelle used to tell me I only think about myself. She was right."

My gut clenched at the mention of his sister, and again, I wasn't sure if I felt my guilt or his.

"I'll leave you alone," he said, turning to leave.

"Wait," I said, guilt consuming me. "You're right; I'm not myself. I didn't mean to turn you into an emotional punching bag."

He slid back down, nodding. "I'm still an ass," he grumbled. "Great way to start a partnership, right?"

Is that what this was?

I held the penny between my fingers. Its surface was dull and worn with age, but it glimmered ever so slightly in the fluorescent lights. "I accept your peace offering. Truce."

A whisper caught my attention—just the faintest hint of a thought. With it, the past few minutes of bickering were abruptly forgotten. My attention snapped to the doors.

"What?" Damani asked as I focused past the doors with rapt attention, listening.

I sensed Art's thoughts the entire time—glimpses of surgical instruments cutting into meat I tried not to focus on. Honestly, Damani showing his ass was a welcome distraction. That is, until . . .

"I don't want to be callous, but your sister . . ." I said in a rush, clambering to my feet. "You said she got hit in the head during a fire? That's what caused her brain bleed?"

Damani rose with me. "Yeah," he said, eyeing me. "Why?"

"You're *sure*? She got a head scan? The doctors checked her out?"

"No. Like I said, she didn't need to. She said she felt fine. Why?"

"Art's done with the autopsy," I said. "Navin's brain—it was bleeding."

"What?" Damani asked, eyes flying to the morgue in sudden, laser-focused interest.

"Art's coming," I said, tilting my head toward the metal doors. "Don't tell him I read his mind."

"The rules?" he asked, but the doors swung open before I could respond.

Art shuffled out, bushy eyebrows pinched and mouth downturned in a grimace.

"Still here, Ms. Gordon?" Art asked sympathetically. He nodded at Damani.

I chewed my lip, formulating a question. "Art? Why didn't Navin disappear? Why didn't he use his powers to escape?"

Gears turned in Damani's mind; his eyes widened in response.

"There are numerous broken blood vessels in Mr. Achar's brain," Art said. "An area of the cerebellum was particularly impacted. Mr. Achar . . . might not have been feeling himself at the time of the attack."

"Could that stop him from using his powers?" Damani asked, breathless.

"I'm afraid understanding of the inner workings of parahuman abilities remains rather nebulous," Art said. "I can only speculate."

"What would cause that?" I asked. "Strangulation?"

"I didn't find ligature marks or any other signs of a struggle that weren't consistent with Ms. Whittaker's description of the attack. Navin was stabbed four times—that was all."

As if getting stabbed four times wasn't enough. I bit my tongue. Art hadn't meant anything by it. Madison was stabbed over a dozen times. Alice was stabbed seven times and suffered multiple cuts, but she managed to get in the water before he could hurt her anymore. Not that it changed the outcome.

"Could it have been from a tactical knife? An ASEK?" a voice asked from down the hall, interrupting my train of thought.

Brittany.

None of us had heard her, suggesting she'd entered at a normal speed. I closed the distance between us in a rush and threw my arms around her, my line of questioning completely forgotten. Her shoulders shook as she cried.

"I got to him as fast as I could," she said in my ear, sniffing. "I thought I got him to the hospital in time, but they couldn't do anything."

"You did more than any of us could," I told her.

"I saw him," Brittany whimpered. "I saw the guy running away. I could have stopped him—I almost went after him—but I wanted to save Navin."

"You did the right thing," I reassured her.

"It's unusual for this guy to be seen. He's usually a lot more careful than that," Damani said.

I cringed inwardly, having already considered the implications.

"Why did you ask about a military knife?" Damani said.

"He threw it in the ocean as he ran. It took me a while, but I found it."

I hadn't noticed until then that Brittany's oversized sweatpants—likely given to her after Forensics took her clothes—were still damp. Behind tears, she was shivering slightly.

It didn't surprise me the killer had a new knife—he left the last one behind too, assuming it was the same killer, but a military knife? Weren't the last two from an expensive kitchen set? My stomach sank. Things were convoluted enough. We needed developments to solve mysteries, not add to them.

"Did you get a look at him?" Damani asked.

"He had a hood," Brittany said, sniffing. "But he . . . um . . . he didn't . . ."

"He didn't look like the guy I described," I said, heart sinking.

"He was small," Brittany said. "Short and really scrawny. I think his hair was dark."

Brittany's description was the complete opposite of the description I had given after Madison's memorial and of Preston Weiss. My stomach twisted into knots. Either we had two stabbers or I wasted precious time and resources focusing on the wrong man.

Brittany didn't want to talk about the man on the beach or how wrong I was—in fact, she wasn't even considering it. She wanted to say goodbye to her friend. I gave her one last reassuring hug and stepped out of her way.

"We won't get DNA or prints off the knife," Damani said as the metal doors swung closed, Art and Brittany disappearing behind them. "Not after being in the ocean."

"No," I said, feeling wretched. Why could we never get a break? Just once?

"They pulled files on APA and Sons of Gaia members," I said. "A few are former or current military."

Damani shook his head. "It's San Diego. How hard do you think it is for a civilian to get hold of an ASEK? There are army and navy surplus stores everywhere."

"I doubt this guy went out of his way to find something that unique. It's too much of a risk. Someone from the store might recognize him. He's screwed if there's surveillance. He probably used whatever was available."

"You're assuming this guy is smart. Brittany nearly caught him."

"She didn't," I countered. "And he was skilled enough to . . . to do what he wanted to do in a short timeframe."

"Do you think this is the same guy?" Damani asked.

His line of thought was finally coming to the same series of questions I'd been pondering since I saw Navin. Unlike me, who wanted nothing more than to go hide under my covers, Damani was *itching* to chase someone—anyone.

Perhaps common sense was kicking in a little too late, but I wasn't sure that was a good thing. "I don't know. Every time something happens, I feel like we get further and further away from ending this. It's chaos, and I don't know which direction we're supposed to go in."

"We?" Damani asked.

"You know what I mean," I said.

He rubbed his face, pensive. "What did Art tell you before I got here?"

"What he just told us: four stab wounds," I said, leaving out the rest.

I wouldn't speculate without talking to Anna first, not with the gleam forming in Damani's eyes. Suddenly, it didn't seem like such a grand idea to give him information.

"Just four stab wounds? Isn't that considered underkill for this guy?"

"You think you could commit a bloodier murder and escape Brittany?" I asked incredulously.

"I'm just saying," Damani insisted. "Doesn't this one feel different?"

"*Yes*, it could be another person, if that's what you're insisting," I said, resolve and common sense tearing like tissue paper under the weight of exasperation. "But first off, I can't handle the idea of a copycat. We have one serial killer and probably two bombers. I *cannot* deal with another suspect. I'll let someone a lot smarter than me—Anna or the FBI's Behavioral Analysis Unit, if I'm being specific—decide if this is someone new. Second, you need to stop pursuing suspects on your own, so whatever it is you're planning with Preston Weiss or anyone else, knock it off before you get yourself in trouble. And finally, this feels just as shitty as the other times my friends died, so *no*, it does not *feel* different."

"Sorry," he said, holding his hands up. "I didn't mean it that way."

"I know." I forced myself to take a deep breath. "I'm just upset."

"What about the brain bleeds? My sister and Navin died different ways. Why did they both have brain bleeds?"

"I don't know," I admitted. "I haven't been at work in a few days. Maybe something happened? Maybe they both had incidents, and it's just bad luck?"

"How would you hit someone precisely enough to cause bleeding in just that area? Have you ever heard of disabling a parahuman that way?"

I shook my head. "I don't know."

271

"Look," Damani said. "I understand if you still want out of the investigation. I really do. This is enough to break anyone, but *please*, consider staying. We're never going to get him on forensics; you know it. He—or, hell, *they*—are too smart. The only thing he can't control is his mind. He can't stop you from getting in. Unless he makes a mistake, we're never going to catch him."

"I haven't even gotten us close," I said.

"You *did*. Once. At Madison's memorial."

I looked at him pointedly. "He got away from Alice. And then he lured her to the same goddamn beach where Navin just died and killed her."

"You're missing my point. He came to gloat—to reminisce or relive the experience or whatever. He's got another chance at my sister's funeral. What if this time we were ready? What if this time we set a trap?"

"But do we think he killed—?"

"Hadley," Brittany said, appearing at the door, her face red and streaked with tears. "Do it, *please*, because I think I'm going to die if I have to live through this again."

I froze, caught off guard. Brittany wrapped her arms around her torso as sobs racked her body.

"Please, Hadley. *Please*," she whimpered.

I reached for her, making comforting shushing sounds as my own tears threatened to make a comeback.

"Okay," I whispered, pulling her into a tight embrace. "Okay, we'll get him."

In hindsight, I should have said no.

CHAPTER 13

Janelle Aluko's—Wildfire's—funeral was on a Sunday. I climbed the steps of the church hours before the crowds arrived, eyes drawn upward to a cross fixed atop the bell tower. The church was a quaint Spanish-style structure with white stucco walls, a low-pitched, red-tiled roof, and rounded arches characteristic of much of the architecture in San Diego. A large stained-glass window rested just above a set of wooden doors. The morning sun caught the window's intricate colors, making them sparkle.

I placed my hand on the heavy iron handle of the entrance and took a deep breath. Family and friends were arriving for the visitation before the service. Already, emotions permeated through the door like smoke billowing through a chimney.

I hadn't known Wildfire was religious. It might have been mentioned in an interview once or twice, but it certainly wasn't something I took note of. Damani didn't give off any religious vibes, and it caught me by surprise when it was announced that, per Wildfire's will, her funeral would be held in the small little-known Baywatch Church of San Diego. Of course, the mayor pushed for a large spectacular funeral at a venue that could accommodate thousands, but in the end, Janelle's family was adamant that her service would honor her, not appease the masses, and her wishes were upheld.

Good for her family, I had thought with a smug sense of satisfaction.

Donna Handler had slunk off to nurse her wounded ego, though I suspected some attempt at theatrics was not off the table. Well, more theatrics. While only family and friends were permitted inside the church, designated areas outside had been cordoned off for public mourners, and the ceremony would be broadcasted live for those in attendance outside and those at home. Mayor Handler had insisted that, since Wildfire had been an idol of the city, it was only right for the public to take part. She might not have been wholly wrong, but I resented the woman enough to be petty on behalf of the Alukos and held the opinion that the funeral should have been completely private.

Of course, a private funeral would've defeated the purpose of my presence. I was there to catch Wildfire's killer, I reminded myself. Or was it Alice and Madison's killer? Maybe Navin's too? Even with Anna's expertise and a consult with the FBI, the Agency still wasn't certain, but we were here to stop *someone*, and if it meant turning Wildfire's funeral into a circus, it might be worth it. With the past as precedent, a knife-wielding lunatic or a bomber was bound to show up.

I drew the hood of my hoodie farther over my head as a handful of early arrivals noted my presence. The last thing we needed was my attendance blasted all over social media before we had the chance to draw San Diego's most notorious madmen out. The few individuals already in attendance placed bouquets of flowers and other tributes along lines of metal barricades. A doll gave me pause, red, orange, and yellow tissue paper glued to her hands to represent fire.

A note written in the scrawl of a child was tucked beneath the doll: *We miss you, Wildfire.* Little hearts and flames were scribbled all over the paper in various colors.

Wildfire was deeply loved. Now, all the city of San Diego had was Livewire.

And Impulse, I thought with a pang of regret, if that was even still a thing. I wasn't the superhero the city deserved. I hadn't known Wildfire well, but I admired her.

What a tragedy the city had been robbed of a real hero.

I tried to push all thoughts of politicians and pettiness from my mind. I would do what I had to do for the sake of Wildfire and everyone who loved her.

It helped that I had an ally against Donna Handler. Ryker had silenced any expectations that Impulse would make an appearance, stating that I had "sustained injuries of moderate severity" at the press conference and "would recover in the privacy of an undisclosed location" for the near future.

I hadn't expected him to go to bat for me after Mayor Handler made it known she was itching for an opportunity to reclaim some goodwill after Wildfire's very public death. The media was frenzied over the political optics. The Agency's reputation was crumbling too, and the public was no longer convinced it could handle the city of San Diego's "Superhero Serial Killer," as the news liked to so boldly include in nearly every headline. Hiding me from the public eye likely brought a lot of heat down on Ryker, but for perhaps the first time, I appreciated him.

It was probably just the shock of me showing up interfering with his ability to think clearly. No one, including me, expected me back in the field.

For now. I'd somehow convinced myself to give Damani two weeks—two weeks to patrol funerals and memorials and practice levitating my ridiculous penny— and then I was done. I could say I tried for his sake and go back to my observation room with its wall of glass without guilt.

Resolution in place, at least temporarily, I pulled the heavy door open and stepped inside. Light shone through the many-hued windows of the church, casting patches of color across wooden pews as I walked down the aisle toward the largest of the stained-glass windows at the back of the building. With its bright windows, bold wooden beams crossing the ceiling, ornate arches, and grand white columns flanking the pews, the interior of the church was striking.

A mahogany casket, a bouquet of white calla lilies placed tastefully on top, was a sobering sight.

I breathed a sigh of relief. The casket wasn't open. An enlarged picture of Janelle Aluko occupied a stand to the right, her bright smile, warm and inviting, in stark contrast with the sniffs of her mother, Maya Aluko, who stood with her husband George to one side of the casket.

Maya Aluko noticed my approach, and with another sniff, she brushed tears from her cheeks. I pulled my hood down and reached out a hand as she turned toward me.

"I'm so sorry for your loss, Mr. and Mrs. Aluko," I said as I took Damani and Janelle's mother's hand in mine.

Their eyes were dark and puffy from days of sleeplessness and grief, but Maya Aluko still managed a small smile of gratitude.

"Thank you," she said.

Their father, George, nodded in my direction but didn't speak, jaw clenched tight.

"You're the one they call Impulse?" Maya asked.

"I am. But, please, call me Hadley."

"Hadley?" Damani's voice came from behind me. He approached, handing a cup of water to his mother.

"I wanted to pay my respects before I started patrolling," I said. "I'm sorry I can't stay for the service. The church is gorgeous."

"She loved it," Damani's mother said, lip quivering.

"I am truly sorry for your loss," I said again.

"Mom," Damani said, placing a hand on his mother's shoulder. "I don't mean to interrupt, but the minister wants to see you."

His mother fixed her eyes on me. "You be careful, please."

I nodded. "Don't worry about us."

Livewire's parents left in search of the minister, unaware that he didn't really need to speak with them. Damani asked him to keep them occupied while the bomb squad did another sweep.

We had learned our lesson.

Damani and I stood in silence, both of us avoiding looking at the casket. He wore a deep-black suit with a white shirt and gray tie. The polished look contrasted starkly with the internal rawness I sensed.

"Sorry for the undercover wardrobe," I said, using my sneakers, jeans, and baggy CSDU hoodie as an excuse to break the silence. The objective was to blend in with the college students in the crowd. "I hope I didn't offend your parents."

"They're grateful. That's the last thing they're worried about," he said. "So am I."

I cast a nervous glance around the church.

"The politicians haven't arrived yet," Damani said, giving me a weak grin.

"Sorry," I said hastily. "I shouldn't make it about them."

"If I could lock the doors and keep them out, believe me, I would."

I fiddled with the drawstrings of my hoodie and tried not to stare at the casket beside me. Its presence felt oppressive, like a void where there should have been life and vitality or a heavy black hole in the world, like a gravity sink sucking me in.

"Are you okay?" I asked finally.

What a stupid question.

"I'll be better once we catch the guy," Damani responded after a long pause, his voice breaking when he finally spoke.

I nodded, hoping my skepticism that today of all days would be the day didn't reach my face. "I'm sorry I can't be here." I gestured toward the pews.

"You came back to catch her killer," Damani said. "As far as I'm concerned, outside of family, you might be the most supportive person here."

Heels clicked on the stone floors. My attention turned to a woman in a black dress and a little boy with tight, dark curls in a suit. The little boy held his mother's hand, sniffing as he kept his attention on his shiny black shoes, refusing to look up as they approached.

"Speaking of family," Damani said quietly.

I nodded.

As he passed, Damani placed a hand on my shoulder. "Be careful out there."

Then, it was just me and the casket. Finally, I turned to look at it, its glossy surface reflecting color-tinted light from a perfectly cloudless day. The lilies on top were freshly cut and delicate. I glanced up and felt the weight of the crucifix above me, the thorn-crowned figure staring down at me from above.

When I woke up with no recollection of who I was— twenty-one years of memories gone in an instant—I had turned to religion and prayer for a time, hoping a higher power would return what had been stolen. It hadn't worked, and religion hadn't stuck. It had unnerved me ever since. I wondered what sort of comfort it had brought Janelle.

"It's a nice church," I whispered under my breath to the superhero in her final resting place. I bit my lip, wondering if there were even words to fit the moment. I shifted uncomfortably under the stare of the crucified figure above and a sense of oppressive finality—my last chance before only a headstone remained to talk to.

"I don't really believe in this," I continued, glancing back at Damani to make sure I couldn't be overheard. "But, uh, it seems like you had a connection with . . . something."

I chewed my lip again, neck growing warm from embarrassment. This was stupid.

"Look," I said. "I don't know if a higher power is really out there, but it can't hurt, right? If you . . . if you can, help us catch him? Don't let him hurt anyone else."

I paused, listening to Damani's and the woman's voices carry in the church.

"And if they're with you, can you tell my friends I miss them?"

Nothing but silence. I rolled my eyes and shook my head. "This is what losing it looks like," I muttered to myself.

"Hey," a voice came from nowhere.

I started as Brittany approached from my left. She was dressed in similar blending-in attire, and yet, despite the bonus of appearing hungover on top of the college student garb, she still somehow gave off a distinct Fed vibe. Even when she wasn't at her best, Brittany still carried herself like she was ready to kick in a door and cuff a suspect at any moment. And yet, recent events had revealed a vulnerability I hadn't been previously aware of.

I noted Brittany's red swollen eyes and gave her a sympathetic smile.

"How are you?" I asked.

"It's an insult to couches to call that thing in the safe house one," Brittany said.

"Why don't you take the bed next time?" I offered.

She shook her head. "I didn't mean to crash the safe house again. Sorry about last night."

"You're always welcome."

Admittedly, I would prefer if Brittany didn't show up at 11:00 p.m. halfway through a twelve-pack of cheap beer two nights in a row, but could I blame her?

San Diego had been rocked by its fourth parahuman murder since May. Even without a graphic video of Navin's murder—and I was sure it would be released soon—the media was frenzied. A heated two days of seeing Navin's face on every TV screen, his name in everyone's mouth, and their opinions about the situation flowing freely—both negative and positive—had left me feeling raw.

The only break in the story was when they'd switched to Wildfire's funeral, which hardly helped. Brittany took it all personally, as had I. We'd inadvertently banded together in our guilt.

"Anything?" she asked me.

"No bad guys yet," I said. "It's probably too early. I just came to pay my respects."

"Yeah," Brittany said somberly. "Me too."

I placed a comforting hand on her arm. "Take as long as you need."

She nodded. "I'll meet you outside."

I passed Damani and the woman with her child, making my way to the doors, nodding my acknowledgment as I passed. If they recognized me, they didn't say anything, though I felt the child's brown eyes on my back. I threw my hood back up, pushed the heavy doors open, and stepped into the sun.

Brittany joined me minutes later, jaw clenched and blinking rapidly.

"We need to stop this. Today."

"Damani said something along those lines," I said, eyes scanning the groups of people gathering.

We needed to move soon or risk being recognized. They weren't supposed to start the live stream for another two hours, but that didn't mean we wouldn't end up on social media anyway.

"We'll get him," I added.

Or *them*. I hoped my tone didn't betray that I fully expected today to be nothing short of another bitter disappointment with Brittany ending up passed out drunk on my couch again.

The only good news, and I wasn't sure it *was* good news, was that Anna still thought it was *possible* we were searching for one serial stabber, not two. Her suspicion that Madison and Alice's killer had military experience was never released to the media, so a copycat killer wouldn't know to use a military-style weapon. Navin's killer also struck at the pier where Alice died. Anna mentioned that some serial killers do that—return to the scene of the crime to relive the moment. It was why Ryker ordered Navin and Brittany to patrol the beach in the first place.

It was a theory that might have proved both accurate and deadly.

"Come on," I said. "The sooner we start patrolling, the sooner we find him."

It wasn't necessarily true. I doubted our suspect would be among the first to arrive. He wouldn't want to stand out like that, but I needed to distance myself from the building emotions emanating from the church. I stepped off the stairs and made my way toward the church's parking lot.

"Christine and Ben are patrolling that area," Brittany said.

"Naturally," I muttered under my breath, turning on my heel and walking in the opposite direction. This was what the Agency got for taking a telepath out of an observation room and tried to make her a field agent. "Fantastic start."

When the church bells rang two hours later, signaling the start of the fallen hero's funeral, Brittany and I skirted along the back of the church, peering at the throngs of people who had gathered. Most took out their cell phones and somberly stood in respectful vigil, images of candles held up toward the sky as the minister began addressing the crowd.

"Still no bad guys?" Brittany whispered.

"No," I whispered back.

My earpiece squawked as Tom and Glenn checked in from their area.

I glanced back at the crowd and grimaced at the roughly two-dozen APA members brandishing signs. It was the area I had seen the doll in earlier. The hair on the back of my neck bristled at the thought of the child's gesture being defiled.

"Well," I said, my face scrunched in disgust. "Not the kind we're looking for."

"It looks like more of them are coming," Brittany said forlornly, peeking out from behind me. The number of protestors was still dwarfed by the number of mourners, who eyed them with clear disdain, but at the moment, they were all I could see. I swallowed my resentment and focused on not letting my emotions cause a scene. Wildfire's family didn't deserve it.

"Maybe he'll be with them?" I said, trying to find a silver lining.

"It's a funeral," Brittany said bitterly. "You'd think they'd find some element of human decency and stay home."

"They're the minority, at least," I said somberly, though the truth was that even one protestor would have been one too many. "We should get out there and mingle while everyone's distracted. It's our best shot."

Said the agent who wasn't meant to be in the field.

Together, we slipped from the back of the church and cut through an alley, ducking past a police line. We flashed our Agency badges at skeptical SDPD officers instructed to keep gawkers from slipping around the back and snapping photos through the windows. Our hoodies probably didn't impress them. We circled around and emerged at the back of the crowd before disappearing seamlessly into the throngs of people, looking like the doppelgangers of more than a few college students in the crowd. For the most part, all the hoodie-adorned, muscular men who made me jump each time they spoke or turned their head in my direction were sympathetic onlookers . . .

But one stood out.

I froze as black waves lapped against my mind, familiar yet foreign at the same time. *He* was in the crowd, his mind a whirl of blood and chaos as Madison and Alice's faces swam before mine.

There was so much rage. I choked, wheezing as raw *hate* pressed into me, and I saw the church through another's eyes. Slowly, I turned, facing the building, but the scene didn't match what I telepathically saw.

He was on the other side of the crowd.

"Brittany," I choked, but she was ahead of me. My voice was lost in the crowd.

My head swam, the world churning.

Why was he so angry?

I was drowning in rage. Was it the large crowd of sympathizers? Was it the unshaken support for a beloved hero? Did he just hate us that damn much?

"Hadley?" Brittany asked, suddenly in front of me. "You okay?"

I tried to form words and winced, ears ringing as my head throbbed, and fought against the invasion of another. He was poison, and my fight-or-flight response was going into overdrive as my mind panicked, wanting to protect itself from the predator. I lifted my hand and pointed into the crowd.

Brittany's eyes grew wide.

"*Here?*" she mouthed.

I nodded. I grabbed her arm and pulled, dragging her through the crowd as I tugged on the unseen threads tethering me to the other mind.

"Potential lead on the suspect," Brittany said, hand discreetly placed on her earpiece. "Gordon and Whittaker in pursuit."

"*Where?*" Ryker's voice pierced my ear.

Where indeed?

My heart hammered in my chest as my eyes scanned the crowd, flitting from face to face, looking for anyone suspicious. He had been wearing a hoodie last time. Would he follow the pattern and have his face hidden this time? Would he stand out? Of course not. Half the men in the crowd could have been him.

Brittany leaned in close to me. "Where?" she asked under her breath.

She was ready to run, but I hadn't found him yet. I shook my head to indicate I didn't know and closed my eyes. The crowd was too loud, telepathically and otherwise, and I could feel Brittany's anxiety building. I shouldn't have said anything yet. Now we were both anxious, and my anxiety alone was enough to distract me, let alone hers.

I heard waves crash from somewhere in the crowd, seagulls crying above. *Heavy breathing echoed in his ears as his feet dug into the sand. There was a splash, and he cursed as his victim plunged into the icy water, her head disappearing beneath the waves. A reddish hue amongst the blue ocean showed where she had gone under.*

He was to my left. I opened my eyes and followed the memory, my stomach sinking when I looked into the crowd of APA protestors. Counter-protestors had formed opposite them; heated yelling intensified as both sides fought to have their message heard over the other's.

Of course he would be with them. What better protection against the Agency than to hide amongst its enemies?

I had a bad feeling about this. Unfortunately, I had committed to pretending to be a field agent for two more weeks, something I was quickly coming to regret.

I nodded in the crowd's direction, and Brittany followed me as we backtracked away and circled around behind them. It would be far too obvious if we walked straight toward them.

I hesitated as my eyes flitted from face to face, wondering which one was the monster.

"He might recognize me," I said, leaning toward Brittany so only she could hear me over the raised voices.

She nodded. "I'll go in. We don't need him calling attention to you."

"That's not what I meant," I said, though I wished it was. The last thing I wanted was to step into a hornet's nest on my own. "He might run again, like he did at Madison's memorial."

Brittany bit her lip, eyes scanning the crowd in search of potential escape routes. "Okay. I'll stick to the outside. If he runs, I'll get him."

I swallowed hard and stepped toward the crowd.

"Hadley," Brittany said, grabbing my arm. "If he runs, don't chase him. Don't call attention to yourself. These people are just itching for an excuse to get ugly."

I doubted anyone would hurt me in front of news cameras, but the Agency was already in hot water. Bad press had whipped some people into a frenzy. I didn't want to be the Agency's posterchild for "overreach" or whatever boogeyman narrative the media could come up with if I set off a powder keg of supremacists.

Brittany held back as I approached the crowd, subtly reporting our situation into her earpiece.

"Hadley's got something," she said as quietly as possible. "We're circling a suspect near the protestors."

My hair stood on end. Hearing her say it raised the stakes a little too high for me.

"Why the hell am I pretending to be a hero again?" I muttered under my breath.

Most of the individuals at the back of the APA mob were newcomers and hadn't yet let the energy of their brethren infect them. They were more civil as they waved their signs and screamed in the church's direction.

Barely.

I muttered apologies and slipped through the crowd, hoping no one would look too closely at a college student in a hoodie, but they didn't pay me much attention.

He was with them. I knew it. I felt myself closing in as I stepped closer to the front of the crowd where red-faced men argued with passionate counter-protestors.

No, he wouldn't assert himself that much. I followed the pull to the outskirts of the crowd, craning my head to see past the bodies that blocked my view.

I saw the hoodie from a dozen yards away, and my breath caught. He stood there quietly, hands in his pockets, fixated on the church. He didn't stand out in any way, but I knew. I closed my eyes, reaching out to the one person who mattered amid the chaos.

He hated her. He hated Wildfire . . . but there was something else. He had *wanted* her, dreamed about her.

So why did he feel so cheated?

The false gods will fall . . . His hand clenched around the pen as he stabbed it into the paper, his knife against the backward minds who worshipped the scourge of humanity. Couldn't they see! It didn't matter. He would make them see. One by one, he'd break down the indoctrination that had been built up in their minds until they could see the truth!

With a shudder, I pulled away from the toxicity of his mind. His guard was down, and hate erupted from him like lava from a volcano. It scalded me every time I reached out. I swallowed hard, anxiety building as I took a step in his direction.

His head turned ever so slightly. A chill raced up my spine as blue eyes flashed beneath a navy hood, the only part of his face visible behind a black balaclava. Why was he wearing—?

He saw me. I knew he did.

He tucked his hands into his pockets, ducked his hooded head, and began moving away. I pushed through the crowd, trailing after him.

Then, fire blossomed, apparent only to me and the mind the memory emanated from. I froze as, in the middle of a parched desert landscape, a bomb went off. An old car was engulfed in roaring, hungry flames to the whooping of intoxicated voices, black smoke billowing up in a thick cloud. Heat seared my face, and I instinctually turned away, though it was only a memory.

"That'll do!" a man shouted. "Those dirty bastards won't know what hit 'em!"

One outraged shout split from the crowd. "The freak got what she deserved!"

I recognized the voice.

I froze in the crowd, eyes wide, paralyzed as the hooded figure in front of me cast a glance over his shoulder and the voice of a bomber rang in the crowd behind me, most assuredly not a memory.

When the hooded figure broke from the crowd, he ran.

What did I do?

Goddamn telepathy! Ryker would skin me alive if we publicly apprehended the wrong man in the middle of a beloved superhero's funeral.

Screw it. If the media wanted to go after me for this, let them.

"Brittany!" I called into my earpiece.

She became a blur at the sound of my voice. I sensed her skirt the crowd, and I pointed toward our runner.

"Him!" I said, eyes locked on the hooded figure as he sprinted toward an alley in the opposite direction of the church.

A blur—Brittany—was on his heels. He didn't stand a chance.

Leaving me, the lone parahuman, amid an agitated mob of parahuman haters.

And a bomber.

"This is stupid," I muttered as I craned my head and looked behind me. I recognized a voice in the crowd, but was he a suspect or just a redneck with an affinity for explosives and beer?

I turned and moved inward, afraid to move too quickly lest someone notice me.

"I think that is," someone said, trying to speak in hushed tones but failing thanks to the noise from the crowd. "I think that's Impulse."

Never mind. Should've guessed they would notice a "college student" yelling into an earpiece. Real smooth.

Eyes turned and focused on me. I needed to get out.

"Freak!" someone yelled.

I didn't see who it was. Voices raised; unintelligible yelling was directed at me.

A hand clutched my shoulder, and I yelped. Then, the world flipped and tumbled. I flailed end over end, a scream erupting from the crowd.

When I finally stopped, a stunned sea of upside-down faces stared up at me. Beneath me, nearly half a dozen people had landed on their backsides from the concussive wave caused by me *blowing myself into the air*. In an attempt to protect myself from a few angry APA members, my poor, broken mind went straight to its signature move for restraining the enemy . . . and used it on me.

So much for not making a scene in front of the cameras. If I survived, Ryker would sacrifice me to the serial killer himself.

I struggled to right myself and gasped as I dropped a foot, my telekinetic hold on myself slipping. This was not what I needed right now! I should've stuck with pursuing the suspect actively evading capture, not seeking out a pyromaniac redneck who liked to make things go boom.

Oh, shit . . . Brittany. Did she even call for backup before she ran? Did I?

I looked out over the crowd, slowly rotating upright, trying to see where Brittany had ended up. She was nowhere in sight.

"She attacked me!" someone shouted. "Did you see that?"

What?

I looked down at a man regaining his footing, his face bright red with rage. A hand gripped my ankle and yanked before I realized there were others beneath me. Shocked, I plummeted downward. I hit the pavement on my back, my breath forcefully exiting my lungs with an *oomph!*

People surrounded me. Panic gripped me as they closed in.

And something else.

For a moment, memory of the fire returned. *An explosive went off, an ill-fated washing machine belching flames and a black plume of smoke reaching for the sky as the door came flying off and it came apart at the seams.*

"That'll do," a man said, his voice eager.

I swear, I had heard the voice before . . .

"*Hey!*" a more than familiar voice shouted, snapping me back to reality just in time to remember I was about to be the victim of a hate crime.

People cried out as a bright light blinded me. I winced and shielded my eyes.

Light sensitivity probably wasn't a good sign for my head.

A loud crack carried through the air, followed by the sharp scent of charring.

The crowd scattered, and Mark's lumbering figure forced his way past fleeing people. He leaned down, and with one swift movement, yanked me to my feet.

My head swam for a moment. When the stars faded, Damani seethed at the edge of the dissolving crowd, sparks flying from his fingertips.

"This is my sister's funeral!" he roared. "Have some goddamned respect!"

Another bolt erupted from his hands and hit the pavement with a *crack!* that sent any lingering gawkers scattering.

I guessed the funeral was over. A pang of guilt shot through me.

"You okay?" Mark asked, checking me over.

I winced as his fingers found a welt forming at the back of my head. What good was a telekinetic fight-or-flight response if it couldn't recognize the dangers of diving headfirst into the pavement from ten feet up?

"Where's Brittany?" I blurted.

Mark pointed in the direction I had last seen the unsub. "In pursuit of the suspect. Backup went to meet her."

Backup included Damani. My voice caught in my throat as he dashed in the same direction as SDPD officers and federal agents. A squawk came from Mark's earpiece, and I realized mine was nowhere to be seen.

I started to follow Damani, but Mark held me back.

"Brittany has enough support. Let's see if we can find Ian."

"I need to talk to Ryker."

"It can wait," Mark said gruffly, using a fatherly voice that suggested there would be no arguing.

"Please, Mark, before I forget."

Mark clenched his jaw, and for a moment, I worried he would fight me. He relented with a disapproving grunt.

I limped in the direction Damani and the other agents had run, a sharp pain shooting up my leg.

"Lean on me," Mark said, throwing my arm behind his neck before I had time to protest. The result was Mark awkwardly hunched over to accommodate my lack of height and me still limping.

"I'm fine," I muttered, embarrassed. "How much trouble am I going to be in?"

"For testing your flight abilities in the middle of a funeral?"

I shot Mark a look.

"Ryker probably isn't too thrilled," he admitted.

I awkwardly leaned against him and hobbled along, closing the distance between us and a group of agents swarming the alley.

"Was it him?" Mark asked. "Was he thinking about Janelle?"

"I didn't see Wildfire's death. Just Madison and Alice," I said, gritting my teeth. Adrenaline was wearing off, the pain growing worse.

"He wasn't thinking about Navin or Janelle?" Mark asked.

"No," I said slowly.

"But you think that's the guy who killed them, right?" he asked, catching my tone.

I stopped, and he looked at me, eyebrows raised. I scanned what remained of the crowd. People were dispersing, officers escorting them away from the church. The funeral was over—ruined. Ruined by me.

The bomber who possibly killed Janelle Aluko— possibly tried to kill Anna and me—was likely long gone.

Damani and his family would never forgive me.

"There was someone in the crowd," I said, looking back at Mark. "After Brittany went after the other guy. He knew how to make a bomb—he *had* made a bomb."

"An accomplice?"

"He was working with others," I said. "But I'm not sure how he fits in. He might have . . . he might be the one who killed Janelle. I'm not sure."

"Can you identify him?" Mark asked breathlessly.

"Maybe by voice?"

"Then you really do need to speak with Ryker." He urged me forward.

My heart sank as we approached the swarm of agents. "No," I said, my breath releasing in a rush.

"He got away, didn't he?" Mark asked, shoulders drooping and mouth downturned in a somber scowl.

I didn't respond. I didn't need to.

Brittany leaned against a wall, arms crossed, staring up at the sky while angry tears slid down splotchy red cheeks.

"Brittany?" I called out to her.

Her brows creased as I hobbled in her direction. "What happened?" she asked, focusing on my injured leg.

"I tried flying," I muttered. "I don't recommend it."

I leaned against the wall next to her and tried not to drown in the waves of misery coming off her.

"He vanished," she said. "Went into the alley and *poof!* was gone. I checked all the buildings. I didn't see anyone with a hoodie."

I nodded toward the agents rummaging through a dumpster across from us.

"You think he ditched the hoodie? We might still get DNA."

"With what time? I couldn't have been more than a second behind him and . . . goddamn it! I was too slow again!"

I didn't know what I could say to make it better. I hadn't even been able to convince myself that it was going to be okay.

"Where's Damani?"

"He stormed off," Brittany said. "Took some agents and wanted to keep looking."

I didn't say it, but I could see how Damani wouldn't take the news very well. Hopefully, I had information that might make the situation the tiniest bit better.

Angry voices drew my attention.

Ryker rounded the corner, his face the color of a tomato. "I want everyone from Forensics here in the next fifteen minutes!" he roared.

He spotted us, eyes boring into us like lasers.

"Gordon! Whittaker!" he barked.

Wearily, I pushed myself off the wall and limped in my rabid boss's direction. Brittany walked beside me, head hung and tears barely restrained.

"Is this guy magical? Is he some goddamned supernatural being? Is there a reason neither of you is competent enough to contain one man? Tell me, what about this is so goddamned hard!" Ryker roared. "You," he snapped at me. "What in God's name were you thinking? I have people filing assault charges against you right this minute!"

I blanched.

His eyes, a combination of ice and fiery rage, held us prisoner.

"Well?" he demanded.

I swallowed hard. If I was wrong, Ryker would find the deepest, darkest pit to lock me in. I'd heard rumors

Alyse N. Steves

of government black sites designed to contain parahumans. If they didn't already exist, Ryker would build one just for me.

It didn't matter. It was about what my friends deserved, not me.

"I can identify the bomber."

296

CHAPTER 14

I awoke with a start after finally falling asleep. Not that it was for long. According to my phone, I'd managed an hour of, well, unrest. My dreams comprised of fire and the same screaming boy who insisted on showing up night after night.

Anna, in her boredom locked away in some undisclosed cabin on a lake she couldn't mention by name, used her spotty internet connection to look into the neighbors. As far as she could tell, no one had lost a child to any sort of tragedy. I had struck up a conversation with Texting Officer, whose name started with a *C*, but the colander that was my mind kept letting his name slip away, so I just called him Texting Officer behind his back . . . Anyway, his kids were fine.

At least, I thought he had kids.

Typically, when my addled brain repeated themes while dreaming, it was after recurrent contact with a mind fixated on them. At home, dreams of a dog buying a bus ticket and disappearing plagued me for weeks until a neighbor mentioned his dog ran off. With no explanation for my child phantom, my mind tried to rationalize the intruding memory, as it was wont to do, by playing it over and *over* again. The recurrent dream was familiar enough that, if I wanted to, a sketch artist and I could probably get a pretty realistic drawing of the boy circulating by the end of the day.

That wasn't going to happen. Ryker wouldn't waste resources on my ghost, even if it meant a good night's rest.

Bam! Bam! Bam!

The much-too-early banging on the door nearly sent me tumbling out of bed. I kicked my comforter off. My face almost had an encounter with the dingy carpet as the comforter wrapped around my ankles. I pried myself free of the trap and scrambled to find pajama bottoms.

I realized what had woken me in the first place.

"Coming!" I shouted. I nearly tripped myself sliding one leg into the pajama bottoms I'd found crumpled in the corner. I winced as I slid my other leg in.

Why did my leg ache?

I rushed out of my bedroom only to nearly have a stroke at the sight of a human body on the couch. I'd been up for all of five minutes and could already tell today would be a *fantastic* memory day.

"Make it stop," Brittany groaned from the couch, covering her face with a pillow and curling into the fetal position. "My head is killing me."

Incessant knocking on the door continued, and for a moment, my brain considered simply overloading and being done with it. Why was Brittany on the . . .

Bam!

Frazzled, I threw the front door open. Damani stepped back as my confused face abruptly materialized before his, and then, bashful, he smiled at me, thrusting a brown paper bag in my direction. The smell of hot sausage and syrup wafted in my direction.

"Damani?" I asked, blinking to clear sleep from my eyes. I ran my fingers through my knotted hair and adjusted the oversized shirt I wore in place of real pajamas.

Anna needed to come home. I needed an adult.

"Sorry," Damani said. "I got anxious when you didn't answer."

"Right," I said, willing myself to reach a level of consciousness capable of human interaction.

Was there coffee in the kitchen? Coffee would help. Maybe Damani had coffee. Wait, why was he here?

"Ready to go?" Damani asked. He nudged the bag closer to me. "Have you eaten? I brought breakfast."

I glanced down at my worn, faded shirt and cringed. "Uh . . . I can be ready in a minute."

I began to step away but paused and turned back, face scrunched in what I hoped conveyed my apologies. "Ready for what?"

Brittany stirred. I glanced at the hungover woman on my couch and back at Damani, trying to remember why I was so popular at . . . what time was it again? I knew I was supposed to do something really, really important today, but I couldn't remember what.

"Jacob Mason?" Damani said tentatively, probing my memory.

"What did he do again?" I asked, heat rising in my cheeks.

"The suspect you identified in the crowd yesterday? The potential bomber?"

I cringed as the debacle that was Janelle's funeral came flooding back. I recalled eating pavement, and my leg twinged.

Ryker had yanked me from the alley and whisked me away to the Agency, where I was thrust upon a Cybercrimes analyst named Neil. Neil smelled like stale cheese puffs and had a mustache that yearned for the generation it truly belonged in, but he was a genius when it came to manipulating video from Janelle's funeral.

Between news footage, social media, and my body camera—at least, what we could get after I crushed it beneath me—Neil managed to zero in on the moment I turned back, drawn to a familiar voice in the crowd.

Separating audio from video had been a tedious task, but after two hours of listening to individually isolated voices, the shout of one man sent a thrill through me. I nearly toppled my chair as I urged my tech-savvy companion to identify who it came from.

Matching audio to video narrowed it down to our new suspect, Mr. Mason, a Sons of Gaia devotee with a long list of assault and battery charges, a history of illegal possession of firearms, and an obvious hatred of the Agency and parahumans with protests, hate mail, and online rants spanning years. He even blogged.

Unlike Preston Weiss, Jacob Mason fit Anna's profile.

"Yes! Come in!" I said hastily, stepping out of the way.

Damani's smile dropped at the sight of Brittany on the couch. She groaned.

"Oh!" Damani said. "I only brought—"

"No food!" Brittany whined, shoving a pillow over her head to block the light. "Dear God, no food ever again."

More memories swamped my addled synapses: Brittany had materialized in the middle of the night, eyes puffy and reeking of wine, which was a somewhat pleasant change from the usual beer smell. She'd been a mess long before she'd gotten to me, and I made her stay again. I stayed up with her until 2:00 a.m. while she sobbed. Vomiting started after that, and I held her hair for another half hour. I offered her the bed around 4:00 a.m., but she insisted on the couch. Insomnia had kept me company after she fell asleep, my mind thoroughly overwhelmed by the deluge of emotion.

No wonder my brain had been repurposed as a sieve.

"Brittany," I said, giving her a nudge. "Get in my bed. I have to work."

She groaned in protest, but she dutifully rolled off the couch and staggered toward my bedroom.

"Morning," she muttered to Damani as she passed.

"You've got a little . . ." he said, pointing to her nose with a grimace.

She pressed her hand to her face and sniffed when it came back with a dot of red. "Stress," she muttered. "It's fine."

As Brittany plucked my comforter from the floor and collapsed into bed, I scrambled for a few potentially matching garments from my closet. I shuffled out and cracked the door behind me, a jeans' leg awkwardly dangling from the wad of textiles in my arms.

"Is she okay?" Damani whispered.

I inclined my head, indicating he should follow me toward the bathroom. I hoped my undergarments were tucked out of sight.

Happy Monday.

"She had a bad night, but she will be," I said, my voice also low. "She took yesterday hard."

"Ryker will let her come back once he cools off."

I raised an eyebrow.

"He suspended her, pending review of . . . well, yesterday."

"Oh! That," I said as if I actually remembered that part. "Dick move on Ryker's part. He can't keep punishing people for doing the best they can."

Damani glanced at the clothes crammed into my arms as a sock threatened to leap overboard.

"I, uh, I should have called." The paper bag crinkled in his hands.

"Let me just, uh . . ."

He nodded as I ducked into the bathroom.

"Are you okay?" I asked through the door.

It hadn't even been twenty-four hours since the beautiful service to say goodbye to his twin sister had devolved into a raging dumpster fire.

"I want to apologize for yesterday," Damani said, overly loud so I could hear him clearly through the door. "I didn't mean to—"

"What'd you do?" I asked.

"I lost my temper," Damani said. "Shouldn't have shot those bolts off so close to people—so close to you. It wasn't safe."

"You're talking to the girl who blows things up when she gets upset. *Believe me*, I get it. It was a bad day."

"Yeah," Damani said. The bag crinkled again. "At least I got *us* unsuspended."

I paused my struggle to get my shirt over my head.

"Forgot about that," I said, forcing the shirt down and shrugging.

"Donna can be useful if you play your politics right."

I scoffed and then winced, remembering that some of the fine gentlemen from yesterday were hell-bent on taking me to court, despite video evidence proving someone from the crowd grabbed me first. Regardless, the media was likely having a grand time making a big deal of it. Impulse sure was turning out to be a shitty superhero. I bet Donna Handler would think twice before putting me in front of a camera now.

I fought back a grin, guilty. Yesterday was far from funny.

"I'm sure Ryker loved that," I said, opening the bathroom door.

Damani stepped aside as I went to the kitchen and dug around for aspirin and a bottled water.

When I nudged the bedroom door open, Brittany was curled up under the covers. I set the water and bottle of aspirin on a nightstand, and she lifted the blanket enough to peek out.

"Thanks," she muttered, sniffing wetly, fingers pinching her nose to stop her nosebleed.

I frowned. I didn't have tissues, so a roll of toilet paper would have to do. I scampered back to the bathroom and returned with my scratchy, papery prize, setting it beside the water.

It was hardly a high-class joint, but I did my best.

"Stay as long as you want," I told her, knowing she had no desire to go home. A thumbs-up popped out and disappeared as fast as it emerged from beneath the blankets. I made my way back to the living room and closed the bedroom door behind me.

"Okay," I said, taking a deep breath. "Let's go get this guy."

Damani and I spent the ride out to Jacob Mason's home in Santee in tense silence. I had to clamp my legs down to keep my foot from tapping the floorboard after Damani's teeth began audibly grinding. It was a wonder Damani had convinced Ryker to let us—the grieving brother and an accident-prone telekinetic who wasn't even a field agent—surveil Jacob Mason instead of the more-than-competent telepath from Atlanta, Graham Allen, and Glenn with his ability to see beyond walls. Guilt quickly quashed the thought; *no one* wanted this done right more than Damani.

The only sound came from the AC blasting, attempting to push back July's intense heat. San Diego wasn't the greenest city, but as we drove farther east, anything green eking out an existence succumbed to drought and became dull yellows and browns punctuated by jagged rocks.

Finally, Damani pulled behind a dented, rusty pickup truck parked down the street from a mobile home that matched the current address in Jacob Mason's file. Shifting nervously as Damani parked, I knew with one glance that the nearly brand-new SUV didn't belong.

"Is this close enough?" he asked.

"Depends on your definition of close," I admitted.

We were too far for me to pick up Jacob Mason's thoughts from the mobile home, but Damani's car stood out on the street of rundown double-wides, some with at least thirty-year-old RVs and other derelict vehicles abandoned in the yards. The street lacked trees, making us feel more exposed than we already were. Getting any closer would be too obvious. The mobile home was tucked as far from the main road as possible, and I was certain the neighbors would notice the strange car eventually. Thank goodness we hadn't taken an Agency SUV.

The landscape was strikingly familiar, I realized as I scanned up and down the street, looking for a better stakeout location. At the end of the neighborhood where the street took a sharp right, a chain-link fence separated civilization from what looked like undeveloped, private land. I couldn't say for sure if it was the area the old car and ill-fated dishwasher burst into flames. To be honest, the desert all looked the same to me, but something about the area gave me goosebumps.

Or was it the familiar tickle at the edge of my brain? Another mind licked at my consciousness like a slavering tongue, and I wrinkled my nose in displeasure. I needed to get closer to pick up thoughts, and I gritted my teeth, deciding I'd rather get this over with.

"Give me a minute," I said, gathering my courage. I threw the door open.

"Wh—hey!" Damani said as I slid from my seat. "If you get something actionable, don't do anything. Ryker wants this done right."

Sure. *Ryker* needed it done right. I nodded. Oppressive heat greeted me as I closed the door, officially leaving the safety of air-conditioning. I suddenly wished my undercover wardrobe didn't consist exclusively of hoodies.

My newfound backbone threatened to flee the second the door thumped closed.

305

"Just read his mind and get back in the car," I muttered.

The thought that it could be over *today* drove me, and my heart rate picked up as I stepped away from the vehicle. We just needed *one* concrete thing, and I could go back to watching Tom and Glenn pick apart suspects in my air-conditioned, dark observation room with potential danger separated by glass.

My friends could stop dying.

I approached the mobile home, head down and hood up. I briskly walked along the edge of the road, as close to the trailer as a dilapidated rail fence would allow. A brand-new, six-foot privacy fence enclosing the backyard stood out against the collapsing rail fence, the sharp scent of green wood and upturned earth still heavy in the air.

I held my phone out in front of me, hoping it looked like we were turned around in the event any nosy neighbors were watching. After all, there was nothing weird about a girl dressed for fall in ninety-degree heat, unable to manage an app to find the main road.

Idiot.

A dirt patch in the lawn caught my eye, a large bare rectangle flanked on all sides by yellow straw that could've been grass if a hose ever found its way to it. A thrill shot through me. Could it be from a car sitting abandoned for years before finally enduring a fiery funeral in the desert? Had I, for once in my life as I remembered it, gotten something right?

I jumped as a dog began barking at the window, spittle flying across glass already smudged with streaks from a moist snout. Maybe the mind I was picking up actually was slobbering . . . I noted the Beware of Dog sign shoved into the corner of the window, the illustration of a boxer matching the dog that snarled at me. The dog never relented as I forced an aura of belonging and tried not to walk faster. I rounded the corner where the road met the old chain-link fence, followed the adjacent street, and looped back around to the car.

I was practically melting by the time I felt the AC again.

"Someone's in the house," I said, pointing a vent at my face. "I feel them."

"What are they thinking?"

I shook my head. "No idea, but don't get closer. There's a dog."

"Of course there is," Damani said, sighing. I leaned forward, biting my lip as I scrutinized the front yard with acute intensity.

"You see something?" he asked.

"Is there a car registered to the property that isn't there? An old one?"

"I'll have someone look into it." He pulled out his phone, inclining his head toward the fence. "Is there a shed in the backyard?"

I could see the roof of a structure just behind the fence.

"I think I saw one when I walked by."

"Could you get a good look at it from the street?"

"Maybe if I was taller." I was very much vertically challenged.

Damani leaned back in the driver's seat, mental gears grinding and eyes focused on the trailer. We sat in silence for the first half hour, watching the mobile home as absolutely nothing of note happened and another agent took his sweet time searching for cars registered to Jacob Mason.

I fidgeted, my eyes continuously sweeping the road. "He's going to notice us."

"I hope he does," Damani said, lips quirking as if amused. "Maybe he'll panic and do something stupid."

I raised a concerned eyebrow.

"*Him*," he insisted. "I told you. I'm doing this by the book."

Rolling his eyes while I stared at him, Damani extended a hand, a quarter glinting in his palm. "Peace offering."

"Peace offering?" I laughed. "What'd you do? What'd *I* do?"

"I've been told I'm not the best at showing appreciation. I don't think I properly thanked you for coming back."

"You just want me to stop squirming," I muttered.

He smiled.

"You've got a thing for change. At this rate, I'm going to be rich." I levitated the quarter out of his hand and into mine. Probably not the smartest thing considering the area we were in, but Damani was right. I appreciated the distraction.

"All I had on me," Damani said. "Besides, you've had enough time with the penny."

I wasn't going to tell him I'd lost the damn penny.

I laughed, and we were quiet again, the quarter hovering up and down, twisting and turning in a midair dance. Damani hardly noticed as he continued examining the manufactured home.

"Why are you still following Preston?" I finally asked.

"Isn't that against your rules?" He tapped his temple.

"Not unless you risk hurting yourself."

"And you think I am?"

I shrugged. "I don't think he killed your sister," I said as I eyed the trailer in the distance.

"You're probably right."

Another long pause, the blustering AC filling the void of conversation.

"She was always better at this sort of stuff," Damani said. "We—uh—we actually didn't really get along."

I raised an eyebrow, begging an explanation. He laughed, but it was bitter. "Janelle was always serious, even as a kid—very focused and driven. She always took the job so solemnly; I think it was a spiritual thing for her. I was just in it for the fame for a while there. I was always the immature one. Everyone used to joke that I should've been born the pyrokinetic the way I ran around like I was hot shit."

"I don't see that now," I said.

Damani shot me a skeptical look.

"Maybe a little."

"Yeah, well." His eyes returned to the trailer down the street. "I ruined a lot of things before I realized I needed to grow up. I lost my son—I'm sure you know by now. His mom took him away. I couldn't—wouldn't—control my temper. My ego was too damn big, so one day, they were both gone."

"The little boy at the funeral?" I asked.

Damani nodded. "First time I've seen him in months."

"I'm sorry." I nodded toward his sun visor. "Can I see him?"

He smiled and folded the visor down, grabbing the picture tucked away in the mirror.

"That's James—Jamie. He just turned eight."

I examined the beaming little boy in the dog-eared picture—tight ringlets, big brown eyes, and missing one bottom tooth. I smiled. "He looks just like you."

"Takes after his mom, thank goodness. He's a good kid."

"Is he . . . like you?"

"You mean can he do this?" he asked, a spark leaping from his fingers as he snapped them.

"Show-off," I said, rolling my eyes.

"He's like Janelle, actually. He's pyrokinetic."

"How does that work?"

"Something about electrokinesis needing both recessive mutations that cause pyrokinesis plus another recessive mutation in a different gene."

"I think I understood half of that."

"It's like hemochromatosis, they say."

"I have no idea what that is."

"Me either," Damani said, laughing. "It's how Mercy Rehab explained it to us. I was too embarrassed to ask."

"He had to go to Mercy? Did his powers manifest badly?"

"Nothing like that. We knew he'd have powers when he was two. It was my fault actually. Mom lit a fire on Christmas, and I was supposed to watch him. Chelsea found him with his hand in the flames. He was fine. Burned his clothes, but there wasn't a mark on him, not that that made it better. Chelsea left not long after that. Jamie's abilities didn't manifest until about a year ago— way older than Janelle and me but still early. Chelsea takes him to group counseling a few times a month. He and some other kids work out how to control their powers there. They've been really great."

"They are," I said.

"I forgot you had to go. How was that? I mean, you woke up with powers and no memories, and then you got tossed into rehab? Sounds like a rough start."

"Mercy was great. Coming home was the hard part."

"Sorry. I shouldn't pry."

I shrugged but didn't offer more. He didn't need to hear me bitch about my mother.

"I need to do better for Jamie—and Janelle," Damani said. "Janelle wouldn't risk any lives until she was certain Preston wasn't the guy. And Jamie . . . I need to be the superhero he thinks I am. So, yeah, I'm following him, and I won't apologize for it."

"You don't have to stalk suspects alone in the middle of the night," I said. "That's a good way to get yourself into more than one kind of trouble."

"Ryker says we aren't pursuing him anymore." His tone was bitter. "We're chasing these guys now. The politicians are barking at him about the press conference. Can't have beloved idols getting blown away on live TV and not make progress in an investigation. Kelley's probably looking to replace him if we can't bring someone in ASAP, so Ryker thinks we should pursue leads that will 'yield results,' as he put it. If I don't look into him, no one will."

"God help the person who tries to get between Ryker and his sense of duty," I said, shaking my head. "Let's hope our new buddy, Jake, has some answers."

"I shouldn't be surprised these assholes took advantage of a serial killer to advance their own agenda."

"You really think that's what happened?"

"You think they're one and the same?" Damani asked. "The Sons of Gaia are bombing and stabbing people?"

311

"I felt more than one creep yesterday. The guy in the hood . . ." I sighed, remembering the man who had escaped, his twisted mind fixated on Wildfire. "The crowd was mostly APA. You could be right. Maybe he's with them. Maybe the APA and the Sons of Gaia are coordinating all of it."

"You think the APA is involved too?"

"I don't know. I told Anna we were chasing a lone wolf, but that was when it was just Madison and Alice."

Just. Jesus, when did two women's deaths become *just*? I shrugged off the memories of the stairwell—of arms wrapping around me—as they threatened to rise up. "I didn't sense anything when Ryker had me crash the APA meeting."

Damani snorted. "The APA is made of all kinds, but the guys catching up around the buffalo dip are Boy Scouts compared to whoever is doing this—all bark with no bite. The dangerous ones aren't socializing. They aren't howling their opinions in public. They're out here plotting behind brand-new privacy fences."

"That's creepy," I said. "The ones at the meetings seem to do enough damage with their barking. I think they've hurt more of us than these guys. It's just not obvious, and it's legal."

Damani shrugged.

"Shit! It's him!" Damani exclaimed as a man with shaggy black hair and a scruffy, short beard emerged from the house, the long-legged brindle boxer from the window tugging on a red leash. We ducked to avoid being spotted.

"Don't look this way," I muttered, heart racing as I waited for him to see us. I released my breath as Jacob Mason walked the dog down the street in the opposite direction, ignorant of our presence as he tried to control the energetic animal and light a cigarette at the same time.

My heart hammered against my chest . . . one beat . . . two beats . . .

"Why not?" I muttered to myself as I grabbed the door handle and slowly pulled. The door opened with a soft pop, and I pushed it gently.

"Now what are you doing?" Damani asked as I slunk out.

"I'll be less obvious reading his mind now than hovering on his lawn," I responded.

"If you get something, come right back. Backup can be here in two minutes."

Quietly, I pressed the door closed as the oppressive heat blanketed me once more. Damani inched closer to the windshield, peering just over the steering wheel. I raised my hand up, all five fingers outstretched, indicating he could send a search party if I wasn't back ASAP. I threw my hood up and power-walked after our suspect.

It occurred to me too late that I probably shouldn't leave the real field agent in the car.

I slowed as Jacob rounded the corner, taking the same path I had earlier, while trying to avoid noxious clouds of secondhand smoke. I frowned, noting Jacob Mason's attire. He looked like a cop. SECURITY screamed in bold yellow across his chest and back. I shuddered. This guy and his slippery thoughts certainly wouldn't make me feel safe. What was his job supposed to be again?

The dog spotted me. Its lips curled, threatening to voice its displeasure.

"Shit!" I cursed under my breath. I liked dogs! What had I ever done to this one? Well, besides trying to put his human in jail for murder and possibly knocking him on his ass at the victim's funeral.

He'd started it.

Tail between my legs, I did an about-face and nearly ran in the other direction, half expecting the owner to come after me.

I approached the car. It was empty.

"Damani?" I hissed under my breath. I scanned up and down the street.

Jacob Mason was out of sight, leaving just me and the still-running car.

I turned toward the trailer.

My stomach flip-flopped. He wouldn't, would he? *He* told *me* we had to do this by the book! I rushed toward the trailer and hovered at the edge of the street, wringing my hands in exasperation. Did I go after him? Was I even sure he was inside? What if he was just going around in the opposite direction to keep an eye on me? I didn't sense anyone else in the house, but that didn't mean it was empty.

"Damani?" I called softly to the trailer.

What was I doing? He couldn't hear me. I sensed him as I inched closer, but from where . . .

A *thud!* from the side of the trailer made me jump. I darted around the corner as Damani brushed dirt from his pants, having landed somewhat ungracefully at the bottom of the yard's six-foot privacy fence.

"Are you *insane*?" I snapped at him.

He grabbed me by the arm and pulled me toward the car, glancing over his shoulder as he briskly escorted me to the passenger's seat.

"Following him was nuts enough," I said as we entered the safety of the vehicle. "I didn't expect you to one-up me! What happened to doing things right?"

"We got him!" Damani said, trembling. His wild eyes held mine.

The world seemed to flip upside down as my heartbeat skipped.

"What?" I squeaked, convinced I'd heard him wrong.

After so long . . . I didn't dare get my hopes up.

Damani held his phone out. I took it when his shaking hands made it impossible to focus on the image. Captured in a picture of the shed's dusty window, there was a grainy shot of . . . what was that? I saw at least five large jugs of acetone and . . . could that weird hunk of metal be some kind of timing device? Like what they showed us in training?

"What do we—?"

"It's in plain view," Damani said breathlessly. "It's visible from the street."

"Seriously?" I asked. It couldn't be that easy.

Damani nodded.

"Call Ryker," I said, nearly choking on the words.

Damani's jaw clenched, and he remained deathly still when, what felt like seconds later, black SUVs turned the corner and rumbled down the road toward us. Mark passed us in AGENCY-blazoned Kevlar, nodding in solidarity, as radios squawked and Ryker's piercing eyes missed nothing from the street.

Mark's knocks on the door echoed like gunshots.

Damani jerked as I slipped my hand into his, but his jaw noticeably relaxed.

The door opened, and angry, urgent shouts of "Hands where we can see them!" were met with exclamations of "You can't do this!" and the sound of handcuffs clicking closed. Somewhere inside, the dog snarled a warning.

Blinds from neighboring homes flipped open. Shocked neighbors watched Mark drag Jacob Mason out of the house while he cursed about his rights and aberrations of nature. Agents rushed through the front door to a barking dog hell-bent on living up to the Beware of Dog sign. Lights flashed and radios crackled and squawked in an assault of stimuli while they searched the house.

Damani tightened his grip on my fingers. I squeezed his hand in return. His eyes never left Jacob Mason as Mark thrust him into the backseat of a waiting SUV and slammed the door, not until the car disappeared from view. Even then, we both remained still despite the turmoil, too afraid to believe it was real.

I didn't remember the drive back to the Agency. I blinked, and then I was sitting inside the observation room.

Ryker's breath was hot on my neck as we studied Jacob Mason from behind tempered glass. The red-faced, cuffed man slammed the table and spat insults at Tom, Glenn, and their mothers. They sat across from him, unfazed, practiced masks of stone-cold professionalism plastered across their faces.

I, on the other hand, was sweating against the waves of rage and *hate* that rolled off Jacob Mason like a tsunami.

And that was just what Jacob was feeling.

"Are you getting anything?" Damani asked.

His arms were clenched against his sides as he struggled to keep sparks from flying. Based on the smell of singed textiles, I wasn't sure he was winning. His mind repeated a sort of desperate prayer that this, finally, was the guy. I struggled against the apprehension that I might have to disappoint him.

316

I focused on the men in the interrogation room, clinging to my chair, bracing myself for what might happen next. Then I surrendered to the onslaught of thoughts besieging me, not exactly welcoming the foreign thoughts and feelings that seeped into me like water in a sponge, but not resisting either.

Emotions reached me first: rage, grief, fear, trepidation, hate . . . hope. Somehow, the last was the hardest to cope with. Trembling, I swam through the emotions that raged around me like a roiling sea, focusing on the apoplectic man across from Tom and Glenn. I reached for his oozing memories, swallowing hard as, internally, I gagged on the sludge that infiltrated my mind.

A stage spread before me. A brunette woman in a tactical vest—AGENCY written across it in vivid yellow—peered out from behind a curtain, her back to me.

I lurched in my seat as Mark approached the woman, and she turned, my own face glancing back at me. I didn't remember Jacob Mason from the press conference—I'd been certain I'd never seen the man in my life—but he had been right behind me, watching.

"What?" Damani asked breathlessly.

"He worked security the day of the press conference," I said, puzzle pieces sliding into place.

"Employment is listed as Ironclad Security," Mark said from beside him, flipping through a file.

"Get me something actionable, Gordon," Ryker growled, but his frustration wasn't aimed at me.

He focused on our suspect with a feverish intensity. Ryker wanted someone to pay for the hell we'd endured over the past few months, and he really hoped that someone was Jacob Mason.

I cast a nervous glance at Damani, who miraculously wasn't smoking. A single clipped nod encouraged me to continue, though his eyes never left Jacob.

A man in a matching security outfit stood beside me. I dropped a cigarette, crushing it into the dirt with my heel as the crowd cheered, Wildfire and Livewire taking the stage.

"Let's see how these freaks like this," I said.

The man beside me snickered. "Kill the freaks," he drawled.

I laughed and pulled a cell phone from my pocket. As the crowd cheered, I pressed the call button.

I sucked in a breath as a fireball erupted in my mind, the phantom odor of smoke filling my nose. I gritted my teeth, Jacob Mason's twisted memories mingling with mine, combining into a hellish vision of fire and resonating screams.

It was him. It was Jacob Mason. He *was* there that day. He had been right behind me. I missed him. I blinked back tears that welled in my eyes; I could blame myself after I finished keeping my promise to Damani.

"Gordon?" Ryker asked.

I looked up. His piercing blue eyes held mine, a need for justice burning bright within them.

"We found them," I whispered.

Damani released a shuddering sob. A wave of grief struck me, and I reeled in my chair. He nodded at me, jaw clenched, and turned for the door.

"Thank you," he gasped, throwing the door open and rushing out, taking his flood of emotions with him. He was gone before I could respond.

I sank into my chair, too disoriented by the deluge of racing thoughts and feelings to follow.

It was over. It was actually over.

Mark squeezed my shoulder. "You got him," he said reassuringly, not oblivious to the sheen in my eyes. "You did good."

Not good enough, but I didn't say it aloud. It wouldn't change Janelle Aluko's fate, and we deserved the peace of closure. Mark rushed out the door, either to put the next sequence of events into motion or to make sure Damani wasn't about to put a lightning bolt through Jacob Mason's skull.

In the end, they didn't need my telepathy to bring charges against Jacob Mason and his coconspirators. The evidence in his shed was more than damning, not to mention his accessibility to the underside of the stage and his computer, which ultimately led to a chat room on a hidden Sons of Gaia black site where he had boasted of the crime. He'd posted a video, which the lawyers would love him for. Still, in Ryker's own words: "We need to make sure not one of these bastards walks."

And there *was* more than one. That much I was certain of as I dug through Jacob Mason's brain, my stomach churning as I saw through his eyes while he packed a bomb full of shrapnel. I lived the moment he watched them pull Wildfire's body from the rubble, the swell of bloodlust intoxicating, emboldening him for the next.

I staggered into my safe house hours later, a pizza in one hand and a two liter of soda in the other. If I remembered correctly, Brittany was a classic pepperoni-and-cheese kind of girl.

"You still here?" I called as I nudged the door open with my foot, but I knew she was waiting, needing to know the outcome.

"Yeah," Brittany said from the couch, muting the TV as I closed the door behind me. "Hope that's okay. I didn't feel like going home."

She caught my expression and froze, barely breathing. A desperate hope glinted in her eyes.

"We have something to celebrate," I said, completely oblivious to what was coming.

If only it had been that easy.

CHAPTER 15

The sharp scent of chlorine from the nearby park blended with sulfur from the Pacific Ocean as a breeze carried the odors across the Agency's terraqueous private courtyard. They mixed with the mild scent of algae emanating from a small pond, home to several curious koi. Equally curious coworkers raised eyebrows and motioned in our direction as they passed the large windows enclosing us, giving the impression I was in a fishbowl myself. Gaping koi gummed the pond's surface, eagerly yearning for dry pellets to rain down.

"Maybe next time, guys," I told the fish apologetically.

The day felt . . . odd—vibrant, maybe? A lunch break with coworkers was a far cry from normal, even before recent events. I'd always been the Agency's pariah, the defective telepath tucked away in a dark interrogation room.

Following the arrest of Jacob Mason and two additional members of the Sons of Gaia for Wildfire's death, an inconspicuous wall—one I don't think anyone consciously realized was there—collapsed. Gone were the stiff smiles at the coffee maker between interrogations. No more eyes shifting to the clock during conversation when people thought I wasn't looking. No more awkwardly keeping my feet from shifting back and forth when I sensed the other person's discomfort as we exchanged canned pleasantries. No more crossed arms and suppressed sighs from behind as my neck grew warm when I took too long in the interrogation room.

I wasn't the San Diego branch's consolation prize anymore, the only telepath the smaller division could attract because the limited pool of telepathic candidates wanted the prestige associated with the larger branches, like San Francisco and Los Angeles. I belonged now, though it came at a terrible cost.

Taking a steadying breath, I turned my attention to a row of cans sitting on the pond's low wall. I withdrew my phone from my pocket and focused the camera on the cans.

"Psychic training continues!" I texted Anna, sending her a picture.

I ached for Anna and Weasel, but until we confirmed that all of Jacob Mason's coconspirators were sharing bunks in a jail cell, Weasel stayed with Jo, and Anna and Elliott stayed in whatever dark hole they were stuffed in. Based on the Agency's progress, they wouldn't have to stay away much longer, and I was eager to show Anna what my new normal looked like.

"Fewer selfies, more crushing!" Damani said, clapping me on the shoulder.

A sense of pride swelled in me as I took in my friends—a newfound support system I eagerly embraced.

"You've got this!" Brittany cheered from a nearby bench, a thumbs-up encouraging me as she nursed a coffee.

Her pulsating headache found me across the courtyard, and I winced, staying as far away from her—telepathically, at least—as possible. She had shown up drunk at my doorstep less since our victory, though her recurring headaches and nosebleeds suggested she was still a mess, self-medicating alone to avoid tarnishing my new sense of competency.

I'd have a conversation with her about it. There was no need for her to isolate herself.

"Remember," Damani said as my brain's throbbing lessened to a dull background ache. "Levitate, crush, drop."

Frankly, Damani and Brittany weren't qualified to train a telekinetic, but the Agency's professionals had tried, failed miserably, and run screaming years ago. I'd rather spend lunch breaks with friends trying the latest thing Damani found on the internet than anything the academics with their limited understanding of telekinesis could come up with.

"I got it," I said, shooing Damani out of the danger zone with a playful shove.

I took a stance before my victims and focused on finding my center . . . or whatever the self-help guru jargon Damani had found was. The first can hovered in the air, turning haltingly on its axis. Then, with a satisfying *crunch!*, the can compressed into a thin piece of metal. It rasped against the brick walkway as it hit the ground, and I cocked my head at Damani, grinning.

"Oh!" Damani rubbed his hands together mischievously. "Getting cocky, are we? I saw that fancy little twist you did there."

The next three cans metamorphosed into scrap metal in a blink. This had been our morning, lunch, and evening routine for the past two weeks. Either Brittany or Damani—Brittany, usually, if she stayed the night—dragged me out of bed in the morning for "psychic practice," as they'd grown fond of calling it. My protests that I was not, in fact, psychic fell on deaf ears. If I'd done well, they kept me busy during lunch and immediately after work. The first few days had been draining, but I felt like I was finally getting the hang of it.

"All right," Damani said. "Memory check. What movie did you watch last night? Brittany, no thinking!"

Brittany snorted behind us.

"Trick question," I said, grinning. "We didn't watch a movie last night."

"We've got a thumbs-up from the audience!" he said, checking with Brittany for confirmation.

I smiled wider, wondering if this was really what life would be like from now on.

It had been a surprisingly good two weeks for my memory. Aside from my usual absentmindedness, I hadn't experienced any major losses or lapses. Hell, it had been a good two weeks in general. The Agency had three bombers behind bars. Jacob's buddies had arrived in cuffs to keep him from feeling lonely not even twelve hours after Jacob himself was dragged from his home and beloved backyard bomb shed. Catching the bombers didn't magically right the world's wrongs, but it helped. We'd still lost too many people, and despite admitting to the bombs, none of the stubborn assholes had confessed to any of the stabbings, forcing an interlude in justice for Madison, Alice, and Navin.

I take that back. They had confessed to the stabbings initially. Their stories had changed as soon as lawyers materialized—they suddenly claimed coercion by the Agency whilst their defense also attempted to drop their charges from murder in the first degree to involuntary manslaughter, claiming the bombs weren't supposed to go off with Livewire and Wildfire onstage. They were only meant "as a message." Damani almost put a bolt through the glass that morning, and Ryker hadn't allowed him in the observation room since.

The APA was having a field day with their story and loved lamenting their plight to any news station that would give them a platform. The media seemed all too eager to capitalize on the drama and give the charismatic hate group an outlet.

Whatever. So long as videos of me supposedly "assaulting" protestors continued to stay off the news, I was happy. Someone probably had a cell phone video of my failed attempt at flight, but whether it hadn't surfaced because the APA and Sons of Gaia thought it made them look guilty or because the Agency didn't want to appear incompetent, I didn't know. Maybe Impulse simply wasn't interesting anymore.

Finding knife sets in the suspects' homes that were consistent with Madison and Alice's murder weapons did nothing to sway them. Quite the opposite actually. Manly shrieks about planted evidence echoed in the Agency's interrogation rooms for days.

Not even Brittany identifying the man who killed Navin changed their tune. She became increasingly withdrawn after she identified Everett Doyle, a cognizant slime mold with a list of priors that rivaled Jacob's.

I knew the experience forced her to relive the day on the beach. She still blamed herself, and I hoped peace would come with time.

Still, the Agency was chasing down final leads, and for the first time in a long time, we were winning. The case was closing regardless of our pain-in-the-ass criminals trying to evade homicide charges, and in time, we would heal. We would never forget, but we could find peace.

Yeah, I could get used to this.

A *splash!* caught our attention as a flattened can skipped across the surface of the pond, koi darting in the opposite direction. Another former can fluttered in an air current that shouldn't exist, swooping and twisting like a butterfly.

"Hadley?" Damani asked as a squished can hovered above his head and the pond spat a second metal disk at us.

"Mind if we join the party?" Christine asked, entering the courtyard through a glass door, Ben and Graham trailing behind her.

"I say we up the stakes," Graham added, brown eyes crinkling in promised mischief.

Graham Allen was the telepath from Atlanta. I'd worked with him multiple times during the past two weeks after our suspects proved surprisingly difficult to read, both of us sitting in on interrogations, tag-teaming and verifying information gleaned from our criminals' malefic minds. He was good. Better than good, and for some reason, he'd taken to me, unexpectedly playing the role of a tacit mentor when I got stuck during an interrogation. The past two weeks were the best I'd ever performed at work. I was going to miss him when he went back to the East Coast.

"Raise the stakes how?" Damani asked, eyebrows raised.

Christine and Ben perched on either side of Brittany, Ben popping chips in his mouth one at a time as he observed us, smirking. Graham pulled a pen from his pocket and wiggled it, eyebrows raised in a way that promised a challenge.

"She can do pens," Damani said, bristling slightly as his training session was hijacked.

I shot him a look and nudged his arm.

Fine, he projected at me. I jumped. A grin tugged at his lips. He knew I'd heard him. I regretted giving him Anna's number. Anna transmitting her thoughts to me was unnerving enough, and Damani wasn't even good at it yet. His thoughts pinged around my brainpan like a shout echoing through a cave.

Graham smiled. "We'll see."

He set the pen on the wall and grinned wider, white teeth flashing amongst a short dark-brown beard just showing hints of gray.

"What's your psionic score?" he asked me. "If you don't mind . . ." He took Damani by the shoulders and positioned him between me and the pond.

I tried to remember my evaluation from Mercy Rehab. "A two?"

"You blew up a car, and they said you're a two?" Graham looked me up and down.

"Let me guess, you're a five?" Damani needled.

Graham ignored him, though an amused glint reflected in his eyes.

"What are you—?" I asked as Graham took my shoulders and faced me in the opposite direction of the pen.

Damani and I stood back-to-back, the top of my head barely reaching his shoulders. Most people were taller than me, but the difference between Damani and me was comical.

"Ah!" Graham chastised, preventing me from checking over my shoulder. "Use him."

"*What?*" I blurted.

Damani's laughter echoed in the courtyard as he comprehended the exercise. "Oh, that's awesome!"

"Damani can see the pen," Graham explained, his tone much too exuberant. "See through his eyes. Float the pen."

"I can't—"

"You got this, Hadley!" Christine cheered from the bench, angular eyes crinkling as she giggled.

Ben gave a whoop for emphasis.

I gritted my teeth. Fine. Peer pressure could win this time, mostly because I feared Ryker walking by and getting twitchy. Ryker had only recently reinstated Brittany after her "unprofessional behavior." I had no doubt he was aware of how we used our breaks; I suspected he permitted it because, for starters, Damani and I were currently the Agency's golden children.

And I hadn't blown anything up. Yet.

I rolled my eyes petulantly at Graham before closing them and concentrating. Damani's mind was familiar. His conversations with Anna had taught him how to leave his thoughts accessible. He was more than happy to leave the figurative door open. I stepped past the metaphorical threshold, sensing a hum of dynamic energy, like electricity through a wire, that I'd come to associate with Damani. He saw my quarry. It was weird, but I saw the pen too. It was like observing an object through a telescope, but it was a crystal-clear image nonetheless.

Good, Graham thought, his voice like a bass speaker blasting in my ear.

I jumped, my concentration breaking.

Sweet merciful! The number of people who knew how to project thoughts was three too many! But where Damani's projection was a flighty echo, Graham's was a honed craft.

"Now, float the pen," Graham said, out loud this time.

I scowled as he chuckled at my discomfort.

Finding the pen was even easier the second time. I grinned as I sensed its smooth, metallic surface.

Okay, now, float the . . .

Damani yelped, kicking his feet as he left the ground. I gasped and dropped him.

"The hard part is convincing your mind that the physical thing you're in contact with is not the thing you want to lift," Graham said, pressing his lips together to suppress an amused smile.

The physical thing was Damani in this instance. My face flushed.

"I'm okay. I've always wanted to fly," Damani said, trying for witty, though his breathlessness indicated I'd rattled him. "Do it again."

Damani gave his best impression of a wounded bird three more times before I finally felt the pen. It wasn't the most effective method, but if I split my focus, I could look through Damani's eyes and, in a sense, telepathically pat around for the pen. I used a similar patting tactic when unlocking the deadbolt to my apartment with

Anna, though I refined that trick long ago, and I didn't need Anna's eyes to do it.

Cheers rang through the courtyard as the pen wobbled and lifted an inch.

"Yes!" I shouted.

I spun at the unexpected rumble of a passing car, heart hammering, and abruptly found myself companionless.

I blinked against the relentless afternoon sun, staggering out of the way of a pedicab blasting hip-hop as tourists laughed and pointed at the USS *Midway* anchored in the distance.

I turned, and the Agency's seventeen-story glass and steel tower glinted in the afternoon sun. I clutched my phone, unlocked with a photo of Weasel and Molly playing on the screen. A timestamp showed I'd sent *They're so cute!* and an embarrassing number of emojis to Jo ten minutes earlier.

Fantastic.

What had I done since the Agency? Perhaps more importantly, where was the bus stop, and how did I get back to the safe house?

I groaned. So much for my not-losing-my-marbles streak. At least I recognized the landscape. The Diner was less than five minutes away. I glanced at my phone, puzzle pieces sliding into place. It was a miracle I hadn't locked myself out of it.

Yet. I shocked myself when I remembered the passcode again. I hadn't made any calls, but I assumed that was my intention. A call to Mark went to voicemail.

Next victim, I guess.

"Hey!" Damani answered on the second ring.

"Hey," I said, cheeks red. "I think today's exercises were a bit much. I can't remember how to get home."

"I told Graham he was pushing too hard," he grumbled. "Are you okay? Where are you? I'll come get you."

"I'm fine. I'm a few minutes from The Diner."

"Oh, God," Damani said, faking a retch. At least, I thought it was fake. "Avoid the food. I'll be there in ten minutes. Seriously, don't eat *anything!*"

I chuckled and pocketed my phone. A kiss of warmth brushed my cheeks, and a crisp breeze from the waterfront tossed my hair as I ambled down the sidewalk.

The Diner's front door signaled my arrival with a *ding!*, and I poked my head in. As usual, there wasn't a customer to be seen or sensed.

"Gladys?" I called.

The front counter where she usually brooded was also empty. It must've been time for her afternoon cigarette.

"Gladys, it's Hadley!" I called to the back as I entered. "I'm just waiting for someone to pick me up!"

I slid into my usual haunt, a booth by the window, and stretched out. I took a deep breath, inhaling the tang of burned coffee, and . . . what was that? Nose wrinkling, I gagged on the stench of acrid charcoal. Had Gladys moved on to burning the food too? That would be an unholy marriage I wasn't sure even The Diner could allow.

I strode to the counter and leaned over. The smell of what was already inedible food being reduced to carbon was unmistakable.

"Hey, Gladys!" I called. "I think something's burning!"

No answer. I bit my lip, waiting.

"What the hell," I muttered, circling around and behind the counter.

331

I didn't have the mental wherewithal to operate a stove, but I figured I could handle turning one off in this instance. I pushed through the stainless-steel double doors to the kitchen and saw the culprits immediately: two heaping piles of hash browns and half a dozen eggs were black and smoking on a commercial grill with significantly more knobs than the one at home. I turned a few of them and felt satisfied when grease stopped spitting at me. I glanced at the ceiling, eyeing a silent smoke detector skeptically.

"Got it!" I called triumphantly to the alley. I had conquered four cans, a pen, and a stove in one day. It was a new high for me.

Something heavy slammed feet from me. I jumped and turned in time to watch the wind force the back door closed again with another jarring bang. It creaked back open, revealing the alley outside.

"Gladys?" I called, my frown deepening when I couldn't sense her surly vibe.

I stepped out the door, a sour, rotting smell from a nearby dumpster assaulting my nose in place of burned food.

"Ugh," I groaned, choking on the stench as I descended the stairs separating the doorway from the alley.

I stepped into something wet, my sneakers squelching. My breath hitched at the sight of my shoes.

Fresh red speckles overlapped brown stains that hadn't been there this morning. A pool of thickening liquid coated the dark pavement beneath my feet, and I knew with certainty it wasn't water.

No! No, no, no, *no*! It was over! We had suspects behind bars! They'd confessed!

"Gladys!" I shrieked. "She's not a parahuman," I said to myself, head swiveling to determine where she was hiding. "No one would hurt her. It's just from the kitchen."

That didn't stop a growing sense of foreboding as dark, sheeny streaks on the pavement caught my attention. They led to the pungent dumpster twenty feet away.

For a split second, time stopped, and I considered running away. I didn't want to repeat this horrible nightmare. I didn't want to be thrust into a horror movie scene *again*. Just once, I wanted to be selfish and spare myself the anguish.

But I'd missed saving Madison by minutes. Brittany had missed saving Navin by seconds. I'd been the same distance from Wildfire when she plunged through the stage.

"Gladys!" I yelled, nearly slipping in the puddle of blood as I scrambled for the dumpster. I flung the lid open.

A strangled cry escaped my lips. I recoiled, choking as my stomach contents rose up.

A man's vacant eyes stared forever past me, milky, their light long since extinguished.

"Tom?" I choked, swallowing hard against quickly rising bile.

Oh, God. I was gonna—

The alley spun.

Why was Tom . . . ?

He wasn't the only one in the dumpster.

A clatter farther down the alley jerked me to attention.

"Hello?" I squeaked.

No one responded.

Panting, fighting the urge to utterly lose my shit, I yanked my phone from my pocket and mashed the call button for the first name that popped up. The red streak I left on the screen didn't register. Hands trembling, I placed the phone to my ear, eyes scanning the alley.

My phone hit the ground with a clatter when I saw the back of the door. A message, painted across it in dripping red letters, had been hidden when I stepped out. KILL THE FREAKS was unmistakable now, scrawled across in still-glistening, much-too-familiar handwriting.

Scuffing came from behind me. Louder—closer!

A hand gripped my shoulder.

My bloodcurdling shriek echoed through the alley. Glass from every window within twenty feet of me exploded with an ear-shattering peal, blowing outward and raining shards.

"Hadley!" Damani shouted, jerking his shirt up to shield his eyes. "It's me!"

I whirled to face him, gasping short, panicked breaths.

"You have blood on your—" Damani's wide eyes stared at my face, but then he saw the dumpster.

I'll never forget his expression.

Hours later, the medical examiner's van waited outside the alley with no sense of urgency, destined to transport Tom, Glenn, and Gladys to the Agency's morgue. Technicians garbed head to toe in white processed the scene while Art finished his assessment of the bodies. Two lumpy black bags had already been laid across the ground. A third body bag lay unzipped and waiting. Yellow crime scene tape cordoned off the area, and strobing lights cast contorted, writhing shadows now that the sun was down.

Damani slid down beside me. I sagged against a black SUV, its lights flashing blue and red in the night, vacant eyes trained on but barely registering the taped-off alley. A clipboard with my statement lay half-forgotten beside me. I'd restarted multiple times after trembling hands resulted in illegible words or falling tears smudged the ink. I was almost out of tears now, my crusty cheeks streaked with their tracks. I silently wondered if I'd run dry too soon. My throbbing head filled their void; the lights didn't help.

"Gladys called the Agency this afternoon," Damani said. "She was worried about some guy who kept hovering outside."

I inclined my head to look at him, my stiff neck protesting as if my head was made of lead. Damani slumped against the SUV, red and blue pulses reflecting across weary eyes.

"Tom and Glenn walked into a trap," I said nasally.

"Yeah," Damani said, voice tight.

The harsh clatter of wheels on pavement signaled Art's examination was finally done, drawing my attention back to the alley. Two white-clad figures guided a stretcher toward us, a lumpy black bag jolting atop it as the wheels clacked and rattled across unleveled pavement. Jaw clenched, I turned away as they passed, the stretcher's metal reflecting the chaos of lights around us.

Damani waited until it disappeared into the van before continuing, though I kept my eyes unfocused on a point in the distance as strained grunts and movement came from the dumpster.

"They went way back, so . . ." Damani started, but his voice failed him as he gazed into the alley.

I refused to watch. I ignored a thump—ground my teeth at the sound of a zipper.

"Pretty sure everyone knew Gladys," I said.

Gladys. She was as prickly as cholla, and I'd never smell a cigarette again without thinking of her. Still, for all the umbrage my existence had caused her, she'd always been there. Her low voice, gravelly from years of smoking, had muttered a constant stream of complaints though she dutifully shuffled to the phone in the back to ring my rescue. Every time. For five years.

Tom and Glenn had been father figures almost as much as Mark was. How many hours had I shadowed them, unseen in the observation room, learning their tells, attentive as they tag-teamed a suspect into a confession? How many times had their eyes lit up with pride and satisfaction as a crucial piece of evidence I gleaned from a suspect's mind provided the break they needed? We'd been a team for my entire tenure at the Agency, even if I'd always been separated and obscured by glass.

My eyes found the alley again. I tracked the forensics team as they systematically scrutinized the scene in their ghostly white garb, bending down frequently to process a piece of glass that hampered their efforts or snap a photograph in a brief flash of light.

"I'm sorry you went through that twice," Damani said.

"I don't remember the first time," I said, voice flat. I'd decide later if I was bitter or grateful.

A convenience store camera across the street had caught the moment I entered The Diner the first time. The Diner's large glass windows provided a perfect view as I sat in my usual booth and texted before something in the back caught my attention, and I disappeared into the kitchen. A different camera courtesy of the restaurant on the corner caught me running from the alley, begging for help and disappearing down the street. It also recorded me when I wandered back in without a clue ten minutes later. Somehow, The Diner's cameras were all pointing in the wrong direction, and I tried not to consider the implications.

Gladys, Glenn, and Tom didn't deserve to be forgotten.

"Why do you think you used your powers the first time?"

"I probably just freaked out. Blew something up," I said, sniffing, swollen sinuses feeding my growing headache along with the lights and myriad of emotions. Was that really my voice? I sounded like I'd aged a lifetime. Maybe I had.

I focused on the soccer cleats on my feet, at least a size too large. Another set of clothes for the evidence locker, another nail trim, and another pair of shoes Lilly would have to miss for a while. The Agency probably had half my closet by now.

A hysterical laugh burbled in my throat. I was wearing a teenager's soccer cleats outside a triple homicide, sitting on my ass with blood dried under my fingernails. Again. I'd get Lilly new shoes. These were defiled.

After all the heartache, I don't know why it was that moment, sitting quietly on the pavement, staring at a child's shoes, when something broke deep inside me. Something I hadn't even been aware I had, that I didn't have a name for, cracked like a mirror—well and truly shattered—and I didn't think I was better without it.

"I'm sorry, Damani. I can't keep doing this. I-I quit," I said, still staring at the cleats.

"Jesus, Hadley," Damani snapped. "No, you don't!"

Startled by his anger, my head shot up to meet his indignant gaze.

"Really?" I asked, heat creeping up my neck.

337

There was an unexpected strength in the anger that blossomed within me. I latched onto it. I'd regret it, but it burned away the heartache right then, and that's what I focused on.

"*Really?* Tell me what I'm doing here other than torturing myself? I lost my shit and contaminated a crime scene *again*, and that was after I fucking forgot about it for ten minutes! If I hadn't wandered back like the damned stray cat Gladys always said I was, they could have been in that dumpster for days before someone found them! Ryker's right. I'm a horrible agent, and I have no place here."

Not even in my observation room. I didn't know what I was going to do with my life—I'd figure it out later—but whatever it was, I wouldn't have to watch my friends die ever again.

"Hadley, you got the bombers. *You.*"

"And missed this guy completely! Again! I couldn't even confirm if the bombers were linked to the murders, and I gave this guy the opportunity to kill again while we were distracted. He's killed half our people—our *friends*. We could have had him long before this if it weren't for me. There wouldn't *be* bombers if it weren't for me!"

Christine had quit half an hour earlier after learning about Tom, Glenn, and Gladys, so the Agency had lost eight people—good people. Good for Christine for knowing when enough was enough. It was time for me to follow her example.

"You don't know that!" he spat in exasperation. "No one else caught this guy either! It's not just on you! He's escaping all of us. Jesus, Hadley, you've got to stop this. You can't keep going off the rails and giving up!"

"I'm not giving up!" I said through clenched teeth. "I'm telling you; I've had enough. She was a little old lady, and she didn't deserve—none of them deserved . . ." I'd nearly whispered the last part and dropped my head, jaw trembling.

There was no shame in choosing me, was there? For finally making one healthy choice *for myself*? Two weeks of a new normal had given me a taste of what my life could be.

I desperately wanted to see where normal could go.

Damani opened his mouth, knuckles taut around clenched fists.

I glared daggers at him. "No! Why is it so important to you that I stay? No one else thinks I should! Tell me, what good do I do *except find dead bodies*?"

He jerked his head toward the alley. "You literally blow up when you get spooked. You could be the most powerful agent in San Diego if you would just stop doubting yourself! Even Graham thinks you have more potential, and he would know!"

"Powerful?" I asked, gaping at him. "Do you even know what I've done? What *power* did? I have a freaking brain—"

"Oh, get off that," Damani snarled. "You're not an invalid. You've just never bothered trying."

If it was physically possible, my jaw would've hit the pavement.

"I mean it," he snapped. "You've let everyone convince you that you're fragile, and you're not. Forget what everyone else told you—you don't need to be protected."

"You don't need to fix me!" I spat, blood boiling. "And I don't need your permission if I want to go!"

"I don't want to fix you! There's nothing wrong with you!" he shouted back. "I just want you to get your head out of your ass long enough to realize what you're capable of. You don't even try!"

"You can be a real ass, you know that? I'm getting an update from Mark," I growled as I rose, needing to retreat before I broke more than windows. Regret was a swift bitch.

"Wait!" Damani said, hand grasping my arm. "I didn't mean to say that. You're right, that wasn't—just . . . wait a minute."

I slumped back down, fuming. He took several slow, steady breaths. My own tension eased with them, but I still refused to look at him.

"That was my temper," he said, straining to keep his voice even. "And I'm sorry. I'm a hypocrite, I know. I shouldn't tell you what to do when I can't even do it myself. I just . . . things don't always come out right when I'm upset."

I bit back the response I wanted to spit at him and chewed my lip instead.

"It's just, we've been a pretty good team, and I need that. I need a team. I need to be around . . . someone like my sister. Nothing's been the same without Janelle, and I like working with you."

My head jerked toward him in surprise.

"I'd really like to keep doing it." He swallowed hard as he averted his gaze. "But I can't if you quit. I know it's selfish of me. I know you've been through a lot, and I'm such an ass to ask you to stay anyway."

"I don't know if—"

"*Please* . . . think about it. I know today's too much. *I know*, but please, don't quit. Don't give up."

I inhaled deeply, closing my eyes against the stench of the godforsaken dumpster, and shook my throbbing head.

"Let's just . . . not talk about it right now," I said, deflating as adrenaline bled away to leave a dull, draining ache at my core. What did you know? I *could* feel worse. I leaned my head against the SUV and wallowed in my misery.

"You're right," Damani said. "I'm sorry for saying anything."

"You're right too," I mumbled. "I don't cope well. I barely have control as it is, and when everyone else's feelings seep in . . ."

In the alley, white-clad technicians heaved another black bag onto a gurney, hitting it with a clang that cut through conversations and shuffling footsteps. I jerked at the sound but forced myself not to look. Probably not Gladys. She was too petite.

"It's probably why you bring out the best in me," I added sullenly. "Your personality is . . . electric."

Damani huffed at my dig, the corners of his mouth sinking farther downward. "I'm pretty sure your response is the most appropriate."

"I'm worried I'm getting used to it," I admitted.

"Yeah. Me too."

I closed my eyes as the wheels of another stretcher—or had I missed the first one come back?—rattled along the pavement, crashing and clacking with each imperfection in the pockmarked pavement. I opened my eyes after it passed.

One to go.

"You really have the ability to piss me off, you know that?" I muttered. "I'm pretty sure that's your superpower."

"I said I was sorry," he grumbled.

"You're gifted at irritating me in many ways. What's the paper you're hiding?" I asked wearily, bracing myself as the third and final stretcher noisily made its way up the alley, guided by unidentifiable white figures.

"Cheating," Damani mumbled.

"You're going to get in trouble if you keep pursuing Weiss," I said. "I've told you that. Repeatedly."

"And I've ignored you every time," Damani quipped, also clearly still irritated with me. "Are you asking because you're curious and don't really want to quit?"

"No. I'm asking because I'm worried, and you're barking up the wrong damn tree. Weiss is a twisted son of a bitch, but he's not our son of a bitch. If I wanted to focus on anyone, it would be the Sons of Gaia, but you're a rabid dog with a bone. What'd you find?"

Damani glanced at the alley, but the gurney had paused, a wheel catching on something. Content that there were no eyes on us, he withdrew a crumpled packet from his back pocket. I shook my head as he thrust it at me. I knew he wasn't supposed to have it, and Ryker was somewhere nearby. Rolling his eyes, he tucked it back out of sight and scooted closer to me.

Real mature.

"Look, remember how his background is spotless?" Damani said in a hurried, hushed tone.

I nodded wearily. "Everything about him is spotless but his thoughts, and that's not illegal. There's a reason we aren't looking at him anymore."

"Hear me out. I started investigating family members. Turns out he had this cousin he was close to. Well, they used to hang out with a kid down the street. Nothing unusual until, one day, the neighbor kid and the cousin are at the cousin's house, and *it burns to the ground*. The cousin died."

"The neighbor was a parahuman?" I asked.

"Yeah. No one knew—no family history until the kid. They got into an argument over a game or something, and the kid started a fire. Didn't mean to. They cleared him of any wrongdoing."

"The Winefield-Drummer Act," I said.

Kids with previously unknown and unmanifested abilities couldn't be charged with crimes if they first activated in adverse ways. They underwent rehabilitation instead. It was a tremendous source of contention with the APA.

"I'd probably hate parahumans if I thought one got away with killing my cousin," Damani said.

"Wait . . ." I sat up straight as a shot of ice raced up my spine. "A little boy died in a fire?"

"Yeah," he said, unaware that my heart was racing. "Really sad. The parahuman kid got out, but the cousin got trapped in his bedroom."

Flashes of flames danced in my mind. A little boy called for his mother as the curtains caught and gouts of flame raced upward, the ceiling roaring as if alive in waves of amber. Oh, God. Was it possible those visions had come from Preston Weiss's mind, obsessing over what could have been the last moments of a loved one? Is that what my nightmares were trying to tell me? Had it been dangling in front of my face the entire time?

But it didn't have to mean anything. Countless supposedly normal people fantasized about dark, twisted delights, thinking they were safe in their own minds. Weiss could hate parahumans, wish for and fantasize about their deaths, but that didn't make him a killer.

"Does that mean anything to you?" Damani asked, gauging my reaction.

"No," I said too hastily.

He raised a skeptical eyebrow.

343

Damn it!

A growing spark danced behind his eyes. He'd had the same expression outside Jacob Mason's house, right before he jumped the blasted fence.

"Okay," I said, hoping for damage control. "I'll help you look into him again, just . . . not now."

"Seriously?" Damani asked, and I realized I'd done the opposite of damage control. "What happened to the Sons of Gaia?"

"You get this last thing out of me, and then you're going to run down every single last one of them once I prove it's not Preston Weiss," I said, hoping he wouldn't notice I couldn't meet his eyes. "Just . . ."

My throat tightened as the sound of wheels resumed.

"Right. Not now," he said, focusing on the alley as the last gurney clicked and clacked toward us.

"Let's meet first thing in the morning."

"Seriously? You really want to investigate him?"

"No. I want to keep you from getting fired—or worse—and I want to move on," I said. "If it's not Preston, *you* need to put your energy into catching the *right* person."

Damani didn't appear convinced. I knew that would spell trouble.

I gave him a pointed look, not liking the distracted, calculating buzz I sensed at the back of his mind. "I know you're still watching him, and I know you want to continue monitoring him. Promise me you'll leave it alone until tomorrow. I swear, I'll give it everything I've got until you're satisfied. Deal?"

Damani rolled his eyes. "Deal."

"I'm serious. This is the last thing. I'm done."

Damani opened his mouth to argue, then settled back, pensive. I didn't trust it, but at least he wasn't arguing.

I'd tell him about the nightmares later, I decided. Guilt ate at me as Damani sat beside me, knowing he'd missed something, but he'd be outside Preston Weiss's front door if I said anything. Sitting outside the alley, turning away as the final black bag clanged past, it felt like the right thing to do.

I'd find out later it didn't matter.

I frowned, confused, as a presence entered the crime scene. A spot of brightness, like a flickering candle flame in the dark, flared behind me and drifted closer. I unconsciously gravitated toward it. I always did.

"What?" Damani asked, noting my confused expression.

"Just . . . someone I know," I said, rising. I peered across the hood of the SUV. What was Jo doing here?

Her eyes found mine, and she beckoned me toward her. Slight creases at the edge of her eyes were the only outward sign to anyone without telepathy that she was agitated.

"Why aren't you answering your phone?" she asked when I was still several feet away, the edge in her voice making me pause.

Jo had passed agitated and was well on her way to scared. Guilt washed through me as I realized what she must have thought. I hadn't reached out to anyone yet, not even Anna.

"It's somewhere in there," I said, motioning toward the alley crawling with ghostly looking technicians.

"I'm so sorry about your friends," she said, surveying the scene. Her gaze shifted to me, sympathetic and . . . something else.

She wanted to hug me—*needed* to be closer, and I flushed, taking a nervous half step back.

345

"Uh . . . yeah," I said, too drained to comprehend the storm of emotion from Jo. "Um . . . I didn't see the suspect. I'm fine; I just got spooked and dropped my phone. You didn't need to—"

My mouth hung open as a wave of shock crashed over me. I knew; I knew why Jo was internally coming unglued. She saw comprehension sparkle behind my eyes.

Her shoulders slumped, embarrassed at projecting bad news. "I'm sorry, Hadley. Someone broke into your apartment. Yours and Anna's, not the safe house."

My head spun, her words distorting in my ears.

"They didn't take anything that we know of . . ." Jo said, watching for my tells.

"Shit!" I yelped.

Jo blinked in surprise.

Was someone looking for me? I turned and gaped at the alley, suddenly trembling. This asshole was clearly escalating. Was I next? What if it really was Preston? He knew who I was! *Should* I say something about the dreams? What if I was wrong, and the Agency spent resources chasing the person who wasn't after me? Not that it mattered anyway. Damani was gone. It was done.

Goddammit, I could never do anything right! Why was everything spinning?

"Hey," Jo said, her soothing hand gripping my shoulder. "Anna's safe where she is, and if you don't want to be alone, you can stay in my extra bedroom. Weasel would be happy to see you."

I took a deep breath, trying to quiet the roaring in my ears. Normally, I found Jo's energy soothing, but as she stepped closer, eyes reflecting increasing agitation, her aura pressing into mine shook me after hours spent holding vigil outside the damn alleyway.

"Uh, it's okay. I'm in the safe house. There's a police officer, and Brittany stays sometimes," I said absently, ears still doing their best impression of the Pacific. I squeezed my eyes closed and willed calmness.

The sound of the last gurney being loaded into the back of the van, the doors slamming in finality, made it that much more difficult.

The van rumbled to life and pulled away from the scene. As it left, a piece of me went with it.

"Oh!" Jo said. "I didn't realize you were . . ."

"Wh—no, nothing like that," I said hastily, heat crawling up my neck. "I appreciate it, but I think it's probably best if I stay in the safe house."

Jo opened her mouth, eyes reflecting worry. She snapped it closed again, jaw clenched.

"Yeah," she said, avoiding my eyes.

Dammit! I was breaking everything tonight.

"Um, I'm sorry," I said, feeling wobbly. "Today's been . . . I'm really not—do I need to make a statement or look at anything right now, or can it wait?"

"Deal with this first. Don't leave the safe house tonight," Jo said. "But yeah, when you've had time to collect yourself. In the morning, maybe? And if you think there's anywhere else someone might look for you . . ."

Screeching claxons blared in my mind. How many of my documents still had my parents' address on them? How many of them were left in the apartment? Oh, God. My mother was going to go absolutely nuclear. But then, what was a more appropriate way to end the night than sending my mother running for her Prozac?

"Can I borrow your phone?" I asked hastily.

At the end of the day, my family was safe, though my mother *had* gone absolutely neurotic and resorted to hysterical crying in an attempt to get me to go to a hotel with them. My apartment with Anna would always feel violated. I still wanted to smack Damani, I wasn't sure who I was supposed to pursue as a suspect, and I just wanted everything to be over. It was too much.

I stumbled into the safe house near midnight, numb.

Are you coming over? Some company would be nice, I texted Brittany from yet another new phone. My old one, like my clothes, would probably be in evidence lockup forever.

Probably not. Not feeling great, Brittany responded. *Freaking nosebleeds today. Sorry.*

She didn't need to apologize. If she needed to process today by herself, I wouldn't hold it against her.

Come get me first thing in the morning, I texted to Damani. *Bring anything you have on Preston. We'll investigate him TOGETHER. TOMORROW.*

I threw the phone on the nightstand and collapsed into bed. I was asleep before I could check for a reply.

He never sent it anyway.

CHAPTER 16

There are some nights I look back on and wish I'd done everything differently. This was one of them.

Hadley . . .

My eyes flew open, jolted awake by . . . something. I blinked, confused by the darkness, and reached for my cell phone on the nightstand. It momentarily blinded me as the screen leaped to life in an assault of light and color.

It was 4:18 a.m.

I groaned and rolled over, tucking one arm under my pillow and nestling my head into the crook of my elbow. Between the grief of losing more friends and the emotional roller coaster caused by the break-in, yesterday had been a never-ending hell, and it was too damn early for my nightmares to keep me up. Just a few more hours, and I might finally put the flames to rest.

I settled deeper into my blankets, not exactly content knowing this was it—I'd go no further after today—but mollified by the understanding that I'd done all I was capable of. Closing my eyes with a detached sigh, I pushed away regret, accepting that doing the right thing didn't always feel right at the time.

Hadley . . .

I gasped, rigid in bed, caught in the awkward limbo between sleep and consciousness. I must have dozed—

HADLEY . . .

I sat up. I was not dreaming.

Please, Hadley . . .

"Damani?" I asked the dark, recognizing the echoing voice.

I reached for the lamp on the nightstand. A flood of light banished any remaining grogginess, and starkly aware, I surveyed my bedroom. Grabbing my phone, I threw my comforter off and stumbled into the living room.

Empty.

Are you talking to me? I texted Damani.

I shifted nervously from foot to foot each moment there was no reply. The text remained unread.

My hammering heart thundered in the silence.

The still-dangling ceiling fan swung above me, and I took a steadying breath, forcing calm. The fan's swaying slowed as I tried to force reason before fear.

If I could hear him, he was close. I rushed to the front door. It opened with a jarring creak, and the stale, cool air of the hallway greeted me.

Silence. No one was there. The only people I sensed nearby were sleeping neighbors.

"Damani?" My voice rang off the concrete walls before being swallowed by the night. "You out here?"

A car engine hummed nearby, and a rhythmic rumble signaled another vehicle crossing the nearby train tracks.

Goosebumps rose on my arms. "Damani? Are you okay?"

Please, Hadley. I need you . . .

Adrenaline lanced through me like a shot. I ran from the apartment and threw myself into the stairwell door.

Drawn by his phantom voice, I followed a crackling, electric pull downward, not stopping even as I lost my footing and stumbled in the darkness.

He *had* to be close, and I had to reach him. A flood of panicked urgency drowned my mind, my breath quickening into short pants as I gulped for air.

He gulped for air. Something was very wrong.

The wall was cold and rough against my back as I slumped into it. It was musty and dark, and the claustrophobia induced by the inhospitable, stark basement walls shifting in and out of focus made the situation even more unbearable as I doubled over, a groan of agony escaping clenched teeth. I pressed my hands against the pulsating fire where my core had once been.

I nearly slipped down the stairs. No, that wasn't me. Damani. Damani needed me *now*. I careened out the door at the bottom of the stairwell, my pace never faltering as I gasped for a lungful of cool night air.

Oh, God. Breathing hurt.

"Help!" I screamed into a listless night.

The surreal stillness was at stark odds with the raging inferno eating away at my abdomen, driving me barefoot toward the cop car parked in the street. I slipped off the curb, ignoring the pang in my ankle as I focused on the police cruiser that meant help. The police cruiser hummed in the dark, twin beams of light from the headlights cutting into the night, yet sat eerily still under the glow of a streetlight. The engine was running, but it was vacant.

Where was Texting Officer?

"Hello?" I limped closer, ankle throbbing, but faltered at the sight of the driver's-side door hanging open, urgent pinging voicing the vehicle's unheeded protests. The officer was nowhere to be seen.

"Chr—" I started, but that wasn't right. "Cha—?"

God*dammit!* What was his name?

Damani's unspoken, jumbled pleading failed to make sense in my mind, and another wave of agony burned through my belly.

My knees buckled, threatening to give out in the street. I was losing him.

The cruiser didn't matter. The officer wasn't there, and Damani needed me *now*.

I bolted down the sidewalk in my pajamas, my bare feet raw against an unforgiving ground. The windows along the street remained dark. Not a single car passed on the road. An otherworldly stillness hung in the air, a blissfully oblivious world sleeping through my sobs begging for help.

No one was coming.

Going . . . to . . . kill me . . .

Damani's fear struck me, tearing and clawing in its primal urgency, and I gasped. A forlorn house lurked ahead, an abandoned husk that had once been a home. Its windows were boarded up and its roof caved inward, graffiti tagging the front door.

Damani was there.

"Okay. Okay," I said, trembling. I punched in the code to the cell phone I had miraculously held onto, my hands shaking.

Texting Officer might be missing, but Damani still needed help, and he needed help *now*.

The lock screen flickered and buzzed as I typed in the wrong passcode.

"No, no, *no*!" I yelled, typing the wrong code again. Didn't I just use it? This was not the time for my memory to pull its shit!

My insides wrenched as the phone locked me out, cutting me off from my only other options for help.

I cast one fleeting glance at the cop car down the street, the cruiser still empty. The officer meant to protect me was nowhere to be seen.

A train's wheels clacking on the tracks broke the silence; its shrill whistle wailed in the night. The sound faded, leaving only my ragged breathing.

I was alone.

I stared up at the dismal house, pulse pounding.

The front door hung ajar, the interior of the home pitch-black through the cranny.

I rushed for it.

I shoved the door open, and the maw of the ruined home swallowed me. Outside, the night remained still, my disturbance already forgotten.

The front door hit the wall with a *thud!*

I stumbled into a dingy, empty living room. Family portraits might have once hung on the walls, but now they stood vandalized with glaring, inflated letters, the words of no consequence as I barreled through.

"Damani?"

A piece of glass bit into my foot, and I winced. A shattered window was the obvious culprit, its dirty curtains languidly rustling in an invading breeze. I staggered, and my phone slipped from my grasp, thumping on the carpet. Pain blunted by adrenaline, I sucked in a breath and yanked the glass from my sole.

I braced against a stained wall. "Damani?"

The absence of the anguish that had called to me became a deafening silence threatening the worst, urging me forward. I left the phone behind. It was useless anyway.

I limped toward the basement door, speckles of blood trailing on the tacky, discolored carpet.

I didn't register the fact that an entirely different blood trail guided my way.

As I reached for the doorknob, a whisper of caution nudged me. I had no idea what waited for me.

It didn't matter.

In the time it took for one last shuddering breath, I threw the door open. Clawing at the rail, I limped down the dark stairwell to the basement. My breath hissed as my bloody foot met each splintered stair.

The walls pressed inward as I descended, and not even the air moved. Only my jagged, panicked breaths kept me company. Every muscle in my body twitched for me to turn and run, but I didn't. I wouldn't leave Damani alone.

Moonlight seeped in from a small slitted window, the only light in the basement. Damani was slumped on the floor, his fingers clutching his side. A dark stain was partially visible behind them.

He groaned at the sound of my shuffling feet. I gasped a sob of relief that he was still breathing. I rushed to him, and he swayed, barely remaining in a seated position.

"I'm here. Stay with me," I begged, placing my hands on either side of his face and patting his cheeks. His eyes momentarily widened in recognition before becoming half-lidded and wandering again.

Oh, God. He was really hurt. I squinted at the basement, eyes adjusting to the dark too slowly. If there was another exit, I couldn't see it. The stairs were the only way out, and I wasn't sure Damani could climb them. The window wasn't an option; it was too small for an adult. Why the hell did I forget the passcode to the damn phone? He needed help *right now!*

"I . . . I knew you'd hear me," Damani slurred.

"What'd he do?" I asked, not sure where to examine first.

I pulled his hands away from his side and swallowed a retch.

It was bad. Oh, God, it was so bad. I couldn't tell if the wound went from front to back. The growing, dark stain obscured my view. My understanding of human anatomy was abysmal. I had no idea if the wound was fatal—if anything vital was there—and the damn thing wouldn't stop bleeding! Trembling, I pressed his hands back into the wound as dark blood pooled and oozed outward. He groaned, neck veins bulging. I applied pressure, warm, sticky blood leaking from between our fingers.

We had to get out of the basement.

"I'm sorry," I whispered, his moans making my stomach clench. "I'm so sorry. It's okay." I trembled, hands shaking as I clutched his.

"He was looking for you," Damani slurred, choking on agony.

"What?" I asked.

The basement suddenly grew colder.

"I heard the cop," he said so faintly I barely heard him. "The woman who came to the alley. I knew it was Preston. When he wasn't home—" He groaned, fighting to stay upright as I struggled to steady him. "I found him here."

"O-okay," I said, pulse thundering. "Is he still here?"

I squinted into the dark, but the corners of the basement were pitch-black, and though Damani was no longer telepathically projecting his pain and his desperate cries for help, I still couldn't feel past the all-encompassing agony and fear rolling off him in waves.

"He left," Damani said weakly. "You were right. He knew I was following him. Knew he couldn't get close, so he used a gun. Didn't even get the door open before—"

"Enough," I said. "Are you hurt anywhere else?"

He winced as I probed for hidden wounds, breath coming out in shuddering groans. His normally dark skin was ashen, and I wasn't sure if it was from blood loss or pain. My hands glistened red in the dim light. He shook his head, confirming my analysis.

Pursing my lips, I leered at the stairs. We had no choice.

"He didn't get you. Not yet," I said, gritting my teeth in resolve. "Put your arm over my shoulder."

"Hadley . . ."

"Get up!" I snapped. "You're not dying. I didn't come down here to watch you bleed out."

He moaned as I shifted his weight and forced one arm around my neck. Straining, I did my best to lift him, his feet pushing feebly against the floor.

He gritted his teeth, the sound he forced through them something between a groan and a roar. Halfway up, his eyes rolled back.

I gasped. "Damani! *Stay with me!*"

His legs gave out, and we teetered backward, the wall catching us.

I managed to drag us into a standing position by sheer willpower alone, braced against cold stone.

Damani wore a dazed expression, sweat beading his pallid brow, but by some miracle, he was still conscious.

"Walk," I gasped, staring at the stairs with dread.

Damani gave a single nod, breathing heavy and ragged.

I pushed away from the wall and practically dragged him, lurching and stumbling. We made it a halting yard before he swayed and staggered.

His knees buckled, and we both went down. He collapsed on his side, moaning. His face grew increasingly ashen, shuddering as sweat slicked his skin.

I scrambled on my hands and knees, pulling his shirt away to reveal ragged flesh. Was the bleeding increasing?

Fuck! I shouldn't have moved him!

"I can't," Damani said. "You need to get help."

I looked up the stairs, a sense of foreboding smothering me. "I'll levitate you. Like the pen. I can do it."

"No," he panted. "You can't risk forgetting. He's coming for you."

"I can do it!" I cried, even though I knew I couldn't. "I'm *not* leaving you here!"

"Hadley, *please*."

He was right. Dragging him three feet left us both trembling on the floor, and he was barely conscious. I couldn't drag a bleeding, semi-conscious adult twice my size up the stairs. I couldn't use my telekinesis and risk a memory lapse, coming to in the living room, oblivious to the past half hour as a serial killer stalked us from behind.

My phone was a useless brick, but the police car was down the street. Texting Officer would be back. He would see me. I could do it.

"If anyone but me comes down those stairs, you fry them," I ordered him, frustrated tears sliding down my cheeks.

His head flopped in weak acknowledgment, but staring at his pale, clammy face and unfocused eyes, I doubted he could generate a spark, let alone throw a bolt capable of stopping an attacker.

But I had to go. Adrenaline driving me, I ignored my throbbing feet and bolted up the stairs.

I should have sensed the black waves. Too late, I heard crackling flames from the past and the cry of a phantom child.

I never made it through the door. As I reached the top of the stairs, it flew open. A boot connected with my hip, and I felt every stair as I plunged downward, never having time to realize what had happened. A pop came from somewhere deep within me, and reality became anguish.

A collision halted my tumble across the floor. A moan told me it was Damani, and we both curled into ourselves, whimpering. My breath came out in shuddering gasps, too winded to scream despite a searing, stabbing pain emanating from my shoulder.

"Run," Damani warned weakly. He was almost drowned out by my ringing ears.

Too late. Damani's wide eyes were the last thing I saw, his hand feebly reaching for me as something slipped over my head and *tightened*.

My breath cut off with a surprised gasp. Someone wrenched my arm, and I shrieked. My presumably dislocated shoulder flared white-hot pain in protest.

My attacker dragged me across the floor, my screams meaning nothing to him. I flailed, desperately clawing at the cloth material covering my head with my free hand, nails tearing at my throat as I attempted to wrench it off. It wouldn't budge.

I couldn't see. I didn't know where he was or what he was doing.

Damani did. I saw Preston Weiss through his eyes.

Gone was the beautiful boy who had sat in the Agency's interrogation room, bright-blue eyes sparkling as if in amusement. Disheveled hair masked those same blue eyes, sparkle long snuffed out. Unfathomable voids replaced them, the raging flames burning behind them visible only to me.

"*Help!*" the phantom boy screeched in my mind, burning over and over again in an endless cycle. Preston's mind burned me as if the imaginary flames had consumed his very soul, devouring every shred of light or goodness he might have once possessed until only hate incarnate remained.

Whatever Preston Weiss was now, it wasn't human. I revolted against the unnaturalness of his mind, desperately clawing for freedom as I realized monsters were real.

Damani watched helplessly as Preston dragged me, kicking and screaming for my life, before slamming me against a wall. My head bounced off with a sickening thud that hurt as much as it was loud. Stars exploded across a sea of blackness, my teeth rattling from the force. Blood from a bitten tongue flooded my mouth. Damani's hands sparked once, but the blood loss had taken its toll. Sparks died on his fingertips; there was nothing he could do.

"*Help!*" the little boy's cry flooded my churning mind.

Just keep looking at me, I silently pleaded as Damani's sight faded at the edges. I had never done this outside a pen, but we were both going to die if I didn't try.

Damani saw Preston in front of me, haggard, pallid face and gaunt frame in stark contrast with the frat boy who had once taunted a roomful of federal agents.

I reached out, and Preston gasped as I telekinetically gripped him, lifting him off the ground. A white-hot pulse of pain burrowed into my skull, and I whimpered. Too much. I couldn't split my focus as I levitated the serial killer into the air. I retreated from Damani's mind, resolving to hold our attacker long enough to get the bag off my head. I gasped in relief as the pain eased.

Blind again, I couldn't see the knife coming.

A cold kiss blossomed across my abdomen, followed immediately by an agonizing, radiating fire that spread in all directions from my midsection.

I clutched my stomach, the pain exploding from my middle beyond comprehension, and a thick, warm substance oozed out of me, flowing over my fingers. The overwhelming stench of copper choked me. There was no scream, just an almost inaudible gasp of incomprehension as my body turned into its own prison, trapping me in hell.

"Hadley!" Damani whimpered, a volume of grief spoken with one cry.

I was dead. I knew I was dead, even if my body hadn't realized it yet. My knees gave way, as did my hold on my killer. Preston Weiss and I fell to the ground at the same time.

I wasn't going to get up again.

Preston grunted as he hit the ground, but the impact was hardly enough to deter him. He stood, triumph radiating from him in waves that barely broke my awareness.

"*Freak*," he hissed.

I shuddered as a cold kiss of metal tenderly stroked my arm, as gentle as a lover but promising something much different.

"Mommy! Help!"

Leaving me bleeding on the floor, Preston approached Damani, confident and unhurried.

His intentions projected loudly from the diseased abscess that was his mind. He would come back for me, and I would suffer. It wouldn't be fast, not if he could help it.

He'd wanted this for Wildfire but had been robbed of the pleasure. He'd grown to hate me nearly as much, and perhaps I'd fill the void of need her death had left.

Hadley . . . Damani pushed through the unrelenting pain that was now my reality, and for a brief moment, I saw again, gifted one last glimpse of the world, ugly as it was. Preston had him by the arm, dragging him toward me, but Damani's focus was on me.

He knew. He knew it was too late, and his sorrow was almost keener than my pain. He was sorry. So, so sorry. I was too.

Damani's voice was a comfort to my mind. *It's okay to get scared, Hadley* . . .

My faltering pulse thundered in my ears, heart straining as my life force seeped out of me. When had it gotten so cold? My hands shook, making it impossible to keep pressure on the wound stretching from hip to hip, turning my entire world into searing agony.

How was it possible to feel so much pain? My hands slipped, and I surrendered to the inevitable, still. The inane desire to laugh filled me, though I remained silent.

Preston was too brutal. He wasn't going to get what he wanted from me.

Flashes of thought darted through my mind. Madison's face, slowly graying as I kneeled over her, praying for her to live. Alice's hair snarled by waves, obscuring vacant eyes. Navin, breathing his last breath in Brittany's arms. Wildfire, Gladys, Glenn, and Tom . . . Someone would have to find us too. I wished I could tell them I was sorry for doing this to them.

Someone had to call my mom.

Weasel wouldn't understand why I didn't come back for him.

Damani's son . . .

Preston threw Damani beside me. His heart raced from the thrill of the hunt coming to its bloody conclusion. The electrokinetic, brother of the firestarter, both hated for horrors their kind had inflicted on him in the past, and the telepath who had eluded him for so long would finally meet their fate.

Flames caught the curtains. The ceiling succumbed to rippling waves of red and orange. A little boy cried.

Hadley, get scared . . .

The bag still plunged my world in blackness, but a rushing sensation told me it was almost over. To be unconscious for the end would be a mercy.

You can get out of this, Hadley. You can do it. Get scared.

It finally dawned on me what Damani was asking.

"No," I moaned, though no one heard it. My body wouldn't respond.

Hadley . . .

It's okay . . .

Something warm sprayed me. A gagging, choking sound filled the air. Then, silence. A ripple passed through reality, as gentle as a moth's wings beating against the night. With it went the sensation of crackling electricity, and I felt the agonizing second I was left alone with Preston Weiss.

Hands gripped me.

CHAPTER 17

I became aware of the smell first. Sweet, hot antiseptic blanketed me. I followed the strange aroma out of the dark; light against my eyelids greeted me next. An occasional *beep!* from nearby or a *click!* from farther away faded in and out. Rough cloth swathed my skin save for where a tightness encircled my middle, but that melted away in time. Warmth came and went—a pressure in my fingers or a gentle caress across my cheek. I lay there in limbo—between consciousness and unconsciousness—for what felt like years.

Then, discomfort. A deep ache radiated from my arm. I flexed my hand, and the pain grew sharper.

I groaned.

"Hadley?" A whisper so soft I thought I imagined it. Anna?

My eyes didn't want to open. Slowly, I lifted the invisible anchors that kept my eyelids closed—kept me out of the light. Night had fallen by the time I willed myself back into the world. The room was dark, curtains drawn, though filtered light from a streetlight snuck its way inside, harsh against my eyes. I turned away. Glaring indicator lights embedded in cold machinery glowed around me, and a steady, rhythmic beeping grew faster. I had the strangest sense of déjà vu . . .

"Hadley? Dan, she's waking up! Hadley, can you hear me? It's Mom!"

I clenched my eyes closed against past memories. Overwhelmed by stimuli, I pressed my cheek into a scratchy pillow. I flinched as warm flesh—hot like fire— gripped my hand too tightly. Every sensation felt raw, as if I hadn't used any of my senses in a very long time.

"Hadley, can you hear me?" Anna asked.

I gave a single weak nod. I tried to open my mouth. It was dry, and the movement hurt my jaw. I licked my lips and forced my eyes back open. Anna's tear-streaked face swam into view above me.

"Do you know who I am?" she choked. Dark circles under her bloodshot eyes became prominent as she leaned closer. She fidgeted with the blankets around me, tucking and untucking the scratchy cloth, her hands trembling.

"Hadley, it's Mom, honey! What's wr—Hadley, what are you doing? Dan, what's she doing?"

"An-na," I croaked, struggling with the syllables.

A strangled sob escaped her. She shuddered a gasp of relief, as if she'd been holding her breath. She clamped a hand to her mouth as tears streamed down her cheeks, her shoulders trembling.

"W-wuh . . . hap . . ." I stumbled over the words, so low I wasn't sure I was audible. "Wuh hap-p-en?"

Sniffs and beeps punctuated tense silence as the seconds dragged on. Anna hiccupped, struggling to form words. I tried not to flinch as she pulled a tangled strand of hair from my face, tucking it behind an ear. I wanted to sit up, to ease the dull ache and stiffness in my body, but the mere thought drained me. Anna slumped into a chair beside the bed, and I realized she'd sat in it all night, waiting for me to wake up.

Anna never let go of my hand, as if afraid I'd slip away again if she let go.

"What do . . . What do you remember?" Anna finally asked. She couldn't meet my gaze.

My gut clenched from memories she tried to shield me from: the sweet fragrance of lilies at odds with the smell of recently churned earth, the eerie stillness of a dark-clad crowd as a single man's consolatory speech competed with the whimpers of a child.

A basement scene oozed across my mind, a dark excavation in the earth that felt as desolate as a tomb. I could still smell mold and oppressive dampness in the air, feel the staleness as it infiltrated my lungs with every panicked breath.

"D-da-mani?" I asked slowly.

"I'm so, *so* sorry, Hadley," Anna said quietly, her voice breaking. "He didn't . . . he—"

I shook my head. I didn't want to hear it. I *couldn't* hear it. I knew Damani was gone, but I couldn't let Anna say it.

It was real if she said it, and I *couldn't* have failed him. But I had.

My eyes focused on the glow of the streetlight behind Anna. I identified the raw ache in my right arm as an IV. I hated them, but I couldn't muster the ingrained revulsion now. I lay there, numb, and acknowledged a hollow sadness blossoming. Senses dulled by drugs and a deep exhaustion that went beyond physical, detached acceptance was all I had left.

"Do you remember what happened . . . after?" Anna asked after what could have been an hour or a minute.

I remembered searing agony in my stomach, and my hands drifted to the area. I expected to find pain and was surprised when there was none. I clenched my eyes against the memory of the knife tearing through fabric and flesh, of the jarring impact from hitting the ground, of lying there, hearing footsteps come closer. I remembered the horrible emptiness I felt as I reached for the consciousness that had once been beside me, clinging to hope that there was still a spark of life and finding none.

The blankets swathing me were suddenly suffocating. Anna leaped up as I flailed in bed, needing to be free. I struggled to push myself into a sitting position on frail arms that refused to bear weight.

"It's okay. I've got you," Anna cooed, shoving pillows behind me.

I leaned into them, sighing and shoving the oppressive blankets off. Anna remained silent as I closed my eyes and simply breathed, focusing on the thumping in my chest and promising myself I'd never again take it for granted.

Thankfully, nothing blew up. Probably had something to do with the sedative in the IV that made my mouth feel like cotton.

The nurses weren't willing to repeat past mistakes.

"Where's . . . what happened to . . . ?" I tried to ask as the sky turned a lighter blue outside, tears springing to my eyes.

I couldn't say his name.

Piercing blue eyes, wild with rage and an unfathomable bloodlust, haunted me when I closed my eyes. I remembered slipping toward the dark abyss of death, knowing it was forever. Footfalls thumped louder as they came closer, and I knew the end was mere seconds away. I had known with no doubt that there was no hope. No one would be there in time to save me, just like I hadn't been able to save Damani. So many faces flashed before my eyes: Anna, Weasel, Jo, my brother and parents, Mark, and Lilly. In those brief seconds, I knew I would never see them again.

Those final moments—the grief and fear of losing them and a deep regret for the pain my death would cause them—were the worst of my shortened life. How could I do that to them? I recognized the cruel injustice of everything good—and there was *so much* good—being ripped from me just as I recognized it. I screamed against it as a last act of raw, raging defiance. The last thing I remembered was fingers clenching my hair, wrenching my head back to expose my throat, and a monster poised to take everything.

"You . . . um . . ." Anna shifted uncomfortably. "Do you remember how they found your car?"

I nodded numbly, though I couldn't comprehend how the day my life restarted five years ago related to where the animal in the basement was now. I slowly became more aware of my body—perhaps the drugs they'd pumped into me were already wearing off. My abdomen felt hollow, and when I shifted, I felt . . . yeah, that was a catheter. I had been unconscious for a while. After all, I had been here once before.

Only this time, five years after I washed up on a beach, my car reduced to scrap metal in a crater on the seafloor, a part of me *wished* my memories had vanished when I'd woken up. I wanted all the tragedy lost to a dark void. I still felt blood on my hands. I still felt the animalistic scream in my throat.

"Hadley," Anna said slowly, bringing me back. Her gray eyes held mine, emotion churning like the stormy sea I'd once escaped. She loved me—had always loved me, even after the person I once was vanished, gone forever.

I glanced down at her hand, still in mine, refusing to let go no matter how long I needed. She was prepared to go through it all again, I realized. I squeezed her hand, feeling everything that could never be put into words. I loved her, too, and as her energy soothed mine, the blood and screams faded, never gone, but not the focus. No, I didn't want to forget Anna. I couldn't imagine life without her.

Concern creased her eyes, and I sensed how badly she wanted to shield me from all the pain, even what had yet to come.

"Tell me," I said.

"You leveled the house," Anna said slowly. "They thought it was a bomb."

Comprehension struck me like Preston's knife. "I killed him?"

"Preston," Anna said. "Yeah, you did. Damani was already . . . You didn't do that, okay? You only stopped the bad guy."

It was quiet for an agonizingly long time, the only sounds coming from the machines that monitored my body. Outside, a touch of orange appeared on the horizon.

"Damani was alive, begging me to save him," I said. "I messed up and killed him."

"Damani messed up when he followed Preston into that house alone. You can't blame yourself for that, but *you* got him, Hadley. He's gone because of you. It's all over because of you. He can't hurt anyone ever again, do you understand?" Anna said firmly, squeezing my hand.

It's okay . . .

Damani's last thoughts echoed in my mind, and I nodded, wanting what Anna said to be true. I was too tired to blame myself anymore.

"I didn't want to kill anyone," I said, needing her to know. I was sure it would hit me later—that I'd taken a life, but at that moment, I had a hard time feeling regret over the monster in the basement.

"I know," Anna said softly. "I'm sorry."

"How am I alive? Why can I remember?" I asked, recalling the gaping wound in my abdomen. Even if I stopped Preston from delivering the final blow, I should have bled to death.

"Jo," Anna said, lips tugging into a grateful smile. "She stayed up all night going over evidence from the break-in. When the officer outside your safe house didn't check in, the station went into a bit of a panic, and then she saw your phone tracker pinging from the house . . ."

"She saved my life."

Again.

"Miss? Are you okay? Can you hear me?"

"She called Mark. The Agency was only a few minutes behind her. Ian got to you in time because of her."

"Are they . . . is everyone okay?"

"Jo was in her cruiser when the house blew. You scared the hell out of her, but she's fine. The officer outside the safe house . . . I'm sorry, Hadley. Preston killed him. Everyone else is a little shaken, but they're okay."

Texting Officer. I still couldn't remember his name. Shamed, I dropped my eyes.

"When did that happen?" I asked, using Anna's left hand as a distraction.

Blushing, she held her hand out to show me the engagement ring.

"Just a few days before . . ." Anna's voice trailed off, and tears pricked at the corners of her eyes again. "We wanted it to be a surprise when we got back, but after they found you, I wasn't sure I'd get the chance to tell you."

"I'm happy for you," I murmured. My voice didn't hold any emotion, but I truly was. "It's about time Elliott listened."

"I should call your mom and dad," Anna said slowly, searching my face for recognition.

"Hadley, stop it! St—help! Someone! We need HELP!"

"Kathy and Dan," I said, answering her implied question while I repressed past memories. "Tell them to bring Collin."

Anna's breath came out in a soft sob, and tears flowed freely down her cheeks once more. "I'm so glad we didn't lose you." She rose and moved toward the door, fishing her cell phone from her pocket.

"Anna?" I called after her. "Do you think they'd let Jo . . . can she bring Weasel?"

Anna laughed through her tears. "Ryker will make the nurses do whatever you want."

Despite the fact the sun was just rising above the treetops, Jo picked up immediately. Anna had barely gotten the words out before Jo said she was on her way. I hadn't expected Jo to show up before 7:00 a.m. with my wriggling ball of fur. Anna gave me a blank stare when I expressed as much. I shut my mouth.

I knew the moment she arrived. My head rose as a press of warmth emanated from the parking lot, growing stronger as it moved through the hospital.

"Please, don't die!" Crashing waves roared in my ears. A seagull cried from above. Footsteps—

Enough. I took a steadying breath.

"Molly!" Jo scolded as skittering nails on linoleum and wet panting warned me of my impending visitor.

A large dog rounded the corner in a burst of energy, zeroing in on my bed in a way that told me she wasn't a stranger to the room.

"Molly, get off her!" Jo exclaimed as Molly, a German Sheppard SDPD K9 unit dropout, dove straight into bed with me. "Watch her IV!"

Weasel apparated from nowhere. He licked my face, paws dancing on my chest. He yapped so vehemently that a nurse popped her head in to tell us he was waking other patients. The nurse shot Jo a look that could melt plastic, but she stopped short of telling her the dogs had to go. Jo and Anna ignored her, struggling to keep tubes and wires away from flailing paws and wagging tails.

"Buddy!" I exclaimed. I rubbed my hands over Weasel's back, fingers mussing his wiry fur as much as the awkward heart monitor on my finger would allow.

I held him close and breathed into his fur, recently bathed, and the world started to feel right again. Molly thrust her head into my hands, refusing to be left out.

"Molly, gentle!" Jo exclaimed, trying to keep the arm with the IV from getting bumped.

We both realized she had hold of my arm at the same time, and she froze, clinging to my elbow and wrist without breathing.

Our eyes met, and I sucked in a breath as a torrent of emotions struck me: elation, fear, excitement, nervousness, grief—just about every emotion a human being could process at once crashed over me. Jo tried— her attempted restraint left her energy tense like a coiled spring—but she couldn't stop the memories that surfaced as reality struck her. I lived. I *actually* lived.

I—no, Jo—stumbled through the debris, ignoring small pebbles that hovered like lightless fireflies, frozen at knee height. They brushed my legs as I pushed through them, though I hardly felt them. My eyes never left the center of the blast where a woman lay supine on a concrete slab, the foundation of what used to be a house. Cracks spiderwebbed outward from her as if she were a fly in a web. The woman's head was covered, and I prayed I was wrong.

I knew I wasn't, but I prayed anyway.

I cleared the ring of debris, pushed outward to circle the woman. The center of the scene was dramatically clear save for a layer of dust that nearly hid the sinister dark splotches dappling the ground.

I dropped to my knees beside the woman. She didn't move, splayed on the ground, unnaturally still. I clawed at a cord lock on a drawstring gym bag, wrenching it off the woman's head. I gasped as Hadley's wan, lifeless face appeared, as motionless and cold as a marble statue.

"Hadley?" I whispered. She didn't move. I leaned forward to shake her but froze as a warm sensation crept through my jeans. I

glanced at the dark pajamas that stuck to Hadley like a second skin, comprehension registering in a startling rush.

Scrambling, I cried out as I peeled away her shirt, gagging at the cavernous wound underneath.

"No, no, no! Don't you dare do this to me," I said, teeth gritted, pressing my hands into the wound and shuddering as warmth oozed through my fingers. "Not to me, Hadley. Please.*"*

A car door slammed behind me.

"Jo?" Mark called. "Where is she?"

"Mark! We need an ambulance! Now!"

Mark's footsteps thundered behind me as he kicked and shoved debris away, clearing a path. He froze, breath leaving him in a strangled cry.

"She's not dead!" I screamed. "Damn it, Mark! Get me an ambulance! She's not dead!"

A pebble floated before me: a beacon of hope. Hadley was still in there, fighting.

"Ian!" Mark bellowed as more slamming car doors echoed in the background. "Somebody get me Ian!"

I swallowed hard against the heartache—the raw desperation—in Jo's memories, unsure if the tears pricking at the corners of my eyes were mine or hers. I'd thought I was alone that night, futilely screaming for help from an uncaring world. Jo had been on her way the entire time.

"Hi, Jo," I said.

Navigating my arms around the dogs, I reached out and wrapped them around her. She shuddered against me, tightening the embrace.

"Thank you," I whispered in her ear.

Her black hair, pulled back in its customary ponytail, tickled my nose. She clung to me, but when Anna shifted in the chair, she broke the embrace. Her eyes glistened, and she blinked rapidly.

"I brought you something," she said, deliberately straightening as she pulled a plastic case from her purse. A metallic CD glinted in the light, "For Hadley #6" written across the surface in black Sharpie. An unexpected wash of regret ran through me as I took the CD. I had been a stupid, *stupid* girl. I never should have pushed her away.

"Thank you," I said, smiling.

Sheepish, she smiled back, and I held her eyes when ours met, searching. A flicker of surprise crossed her face, and she looked away first, fidgeting as a blush colored her cheeks. I brushed my own cheek, again wondering if the warmth I felt was her or me.

Weasel yipped in my face, punctuating his protest with a whine and a sneeze.

"O-*kay*, Mr. Jealous!" I exclaimed, putting my hands back on the demanding mutt.

The new collar on Weasel's neck caught my attention. I took the name tag in my hand and noted the address on the back. It wasn't mine: "If found, please call Jo."

"I'll get it fixed soon," Jo stammered. "Molly chewed the other one, and the doctors weren't sure if . . ." She pursed her lips.

"I'm glad you were looking after him. Thank you." I dropped the tag, not needing any more reminders that I almost didn't come back.

Voices carried down the hall.

Anna got up and poked her head out the door. "Your family's here," she said.

A brief flicker of nervousness crossed Jo's eyes, and I resisted raising an eyebrow.

"What's wrong with her?" a voice shrilled.

"Mrs. Gordon, I need you to calm down. We called Mercy. They'll be here soon, and everything will be all right."

"Mercy?" the voice grew harsher. "My daughter doesn't need that place! She isn't one of those freaks! What the hell have you people done to her?"

"Mrs. Gordon, I need you to c—"

I jerked at the sound of breaking glass, and a nurse rushed to the doorway. Her eyes grew wide at the sight of the shattered window.

"It's okay," she said, holding up a trembling hand. She didn't move past the threshold. "You just sit tight. We're getting you some help, okay? Just—just stay calm, okay, sweetie? Can you do that for me?"

I gritted my teeth against the past. A rush of heat coursed through my blood.

"Here comes the Kathy show," I muttered under my breath, preparing myself for my mother's personality to envelop the room.

Anna's expression told me she wanted to say something, but she held her tongue. A flush of guilt blossomed in my chest. I almost hadn't gotten to wake up to a neurotic mother.

Old habits died about as hard as I did.

The room fell eerily still as a shadow crossed the doorway, my mother's anxious energy preceding her. I braced myself as Kathy Gordon strode in, her blonde highlighted hair somehow perfectly in place. It hadn't even been an hour. When the hell had she found the time to do her makeup? She walked over and slowly sat down in the chair Anna had occupied, setting her purse on the ground. My mother took my hand, brown eyes glistening, and was quiet.

"Hi, Mom," I finally said, fidgeting in contrast to her stillness.

Her blush-colored lips trembled, and she sniffed. "Losing you would have killed me," she choked.

She threw her arms around me, and for a moment, I froze . . . as did hell. Slowly, I wrapped my arms around her, staring at my dad and brother hovering in the doorway, the question of *What the hell?* obvious in my eyes.

"How are you feeling?" my dad asked as my mother clung to me. He looked older, brown eyes bloodshot and graying hair tousled. In contrast to my mother, Dad looked like he'd leaped from bed and thrown on the first clean thing he could find.

"A little rough," I said tiredly.

"But you remember everything?" Collin asked hesitantly. My wiry little brother, pencil thin and not yet having grown into his height, shifted nervously from foot to foot.

"Everything seems to be there," I said, reaching around my mother to tap my temple.

I left it at that. I didn't want to talk about the basement, and mercifully, no one else did either, though the memories danced in their minds: a tube down my throat as I struggled to breathe on my own, the staples holding my stomach together after my intestines had nearly fallen out, the bruises and black eyes from falling down the stairs, and the sling that held my dislocated shoulder in place.

It had been a rough two weeks. The faint scar on my abdomen was the only vestige of that day. That I didn't have an ostomy bag told me Dr. Patterson was a miracle worker. Of course, I had already known that. How could I ever thank him for saving me a second time?

"When do the doctors think I can go home?" I asked Anna, knowing by the dark circles and the fact she could barely stand that she'd been my primary guardian.

"Don't rush to leave," my mother chimed in. "Let the doctors make sure you're okay first."

"You can stay with us, if you'd like," my dad added, looking to my mom for confirmation.

She nodded, eyes alighting in hope. My brother's equally expectant energy radiated across the room. I didn't respond for a moment, wondering instead if I'd woken up in an alternate dimension.

"I'll, uh, I'll think about it," I finally stammered.

Mark and Lilly showed up around 8:00 a.m., and with my hospital room about to burst at the seams, Jo volunteered to take Molly and leave the visit to family. Molly whimpered as Jo guided her toward the door. Weasel squirmed in Anna's arms, realizing he wasn't going with them. An acclimatization period would be required for many of us before life could return to normal.

Normal. I wasn't sure what normal meant to me.

"Officer Ramirez?" my mom said as Jo encouraged her dog around my crowd.

Jo froze, eyes trained on my mom as if she'd just pulled a gun on her.

I swallowed a laugh. So, there was one thing Jocelyn Ramirez was afraid of . . .

"Ma'am?" Jo asked.

"It's good to see you," my mom said.

Jo nodded, mind buzzing. Mom nudged my leg as Jo passed the doorframe, and I nearly jumped. She jerked her head in Jo's direction.

"Hey, Jo?" I called after her before I realized I'd lost my damn mind.

She paused in the doorway.

"Weasel likes the dog beach. Can Molly come some time?" I asked.

Dumb question. Jo was the one who had taken Weasel to the beach for the first time.

Regardless, an unexpected thrill surged through Jo. My own machines chirped in response.

When she responded, though, her voice was even: "What do you think, Molly? Would you like that?"

Molly's tail wagged in response.

"I'll call you soon," I promised.

A grin spread across her face before she vanished from view. I tried to avoid looking at my parents as smugness radiated off my mother. My cheeks burned.

About time, Anna projected at me, also smiling, and the room grew even hotter.

My visitors made room for Mark's hulking form, and he stepped inside, his mass enveloping me in a hug.

"You didn't have to get here so early," I said as Lilly hovered behind him.

"I promised the kid I'd tell her the moment you were up," Mark said in my ear. "She took it hard."

I beckoned Lilly over, and the teenager threw herself on me.

"Gentle," Mark murmured as she curled into me. I stroked her hair as her wracking sobs set off my mom, and within a few seconds, everyone in the room was blinking rapidly and focused on things in the corners.

After that, my day was a revolving door as parahumans from the Agency flooded in, flowers, chocolates, and balloons in tow. Anna left after lunch to reunite Weasel with a patch of grass and our apartment, which she warned me had new locks on the windows and doors I'd have to get used to. She promised to be back later with Elliott and a more substantial dinner than hospital milkshakes. By that, I was pretty sure she meant pizza. I doubted I could keep it down or that the nurses would let me have it, but I smiled anyway. My parents left late in the afternoon.

"When you're ready to visit," my mom said. "There's peanut butter ice cream in the freezer."

I gaped at my mom and dad, mouth opening and closing like a goldfish, before finally nodding.

"I'm glad you're okay," my shell-shocked brother told me as he gave me a parting hug.

"Keep an eye on Mom for me," I whispered into his ear. "Something's wrong with her."

Collin chuckled. He tried to pull away, but I held him closer.

"And calm down. I'm okay."

My brother's face crumbled, and blinking hard, he said his goodbyes, rushing out the door before his macho-man facade could take a hit.

For a short time, after a parade of friends and family, I was alone.

My last visitor arrived late in the day, the click of her shoes signaling her arrival. She stopped outside the door, just out of view, and stood there for a long time.

"You can come in, Mrs. Aluko," I finally called to her.

Damani and Janelle's mother stepped through the doorway, clutching her purse in both hands. She twisted the handles, and I remembered Damani's similar nervous habit with a grief-stricken pang.

"I hope I'm not intruding," she said, shifting her weight from foot to foot as she looked past me out the window.

I motioned to the chair beside my bed, and she stepped around and sat down. She clutched at her purse for several more minutes before she spoke.

"I'm afraid George wasn't feeling well, but he wanted me to tell you he's glad you're awake."

I nodded, unsure how to respond.

"Damani spoke highly of you," Maya Aluko said. "I have to admit, I think my boy was a little taken with you."

A smile tugged at my lips, but it didn't quite form.

"He's . . . he was good at seeing the potential in people," I said quietly. "Even if they can't see it themselves."

"Hardheaded and willful is more like it," Maya said, chuckling.

This time, I laughed.

"I came to see you after . . . I came to see you. You look better."

"Thanks," I said weakly.

We were both quiet. Finally, she pulled something from her purse. She slipped a photo into my hands, and my jaw tightened as Damani smiled at me. Brittany and I stood on either side of him. He held up a crushed can, grinning and pointing at it like it was a prized bass. I remembered the day but not taking the photo.

"I wanted to thank you," Mrs. Aluko said gently, closing my hands around the picture.

"Thank me?" I asked. I couldn't look at her, my eyes focused on the picture.

Where did my quarter go?

"You stopped the men who took both of my babies. I don't think I can thank you enough."

"I'm not so sure they would be gone if it weren't for me," I whispered.

Mrs. Aluko chuckled, though there was little mirth in it.

"Let me tell you something about my children," Mrs. Aluko said. "I knew they would be trouble from the moment they were born. I knew my family had the fire gene in our blood—my mama and her mama had it. I

381

wasn't blessed with the gift, but I knew my children would be. They both started early. Janelle started burning her teddy bears when she was six months old, and the first time Damani shocked me—boy, was that something!"

I focused on her, visions of laughing children dancing in her mind. Maya's eyes looked far off, lost in distant memories that played out for me to view. I saw Damani swaddled in a blanket and smiled.

"Those two were always running toward danger," Mrs. Aluko continued. "The two of them together—I don't know how I handled them. Janelle had her sense of purpose, and we both know Damani was uncontrollable. They were born to fight for others. My babies burned bright and did their jobs with an unbridled passion, but there was a price in that. They thought they were invincible. I always worried that one day they'd meet someone stronger than them, and then they did. I don't think you played any part in what happened. They always would have run headlong into those terrible men, regardless of the consequences. It's who they were."

"I don't understand how you can forgive me when I was there for—I was there for both of them and failed both times."

"I know what Damani thought about it," Maya Aluko said. "He came by the day you two caught the men who killed . . . who killed Janelle. He called you a hero. He said it wouldn't have happened without you. I think the biggest tragedy would be if any of those men were still out there, terrorizing people. *You* stopped them."

Maya patted my hands with the picture folded in them. "I think the thing that would hurt Damani and Janelle would be if they died in vain—if parahumans were still terrorized simply for existing, and if monsters were still making the world harder and scarier for people who did nothing but live their lives just like everybody else. You made sure what they stood for lives on, and that gives me some comfort, even if it doesn't bring them back. I needed to tell you that. Damani said you have a habit of being hard on yourself. He wouldn't want you blaming yourself, and neither do I."

It's okay . . .

"I—" I began, eyes focused on my hands.

"Hadley," Maya said firmly, interrupting me. "Drowning yourself in guilt is not how you honor my son's memory. It's not what he'd want."

I didn't know how to respond.

"Are you going to be okay?" I asked instead.

"It'll take time," she said.

I wrapped my hand around hers and nodded.

"Would it be okay if I visited again?" Maya asked. "I think it would do Jamie some good if he could meet you."

I nodded, trying to swallow the lump stuck in my throat.

"If you don't mind," I said, voice shaking. "You have beautiful memories. Could you stay a while longer?"

She smiled at me. "I'd like that too."

They sent me home the next day, though I had weeks of therapy in my future, both physical for the shoulder I couldn't lift all the way and mental for the emotional scars hidden just below the surface. My body was so weak that making it from Anna's car to the couch left me exhausted for the rest of the day. My mother fought us harder than I expected, insisting that I come home, but the danger was past, and as grateful as I was to have a chance to rebuild my relationship with my mother, let alone have the feelings reciprocated, I needed time. Anna finally convinced her that, between herself and Elliott, I'd have every need met. It hurt her feelings, but my mother was not what I needed. Not yet.

I spent two days lying on the couch, only getting up for the bathroom or the fridge and to move to my bed. Anna acted as a round-the-clock nurse, Elliott stopping by frequently to help, both understanding I was processing, but I resolved to be okay. If not for me, then for everyone else.

When Jo called, I answered, and she didn't mind that our conversations never lasted long, exhaustion coming easily. Weasel acted as my sentry, tucked under one arm as we watched TV together. When I became too tired to watch TV, Weasel and I crawled into bed at any hour and slept.

It was a good tired, and each morning I awoke, I felt like Damani's last thoughts might be true. After everything, I'd be okay. I wanted to be.

Weasel growled early on the third morning. At least I'd had that long.

CHAPTER 18

A shape slunk through the shadows, ragged breathing echoing against block walls. Unintelligible whispers were punctuated with low growls, the click of claws on concrete sharp in contrast. The prowler stuck to the dark recesses of the room as I took my seat at a cold metal table. I squinted at a black corner, cast in deep shadow despite the glaring light above, a mere bulb lacking a shade. The corner appeared empty, and yet . . .

A man across from me whimpered, wrists chained to the table and head obscured by a black hood. I turned my attention to him, the unknown creature in the corner temporarily forgotten.

"I need to know who the killer is," I said.

"I already told them!" the man shrieked.

Whimpering continued under the hood. I leaned forward, taking the man's hands in my own. He jerked back, the shackles on his wrists slamming against the table with a metallic clang as he fought against me.

"Right," I said, venom dripping from my voice. "Preston, right?"

"Yes!" the man yelled. "Yes, it was Preston!"

"You know," I said, voice promising violence. "I really hurt Preston. You don't want me to hurt you, do you?"

"Please!" the man whimpered. "I told you who the killer is!"

"You told lies!" I snapped.

The man screamed. He writhed in my grip, veins bulging from his neck as he wailed. I winced, breathing deep as searing pain crept up my arms. A sensation akin to my nerves being flayed one-by-one spread further and further. When sweat began beading my forehead, I let go. I breathed deep, refusing to show the pain. I couldn't let them see the pain.

"Tell the truth and all of this ends," I insisted.

"I told the truth!"

I braced myself, jaw clenched as I squeezed the man's fingers. Nerve pain shot up my arms once more. The man wailed as I clutched his digits, my own breaths coming out in ragged shudders.

When I let go, Preston Weiss smiled at me, once again the beautiful boy I first met.

"Too late," he goaded, his teeth flashing as his triumphant cackle echoed in the room.

The shadows shifted, and I squinted, tracking the animal-like shape as it moved along the wall. Its haunches bunched, poised to strike. Yellow eyes blinked from the blackness. Weasel growled, low and sharp.

"Weasel?" I asked as the abomination separated from obscurity, catlike haunches bunched as it slunk toward my dog, helpless in the center of the room. A dog's head, snout flat and

sharp teeth protruding from a mouth dripping red-tinged foam,
swiveled to home in on my helpless pet.

"Weasel, run!" I shouted as the apex predator pounced.

Weasel growled again. Then, silence. Wrenched from
sleep, I bolted upright in bed, sensing the intruder too
late.

"Weasel!" I squeaked in the dark, reaching for his
fuzzy body.

My hand brushed against furless human skin, and I
recoiled.

"Hi, Hadley," a strange masculine voice growled.

The sound I made in response was somewhere
between a scream and a gasp. I blindly lashed out,
swinging toward the voice, my arm passing through
empty air as I missed.

Weasel screamed, a keening cry that sent my heart
racing. Then, it cut off.

The room was silent.

Eyes still unadjusted to the dark, my hands raked the
bed, searching for my dog.

"Behave," the intruder commanded.

"P-please. Leave him alone," I whimpered. "What do
you want?"

I jerked as a finger caressed my face. A rough,
calloused hand stroked my cheek before running
through my hair. I shuddered, frozen in place. A ringing
echoed in my ears, and the grasping fingers withdrew.

"Didn't you ever wonder why the bombs never
matched? Why those second two were so sophisticated,
so perfectly tailored for their purpose? You never
wondered how Preston was always in the right place at
the right time? How I made sure he always had an alibi
after you identified him? Wasn't it so strange how those
Sons of Gaia bastards took back the stabbings? Surely

you noticed how they seemed to have no memory of it at all? Hell, did you forget all about the brain bleeds? That right there should have told you!" the man said, his voice a knife cutting through the dark. "None of that seemed weird to you?"

I remained perfectly still and silent, barely breathing.

Beside me, a lamp flipped on, flooding the room with light. A surge of adrenaline coursed through my veins as I was temporarily blinded, and I blinked furiously to restore my senses.

Regaining my sight didn't make the situation better.

A man crouched beside my bed, Weasel in one arm, gripped tight to his chest. Weasel remained perfectly still, staring up at the man with wide, panicked eyes, as if he too knew one false move meant disaster.

I stared at the stranger, trying to place him. His appearance—dark, predatory eyes and stringy brown hair, unkept and tousled—was the exact opposite of Preston Weiss's. He clearly knew who I was, but I had never seen the man in my life. I focused on Weasel in his arms, and tears pricked my eyes.

"Let him go," I begged.

The man glanced down, a smirk tugging at his lips. "In a minute. We're talking."

"Okay," I whispered, heart hammering. "Just don't hurt him."

My eyes darted to the doorway and Anna's room across the hall. Anna's door was closed, and I sensed her sleeping inside. She was alive and unhurt, thank God.

I started to scream for help—

Damani's terrified face flashed before my eyes, pain from a gunshot wound wracking his body. Crimson oozed from him, staining my hands, and I couldn't stop it.

The scream died in my throat.

No.

Not Anna. *Never* Anna.

I wouldn't put her in danger.

An unnatural numbness spread through me, and two concrete thoughts shone through the darkness of fear, beacons of light highlighting the only things that mattered: keep him away from Anna and get Weasel back.

My focus returned to the man, afraid I'd drawn his gaze away from me, though my attention had only wavered toward Anna's door for a split second. His lips twitched as my attention flicked back to him, eyes cruel.

Preston Weiss had the same eyes, the same bloodthirsty look as he stood over me with a knife. I sensed the strange man's excitement, like a cat playing with a cornered mouse. I certainly felt like prey.

"You know things won't go well if you use your abilities on me."

He wasn't asking, but I nodded anyway, afraid to make sudden movements. He surveyed me with his eyes, expression an unholy marriage of predatory lust and righteous rage. His eyes lingered on my forehead before traveling downward and resting on my abdomen. Swallowing acrid bile, I resisted the urge to pull my blankets over my body. My fresh scar ignited beneath his gaze; the burning made me squirm.

"Preston was a brutal one. I have to give credit where credit is due: the man was an artist. No abilities and barely more intelligent than livestock, and he still took down six agents with his insipid little knives. Granted, he wanted all of you, but I couldn't let one puppet do all the work, especially after the idiot exposed himself. It would be too obvious, wouldn't it, and I had to see the plan to completion."

He flashed a smile; his yellowed teeth looked like fangs. "Almost done now, aren't we?"

"What do you want?" I asked slowly.

"Take a look at this. Tell me what you think," the man said, ignoring my question.

I flinched as he thrust a phone in my face. Impatient with my lack of focus, he forced the phone closer, and I took notice of the video.

A boat sat quietly and unassumingly anchored in the bay . . . until it didn't. With a low groan of protest, fingers of water emerged from the bay, constricting around the boat for a brief moment before snapping it into splinters. Waves splashed in all directions, water spraying in the air as the vessel was devoured by the deep.

Wait . . . was he? I glanced at Weasel, frozen in his arms, blinking slowly and breathing in shallow gasps. Weasel wasn't remaining still by choice. Realization washed through me like a wave.

He was a parahuman.

Was he controlling—no, wait, a hydrokinetic couldn't do that. I couldn't think straight long enough to figure out what the hell he was.

"Beautiful, right?" he asked, calling my attention back with a jolt.

"Wh—what do you want?" I asked again, hysteria rising in my voice. I tried to swallow it, thinking of Anna in the other room, but what the actual fuck did a sinking boat have to do with a lunatic *parahuman* in my bedroom, and why the hell would a parahuman want to attack me anyway? Hell, why would he want to attack any of us at the Agency? He was one of us!

Anna wasn't. I glanced toward Anna's door again, grateful she was still quiet, though a part of me remained torn between the desire for her to wake up, to hear the man speaking, and call for backup, and the urge to keep her as far away from him as possible. Maybe he didn't know she was here? It had to stay that way.

"Well, honestly, I wanted you dead at first," the man said, bringing me back to attention in a bone-chilling instant. Few things got one's attention quite like the threat of death. "You really pissed me off when you messed things up with the Madison situation. I thought for sure you were going to identify Preston, and then I was going to have to get *another* pawn. Do you have any idea how long it took me to warp that dense oaf's sad excuse for a brain? Oh, sure, there were the others, but Preston was the foundation of the entire operation, don't you see? You do see it, right?"

In a flash, his free hand lashed out and gripped my wrist in a vise, his long thick fingernails digging into my skin. Vertigo seized me, and the room spun. My heart hammered in my chest.

Miraculously, nothing exploded. I held my breath, praying to keep control, to not do anything that might send Anna running into the room or cause this sociopath to hurt Weasel. Hysterically blowing up our furniture could wait until later.

If there was a later.

As it was, I saw no way to escape.

If I tried to use my powers, Weasel . . .

I didn't understand what was wrong with Weasel. He stared at me, eyes rolling in fear, but he neither moved nor made any noise. He was simply . . . paralyzed. Maybe I could . . . but Anna and Weasel were in the apartment, and what the hell was he doing to my dog?

I didn't know what to do. Why didn't I ever know what to do?

I took a gulp of air.

No hysterics, remember?

The man clenched my wrist tighter. Ringing resounded in my ears. I suppressed a wince and breathed deep, willing calm. The man frowned as if disappointed, as if he expected something to happen.

"You know," the man said, maniacal grin reappearing in a blink. "I can make *anyone* do *anything*. At least, I could until the day you and Alice Cho chased Preston through the park. You don't remember—I know, but I grabbed you that day, right after Alice went into the water. It was the perfect opportunity: one touch, and your heart was supposed to stop. Poof! No more Hadley Gordon to get in the way." His smile fell. "Imagine my dismay when it didn't. You just—*poof!*—got all glassy-eyed for a minute and came to, not knowing which end was up. A freaking brain lesion! *Really?* You're the most ineffective agent the Agency has ever had the displeasure to employ, and the fact that you're completely fucked-up is what saved you!"

I was right. He was a parahuman. I didn't know what kind. Could hydrokinetics even cause a heart attack with one touch? Strokes for sure, but heart attacks? It didn't matter. I didn't want him to stick around long enough to figure it out.

I glanced back at Anna's door. He'd kill her if she came in, I was certain of it, and the longer the crazed parahuman yelled at me—

"Oh, she's not going to wake up yet," the man said. "We need to have our conversation in private. If you're good, I'll wake her *and* the dog."

The earth seemed to collapse beneath me. He had found her, and I'd slept through it.

"Don't hurt her!" I begged.

A fracture appeared in my resolve like a crack in a dam. I moved involuntarily toward Anna's door, but the man squeezed my wrist again, nails burrowing in for good measure.

"Oh, relax. Killing her won't do me any good. Not right now, at least," the man said, rolling his soulless eyes. "That would mess up the plan!"

I had to get to Anna. I had to deescalate the situation. What had they taught us about crisis negotiation at the Agency? Or was it a class from school? It didn't matter. They had a name for what I had to do, and I scrambled desperately for the knowledge I prayed was stored in my brain, not lost to some godforsaken lapse. Step one was listening. Step two: who the hell knew? I couldn't remember, but screw it, I'd wing it. I didn't have a choice.

"What plan? What do you want?" I asked again, forcing my eyes away from Anna's door to hold my attacker's attention. "How can I help you?"

"I tried to be fair," the man said. "It was only supposed to be the Agency at first, but the world . . . it just isn't right. The system needs to be *completely* dismantled and reconstructed."

"What was supposed to be just the Agency?" I said, trying to project empathy with my trembling voice.

I couldn't challenge him. I had to keep him talking— agree with whatever he said and keep him calm. I did my best to drop my shoulders and relax my back. If he didn't think I would run, maybe he would let go.

Now, if only I could figure out what the hell he was rambling about.

"No one cares about us," the man continued. "They want to control us—but we can't let them!"

He wasn't making sense. I tried to still my pounding heart and focus my mind. If I could just reach out and see what he was thinking, I might be able to get the upper hand and steer the conversation in the right direction.

His eyes flicked toward me, pupils contracting like a predator about to pounce. "Don't do that! You stay out!"

I froze, eyes wide. What the *hell?* Non-telepaths couldn't feel telepathy!

"You shouldn't be on their side," he said. "Not after what they did to you."

"*What?*" I blurted. I snapped my mouth shut, concerned I'd said the wrong thing.

Smiling that twisted, predatory smile, the man laid Weasel on the bed. My heart skipped a beat when Weasel didn't move, sprawled across the sheets in a heap, his fur rumpled. I experienced a moment of relief when his chest rose and fell.

Then, the parahuman's focus rested exclusively on me. Never releasing my wrist, the man rose and crept toward me. I tried not to wince as the bed creaked under his weight. I kept my eyes focused on him, trying not to let fear reflect on my face. My bravado extended *only* to my face. Internally, I was certainly losing the battle. He could probably feel my hammering pulse in my wrist.

"The Library Lounge," the man said, his breath hot against my face.

I frowned involuntarily. Why did that sound familiar?

"Do you remember your birthday party? You told your mother you were going to the library with Anna. It wasn't exactly a lie, you naughty girl."

I opened my mouth and closed it again. He was baiting me. That was in the newspaper: "Inebriated Girl Plunges Car into Ocean after Binge Drinking at The Library Lounge," or something to that effect.

"I remember it," he whispered. "It wasn't like they told you."

I didn't move as his face came within inches of mine. I wouldn't react like prey. I hadn't enjoyed my first experience with a hunter.

"They don't trust us, so they hunt us. They hunted you. You were lucky. You fought and got away."

"Who hunted us?" I whispered, playing into the narrative.

"*The Agency,*" the man hissed between clenched teeth. "But not the one everyone else sees—the other one. The one they hide. We're their *hostages*, and the things they make us do . . ."

He was an inch from my face, looking directly into my eyes. His reflected an uncanny intelligence. He was mad for sure, but I was a dead fool if I took him for stupid.

"We have to make them stop."

"What are we going to do?" I whispered, praying my choice of words wouldn't be lost on him.

Slowly, a grin broke across the man's face. I waited for an agonizing eternity as he hovered over me, flashing his teeth at me like a predator closing in for the kill.

"You'll help me make them stop," he said slowly.

It was a statement, not a question, and it terrified me. "Yes," I choked.

"I want Kelley," the man said. "It's always been Kelley."

Marshall Kelly? Ryker's boss?

"I don't—"

"You're close to Kelley. You were on the news together, Impulse and Kelley."

I bit back a retort. I couldn't argue with him.

He was relaxing, and though I didn't see an escape yet, I also wasn't dead.

"What do I need to do?"

"I want him dead."

"Wh—why?"

"I want him dead. You agreed to help. Does it matter why?" the man said, grinning.

"I just want to understand," I said.

"They're too smart. They won't believe it if I do it. You're the hero. It has to be you. They'll listen to you."

"Tell me what Kelley did. If—if Kelley has done something, there has to be a way—"

"You don't believe me!"

"No!" I shouted as he rose, a wild look in his eyes. I'd lost him. I was stupid if I thought I ever really had him. "I believe you!"

"They didn't believe me either! I tried to get them to listen!"

"Then let's go tell them together! It's like you said— I'm the hero! Let's go tell them together, and they'll believe it!" I yelled. I didn't know who the hell "them" was, but I'd agree to anything if it meant Anna and Weasel would be safe. Well, almost anything.

"No!" he snapped, slamming his free hand on the bed and facing me with veins bulging in his neck. "Kelley controls them all! Kill him, and we're all free!"

He was out of control. He was going to kill me, Weasel, and Anna.

"Okay," I whispered. "Okay. I'll do what you want. I'll do it. Just give me back Anna and Weasel, and we'll do it your way. I'll do whatever you want."

"I don't think you will," he said, his eyes still wild. "But I'll make you."

He stood, rigid, sweat glinting off his forehead, and licked his dry, chapped lips. "You weren't good, but I'll give the dog back. But only if you let me leave."

I looked at Weasel, pupils so wide from fright that his eyes appeared black. His legs twitched as if he were having a nightmare, but the poor dog was certainly awake.

"Okay," I whispered. "You can leave. I won't do anything."

He reached down, picking up the prone canine, and I resisted the urge to lunge at him. I released my breath with a shudder when he let go of my wrist. Slowly, he backed toward my bedroom door, Weasel clutched in his arms. I scooted toward the edge of the bed, and when he didn't make any move to stop me, I rushed out the door after him. He vanished around the corner into the living room.

I paused outside Anna's bedroom. I heard her rhythmic breathing inside, and tears sprang to my eyes.

"What about Anna?" I asked, my voice breaking. "What did you do to her?"

Silence.

I rushed into the living room. Weasel shook on the floor, tail between his legs and a puddle at his feet. He whimpered as I lunged for him and scooped him into my arms, clutching him to my chest.

"It's okay," I sobbed as the confused animal trembled. He licked my chin, his whining high pitched and distressed.

On shaky legs, I rose and bolted for Anna's room. I burst through the door and threw on the light.

Anna lay on her stomach, one foot hanging off the bed. An arm was tucked beneath her, the other one clutching her pillow. It's the way she had slept for as long as I could remember, but there was no way she'd slept through what happened across the hall.

"Anna?" I asked, hesitantly approaching the bed.

Her curly hair obscured her face, but her torso rose and fell. She was breathing, but she didn't respond.

I set Weasel on the bed and sat down slowly. Still, she didn't respond. I fought hysterical sobs that threatened to erupt from my throat.

Not Anna . . .

"Anna? *Please*, wake up," I sniffed, tears rolling down my cheeks. I placed one hand on her shoulder and shook.

She didn't move.

CHAPTER 19

Monitors beeped steadily, filling the room with sharp chirps and rhythmic mechanical sounds. I hovered in the doorway as Elliott gripped Anna's limp hand, head bowed in stunned silence, the shock still too new and raw for him to make sense of.

He never relaxed his white-knuckled grip on the steering wheel as we'd chased the wailing ambulance through red lights and artificially lit streets, and even now, he hadn't figured out how to express his heartache as his fiancée lay motionless, oblivious to his desperation as he waited for a spark of life. My own eyes were red and swollen after watching Anna being removed from our apartment on a stretcher and taken away in shrieking flashes of light, Weasel whining and shaking in my arms as one of his beloved humans was taken away for reasons he didn't understand.

The last time I'd seen stretchers, my friends had never come back. I clenched my eyes shut against the sight of Anna's prone form, willing calm for Elliott's sake. He deserved at least that much.

We both knew it was my fault. Never mind the fact I should have sensed the intruder in our apartment— Anna shouldn't live with me at all.

My gaze fixed on the ring on her left hand, and I nearly drowned in a flood of guilt. Dammit, she should be living with Elliott! The only reason she wasn't with him was because I couldn't live alone, and now she was . . . she was—

Jesus, not even the doctors knew! She wasn't asleep. They didn't know if it was a coma. They weren't even sure if she was conscious but paralyzed. They were running every test imaginable, but every time I asked for an update, the answer remained the same: "None of the results are back. We'll let you know as soon as we know something."

But they didn't know anything.

Voices carried down the hall, and I held my breath: Anna's parents had arrived.

"Hadley!" Anna's mom called, rushing to me. Her heels clicking as she ran were rapid-fire gunshots to my nerves.

"Hadley, what ha—oh my God!" Desiree Kinney's face crumbled, hand flying to her mouth at the sight of her only child, deathly still with tubes and wires erupting from her: every parent's worst nightmare.

"I'm so sorry," I said, sniffing as she pushed past me.

Anna's parents had never wanted her to join the Agency. She had been going to school for clinical therapy before my accident, but she had followed me to the Agency to become a profiler instead.

Elliott stepped away from Anna and approached Desiree, wrapping his arms around her, rocking her as she wept.

Anna's father, Sam, stood frozen in the doorway beside me. Without a word, he clapped one hand on my shoulder. He left it there for a moment, squeezed, and stepped through the door without casting me a glance.

I didn't know what to say. I couldn't make it better, so I just stood there as Desiree brushed a strand of wild hair from Anna's face and Sam hovered, haunted, too afraid to touch her and make it real.

Elliott approached me, and gently taking my arm, pulled me into the hall.

"I think you should step outside for a bit. Let me talk to them," Elliott whispered.

"I don't want to leave—"

"Nothing will happen to Anna," he said quickly. "But, Hadley . . ."

He paused and pursed his lips, trying to find the words. I already knew what he was thinking, and I tried not to let it reflect on my face.

"They're in shock. No one is thinking clearly. You shouldn't have to take the brunt of it. You've been through enough."

What he meant was they all blamed me.

Hell, I blamed me.

I clenched my jaw and fought back tears. "I'm sorry, Elliott. I'm so, so sorry!"

"Hadley," he said gently, taking a deep breath. "I know you . . ." His voice faltered and broke. "I *know* it wasn't you. We all love you, and it wasn't your fault. I know you'd *never* intentionally let Anna get hurt, but . . . everyone just needs a minute to be angry at the situation, okay? Let's not hurt you doing it. I'm not asking you to go away. Just step outside so you don't have to feel us process."

He meant it to protect me, but it just hurt.

Anna had been safe! She'd been safe with Elliott, and then she'd come home to me. That was the situation. That was what everyone was so goddamn angry about: Hadley couldn't function, and Anna had to take care of her. Anna had to put her life—her future with a great guy—on hold *for me*. That's why Anna had been in the apartment when the madman came.

Broken whimpers drifted from Anna's hospital room. Sam turned to face the window while Desiree bent over Anna, making sounds no parent should ever make for their child.

Anna's room was across from the one I'd been in nearly four days earlier, and I eyed the door down the hall, wondering if it would be better if I was still behind it.

Elliott squeezed my shoulders, expression pleading. "Please, Hadley. Go outside for a bit. Check on Weasel. The Agency should be here soon, right? Go wait for them."

Anna's life was better when I was gone, so I nodded, and without another word, I turned on my heel, marching toward the exit as I swiped at my burning eyes.

Cool nighttime air rushed into my lungs as I threw the doors open and burst outside, head spinning. I stumbled into the parking lot and leaned against Elliott's car, gasping quick, angry breaths. Weasel yipped from the driver's seat, poking his nose through a gap in the window. I wouldn't leave him alone in the apartment after what happened. Hell, we were never going back to it.

Eyes clenched as I steeled myself against reality, I couldn't see I wasn't alone. A foreign presence tickled my mind, and I frowned. It was 2:00 a.m. Who else would be in the visitor's parking lot—

Someone was watching me.

Eyes flying open, I straightened abruptly, whirling to face him. I probably should have been scared, but the person watching me from the gray sedan at the edge of the parking lot wasn't the parahuman. In fact, I didn't get the sense he was a parahuman at all. And yet, I knew he was working with *him*, watching me and reporting back to . . . his boss? Coconspirator? A terrorist cell's slavering attack dog? I couldn't imagine where in the convoluted network of anti-parahuman extremists the parahuman fit, nor why a group of people who clearly hated them was working so closely with a certifiably psychotic one.

I telepathically reached out to the stranger, probing for answers and intentions. Whatever haphazard anti-telepath barrier he'd constructed to shield his mind imparted a falling sensation, and I lurched back, vertigo disorienting me as if I'd been sucked under a churning wave.

My fists clenched. Someone had broken into my home and attacked my loved ones. I was standing outside the hospital, Anna's life hanging in the balance, and they had the nerve to try to intimidate me *here*. I wasn't about to roll over, not this time, not with Anna lying helpless just beyond the hospital's walls. Oh, no. I wasn't scared anymore; I was *pissed.*

"I'm going to kill him," I told my dog. "I'll kill him!" I shrieked louder, voice echoing in the night.

Weasel barked and whined, ears pressed against his head as I braced against the car for support, shaking with rage.

Not Anna.

Anna's hospital room was visible from where I stood. The light from within was bright against a still-dark sky, and it seemed appropriate that, even now, trapped within her own body, her presence should glow like a beacon. She'd always been my guiding light—my sister. I fought for her when Preston Weiss promised to take it all away.

I wasn't going to let his goddamn partners ruin that.

"He said he'd make me do what he wanted," I whispered. A hysterical, bitter laughter bubbled up. "Fuck that."

Never Anna. Clenching my jaw, I shoved away from the car and marched across the parking lot, Weasel's whimpering protests ignored. This time, I wasn't waiting for someone to find my friends first.

"Hadley?" a voice called after me. A cold surge of adrenaline stopped me in my tracks.

Oh, *shit.* I'd texted her and asked her to pick up Weasel. I didn't think she'd see it until she woke up, supposedly hours from now. Molly loped toward me, tags jingling on her collar, Jo not far behind.

"What happened to Anna? Is she okay?" Jo asked, hands shoved deep into her coat pockets.

Dark circles ringed her eyes. The sight of her was immediately sobering. What was I doing to her? She'd dragged me from the brink of death—twice. She had been one of my only visitors in those early days at Mercy, the only person who'd showed up without expectations, simply happy I was breathing. She was one of my first friends, but when I sensed her feelings for me transform into something deeper, I pushed her away. I built a wall when she didn't deserve it. Still, when I called, treating her like nothing more than my dog sitter, she showed up.

She wasn't. I'd been so childish.

I turned rigidly, putting myself between her and the sedan, hoping I could obstruct the driver's view but knowing it was futile. I didn't sense malice from the occupant. Hell, a raging telekinetic coming at him hardly elicited a response, and I hoped he'd continue to be content lurking while I encouraged Jo to leave.

Dammit. Now, I had another problem: they'd seen Jo.

"It was another parahuman," I said slowly, head hung. I couldn't meet her gaze. "He broke in."

"How bad is she hurt?" Jo asked, looking at the hospital, oblivious to the situation I'd put her in.

"I don't know," I said, my voice cracking. "She won't wake up."

"Did they catch the guy?" Jo asked.

I snuck a glance behind me and fidgeted. Nothing from the car. Jo needed to leave. I stepped around her as if I was heading back to the hospital. Jo turned and followed like I hoped she would, her back to the car.

"Not yet," I said, turning to face her. I liked having Jo between me and the car even less. I glanced at the hospital. If we walked inside, she might stay. She needed to get away from here.

"The Agency won't let him get away," Jo said. She placed a reassuring hand on my shoulder.

I flinched involuntarily, still unable to meet her eyes. My own flicked past her to the car.

405

Jo—damn her—was a good cop; she could recognize suspicious body language as quickly as I could read someone's mind. She scanned the parking lot. Surprise etched her face, and my heart skipped a beat.

"They're sure taking their sweet time getting here, aren't they?" she asked slowly.

My shoulders sagged with relief. I thought she'd seen the car.

Wait, shit. *That.*

"I didn't call them," I blurted, unable to lie to her, and my cheeks burned. "I told Elliott I did."

Stupid, stupid, *stupid.* I should have told her I called them.

"Wha—why? Hadley, what happened?"

I shifted from foot to foot, pulse quickening. She interpreted it as concern for Anna, not realizing she was in the crosshairs too.

"I'm sorry," I stammered, voice trembling. "I didn't mean to text you so early. You probably want to go back to bed—"

"Hadley," she insisted, stepping closer, her dark eyes searching my face. "Talk to me."

I looked past her at the sedan.

"He said he'd make me do what he wanted," I choked, wondering how long it'd take them to identify her. "He'll kill Anna if I don't."

"He said he'll kill Anna if you call the Agency?"

It suddenly dawned on me that, if I didn't want law enforcement involved, I probably shouldn't have begged a police officer for help in the middle of the night. God, I was an idiot in so many ways.

Jo was going to call the Agency. How the hell did I make her leave without calling in the cavalry?

"He didn't have to say it," I said in a rush, trying to impress upon her the direness of the situation. "He—he wants me to kill someone in the Agency. I know he'll kill Anna if I don't do it. He hates the Agency, Jo. What'll he do if I call them?"

"Okay. Hadley." She took my shoulders and forced me to look at her. "I know you're terrified right now, but he's not here, and Anna will be much safer with some agents outside her door, okay? I'll take Weasel, and I'm sure Ryker can put you in a safe house. No one is going to get hurt."

Right. Because the last safe house worked out so well.

Which made me wonder for the first time how Preston had found me. Was it the parahuman? I shivered, wondering for how long I'd been an unwitting plaything, helpless prey without a clue. Apparently, an entire freaking network was hunting me. My eyes flicked to the car again. Jo needed to go.

"He can make anyone do *anything*," I whispered. "That's his power. That's what happened to Anna. She won't wake up because he touched her. It doesn't matter who you put at the door. If he touches them, he can make them kill Anna."

Jo blinked slowly, staring as if she'd misheard me. I appreciated the utter insanity of it all. No parahuman was capable of *mind control*. I wouldn't believe it myself if I hadn't seen what he did to Anna and Weasel. And a parahuman with such dramatically different dual abilities? Dual abilities weren't that uncommon: I had telepathy and telekinesis. Mark had superstrength and invulnerability. But dual abilities were always concomitant. Hydrokinesis and never-before-seen mind control? No. A unicorn broke into our apartment. A murderous unicorn, but a mythical creature nonetheless.

407

Jo—bless her—recovered quickly, and if she didn't believe me, she didn't say it.

"Hadley, the Agency is trained to deal with all types of parahumans. I'm sure there's a protocol for handling whatever this guy is, but you have to call them."

I looked at the car again. The driver was still just sitting there, watching. As I tried to figure out what the hell I could possibly tell a police officer to make her drop a conversation and *freaking leave*, Jo frowned, realizing my eyes had focused on something behind her one too many times.

"No!" I shouted, clutching her shoulder when she started to turn.

Her eyes widened at my raw panic. "Hadley?" she asked, tensing as my nails dug into her. "What's going on?"

I could've lied—probably should've, but it was Jo. She was the *one* person I'd had from the beginning who wasn't completely gutted reconciling two opposing versions of me, and I wasn't about to create some two-faced version of me by lying now. Call me selfish, but I needed one person who just saw *me*.

"If I asked you to trust me," I said, my voice a trembling whisper. "If I asked you to take Weasel and go home without asking questions, would you do it?"

"I trust you," Jo said, eyes searching me as she became increasingly rigid beneath my claws. "But I'm not doing that. What's going on?"

My eyes pleaded, but she planted her feet and crossed her arms, anchored in place. I bowed my head, knowing I was dragging her in.

"Someone's watching me," I said, so low Jo didn't comprehend at first.

When she did, she had me by the arm in a blink. Pulling me in the hospital's direction, she reached for the phone in her back pocket as she scanned the area. I stumbled behind her, fumbling to voice incoherent half protests.

"I'm calling the Agency. They'll get protection for you and Anna. Molly, come!" she said quickly, checking over her shoulder for moving shadows.

No, no, *no*. This was falling apart. The man in the car could take me to the parahuman. I *needed* him to take me to the parahuman. I had to stop this—to fix Anna.

Another surge of panic gripped me. If he told the parahuman I made the wrong move, he'd kill Anna. Did he know about everyone in my life already? Would he then move down the list of family and friends: Jo and Brittany? Mom, Dad, and Collin? What if Mark and his kids were targets? Someone could be dead before the Agency had time to act.

I'd already lost so many people. I couldn't lose anyone else. I couldn't.

"No! Jo, stop!" I shouted.

We were both surprised when she froze in place. She blinked rapidly, staring at her dangling feet as she hovered an inch above the ground. She let go of my arm as I released my telekinetic hold on her, and I stumbled back, appalled at myself.

"I'm so sorry!" I squeaked. "I didn't mean to!"

I continued backing away from the hospital, putting distance between us—putting myself between her and the car where I should have been the entire time, but she clutched my wrist. Her energy pressed into me, pleading, raw and earnest. Her eyes searched for mine, but I couldn't meet them. I focused on a moth-swarmed floodlight in the distance, holding my breath. I didn't want to see the look on her face, to see what she thought of me. At least I hadn't blown her up.

"Hadley, I'm not mad, but you need to come inside with me."

She genuinely wasn't, which surprised me. Oh, sure, she wanted to wring my neck, but I didn't scare her—I never had, and I didn't understand why. Her police cruiser still had dents in it from raining chunks of house.

"He can make anyone do anything he wants with *one* touch," I said, unyielding as Jo closed the distance between us, still not letting go of my wrist. I squirmed as her warmth drew nearer. "Anna's in a coma because he touched her. That's all he had to do, and I don't know how we're supposed to protect her. Can we even wake her up without him? If the Agency catches him, does she die? If they don't, will she still die? The Agency can't fix this. They couldn't even handle Preston."

I hadn't voiced the last part before, and hearing it spoken aloud, I realized there was a horrible truth in it: I didn't trust the Agency anymore. They hadn't protected any of us. Eight agents—my friends—were dead. I'd nearly joined them. Anna might be dying. No, I had lost my faith in the Agency.

I looked up at Jo, tearful eyes pleading for her to understand.

"Hadley," Jo said uneasily, still scanning the parking lot, grip tight. "Anna's in the best place possible, but *no one* is safe if that guy is still out there. *You* aren't safe. Call the Agency. Ryker will handle this."

"How?" I asked bitterly.

Jo saw the gray sedan now too, a surge of adrenaline racing through her as she realized I was right: we were being watched. Her free hand twitched, reaching for her side. A flicker of frustration crossed her eyes as she realized her gun was in her safe at home. In another heartbeat, she considered if it was better to keep her eyes on him or switch positions with my stubborn ass and put herself between us.

Then there was the part of her that wondered how hard I'd fight if she just dragged me inside. I listened to her inner turmoil as we both stood resolute, silently fighting conflicting battles to protect the other.

"It's not him," I said. "The guy in the car isn't a parahuman."

That didn't ease her anxiety. From experience, non-parahumans did just fine with bombs, guns, and sharp knives.

"Let's talk about it inside," Jo insisted, her unspoken thoughts begging me to be reasonable, but he had hurt Anna. Reasonable had left the station.

"I don't want to go inside, and I'm not calling the Agency," I said. "I-I want you to go home."

She jerked back as if I'd slapped her.

"Hadley . . . I know, after everything you've been through, that everything feels hopeless right now. I know you're grieving for your friends; I know how much Anna means to you. I'm so, so sorry for everything that's happened and that it's not over. I understand that you're terrified and confused, and I know the Agency let you down, but you have to believe me when I say that the Agency *can* bring this guy down. You have to talk to them," she said, misunderstanding my resistance.

But she wasn't wrong. Any faith I'd had in the Agency had died in that basement.

"He can't touch me," I said. "His abilities don't work on me. He used Anna to get me to do what he wants because I'm immune. That's why he hurt her."

"What does he want with—" Her eyebrows knitted in confusion. Then, her eyes widened as she realized I'd lost my damn mind.

"Hadley, no. *No.* You're not going after this guy. You can't!"

"I stopped Preston!" I snapped, immediately regretting it.

She flinched, startled that I'd yelled at her, but she didn't release my wrist.

"At what cost? The rest of us got to stand at the foot of a hospital bed for two weeks and hold our breath every time one of your monitors gave an awkward chirp," she said slowly, a haunted look behind her eyes. "Please, Hadley, don't do that to us again."

Blood soaked my jeans, sickly warm. The same warmth oozed through my fingers, yet grateful tears pricked my eyes, knowing it meant there was still life—still a chance.

I bit back a hiss as memories suddenly bubbled from Jo like a pot boiling over. Her normally controlled veneer cracked, emotions seeping out.

"I'm the only one he can't hurt," I said belligerently, attempting to throw up a mental wall. "He told me. My brain is too fucked-up for him to control. If I just . . . if it's just me, no one gets hurt."

A flash of emotion crossed Jo's face, her frown deepening. I stepped back as she pressed even closer, wondering if she really might sling me over her shoulder and drag me inside. She was probably half a foot taller. I didn't doubt she could do it. Her energy wasn't angry though; it was scared. She was scared for me.

"Damn it, Mark! Get me an ambulance! She's not dead!"

"You can't know that for sure," she whispered.

"He tried—"

"You know who else had that mindset? Damani Aluko. He didn't think anyone could touch him, either. Someone did."

"Don't bring Damani into this. It's not the same thing," I retorted, jerking my arm back angrily. I clenched my teeth, blood pressure rising when her grip didn't loosen.

"So, what?" she asked, not backing down. Her eyes held mine, color creeping up her neck. "I just let you go? You want to see if you can use your superpowers and what? What's your plan here, Hadley?"

Ian dropped beside me—no, Jo—throwing his hands on Hadley's bloody body. I gasped when he moaned, shuddering as if he would be sick.

"Let go," he choked, and I reluctantly removed my hands, wondering if it was the last time I'd ever touch her—me—alive. I stared down at the glistening blood on my hands and choked back a sob.

"I don't know," I muttered, averting my gaze. A sickly churning twisted my stomach, and I breathed deep, trying to keep Jo at a distance in more ways than one.

"You're just going to go out there and dig in his head to see how to fix Anna?"

"I don't know," I winced, nausea clawing at my insides. She was really hurting me. She'd always been so controlled around me, keeping her energy to herself like the nurses at Mercy taught her. Now, it was like a dam was collapsing; a rush of emotions pooled around me.

"How do you plan on catching him? You going to dangle him by his ankles until the cops come?"

"I don't know."

"What if he's immune to *your* powers?"

"Jesus, Jo!" I snapped, jerking my arm again. Again, she didn't let go. "I doubt he's immune to getting blown up!"

The ambulance wailed as it raced away. I slumped beside Mark against the hood of my cruiser, staring at my red-stained, trembling hands, wondering why I'd given her away to strangers. Again. An ambulance had carried Hadley away once before, only this time, I knew what they took with them. Why? Why had I never taken the chance . . .

"Tell me that wasn't the last time I'll see her," I whispered.

Mark didn't answer.

I clenched my eyes closed, stomach churning as tears pricked my eyes. She was projecting. She was showing me on purpose.

Jo was quiet while I reeled, eyes pleading. When her hand slipped from my wrist into my hand, my breath caught, anger giving way to shock. I stared at her, trembling, quelled by the look of desperate longing she gave me.

"That's not you," Jo whispered.

"It is," I said, surprised by a deep, aching regret. Preston Weiss was a monster. He deserved what he got, but I didn't mean to let him turn me into a killer too. "You saw what I did."

Jo shook her head, hand warm in mine, and I heard everything she didn't say.

"Come inside with me," Jo pleaded.

I glanced over my shoulder at the gray sedan, the desire for revenge overshadowed by my thunderous heart.

"Please, Hadley. Don't. Don't make me find your mangled body again."

I—Jo—sat at the edge of the hospital bed, the woman in it scraped, bruised, and so very still.

"I'm sorry," Jo whispered. "I'm sorry I was too afraid to say anything."

I turned away from the car to stare at her, internally reeling. I hadn't been sure if she was aware of the feelings that had awoken in her all those months ago as we sat on her couch, laughing at some godawful sci-fi movie I'd picked out. I guess she'd figured them out.

Tears slid down her cheeks, and she made a choking sound. She averted her gaze, jaw clenched tight.

"Look," she sniffed, voice shaking. "I understand if you see me as just a friend, and that's okay, but I—you aren't just . . . you don't know what you mean to me."

But I did. I stood frozen in place, pulse racing. Her jaw clenched as she tried to find words you don't come back from, words I'd been terrified to hear her say. I'd panicked that night on her couch, convinced it wasn't what I wanted, convinced it was just Jo's second drink after a long day talking, convinced nothing would change if I just put distance between us until the moment passed.

"Don't make me find you a third time, okay? Promise me that," she said, still not looking at me. She brushed her cheek forcefully and sniffed, standing up straighter.

My heart sank as her hand left mine.

She folded her arms, closing herself off from me. The color in her neck reached her face. I held a hand out for her, realizing I wanted more than anything for her to continue. I didn't care that some creep was watching the messy details of my life play out; I needed her to say it.

"Jo, I—" I froze midsentence, when a ripple passed through the parking lot—a minute disturbance in the ebb and flow of the world.

I was all too familiar with the disturbance death left.

"Anna?" I squeaked in panic, spinning to her window, but the disturbance wasn't from inside the hospital.

Jo was too slow as I turned toward the parking lot and ran. The gray sedan practically glowed in the dark under a streetlight.

"Get a nurse!" I screamed as I ran toward the car.

"Hadley! No!" Jo shouted.

Molly's agitated barks echoed behind us. Weasel parroted her disturbed howls as I ran with Jo on my heels.

It was too late by the time I threw the car door open. A balding man slumped to the left in the driver's seat, head arched back at an awkward angle, eyes staring at nothing. Beads of blood rolled toward his lips from both nostrils. I recoiled, and Jo gasped as she slid to a halt behind me.

But he was an accomplice, wasn't he? He was watching me! How could he just sit there and die in a hospital parking lot and *just watch me?*

How? The parahuman had said he had to touch people to kill them. He said he had to touch them! I spun, searching the dark. Had some twisted hydrokinetic ability done this? What the *hell* could the parahuman do, and how close did he have to be to do it? I didn't sense anyone, and it only disturbed me more.

"Hadley, get inside!" Jo shouted, arms wrapping tightly around me before she yanked me away from the car.

"Sir?" Jo asked, leaning in before I could stop her. She pressed her fingers to the man's neck.

I let out a breath when nothing happened, no parahuman-induced backlash rebounding onto her. Her shoulders sagged, confirming what I already knew.

Why hadn't I helped him? His mind . . . how could I not know? Why hadn't I realized he was hurting?

I stumbled back, dazed, as Jo grabbed her cell phone, dialing the Agency in one swift movement. She shoved me farther behind her, keeping herself between me and the car.

"Hadley, get inside the hospital. Go!" she pleaded as the line rang.

I stood frozen in place, gutted. He wasn't the enemy. He wasn't hunting me. The poor man was a message: I would do what I was told, or people would die.

And I had let him.

CHAPTER 20

I wondered how pissed Ryker would be if the camera in the corner had an "accident." Its red light had been blinking incessantly since I grudgingly parked myself in a cold, uncomfortable chair to go over the night's events with Mark. Per Ryker's request, Dr. Patterson joined us after half an hour so I could recount the details "with more clarity." Translation: Ryker blamed my emotions for my inability to coherently take Mark through the home invasion that had landed Anna in the hospital. Truthfully, I was doing better than I thought I would be. Turns out, when you survive getting gutted like a fish by a serial killer, you come out the other side a little more resilient.

At least, I hoped that was the case. There was still time for shock and adrenaline to wear off and for me to crumble in traditional Hadley fashion. In the meantime, I was having a difficult time recounting the details Mark asked me, like what the invader might have touched, what he was wearing, how he might have gotten in, etc. Understandably, I hadn't been focused on those things when a madman had hold of my dog, but let's be honest, I was still me. Remembering wasn't my strength on my best day.

As if having two parahumans in the room with me wasn't enough, Graham lurked in the observation room on the other side of the glass, and for the first time, I understood what it felt like to be a suspect with a telepath rummaging through their brain. Well, almost. I felt Graham in my mind, rifling through thoughts like documents in a filing cabinet. I couldn't tell you what telepathy was—whether it was made of protons and electrons or had mass, but it existed with its own set of rules and properties, and our respective telepathic abilities converged in my mind like two magnets of the same polarity meeting. A strange tickle, like a stray hair across my arm, pestered my brain as Graham delineated facts when words failed me.

And then there was Ryker, who I concluded did, in fact, live in his office. He was at the Agency, pristine black suit polished and not a single white hair out of place, when Mark and I arrived from the hospital. Despite being in the observation room with Graham, his presence still dominated the interrogation room.

Jo returned to the hospital after taking Molly and Weasel home, promising me she would sit outside

Anna's room until a protective detail arrived. It was exactly what I'd feared would happen—Jo and Anna both directly in the line of fire, and I squirmed in my chair, wanting nothing more than to be back with them.

That was hours ago. The sun rose, and sagging, swollen eyelids, dark circles, and bedraggled hair—reflected in the one-way glass for me to behold—perfectly expressed the bitter, desolate ugliness I felt inside. The door opened, and Mark took a folder from an umber-colored hand that likely belonged to Ben.

Most of our skeleton crew was here, running on fumes. Appeals to other departments and branches for additional personnel went conspicuously unanswered. Not even Major Crimes, Damani and Janelle's glory-seeking department, would touch us. I couldn't blame them. This case spelled death for anyone dumb enough to pursue it. Ryker's attempt at cross-agency cooperation was being held up by red tape, but there was a chance the FBI would support us, if only to show us up as the better federal agency.

Let them. Maybe they could protect the Agency's people better than we could.

"Looks like CCTV got something," Mark said, pulling a picture from the folder.

"This is him?" I asked, staring at a grainy photo taken by an exterior camera from the grocery store down the street.

Although the image was pixilated, the man's face was clear enough. It helped that he had looked directly at the camera. Facial recognition would eventually identify him, but the flicker of a grin on his face told me he wasn't concerned. I shivered at his dead yet predatory eyes, their appearance both hollow and fathomless, like a shark's gaze before striking.

"You tell me," Mark said. "Time stamp fits. Not even twenty minutes before you called the ambulance."

I stared at the pixilated photo: stringy, long hair covered his ears, his gaunt cheekbones were sharp, and those eyes . . . they were hauntingly familiar despite lacking definition.

"It's him," I said, shoving the photo away in disgust with the arm Dr. Patterson wasn't latched onto.

He'd been oddly quiet, but perhaps it was because he'd come from Anna's bedside before joining us, his background thoughts a kaleidoscope of confusion as he processed what he'd felt from her body.

That not even Dr. Patterson could help only made me more irate.

"You're sure?"

"Absolutely."

I resisted the urge to scratch my temple as Graham dug around, looking for a memory of the man who had broken in. Obviously, Ryker wasn't going to take my word for it. I made it easy, shoving a memory at him: my bedsprings squeaking as the man leaned in, stinking breath hot on my face. Graham telepathically recoiled at the too-intimate recollection, the tickle in my brain easing slightly.

Okay, maybe that was a little mean. Dr. Patterson shifted in his seat, rolling his shoulders as my crankiness put him on edge.

"We'll get the photo circulating," Mark said. "Identifying him will go a long way."

Somehow, I doubted it.

"If only he dropped his wallet," I muttered irritably.

A surge and then recession of sensation under my skin, like a wave crashing to shore and receding, conferred an increased sense of calm. I glanced at Dr.

Patterson as he squeezed my arm, his own tension palpable. A little presumptive, but I didn't blame him. I was becoming increasingly impatient and angry. Angry Hadley could blow things up too.

Mark slid a laptop across the table. Sighing, I pulled it closer and scanned the headshots of army personnel for the third time. We filtered the eMILPO records of every active duty, reserve, veteran, retired—hell, even military spouses—male who could be in San Diego for eye color, height, weight, hair color, and age range, which still left me with thousands of faces.

For once, I wished discharge records would state if the Parahuman Honorable Discharge Act had been invoked, as it had in Mark's case. How many of these "medical discharges" were actually parahumans who weren't allowed to serve?

That was assuming I was even right regarding his ability . . . or abilities. I kept scrolling, wondering how big the bag of cheese puffs would need to be to lure Neil here. This was Cybercrimes' forte.

"You're certain he has a military background?" Mark asked.

"He's the guy who stabbed Navin with the ASEK. I know it," I said without taking my eyes off the sea of faces. "And I think he has a background in bombs. I think he set off at least one of them. He has to be military."

"Brittany identified Everett Doyle as the man who killed Navin. Jacob Mason and his buddies admitted to the bombs—all of them."

"Brittany is self-medicating away grief," I offered in explanation. "And I wouldn't put it past Jacob Mason to protect his mission, even if it required protecting a parahuman."

That part still didn't sit right.

"Hadley," Mark sighed, clearly thinking the same thing. "Neither the Sons of Gaia nor the APA would be caught dead working with a parahuman, and why would a parahuman work with them to kill other parahumans? It makes no sense."

"I never said it did, but he admitted to working with Preston Weiss, and he knew about the bombs," I grumbled.

"We're their hostages, and the things they make us do . . ."

My skin tingled, and I rubbed my arm, the faint memory of my nerves lighting up in pain making me wince. It had just been a dream, but . . .

"What?" Mark asked as my gaze became unfocused.

"I think they made him torture people with his ability," I said.

"That would break a very long list of laws, both foreign and domestic," Mark said. "Parahumans *can't* serve. The superpowers of the world would scorch the earth killing each other with us."

Right. Because nukes and missiles kept them much more civilized . . .

"They can serve if no one says anything," I muttered.

Mark's eyebrows rose. I shoved the computer away, somehow knowing he wouldn't be in anyone's system.

"Is it possible he was black ops? Something that could fly under the radar? Maybe he was part of a group willing to look the other way? He seemed convinced of some sort of secret group: a hidden Agency. Could that be true?"

"The guy is unstable," Mark said. "Parahumans can't serve. There's no secret group of elite parahuman soldiers out there. Whatever he told you, it was just to seed doubt. He wants to isolate you so he can manipulate you."

"I know. It's just . . ."

Just what?

He was gaslighting me. That's why he brought up the worst day of my life. I drove drunk. I crashed and should have died. There was nothing else to the story. I knew I couldn't trust anything the madman said. And yet . . .

Mark's expression became pained as my questions brought up old memories of the IED that activated his dormant parahuman genes and revealed him for what he was. The army hadn't even waited a week before medically discharging him, the fateful IED an ironically perfect cover. Somehow, I was certain someone made an exception for the parahuman hunting us.

I glanced at the glass. If anyone had heard whispers of parahumans illegally serving in the military, it would be Ryker, but if my comments caught him off guard or set his mind abuzz, he didn't give anything away. In fact . . . he wasn't there? Where was Ryker? Where had Graham gone?

Some telepath I was. Maybe Graham picked up something useful in my brain, and they'd gone to do something worthwhile? Oh, well. They could review my probably treasonous conspiracy theories later.

"He isn't in our database," I said confidently, closing the laptop.

Mark frowned, clearly disagreeing. I couldn't blame him. I wasn't even certain what I'd picked up on to make me so confident.

"Let's take a break," Mark grumbled. "I'll get you a coffee."

I'd already downed two, and they hadn't brought the expected energy I so desperately needed. Ryker would probably kill me if my bathroom breaks became more frequent, but I nodded anyway as Mark rose.

Dr. Patterson squeezed my arm in forewarning, preparing me for the flood of emotions I was about to experience. I nodded and stiffened, bracing against the coming onslaught. With a not-so-subtle sigh of relief, Dr. Patterson released my arm. His hands trembled as he slipped his gloves on. He'd left me just enough anger to keep me sharp; I hadn't realized just how much he'd been absorbing. I squeezed my eyes shut as a wave of panic intermixed with grief and exhaustion cascaded over me, constricting like a vise. Beside me, a chair toppled over, hitting the ground with a clatter. Dr. Patterson scrambled forward, reaching for me, but I shook my head.

"I'm okay." I took a deep, shaky breath. I would *not* blow up the Agency today.

Visions of a psychotic intruder lurking at the foot of Anna's hospital bed, Jo dead in the hall, pummeled my mind. I focused on my breathing as the urge to check my phone suddenly became overwhelming.

"Sorry, Hadley," Dr. Patterson said.

"Don't be." I clawed at my pockets and fished my phone out, slumping back in relief when I saw a text from Jo time-stamped fifteen minutes earlier. "You're a lifesaver."

Literally.

Dr. Patterson relaxed in his chair, satisfied that nothing else would go boom as I scrolled through my phone.

"You should see someone," the doctor said.

Jo's texts said Elliott and Anna's parents had passed out, asleep. No one but nurses had come by. No updates from the doctors.

She had to be exhausted. She'd been with them all night.

"I'm hopelessly single," I said absently.

Dr. Patterson shot me a look, and I blushed, realizing what he meant.

"For the emotional trauma or the physical wounds?" I asked, more sarcastically than I meant to.

Dr. Patterson raised an eyebrow.

"Sorry," I said quickly, embarrassed I was taking my frustration out on people who only wanted to help.

I scrolled through my phone, clinging to every update Jo sent, though they were all the same. Tears pricked at the corners of my eyes as I scrolled up to a photo of Weasel and Molly curled up on Jo's couch.

"It's okay to not be okay," he said, assessing my haggard, heartbroken expression. "You've been through a lot. You're parahuman, not superhuman."

"I know." I looked up from my phone, smiling, though there was no warmth in it. "But I'm tired of not being okay. I'd like to be angry today if you can handle it."

He nodded in understanding and stood, massaging his neck.

"Dr. Patterson?" I asked, a thought coming to me.

"It's Ian, Hadley," he insisted, a weak smile failing to reach his dark-rimmed brown eyes. "I think we've been through enough together to drop the formalities."

"Ian," I relented. "How do your powers work?"

"I heal people," Ian said quickly, taken aback.

"But how?" I asked. "You make people's bodies do things."

Comprehension dawned on him. "Like Anna's attacker."

I nodded.

"I can only correct things that are out of balance," Ian said.

"But, theoretically, could someone else like you have the ability to impact things that aren't out of balance?"

"Parahuman abilities exist on a spectrum," Ian said. "We don't completely understand the biology. Why is it that some telekinetics struggle to move an empty can while others can level a building?"

"Good point," I said, wincing at memories I was desperately trying to save for the therapist Ian knew I needed.

"I suppose he and I could be on the spectrum of a similar ability, though I've never heard of someone like him," Ian conceded.

"When you use your ability, you feel what the other person feels, right?"

Ian nodded.

"Do you have to heal yourself?"

"Heal myself? As in, do I take on the person's injuries myself?"

I shrugged, though I wasn't sure that's what I meant. "Sure."

"No, I don't get hurt. I feel their pain, but that's where the shared experience ends. Spending energy to heal someone is what takes a toll. There's a recovery period, yes, and my abilities do aid me," Ian said. "Why do you ask?"

"The parahuman . . . he felt like a flayed nerve. He was in physical pain. What if he's like you, but his ability goes beyond empathy? What if it's more like . . . a mirrored response, and his ability to manipulate his own body is on the lower end of the spectrum? What if he doesn't recover like you? What do you think years and years of hurting others would do to him?"

I didn't have sympathy for him, but I needed to understand what had turned him into a monster. I needed something to make sense.

"I think using that ability would be the very definition of hell, especially if he's using it as you say he is," Ian said. "It's an interesting theory, but regardless of his misfortunes or what happened to him, he must be stopped, and if there's any helping him, we'll let our justice system decide."

I nodded, not disagreeing, though I not so secretly hoped Ryker had a black site he could simply lose the madman in. A cavernous pit would also do.

Ian exited the room in search of a hard-earned reprieve from my emotions. Mark returned a moment later, the promised cup of coffee in hand. He picked up the toppled chair beside me without a word.

"Hang in there, space cadet," Mark said sympathetically.

I leaned back in my chair and sighed, inhaling the rich scent of the beverage.

"It's too much, Mark," I admitted, feeling defeated. "Whoever these people are, they're too well-organized. How can we possibly beat them?"

"It's way too much," Mark said. "And I'm sorry it's fallen on your shoulders, but we're going to stop them."

Before or after we all ended up in body bags?

"Did Art finish with the guy from the hospital?" I asked, fighting the urge to be flippant.

"Burt Summers. No ties to the APA or Sons of Gaia. He was an accountant," Mark said. "Intracerebral hemorrhage. He died of a brain bleed."

"How long would that take?" I asked, stomach churning.

It was better when the guy didn't have a name. I hoped he didn't have a family.

"It was slow. Art didn't say, but it probably took a while. The good news is, Art doesn't think the parahuman did it from a distance. He probably had to be in contact with the guy, and then nature took its course from there."

That was good news?

"Oh, God," I said, staring up at the ceiling. "I just stood there while he slowly died."

"You didn't know," Mark said.

A new thought occurred to me. "Anna!" I shouted, sitting up straighter and scrambling for my phone.

"Anna will be fine. Her scans came back clear, remember? We'll ask them to redo them later today to be certain," Mark said. "She's okay."

I didn't consider a coma okay.

"Assuming the asshole doesn't come back or hijack a nurse to murder her," I muttered irritably.

"Ryker's got agents swarming the hospital, and Jocelyn is camped outside Anna's door. God help the person who pisses her off," Mark said. "He's not getting to Anna."

"Jo shouldn't have stayed. All he has to do is touch someone, Mark," I muttered. "One touch, and they die of a heart attack or their brain bleeds."

"Good luck getting rid of her," Mark said, smiling as if he knew a secret.

I rolled my eyes.

He threw his hands up, still grinning. "Sorry. Not my place."

He wasn't sorry, and the corners of my mouth tugged upward. She stayed.

I leaned forward in my chair, hoping coffee would help my life make sense again. Sipping it, I brought the photo of our unidentified psychotic asshole to me again. What had the Sons of Gaia offered to make him work for them? Revenge? Money? Were they blackmailing him? Did he just like watching the world burn? Hell, I'd accept that he and Preston were lovers. Anything to make it make sense.

"Where's Ryker?" I asked, rubbing my likely very bloodshot eyes. "I want to finish this and go back to the hospital."

Mark shook his head. "You need to get out of the city."

"What?" I yelped. "No! I'm not leaving—"

"Hadley, enough," he said firmly. "You've been through enough. You almost died. These people broke into your home—*twice*, and now they're following you. You've earned the right to disappear to the ends of the earth to heal and grieve, you understand?"

"Everyone here has suffered," I snapped in response. "I'm the only one he can't hurt!"

"You don't know that for certain. Damani thought Preston couldn't hurt him until he had a bullet in his abdomen."

"Why does everyone keep bringing up Damani?" I snapped, frustrated tears forming. "He died, you know? He doesn't deserve to have everyone shit on him!"

"No," Mark said, lowering his voice. "He doesn't, but you need to learn from his mistakes. Damani went rogue, and it cost him."

"I'm not saying I want to go rogue!" I shot back, ignoring the fact I had intended to do exactly that a few hours earlier. "Let me stay so it doesn't cost *you*."

"It's not my call," Mark mumbled.

I glared into my coffee cup. Ryker was *not* sending me away. I wasn't leaving this time.

Mark sighed and leaned back in his chair, crossing his arms against his chest. We were both quiet for what seemed like an eternity, the only sounds coming from the ticking clock on the wall.

"I'm going to see what grabbed Ryker's attention. You want me to steal a muffin from the break room?"

"No," I said petulantly.

"Suit yourself," Mark muttered as he heaved the bulk of himself out of his chair. He disappeared out the door without another word.

I leaned heavily against the table and placed my head in my hand, rubbing at a tickle at my temple. I stared down at the blurry face from the convenience store's camera. "Who are you?"

Tick!

Between the blinking security camera, the ticking clock, and the damn tickle that was growing into an itch, I was certain I would go crazy soon. Well, crazier.

Tick!

One more second went by with no answers.

Tick!

Another second Anna was in a coma.

Tick! . . . Tick!

Two more seconds. Someone could be dead.

The table vibrated beneath me, a metallic thrum resonating in the small room. I clenched my jaw and pressed my palms into the table, willing control. And dammit, *what was that tickle*?

Tick!

Hadley . . .

My head shot up. Why was Graham—?

Hadley . . . he wanted you to know . . . you weren't good . . .

Fuck!

I was running in an instant, my chair clattering behind me as it toppled over. The interrogation room's door boomed, colliding with the wall as I barreled through it. I nearly tripped over my own feet as I scrambled to warn the others. After all, the only thing more terrifying than a parahuman psychopath who could kill you with one touch was a brainwashed telekinetic who didn't even have to touch you.

"Mark!" I screamed as I slid into the Agency's common area, following the smell of freshly brewed coffee. "He's got Graham!"

Mark stared at a TV mounted in the room's corner, slack-jawed. He turned toward me, eyes wide, a haunted expression on his face. "I just saw—"

Whatever it was, it could wait. I grabbed his arm and yanked, but it was like trying to drag a refrigerator. When he didn't budge, I used other methods.

"Jesus, Hadley! Stop!" Mark shouted, eyes growing even wider as I telekinetically slid him across the floor and into the hall, the soles of his shoes making a shrill, nerve-flaying squeak against the break room's linoleum.

"Mark, fucking run or die!" I snapped at him.

A red fire alarm down the hall gleamed like a beacon. I reached out for it telekinetically, and the glass exploded, sending shards in all directions. The handle flipped down, and a wave of relief washed through me as the building exploded into chaos with strobing lights and a piercing bell so loud I heard white noise as the sound waves assaulted my eardrums. Hopefully, everyone would evacuate before Graham found them.

As for us . . . I sensed the other telekinetic down the hall, moving ever closer, and cursed. The closest stairwell was behind him. I turned and ran toward the other side of the building, where Ryker's office was located, and hoped we were still out of Graham's range. Did Graham even have a range?

We were so dead.

"*Hadley, what the hell?*" Mark shouted after me, his footsteps thundering behind me over the noise of the alarm, the vibrations making the office windows shake.

I rounded a corner and yelped as Mark's arms closed around me. He yanked me into an office with its door ajar. We nearly sent Ryker hurdling to the ground as we collided into him. So much for the fire alarm working.

I went limp, wiggling, and dropped from Mark's arms as he grabbed for me like I was a bar of soap. I lunged at the door and slammed it shut. My shaking hands struggled with the lock. I froze, a hysterical laughter threatening to erupt. What the hell was I doing? What kind of telekinetic locked a door against another telekinetic?

"What the hell is happening to my Agency?" Ryker snapped, face red and neck veins bulging.

"Hadley says the suspect is in the building," Mark said, turning to me, bewildered, for confirmation.

"No!" I hissed, peeking through the blinds. "It's Graham! He brainwashed Graham!"

Oh, God. The parahuman wasn't exaggerating. He really could make anyone do anything, and he was making Graham kill us. We needed to get out of the building. An office door would do nothing to stop a telekinetic.

"I just sent Ben and Graham to deal with the mall situation. Your goddamned suspect is there!" Ryker snapped at me.

"Graham is in the—"

Everything became eerily still and quiet as the fire alarm suddenly fell silent.

"Shit!" I muttered. "We need to get everyone out of the building."

"Ms. Gordon, no one's here. Every available agent is responding to the goddamned parahuman on a stabbing spree at the biggest mall in this forsaken city."

"*What?*" I whispered.

I knew better. I *knew* Graham was here . . . but that also meant there was no one else here to help us survive him. A surge of mixed emotions—relief and dread—competed within me. All we had was Mark's muscles, my unpredictable abilities, and Ryker's temper to combat a seasoned telekinetic.

We were going to die.

"The news, Hadley," Mark said. "It just happened."

I wasn't paying attention, my eyes still trained on the hallway, waiting. Mark grabbed my shoulders and turned me to face him.

"Hadley . . . from the description, it's Brittany."

"It's Brittany what?" I asked, suddenly forgetting we were about to have our spines ripped through our mouths.

"They estimate about fifty people were stabbed in under three minutes."

"But, that's not . . . how can you say that? Brittany wouldn't do that."

When was the last time I'd seen Brittany? Hadn't she come by the hospital before they discharged me? She'd been fine. There was no way she was planning a stabbing spree. A parahuman with unnatural speed might have attacked the mall, but it wasn't her.

"I need you both at the scene *right now*. The Agency is crippled, and we're going to need all the manpow—" Ryker sputtered.

Shattering glass interrupted him.

Oh, right. We were about to die.

Whatever the hell else was going on, it would have to wait. Slowly, the hall lights grew dimmer . . . and went out. I flipped the light switch down, plunging Ryker's office into an artificial gray gloaming despite the window behind us. Not that it would do any good against Graham.

A strong breeze picked up in the hall, whistling through the crack at the bottom of the door.

Office buildings don't have breezes.

"You said Ben was with Graham?" I squeaked, realization rising as quickly as the wind. I really, really hoped someone had just turned the AC all the way up.

"He and Graham confirmed they were at the scene," Ryker said, his voice markedly lower now that it sounded like a hurricane outside.

Finally, it was sinking in. Yes, I was the world's most unreliable agent, but I could be right . . . sometimes.

"I don't think they ever made it," I whispered as the whistle at the door grew into a roaring moan, nearly drowning out my voice. With a *crack!*, the door swung free of the doorframe. I lunged forward, shoving my body against it, attempting to force it closed again. It finally moved when Mark stepped in.

With the door closed, I leaned my back against it and closed my eyes, searching.

In the office, wind raged like a tornado. Objects began slamming into the walls, breaking my concentration.

A chair crashed into the window beside me, shattering it, and the blinds flailed wildly at us.

I shrieked unintentionally and ducked to avoid a direct hit to the face as something red and fire extinguisher–shaped sailed inside and hit the floor with a *thunk!*

Office supplies became projectiles, a stapler flying towards my head.

"Down!" Mark shouted, dropping low. He pulled me away from the doorway to his side, wrapping his arms around me and attempting to shield me with his body.

"Gordon!" Ryker shouted from the floor, hands covering his head as loose sheets of paper and various pens assaulted him. "Control this!"

Control a tornado? How?

"Now, Gordon!" Ryker barked.

My heart thundered in my chest as the wind whipped my hair into my eyes. Something lanced my shoulder and was gone before I cried out. I gripped Mark's shirt, holding onto him for dear life. A flying horde of office supplies raced around us, a dizzying frenzy held aloft in a thundering stream of air. There were too many. I couldn't keep track of everything coming at us. I couldn't stop that many projectiles at—

But I had. I'd done it that day in the parking lot when a bomb packed with shrapnel should have torn Anna and me apart. I squeezed my eyes shut, desperate to remember how we survived that day.

Anna leaned against her car. My mother was speaking.

I yelped as something slapped my face and flew away. Mark wrapped an arm around my head as I buried my face in his shoulder.

Focus. *Focus.*

My mother was speaking. Then, Anna was screaming. Anna was *screaming*.

A pulse rippled through the room, rocking the floor.

For a dizzying second, I felt connected to everything in the room at once. My eyes flew open, and I gasped.

The objects assailing us tumbled as if blown away by a blast. What didn't embed in the walls flew back at us. I recoiled as a pair of scissors came at us, squeezing my eyes closed once more.

I remembered Anna curled at my feet and car alarms blaring around us, the smell of burned plastic, and the frantic look in Anna's eyes.

This time, when the floor rocked, I held Mark tight, willing the telekinetic eruption not to dissipate. I opened my eyes, panting with effort. The wind was gone, though objects continued to race around the room, ricocheting off an invisible bubble that encircled us.

Mark gaped at me, and I stared back with wide eyes. I didn't know I could do that either. I released my death grip on Mark's shirt, leaving behind indentations where my nails had dug in.

"Can you hold it?" Mark asked.

Did I have a choice?

"I don't know," I panted, sweat beading my brow.

Mark stood, and Ryker lifted his head.

The wind switched direction, and I nearly dropped our protective bubble as the windows blew out behind us, objects whizzing past as if a vacuum had been applied to the building. I wondered how many government secrets sailed out the window as Ryker's computer launched off his desk and into a seventeen-story oblivion.

"We need to get out of here," Mark said.

Ryker's desk began sliding across the floor, a shriek like nails on a chalkboard setting my teeth on edge as it scraped the ground.

"I think I can keep us in the bubble if you stay close."

I didn't really. I needed to maintain cognitive function through it, but I decided it wasn't a good idea to bring that up.

Mark offered me a hand, and I stood slowly, my head spinning from the effort of doing too many things at once. And by too many things, I meant breathing and blinking.

"Good, Gordon," Ryker said as he rose, brushing off his suit. A trickle of blood marred his face where something had struck him, but he was otherwise unharmed.

Then, Ryker was upside-down. No, *I* was upside-down.

Shrieking, I sailed toward the shattered window and the seventeen-story drop beyond.

I lurched just before the gaping void, hovering horizontally off the ground. I strained, arms and legs kicking frantically, fighting the telekinetic in the hall, pushing against him for dear life as he attempted to shove me outside the building.

Projectiles began assaulting Ryker again, and he dropped to the floor. Mark remained unaffected as objects bounced off his hulking body. He reached for me . . . then collapsed, groaning.

"Gordon!" Ryker croaked. He clawed at his throat, gagging.

Mark coughed beside him, veins bulging in his neck as he slumped on all fours. Graham would choke them to death if I didn't do something quickly.

Still floating, I righted myself, arms flailing inanely, trying to get oriented while projectiles pummeled me.

I sensed the other telepath in a way I didn't feel most people. I felt his invisible grip on me as he pushed, trying to force my body out of the hole in the building—I was the weaker one.

Yelping, I slipped, throwing my hands out and panicking when I realized I had hold of the window frame. Heart hammering, I blanched at the drop visible from the corner of my eye.

I cried out as another telekinetic jolt threatened to remove my grip.

I dug my nails in.

Mark and Ryker choked on the floor, gasping—dying.

I blinked, and I was in the basement again, Damani choking on his last breath beside me.

It's okay to get scared, Hadley... Damani's voice whispered in my ears.

A vision of a house ripping apart brick by brick flooded my mind. I clawed at Preston Weiss as he raised a knife above my head. Then, the walls had exploded outward as if forced apart by a bomb blast.

Get scared...

So I did.

"*Get down!*" I shrieked, but Mark and Ryker were already gasping on the floor.

In my mind, a knife glinted in the moonlight. I remembered the searing agony of it digging into me. I remembered the horrible moment I realized I was going to die. I lashed out at the memory with everything I had.

The air in the room rushed out with a *boom!*

The door slammed and buckled, cracking through the middle as I forced everything in the vicinity in the opposite direction.

Ryker grunted, tumbling, before rolling into Mark, who rooted them in place. I pushed harder, the knife gleaming in my mind. I would push it as far from me as humanly possible, and then I'd keep going. It would never touch me again.

I screamed, the same heart-wrenching cry I'd screamed as bricks had torn away from basement walls and the first floor of a derelict house had come crashing down before exploding upward. With a sharp *crack!*, a gaping hole formed where Ryker's office door used to be, chunks of wood sailing into the hall.

I gasped as Graham launched across the hall. I lurched away from the window as his opposing force vanished in a blink. I couldn't see him, but I heard a thud as his body landed away from us. It was nearly perfectly in time with the sound of my own body hitting the ground. My head bounced off the floor, stars dancing across my vision.

"Gordon?" Ryker asked, his voice raspy. He craned his head toward the hole in his office where a window once was. He found me on the ground, exhaling heavily and rubbing his throat.

Mark's red face swam into view. His voice sounded far away when he spoke. "Hadley? Hadley, talk to me. Are you okay?"

The wind in the room had stopped. Had I neutralized Ben too?

"I beat him," I croaked in disbelief, head spinning. I had done it, but I realized it came with a cost as a void began blooming within my brain. A lapse was coming.

"Up," Mark told me, pulling at my arms. "He won't stay down."

I choked in a breath as the room whirled around me. Mark pulled me toward the door, Ryker leading us down the hall. I staggered against the frame, knees buckling as my ears rang.

"Carry her!" Ryker ordered. He threw the stairwell door open.

Mark slung me over his shoulder, and my head reeled all the more, vision growing darker at the edges. I waited for darkness to come, for the last few moments of my life to vanish in a blink, the cost of me using my powers.

The door slammed shut behind us as we entered the stairwell, Mark and Ryker leaning heavily against the railing. Their clomping footsteps echoed as they raced down spiral staircases, the jolting corkscrew motion making my stomach churn.

The wind picked up.

I became all too aware of the seventeen-story drop in the middle of the stairwell.

We weren't alone.

"Hadley, please tell me you're still with us," Mark muttered.

"Barely," I whispered. Maybe if I lapsed now, I wouldn't realize we were taking a nosedive to our deaths.

Mark grunted, one arm securing my legs to his chest as I dangled unceremoniously over his shoulder. Mark gripped the rail with his other hand, his eyes watering from the wind. A powerful gust upset Ryker's footing, and he stumbled toward the abyss with a shout. Mark's hand shot out, steadying the man before returning to the railing.

"Where is he?" Mark shouted.

I glanced up, eyes watering against the onslaught of air, but I couldn't see Ben lurking above us.

"Gordon!" Ryker shouted. "Subdue him!"

The stairwell spun, but I couldn't tell if it was my head or the wind.

"It's okay to get scared," I whispered, harnessing the memory of the basement. In my mind, I transformed it from a memory of fear, repurposing it as a weapon.

There was a *crack!*

I blinked as sunlight blinded me, and Mark set me down in the middle of the parking lot. I sat on my backside and stared at a gaping hole in the building's side, chunks of debris littering the once-pristine grounds.

"What happened?" I slurred.

"Later," Mark said.

Ryker stumbled beside him, hand pressed against a freely bleeding head wound. His white hair made the red look even more striking. I didn't remember him having the injury before we entered the stairwell, and my stomach twisted.

"Remind me to never piss you off, Gordon," Ryker mumbled, looking ill.

"Did I kill Ben?" I asked, heart sinking.

"Doubtful," Mark grunted. "Kid can fly."

I should have been more worried about Graham. I sensed the other telekinetic a moment too late.

An SUV flipped on its side and slid across the asphalt toward us. I threw my hands up, and the SUV groaned to a halt, the sounds of metal crunching and glass shattering filling the air as Graham and I fought for control of it. Darkness tickled my sight once again, and I panted, knowing I was about to lose myself once more.

"I can't!" I cried.

Mark rushed forward and gripped the car, fingers crumbling the frame like a tin can. Gasping, I let go as Mark lifted the car and flung it away, his brute strength overpowering Graham's telekinesis. I panted, head spinning, and scanned the area for our attacker.

Where did Graham go? I reached out, feeling for the telepath that circled us like a predator.

"I'm going to need you to hit Graham a little harder," Mark said, eyes darting in all directions.

How close did Graham need to be for his abilities to reach us? How close would I need to be to fight back?

Needles sinking into my chest answered my silent questions. I clawed at my shirt, feeling for a wound that wasn't there.

"Dammit!" Mark wheezed as he doubled over. Ryker dropped to the ground beside him.

I hyperventilated against the crushing weight in my chest. I lurched, blood no longer pumping in my veins as Graham telekinetically crushed our hearts.

Admittedly, I didn't know we could do that.

I was lying in the basement again, life force draining from me. I remembered the slowing of my heart, my breath leaving me as an eternal darkness came.

Panicked, I lashed out the moment I identified the person who wasn't Mark or Ryker, attacking the past and present at once. A *crack!* pierced the air from across the lawn, followed by a howl of pain.

Graham dropped, clutching his arm.

I stared at him, eyes wide in horror at what I'd done, and his gaze found mine. His eyes held mine, and for a moment, I saw something familiar, as if the real Graham had woken up and recognized me. Then, the moment passed. He rose, arm dangling at his side. His energy reached for us, poised to strike again.

He wasn't going to stay down. He wasn't allowed.

I wasn't a match for Graham. If I didn't do something drastic, he'd kill us all. Damani had begged me to do something drastic once, and I'd hesitated. It had nearly cost me everything. It cost me him.

I couldn't hesitate again.

"I'm so sorry," I whispered as Graham choked, clutching his throat.

I held on, tears streaking my face as his panic set in. He clawed at his shirt. My grip on his lungs tightened as I simultaneously compressed his ribs. At least, I thought the hollow meat sacks I sank my telekinetic claws into were lungs. I saw through Graham's eyes as the edges of his vision grew dark and hazy, and I knew the exact moment his sight went dark.

Graham dropped like a rag doll. Immediately, I let go. I sensed his heart still beating and let out a sob of relief.

"I'm so sorry," I repeated, rocking on the ground as tears streamed down my cheeks. I stared at his prone form, part of me praying for him to get back up. Mark and Ryker gaped at me, frozen on the ground, and I hung my head, unable to look at them.

"He's alive," I whispered.

"It's okay, Hadley," Mark said reassuringly, rising and wrapping his arms around me. "You did good. He'll be fine."

I buried my face in his shirt to stifle my sobs. One arm still wrapped around me, he encouraged me up and away. I leaned into him, obediently following.

"I didn't mean to hit him that hard. I just wanted to push him away," I whimpered into his chest. "I panicked."

"You didn't do anything Ian can't fix," Mark said, pulling me in the opposite direction of the prone man.

"Oh, God. Did he get Ian?" I asked.

"If he didn't, Patterson will be at the crime scene," Ryker said, approaching slowly. He eyed the downed telekinetic, then turned his calculating eyes to me. His hornet brain wouldn't let me glimpse what he was thinking. "I'll send a containment unit for Mr. Allen, but the situation at the mall is urgent. We need to go."

"We can't just leave him," I pleaded. I had no idea how badly I'd hurt him.

Would he be unconscious for a few minutes? Hours? Would he ever wake up at all?

"He's going straight to the hospital. There are people at the mall who are in worse shape," Mark said, practically dragging me to the SUV.

My eyes remained fixed on Graham as Mark urged me away.

"We've really got to go, Hadley. Brittany needs us too," Mark insisted.

That got my attention. I let him shove me into the back of an Agency SUV.

"What happened to Brittany?" I asked as he climbed in beside me.

Mark's shoulders slumped, eyes pitying as I stared at him, eyebrows knitted in confusion.

"We'll talk about it on the way, okay?"

As Graham's prone form faded from view, I buried my head in my hands.

"I'm so, so sorry."

CHAPTER 21

I slumped on the mall's ground floor, an immobile escalator's cold metal pressing into my aching backside. White PPE swathed me from nearly head to toe, crinkling like a bag of potato chips each time I moved. I pulled the hood down after my hair stuck to my sweaty neck, the disheveled brown strands the only things distinguishing me from federal agents and police officers patrolling the level above me, searching for more victims or laying down numbered evidence markers and snapping pictures. The occasional jingle of tags signaled a nearby search dog, but with jumbled scents from thousands of visitors spanning the expansive mall, the dogs had their work more than cut out for them.

Head hung, I stared through limp strands of hair at the mall's food court. Normally bustling with activity from a myriad of diners, the food court was eerily silent now, the aromas from countless varieties of food long since dissipated.

Where families usually sat enjoying pizza and Froyo, fifteen black bags now lay in tidy rows, the individuals inside found scattered from one end of the mall to the other in tacky pools of blood. The last body arrived half an hour earlier, but that didn't mean there weren't more to come as agents and officers broke down dressing room doors and checked back rooms. The Disaster Mortuary Operational Response Team had only just arrived, bringing with them enclosed white canopy tents from which they could perform their work identifying the victims. The number of those killed had already overwhelmed the Agency—at least, what remained of it—and the FBI's resources.

Technically, the FBI had jurisdiction now. With Counterterrorism's personnel dead, brainwashed, or well, *me*, an investigation into the invasion of our own headquarters looming, and the hunt for our rogue, weaponized agents taking priority, the Agency didn't have the capacity to investigate the mall massacre.

Ryker had called the FBI for assistance before we arrived at the scene. It was unnecessary. SDPD officers—reeling over a crime scene streaked with blood across acres and cries for help echoing from every corner—had reached out to them when the Agency's lines went dead.

SDPD and the FBI were less than thrilled about that. Tempers cooled after we explained we had been trying not to die ourselves. All the blood and limping really sold it.

The FBI already had things under control. I hadn't seen Ryker—whisked away for a debrief and questioned by the FBI's Special Agent in Charge shortly after stepping foot on the scene—in a while. Mark had also vanished the second the FBI and SDPD realized someone with superstrength was at the scene. With most of our agents suspects or missing, the Agency couldn't do anything more than provide manpower in the search for survivors. I'd found two people clinging to life in a barricaded utility closet, a meager number considering how many were wounded.

At least we showed up. Major Crimes remained blatantly absent.

In addition to the dead, forty-seven victims had been rushed to the hospital. Chuffing from Trauma Hawks had abated two hours earlier, as had wailing sirens from a swarm of ambulances racing toward hospitals already overwhelmed by one of the worst mass casualty events in San Diego's history.

I rested my head on my knees, stiff PPE crinkling around me, and reached out for what had to be the millionth time, but if there were any overlooked survivors, they weren't conscious. I wouldn't hear them with all the shell-shocked minds droning around me. It was like listening for a whisper with a jackhammer beside my head.

"Kelley's en route from DC," Mark said, heavy footfalls behind me sounding his descent down the shuddering escalator. "He'll be here in a few hours."

"Does Kelley know he's a target?" I asked.

"That probably just pissed him off," Mark said. Having met the unnerving man, it wouldn't surprise me.

"We're going to need more than Kelley," I said, lifting my head and rubbing my sweat-slick face. I cringed, having forgotten my clammy hands were stuffed inside suffocating purple nitrile gloves.

San Diego's top parahuman investigators were deceased, missing, or part of Major Crimes and likely pissing themselves, leaving only Mark, Ryker, and me.

The Agency's containment team might be able to handle one parahuman, even if his ability was, until now, undocumented, but three with wildly different abilities? That shitshow would wind up as a case study. We needed support if we were going to find Brittany, Ben, and the madman controlling them—assuming Ben was with him and not lying dead somewhere from a telekinetically crushed skull—and we needed it quickly. If the suspect could do this much damage before lunch, I didn't want to know what else he could accomplish today.

Unfortunately, the larger better-funded FBI was ironically ill-equipped to deal with parahumans. They couldn't pick up the slack. They could handle dead and bleeding bodies at the mall so long as no one combusted, but until Agency reinforcements, either parahumans or one hell of a trained containment team from LA or Atlanta or Toledo came—they could come from the depths of hell for all I cared—Brittany and Ben were chum for a shark.

"Anything from Cybercrimes?" I asked.

"Nothing actionable," Mark said. "The best thing we can do is—"

"I know," I cut him off, perhaps too abruptly. "We need to help here. These people need us too. I'm just worried."

"Me too," Mark said.

He leaned against the escalator's rails and sighed heavily, dark circles under his eyes making him appear a decade older. He was a boon in the search for survivors, cutting down the time it took rescuers to reach victims behind locked doors, but even the strongest man in San Diego could only run at full bore for so long.

"It doesn't make sense," I said, staring at the scene. "The Sons of Gaia wouldn't orchestrate *this*."

"Looks like the bastards' rabid dog slipped his leash," Mark muttered.

Goosebumps rose on my arms. Somehow, I didn't think that's what had happened. It didn't matter. Brittany, Ben, and Graham were caught in the crossfire, and no explanation could justify their exploitation.

Brittany.

I stared at the black bags laid out before me. A camera had recorded her at the scene, standing on a terrace just . . . staring. She looked like she was about to fall over the railing, pupils dilated and gaze vacant and unblinking as she appeared completely unaware of where she was. That was seconds before she vanished and a blur began dropping bodies. She hadn't responded to a single one of my calls.

I'd seen the video, but I still couldn't believe it.

"Poor Brittany," I whispered, a storm of emotions churning in me. I wasn't sure if I wanted her to be okay, catatonic, somewhere nearby, or halfway to a country with no extradition.

Mark groaned and shook his head, at a loss for words of comfort because none existed for the situation.

"That's your statement?" Mark asked instead, nodding at the notepad beside me.

"Everything since the bastard broke into my place this morning," I muttered, straightening and reaching for the notepad. "It's been a day."

"Whatever his endgame is, he's done hiding. This is only going to get worse."

"You really know how to give a good pep talk," I muttered.

Mark took the notepad and flipped through the pages, eyebrows raised. "This is lucid. Didn't you have a memory lapse?"

"Ian is a saint. I don't think I'm going to remember the stairwell, but everything else seems to be there. What a time for my memory to stick around," I said, sighing.

"You're doing better," Mark said.

"In the whole three and a half days I've been out of a coma?"

Mark nodded an implied *touché*.

"I'll take my wins where I can find them," he said, eyes drifting to the black bags. "Not much to celebrate lately."

"Like the shitty thing in your pocket you don't want me to know about?" I asked, giving up the facade of being tactful.

I was a kind of exhausted I didn't think a human being could physically be, everything ached, my friends' minds and bodies had been hijacked, and I was staring at bags of dead bodies. Whatever Mark was hiding could join the damn party.

He shot me a look meant to make me feel guilty for prying, but I already felt as low as I could. He pulled out his cell phone and handed it to me with a pinched *I warned you* expression.

"They found this pinned to a dressing room door with a knife. It's likely the one used in the attack," he said.

I expanded the image on the screen, doing my best not to think too hard about the red stain spread across the top of the paper, and noted the large blade, one edge serrated like a miniature saw.

"Another ASEK?" I asked. "Did he really make Brittany kill these people with the type of knife that killed Navin?"

"Bastard has no humanity," Mark muttered.

I examined the image, eyes widening with every scribbled word.

"What *is* this?" I asked in disbelief, dangling the phone away from my face as if it reeked.

"A manifesto, it would seem. It's a call to arms, encouraging parahumans everywhere to rise up against those who have oppressed them and let murderers slaughter their kind."

"You know Brittany didn't write this shit. It's not even her handwriting," I said, forcing the phone back at Mark before I finished reading it.

"I know. An electronic copy was anonymously posted to social media, along with a video of . . ." Mark paused. I didn't need him to tell me what the video was. "We took them down, but not before some people could download them. The FBI is helping us get ahead of it. I don't think anything can be traced back to Brittany. The video never showed the unsub, but . . ."

"Jesus," I mumbled.

We had to find Brittany before the entire country demanded her head. The media was already speculating, and it's not like there were many speedsters in the West. If the video of her on the terrace leaked . . .

452

Of course, convincing people that Brittany was under the influence of an ability no one knew existed came with its own problems.

Baby steps.

"He's making her do this," I insisted. "You know she'd never hurt anyone."

"I know, but we need to get to her and prove it before she does anything else. If this keeps up, it won't matter how innocent she is, it'll only matter what the public thinks is the truth. Every anti-parahuman group in the country is about to foam at the mouth."

"I don't get it," I said, shaking my head. "Even if he slipped *whoever's* control, he told me he wants Kelley dead. He said he wants to bring the Agency down. First, he helps kill half the parahumans in Counterterrorism, along with Janelle and . . . and Damani. *That* fits his agenda, but then he turns the other half into murderers slaughtering non-parahumans and writing manifestos. What's he doing? If he wants our leadership, why isn't he going after them? None of this"—I waved my hand across the scene—"does anything to get him closer to Kelley."

"It gets Kelley in San Diego."

I rolled my eyes. "If he has Brittany, he could be in DC in less time than that flight will take. Ryker's been here the entire time. He's literally gone for anyone else. It doesn't make sense."

"He's unstable," Mark said. "I don't think he has a plan beyond chaos."

I put my face in my disgusting gloved hands and groaned. "And he has poor Brittany and Ben. We still don't have any idea where they are?"

"Cybercrimes is doing the best it can, but all the mall cameras mysteriously went down about a minute into the attack," Mark said, giving me a pointed look. "A security camera from a business across the street caught Brittany exiting toward the highway on foot. SDPD just missed her. No idea where she was heading."

"Was the parahuman here?" I asked.

"There were several guys who matched the suspect's description, but they all got taken to the hospital or . . ."

Mark's eyes drifted to the black bags.

"Did any of the security cameras at the Agency get him? What about Ben?"

Before I reduced the Agency to glass and rubble, of course.

"All we've got is Ben and Graham leaving the Agency. Their SUV comes back ten minutes later. We think he got them in transit. There's no footage after that. We're checking the CCTV between the mall and the Agency."

"Just like the mall," I groaned. "How the hell did he get them in the SUV?"

"He must've gotten them to stop for something."

"Or someone," I said, thinking of Brittany. I'd pull over for her without hesitation.

"Chances are Brittany or Ben will lead us to him. We just need to be patient."

"You're assuming both are still alive," I said somberly.

Mark sighed, once again at a loss for words of comfort. He looked out across the food court, his eyes lingering on the frozen yogurt shop he liked to take his kids to, now marred with numbered evidence markers and red-brown stains. He blinked hard, clenching his jaw.

"They picked up Graham. Ian will evaluate him," he said, clearing his throat. "They've got him heavily sedated, so no telekinesis. He's secure until we can figure out what's going on with his brain. They don't know how long it'll last."

"Do you think it's permanent?" I asked, remembering Anna. A pang shot through my heart as I thought of Jo, too, likely still sitting outside her door based on the last text I'd read before the world went to hell. Well, even deeper into hell.

"I don't know. Hope not."

Ryker rounded a corner, running a hand over his face. He paused when he saw us, his normally perfectly combed white hair sticking out at odd angles and black suit ruined with dirt, one arm torn at the shoulder. He had wiped most of the blood off his face, though I could still see it in his white hair. A deep red crust marred his ear; a similar stain was prominent on the collar of his shirt. He'd let the EMTs look at him but refused to go to the hospital. He probably had a concussion, and I winced inwardly, wondering if it was the debris I created in the stairwell or Ben and Graham who did that to him.

He directed a curt nod at Mark.

"Time to go," Mark said. "The FBI has this covered. Nothing more we can do."

I was all too ready. I knew we had to be here; I knew we owed it to the victims to help. Family and friends needed to have their loved ones accounted for, but so did I. Brittany and Ben had vanished hours ago, and every minute we didn't know where they were was a minute something horrific happened to them.

I stood slowly, wincing. You never notice how injured you are until adrenaline stops and crushing fatigue takes over. My adrenaline had worn off hours ago, and my sore body yearned for about two days of sleep and a pharmacy's worth of painkillers.

"It's going to be a long damn day," I muttered, tears springing to my eyes as I put weight on my left leg.

Eyebrows knitted in concern, Mark offered me a hand. I gratefully reached out for it. He pulled me to my feet, and I gingerly avoided putting too much weight on my left side, lest my hip decide to send out stabbing pains to let me know what it thought of me and the life choices that had led us here.

"Diane mentioned something about a bottle of painkillers and a hot bath," Mark said, as if reading my mind.

Wait.

"Diane?" I asked. I looked to Ryker, whose attention was on a member of DMORT, then back at Mark.

"We're going to find Brittany and Ben," I insisted, confused. "Aren't we going to rendezvous with Kelley?"

"Hadley," Mark said, placing a sympathetic hand on my shoulder. "You got out of the hospital four days ago. You're supposed to be on leave, and you can barely stand up. You saved our asses. That's enough for today."

Bedsprings creaked in my mind, animalistic eyes piercing in their intensity and breath hot on my face. I shuddered against the memory.

"N-*no*," I stammered. "He has Brittany and Ben. We can't just abandon them. You don't understand. He's not—I can help. Call Ian or HR or the psych or whoever you need to give the okay, and let me help. I helped with this. I'm okay. I can make it through the rest of the day."

And tomorrow, and the day after that. However long it took to get Brittany and Ben away from the parahuman. *Alive*.

"Kelley's coming," Mark said. "He'll bring people more capable than us. We should get out of their way."

"We're just supposed to, what, wait by the phone and hope the rest of our friends don't come back in body bags?" I asked, blinking back tears. I looked at Ryker, but his attention was still with DMORT. "I can't do that. I-I didn't do enough before, and—I can't."

I took a wobbly step toward our boss. I had no idea what I could say to convince him, but dammit, I would.

Mark blocked my path. "You did do something. You fought a serial killer and barely lived. You got out of the hospital, and then you survived a home invasion and kept Ryker and me alive a few hours later. You got your ass kicked in the process. You had a memory lapse. You need to rest, and I need to get my family to safety. I'd appreciate your help with Lilly. She listens to you."

I scowled at him. "Don't use your children to manipulate me."

"Please, Hadley. If it helps, Ryker ordered both of us out of here. I'm going too."

"It doesn't help, you ass," I muttered under my breath. I took another step forward, and when he didn't move, I attempted to shove past him.

He sidestepped and easily blocked me. "What are you going to do? Ryker's not changing his mind. You plan on following Damani's example and chasing him down yourself?"

I stepped back as if I'd been slapped. "I'd be dead if not for Damani. Did that ever occur to anyone? No one else saw Preston Weiss coming. No one was even looking."

This time, it was Mark's turn to look surprised. He glanced back at Ryker, a flicker of doubt in his eyes. "Our eyes are open now," he muttered. "Look, you aren't a field agent. We never should have asked you to be one. It's just . . ." He rubbed his face. When he looked back to me, guilt reflected in his eyes. "You weren't trained for this, Hadley, and that's not your fault. It doesn't change the fact that . . . that you can't help in this situation."

My resolve shattered in an instant. I staggered back, ducking my head so he wouldn't see the hurt in my eyes. "Okay."

"Hadley, I'm sorry. I don't mean—"

"I said okay. Let's just go."

Mark rubbed his face again, then nodded, expression pinched. "I called your parents. They're meeting us at my mother's."

My eyes nearly bugged out of my head. "Are you kidding me? No! I'll go—"

"There's nowhere to go," Mark said hastily. "Your apartment isn't safe. Our last safe house was so compromised it almost cost you your life, and this guy obviously has an interest in you. We can't risk it. Your parents have agreed to take you out of the city. They aren't going to tell us where."

"Oh my God! You're trusting *Kathy* with my life? That's where we are? What about the other parahumans who live in the city? What if he goes after them? Should we ask my mom to hide them too?"

"Don't be an ass. Ryker's already called a press conference," Mark said. "He's recommending parahumans leave the city. Those who stay will be subjected to a mandatory curfew."

"That's insane. There's no way to enforce that. We're going to have vigilante groups taking to the streets on witch hunts. You can't even tell who the hell is a parahuman unless they use their abilities right in front of you. *No.* I'm not leaving Brittany and Ben to die. I'm not leaving Jo and Anna behind."

"Hadley," Mark sighed. "They're after *you*. Jo and Anna aren't safer with you drawing attention to them."

"No," I repeated, though I'd already given up.

He was right. Anna wouldn't be in the hospital if she'd stayed away from me. Damani would be alive if he hadn't tried to protect me.

"Hadley, there is nothing we can do. *Please*, I'd like to see my family. Diane is handling the kids by herself."

I rubbed my face, fighting frustrated tears. "Okay. Okay. I'll help you with the kids. But I want . . . I want Ryker to know I'm available if he needs me. Maybe . . . maybe there's something I can do."

But there wasn't. There never had been.

Mark held up my notepad. "Let me get this to Ryker, and we'll get out of here. Jo will watch Weasel."

"Who has a weasel?" I asked.

Mark paused. He opened his mouth and closed it again. He clapped a hand on my shoulder.

"When you remember, just know he's fine."

I leaned heavily against the escalator railing as Mark spoke to Ryker. They were too far for me to overhear, but I caught Ryker's glances in my direction. Mark returned a moment later and wrapped an arm around me. I leaned against him, resigned, and let him lead me away.

Gordon . . .

I would have jumped if my leg allowed it. I glanced back at my boss, his piercing blue eyes fixed on me.

You did good.

Ryker turned away. I stared at his back as he disappeared. I admit, I almost turned around. I almost said something.

I didn't.

I hobbled toward the exit, avoiding looking at the black bags on the ground. Once, a scene like this would have driven me to a meltdown. After hours of watching the black bags come in, I was empty. I wasn't sure it was a change for the better.

"You okay?" Mark asked, eyeing me sympathetically.

"Nothing an entire bottle of ibuprofen can't fix," I grumbled, unable to meet his gaze.

"Better a five-foot fall on your ass than a seventeen-story swan dive into the parking lot."

I groaned again in response and tried not to remember how I almost turned into a splatter at the base of the Agency. It was yet another experience I could unpack at a future date, probably in a later session with a therapist after we moved past my family trauma. Actually, the more I thought about it, the more the splatter option became more appealing than having my mother stand between me and a serial killer with super abilities. My father had probably called the local pharmacies in search of horse tranquilizers for my mother after Mark's call.

We reached the SUV, and I leaned against it, wincing and whining my way out of my PPE, nose wrinkling as it peeled away from my perspiring skin. PPE did not mix well with San Diego's arid weather. I handed Mark the white garb, and he opened the passenger door for me. I let out a sharp breath as I tried to scoot my shrieking tailbone into the passenger's seat. Mark had dealt with his PPE by the time I closed the door and reached for my seat belt.

He slid into his seat, eyebrows pinched in concern. "You need a doctor."

He frowned as I blinked back tears.

"Ian would have said something if it was bad. I think I'm just bruised," I said through clenched teeth.

"Don't be stubborn," Mark said, closing his own door. "You should've let Ian deal with that when he worked on your head. I'm still not convinced you didn't rush him through that either."

"Ian's got other people to fix," I said. "Things have been a bit noisier, but my memory's been fine for hours."

Mark shot me a look.

The *crack!* of a snapping bone reverberated in my mind, and I squeezed my eyes shut, forcing the memory back down. I'd welcome that one being lost to a lapse.

Mark read my face like an open book, damn him. "You better not blame yourself for what happened at the Agency. There'd be bodies if it weren't for you. I get to go home to my kids."

"I broke a man's arm and then suffocated him," I said defensively. "He couldn't help what he was doing."

"If Ryker had his gun, he'd be full of bullets. He's alive. We should all be damn grateful."

"What about Ben?"

"Still no sign of him," Mark said.

"And you're sure I—?"

"No," Mark said, cutting me off. "You created more than a few widow-makers in that stairwell, but I'd tell you if I thought he took a hit. I think Ryker got it the worst."

"Great," I muttered, though I believed him about Ben.

"He owes you his ass."

I pursed my lips, silent, sore, and cranky. Mark grunted in exasperation, equally cranky. "Take the damn win, Hadley. For once, just take the damn win. Stop torturing yourself for things outside your control."

I stared pointedly out the window and avoided Mark's irritated gaze.

"I don't think they wanted to kill us," I mumbled.

"Graham tried to toss you out a damn window," he said. "And never mind what they wanted. They weren't in control."

"Graham has more than enough ability to pull your brain through your nose, and you know it. Ben could have easily ripped the oxygen from our lungs and burst them. He didn't."

"Okay," Mark said, trying to exude patience. "So he made them homicidal and stupid. Good for us."

"I think a part of them was cognizant and fighting."

"Well, thank God for that."

"That means Brittany's aware. She knows what she did."

"Yeah. Say she does. You can't fix it. I can't fix it. *She* can't fix it. There is absolutely no point in punishing yourself for things you have no control over. We'll get Brittany and Ben back, and then there will be plenty of counseling for everyone involved. We'll heal. She'll heal."

I bit my lip. I opened my mouth to say something but thought better of it. I crossed my arms and stared out the window.

"What?" Mark asked grumpily.

"What if Preston Weiss didn't want to?" I asked, voicing my concern for the first time since the parahuman appeared in my apartment, making his abilities apparent. I'd shoved it down, denied it, but . . .

"What?"

"The parahuman said he had to warp him. Those were his exact words. He said it took a long time. What if Preston was actually a good guy? What if he was a victim, and I killed him instead of helping him?"

I whispered the last part, desperate eyes looking to Mark for answers, for him to tell me I was wrong and hadn't killed an innocent man.

Mark sighed and ran his hand through his hair. "Jesus, Hadley. It could have been one of a thousand scenarios. Maybe he was a victim. Maybe he was always a murderous bastard just waiting for his chance, and the psycho who broke into your home gave him one. The facts are that he opened Damani's throat right next to you and you were dying yourself. You did what you had to do. Was it fair? Hell no, but as far as I'm concerned, it was your *only* option. Don't torture yourself playing *what-if?* It won't do anything but fuck you up worse."

Mark signaled his exit, and I glanced at the sign as we merged onto I-8 East, heading out of the city.

"I want to stay," I whispered, though I couldn't think of a single thing that would convince him to let me.

After a lifetime as I knew it of rolling over and screaming *poor me* anytime things got hard, I didn't want to cut and run. It was also the one time I was being ordered to. The irony wasn't lost on me.

"There's nothing you can do, and you don't get a say," Mark said firmly. "Ryker wants all parahumans to get the hell out of the city, and I don't blame him. We don't need a bunch of living weapons running around."

"And Kelley's going to be able to deal with him?"

"Last I heard, he might be able to get the National Guard involved. He's got agents coming in from all over."

I sniffed in disgust. "Sure would have been nice if he'd put that much effort into stopping a serial killer and some bombers."

"It's sad when it's a bunch of parahumans," Mark said grudgingly. "It's unforgiveable when it's everyone else."

"They'll kill Brittany and Ben. How else will they be able to contain abilities like theirs? Good luck getting a tranq in Brittany. Ben alone can flatten a building."

So could I, I remembered with an inward wince.

"They might," he admitted softly. "But not if Ryker has anything to say about it. Say what you want about

463

him, but he's married to his sense of duty, and that includes his agents."

I bit back a sarcastic quip and crossed my arms instead, staring out at withered golden hills and boulders on either side of the highway in silence. Mark turned off the exit, a hotel visible up the road. My stomach clenched as we turned into the parking lot.

The side door of Diane's minivan slid open, and Lilly leaped out, running toward the SUV as we pulled into a space. Mark barely cracked the door before she had her arms around him, sobbing.

"Hey," he said reassuringly. "Everything's fine. We're fine."

I attempted to slide out of the passenger seat without looking too feeble.

Diane met me at the door, balancing Logan on her hip, and held it open for me. "Are you okay?" she asked, her voice low. "Mark said—"

I shook my head, cutting her off. Logan understood more than Diane thought, and Lilly's anxiety already left me wanting to vomit.

"This is Gilman." Mark's surprisingly professional voice came from the other side of the car.

I peered through the driver's window at the cell phone pressed to his ear. He noticed me and shook his head. I understood: *no Brittany update.*

" 'Adwee," Logan blabbered, redirecting my attention. He reached his chubby arms out to me.

"She'll play later," Diane said.

Her eyes widened as I finally forced myself from my seat, the purple-and-black bruise on the left side of my jaw becoming visible. I pulled my hair from behind my ears in the vain hope of concealing it. I refused the hand she offered, mostly so she couldn't feel my Lilly-induced shaking.

She hovered alongside me as I hobbled to the van and pulled myself inside. I did my best not to whine for the kids' sakes. I gingerly navigated around car seats, toys littered across the floor, and a handful of castaway Goldfish, careful not to wake the sleeping baby. I noted the suitcases and stroller shoved in a haphazard pile in the back.

Lilly opened the other door and heaved Logan into his car seat, shushing the toddler as he fussed. She attempted to force his arms inside the straps as he wriggled like a fish and clenched her shirt.

"No!" he wailed, tears sliding down red cheeks.

"We don't have time for this, bud!" Lilly said through clenched teeth. She wrenched one arm under a strap, only for Logan to pull the opposite arm free, his face growing redder as his wails grew louder.

A set of plastic keys rose from the floor and floated in midair.

"Sit still and we can play," I told the toddler as he focused on the toy with a laser-like intensity.

Lilly stared at me with a cornered-deer expression.

"It's fine," I said. "I'm fine." It was worth a memory lapse if the kids would calm down.

Lilly secured her brother and climbed in beside me, crushing a Goldfish with a crisp *crunch!* as she navigated the toys. She chewed what remained of her bleeding cuticles, her feet tapping the floor.

I focused on making the plastic keys dance, the energy in the minivan notably calming as the toddler giggled.

Diane climbed into the driver's seat and rolled the window down, leaning out toward Mark.

My heart sank.

"Call me as soon as you get there," he said, leaning in and counting heads. His eyes lingered on Jonah, asleep in his car seat, before focusing back on his wife.

"Dad?" Lilly squeaked. Her hand found mine.

I sucked in a breath as she clamped down on my fingers with force, and she recoiled.

"I'll meet you at Nana's house," he reassured her.

Lilly looked at her stepmother, her eyes wide, then at me.

"They need me to come back for just a bit. It'll only be a few hours," he said gently.

I reached to unclasp my seat belt. Mark shook his head, eyebrows pinched and lips pursed in a way that suggested I didn't have an opinion in the matter. I opened my mouth to argue anyway, but the sight of Jonah and Logan in their car seats made me pause.

If I had been out of the way, if I hadn't been around for Damani to worry about, would Jamie still have a father? Mark was right: I attracted psychopaths like flies to a corpse, and I didn't have the capability to handle them. Mark didn't need a liability.

I shut my mouth and sat back.

Mark kissed Diane on the cheek, and Lilly shook like an overstimulated Chihuahua. Tears dripped off Lilly's cheeks and onto her shirt as we pulled away. We pulled onto the highway, and Mark disappeared.

Damn you, Mark, I thought, feeling the anguish of his distraught children.

The tense hour to Mark's mother's house was highlighted by Logan screaming for a toy that had been left behind, Jonah screaming because his brother was screaming, and Diane and Lilly both bribing them with snacks that ended up joining the Goldfish on the floor.

I didn't blame the kids. It wasn't about a toy. The emotions churning in the car were palpable, even if you weren't a telepath. When the minivan pulled into the driveway, I threw the door open and, hip willing, crawled outside, grateful for open space, fresh air, and the fact I hadn't blown anything to bits while trying to control my own racing mind and force out the hysteria of four others.

"Hadley?" Diane called as she carried Jonah toward a quaint brick house.

The door swung open as Lilly and Logan rushed up the sidewalk, revealing a very concerned looking, stooped older woman with stark white hair and a kind face. I shuddered. I couldn't handle one more emotional person right now.

"Give me a few minutes," I said, my voice drained of emotion.

Diane nodded empathetically and went inside, leaving me blissfully alone under a cloudless sky. How could it possibly be so beautiful while nearly fifty people fought for their lives in hospitals, more than a dozen others lay in black bags, the Agency prepared for a confrontation with an unhinged parahuman, and the only friends I had left were suffering, possibly dying?

All while I had been forced away in a minivan full of children.

There was a swing set in the side yard, and I sunk into a seat that was much too low for me. My knees awkwardly positioned higher than the pelvis that still throbbed, I rocked back and forth as much as my aches and pains would let me, which wasn't much.

My own grandparents had a similar swing set in much poorer condition in their yard. It hadn't been touched in years, and I wondered if I had enjoyed it when I was Logan's age.

At that moment, I wished more than anything to remember a happy childhood memory to hang onto amid all the sadness—some vestige of ignorant bliss to remind me the world still had happiness in it—but I couldn't remember a time when I felt like that, and I hung there in a child's swing, limp and defeated.

Shouting came from the house, and my stomach twisted. The front door slammed open, launching the outer screen door into the wall. I blinked in surprise as it tore from a hinge, dangling at an awkward angle. My surprise was short-lived. I wished nothing more than to be invisible as Lilly stomped toward me, face red and tears streaming down her cheeks.

"You knew!" she screamed, mouth twisted into a grotesque snarl. "You knew, you *liar*!"

"He'll be back soon," I said. "He's just going to help Ryker and Kelley coordinate their response. They need his military expertise, that's all."

"Liar!" Lilly snapped at me. "They're sending Dad after *him*!"

"*What?*" I asked, dumbfounded.

"Talk him out of it," Lilly demanded, shoving her phone at me.

I grabbed it and dialed her father without hesitation. Like hell he was going after that madman.

"Lilly . . ." Mark sighed on the other end.

"Not Lilly. What the hell are you doing?" I snapped at him.

"They found him, Hadley," Mark said. He sounded far away—distracted.

"Uh-huh," I said. "And now Kelley and the National Guard are going after him, just like you said."

Silence.

"Mark, tell me they aren't sending you after him."

"I'm leading the team in."

"Mark—"

"I have to do it, Hadley," Mark said, cutting me off. "We don't know who he's got in there with him; they need someone with experience. He's going to cut through these guys like butter unless—"

He paused, but I knew what he was going to say. *Unless they sent in a Tank.*

"Mark," I said slowly. "This guy doesn't use knives or bullets. If he touches you, you're dead."

Lilly stifled a sob beside me. I tried not to look at her.

"We're covered," he said.

"With what? We don't know anything about this guy," I said. "How are they supposed to know if a layer of fabric or whatever the hell you're wearing is enough to block his abilities?"

"What do you want me to do, Hadley? He's going after kids now!"

"Kids?"

He sighed, the sound nearly drowned out by the increasing drone of voices and commotion in the background. "I'm sorry, Hadley. Mercy Rehab just burned to the ground. They were having a session with some kids, and one of them . . ."

"No," I whispered.

My heart broke for the first place I'd ever thought of as home, for the nurses I thought of as family long before mine accepted me. Well, tried to. Beyond that, I knew without a doubt which child it was. Damani's son was the victim of a madman.

"Jamie," I said, his name coming out in a gasp. "Is he okay? Is he—"

"He's fine. Ian saw to him. No brain bleed. Everyone's fine, but they lost the building before they could contain the fire."

I closed my eyes and took a deep, steadying breath.

"Mark, this guy is a piece of shit, but that doesn't mean—"

"Did Lilly tell you she had to quit soccer?"

"I don't see how—"

"She kicked a ball into the goal frame. Burst the ball like a balloon and bent the frame."

I blinked slowly, comprehension taking a moment to overcome shock. I stared at the door hanging from one hinge, then at Lilly. She watched me with wide eyes, barely breathing. She was a few years too old for her abilities to be manifesting, but who was I to say anything? Mine had waited until I was drinking age.

"Today was supposed to be her first time at the support group at Mercy. I don't want her to know what happened."

"*Shit*," I hissed under my breath. "Why didn't you say anything?" I lowered my voice to a whisper and stepped away, hoping Lilly wouldn't hear. "Mark, he can't get her."

"Not if I'm there to make sure this goes right," he said.

"Send me," I blurted out. "He already admitted he can't hurt me. Send me instead."

"Hadley . . ." Mark sighed. He sounded exhausted. "You know you can't."

"Better me than you!" I snapped. "You have three kids! What happens to them if you don't come home?"

Lilly let out a wail beside me, and I mentally kicked myself.

"Look, tell them—" His voice broke. "Tell them I'll be back as soon as I can. And I'm—I'm sorry for what I said at the mall."

He hung up.

"Goddammit! Mark?" I hissed, staring at the phone in disbelief.

"What did he say?" Lilly squeaked, breath coming out in rapid pants.

I stared at her, words failing me.

"Hadley, what did he say?" she nearly shrieked, her shrill voice rattling my brain as much as her emotions. If she didn't break something else in the next few minutes, I would.

"Hey," I cooed. "He's going to be fine."

I reached out for her, but she jerked away, wrapping her arms around her chest and shaking her head.

"I need my dad!" she sobbed. "Hadley, I need my dad!"

I needed Mark too. I needed Brittany and Ben to come home. I needed Anna to wake up.

I needed to actually *do something*. To hell with what Mark or anyone else thought.

I grabbed the crying teenager and forced her to look me in the eye. "Lilly, I'm going to get your dad. He's not going! You hear me? He's not going after him."

I looked past the girl to the minivan parked in the driveway, keys left in the ignition and forgotten about amid the chaos.

I was going to owe the Gilmans the biggest apology.

471

CHAPTER 22

I didn't think it was possible for the drive back to the city to be more stressful than the drive out of it, but of course, I hadn't imagined stealing Diane's minivan from her mother-in-law's driveway and racing down I-8 West at speeds over one-hundred miles an hour when I'd woken up that morning.

Outside of failing my driver's exam, this was my first driving experience in five years. Considering that the last time I—Old Hadley, specifically—drove a car by myself resulted in a traumatic brain injury and rehab, I had reservations that this plan, and it wasn't really a plan if I was being honest, was doomed from the start. I wasn't Old Hadley, and I was discovering that nothing was more terrifying than trying to figure out how much brake pressure to apply while barreling down the back side of a four-door sedan.

Well, almost nothing. There was always the sense of impending doom that I'd be too late to stop Mark from getting himself killed, Brittany and Ben would be killed by the National Guard, Anna would die in a coma, and I'd lose all my friends, then my family, to a terrorist cell's unfettered homicidal maniac.

"Shit!" I shouted as my exit materialized on the right. At least, I thought it was my exit.

I threw on a blinker—possibly the wrong one—and jerked the minivan over. Other drivers laid on their horns as I cut across white chevron markings separating the highway from the exit and barely made it.

"Jesus," I muttered under my breath.

At this rate, I'd kill myself long before I reached Mark. The Agency loomed in the distance, and my shoulders relaxed as I realized I'd almost made it.

Now, to convince Mark not to be a hero.

Tires shrieked as I careened into the Agency's parking lot, the smell of burning rubber and hot engine permeating the air as I slammed the car into park before it came to a full stop. If I lived through the day, I probably owed Mark and Diane money for vehicle repairs.

I stared at the front of the once-flashy building, heart sinking. One side of the structure was noticeably crumbling with glass windows blown to oblivion starting from the seventeenth floor. Onlookers gawked from the sidewalk, snapping pictures. A few directed their cell phones at me while others snapped selfies. No one dared get closer, though they'd yet to tape off the building. An obvious dearth of reporters told me action had to be occurring elsewhere. The parking lot should have been crawling with speculating news crews.

I'd anticipated the Agency mounting a response from headquarters, but looking at the razed edifice, I knew I'd made a terrible misjudgment. The damage was worse than I remembered. The Agency couldn't work from this building. They were coordinating their response from someplace else, but I had no idea where.

I was alone.

"No! *No, no, no, no!*" I muttered, snatching my phone in a panic.

I winced at the sight of thirteen missed calls from Mark and seven missed calls from Diane. I shuddered at the missed calls from my mother. Where their attempts stopped, Jo's missed calls started. Even my brother had called. I swallowed my guilt in a hard lump and tried to convince myself I was doing the right thing.

I dialed Mark.

"Pick up," I begged. "Please, pick up."

My call went to voicemail. Frustrated, I threw the car door open and gingerly slid out. The police department, city hall, and several other government buildings were nearby. It made sense for them to move to one of those locations.

Swallowing my rising anxiety, I squeezed my eyes closed and prayed for the ability to concentrate. Chuffing from a distant helicopter caught my attention. Somehow, I knew they were there, but where was it?

My phone buzzed, and my breath released in a rush.

"Mark?"

"Where are you?" Mark asked.

I paused for a moment, voice stuck in my throat as I searched for the words I needed. How on earth did I convince the most dutiful man I'd ever met to abandon his obligations? Especially if he thought he was doing them for his children?

In the distance, a siren wailed to life, its urgency jolting me to action. I'd convince him. I had to.

"Where are you?" I asked, ignoring his question. "Have you gone after him?"

"Hadley, Diane is hysterical, your mother's off the rails at *my* mother's house, and Jo is driving the streets looking for you. *Where are you?*"

"Are you going?" I asked. If he was going to ignore my questions, I could be childish and ignore his. Never mind the fact I'd started it.

"Dammit, Hadley!" Mark snapped. "I can't do this right now! Your phone says you're at the Agency. Jo will be right there."

Damn that freaking tracking app!

"Mark, no—"

Goosebumps rose on my arms at the sound of a whistle. Behind me, a mess of thoughts crashed like waves in a hurricane, chilling me. A blackened aura slithered into me, and I whimpered, overwhelmed by raw poison that burrowed deep.

In a heartbeat, I became prey. I should have known I couldn't play the hero.

"Mark?" I whispered, comprehending how utterly doomed I had become in the span of half a second.

"Hadley, Jo's coming. End of discussion. I have a job to do. We'll discuss this later."

"Mark, don't hang up," I whispered, unsure what would happen if I was overheard. "I messed up."

There was a pause. The siren in the distance became disturbingly louder, as if heralding my fate.

"Brittany's behind me. She's not okay," I whispered.

The siren wailed as Mark's breath caught.

"I'm coming," Mark said, fear edging his voice. "I don't care what you have to do, Hadley, but you hang on. I'll be right there—*BILL!*"

"I'm really sorry. You were right," I whispered.

A hand brushed my face as it reached for my phone.

"Hadley, don't—!" Mark's voice rang in my ear as Brittany took the phone from my hand.

There was a decisive beep as she ended the call. A tense silence fell, punctuated by that damned siren and the sound of my heart hammering in my ears.

A little girl kneeled by her bed, hands clasped against her forehead. Blonde hair fell around her shoulders, bright-blue eyes staring up at the woman hovering over her.

"What are we praying for today?" the woman asked. The little girl cast her eyes to the side, watching a man who leaned against the doorframe. He looked away, neck burning an angry red, and the little girl dropped her eyes, her own shame blooming.

"To make it go away," the little girl whispered.

"You know why He's punishing you?" the woman asked.

The little girl shook her head.

"Yes, you do," the woman scolded. "Only bad boys and girls get the curse."

"I'll be good," the little girl whispered. "I won't do it, Mama. I won't go fast anymore."

I struggled against the memory as if fighting an undertow, resisting feelings of shame, confusion, anger, and a suffocating *need* for vengeance. Taking a deep breath, I turned to face her, saying my own quick prayer.

She didn't look like the Brittany I knew. Unwashed, knotted hair hung limp around her ashen, gaunt face, giving the impression she'd been ill for some time. Her once bright-blue eyes were bloodshot and rimmed by circles so dark they looked like bruises. I tried to dig into her churning mind—to see what she intended to do— but her thoughts outside that painful moment of the past were gossamer, slipping between my metaphorical fingers. I wasn't sure Brittany could hold on to them either. Decades-old memories repeated in an endless loop in a way I'd never felt before. She was drowning, events from long ago playing on a forced cycle she couldn't break.

No, I *had* felt this before, I realized with chilling clarity. When Preston Weiss stood over me in that godforsaken basement, a screaming boy perished in flames over and over again in his memories.

I resisted the urge to vomit. The parahuman was doing this to Brittany. What if he had done this to Preston Weiss?

"Hey," I said to the drone who had once been, and maybe still was, my friend.

She stared at me, her pupils dilated. She blinked and cringed, shaking her head as if trying to rid herself of something. Slowly, I raised my hands, hoping she would take it as a sign of submission.

"Are you okay?" I asked.

I chanced a glance down and swallowed a gasp at the sight of rusty-brown stains on her shirt and pants. Her arms and trembling hands were tinted a similar color; her nails looked like they had dirt caked under them. I knew it wasn't dirt.

"We thought you ran," Brittany said.

"I couldn't leave—"

"It wouldn't matter," she said, cutting me off. She looked past me, her voice detached.

I wasn't sure if she was threatening me or not. I opened my mouth and closed it, unsure of how to respond.

"You know they're looking for you, right?" I asked.

She nodded. "It wasn't me," she said, still looking past me.

"I know," I said. "I know you'd never do that. We can stop him. Mark's on his way here. We can go to Ryker and figure out a way to stop him."

Her eyes snapped to me, and I realized I'd shown my hand. She took a step toward me, and I took an involuntary step backward. Behind me, a wailing siren abruptly cut off.

"He wants you," she said.

The hair on the back of my neck stood on end. I stood rooted in place, brain buzzing in alarm. I needed to backpedal, and I needed to do it quickly.

"He said he can't control me," I blurted.

"He can't. That's why he wants you." She took another step closer.

I couldn't outrun her. I couldn't fight her. Trying to maintain a telekinetic grip on her would be like trying to lasso a jet. My only option was to stall until Mark arrived, but even then, I wasn't sure an army could stand between us if Brittany wanted to hurt me.

The point was moot.

Mark wouldn't make it. The cold weight of acceptance settled on me. She was going to do whatever she'd been instructed to do.

"Brittany, *please*," I whispered, stumbling backward.

She took another step in my direction, and this time, I recoiled, throwing my hands up in self-defense.

"Brittany, stop!" I begged, thrusting my palms out toward her. "Whatever he told you to do, please fight it. Please!"

"*Hadley!*" Jo's terrified voice pierced the air like a gunshot.

No. Brittany would kill her.

Startled, I turned my back on Brittany.

Jo stood outside her cruiser, lights flashing but siren silenced. Her hands clenched a gun, finger resting beside the trigger. Her gaze flickered between me and Brittany, an inner war raging behind her eyes.

My breath caught at her expression of grief. Her eyes were wide and haunted, her thoughts racing behind them. The glimmer of hope they held rapidly dimmed as she realized her nightmare was playing out in front of her.

I knew that look. She knew she couldn't do anything but watch. Brittany would move the moment Jo's finger reached for the trigger. She'd be dead before it got there.

Unfortunately, Jo was going to try anyway.

A whistle of wind and rapid footfalls sounded behind me.

"*No!*" I shrieked.

Jo's expression twisted into one of abject horror. Whether it was because she realized she was about to be ripped limb from limb or because her gun was abruptly telekinetically ripped from her hands and flying across the parking lot, I wasn't sure.

Actually, it might've had something to do with her feet leaving the ground. I jerked her straight into the air, her arms and legs flailing.

"Hadley!" Jo cried.

I'd probably die for the next part.

I screamed, lashing out across the parking lot with a telekinetic assault. The police cruiser's windows blew out in an explosion of glass, the cruiser rocking on its wheels and alarms wailing as my invisible force struck it.

Brittany became visible, tumbling across the pavement, and I gasped.

I hit her! I hit—

Oh, *shit*. I hit her.

Brittany regained her footing and turned toward me.

"Hadley, *no*!" Jo screamed.

Fuck.

I lashed out again, but Brittany was ready for me this time. I lifted my head toward Jo at the sound of whistling, but I was too slow. I'm not sure what I would have said anyway.

Arms wrapped around me, tightening against my chest and cutting off a shriek, and my feet left solid ground.

I found myself moving at an impossible speed and willed myself not to blow anything up—to not blow *us* up.

My heart hammered against my rib cage, inaudible against the buffeting wind roaring in my ears like a tornado. I expected Brittany to drop me in front of a train or off a cliff. Instead, she stopped under a flickering streetlight.

She dumped me from her arms, and I gasped a lungful of air.

Legs unsteady, I stumbled against the closest building, vertigo making my stomach churn. I turned to run, but the world tumbled around me. I didn't realize I was falling until I hit the pavement, my hands scraping against the ground. I attempted to crawl, but it was pointless. I couldn't escape Brittany by *crawling away*.

I turned to look at her, shaking, expecting her to be angry. I braced myself for an assault. Instead, she stared straight up, unfocused eyes following something I couldn't see.

"I didn't do anything wrong!" a teenage girl screamed, slamming her bedroom door. She rushed to her closet and threw it open. She stared at her clothes, uncertainty clouding her face, before rushing forward and grabbing handfuls of shirts. She tossed them on the bed as someone pounded on the door.

"Brittany Ann, you open this damn door!" her mother shouted from the other side.

The teenage girl brushed angry tears from her cheeks, willfully ignoring the woman outside her room.

"Open the door, Brittany!" her father shouted.

"No!" Brittany shrieked, whirling to face the door. "I'm going to Grandma and Grandpa's!"

She wasn't going to hurt me.

"Jo?" I wheezed, struggling to catch my breath both from Brittany's smothering memories and dizziness.

"Fine," Brittany said, eyes unfocused and distant as she stared up at the streetlight, though I didn't think she saw it.

"Thank God," I gasped, my concern replaced by guilt. Whatever happened next, I hoped Jo wouldn't blame herself. "Did I hurt you?"

"No," Brittany said absently, still not looking at me. "You should've."

That was reassuring.

"I can't stop," Brittany said.

I willed my stomach contents to stay put. It would help if Brittany could stop the waves of rage coming off her.

"He didn't tell me to hurt you. But I will if he tells me to. I have to do what he says."

481

"I'm not sure how to take that." I sucked in another lungful of air. "You know," I added, making what I knew was a feeble attempt at distraction, "the day I moved out of my parents' house looked a lot like that."

Brittany's face scrunched in confusion, and I tapped my temple.

"I don't want to hate them, but he wants me to. It's all I could feel when . . ."

She glanced down at her stained hands, and for a moment, awareness flickered behind her dazed eyes.

I didn't have time to get my hopes up.

The Brittany I knew vanished as quickly as she'd come, a cloud settling back over her mind.

Slowly scooting toward the wall and settling against it, I stared up at a darkening sky and desperately wracked my brain for a way out.

Maybe I *could* attack her. I had been fast enough at the Agency. Maybe I could grab her lungs like I had Graham's.

Catching Brittany's suspicious glance, I realized I'd already used my one chance. She wasn't as dazed as she looked. If I wasn't fast enough or she slipped from my grip, I could probably dig my own gr—

I nearly leaped up as a hard lump in my pocket pressed against my backside. My hand jerked toward the phone I shouldn't have had, but Brittany's head snapped in my direction, her intense, suddenly all-too-focused gaze commanding me to leave it alone. Bewildered, I dropped my hand to my side.

Brittany knew there was a tracking app on my phone. Everyone knew. Why would she put it back in my pocket?

I have to do what he tells me . . .

Had she found the will to defy him? Was my friend still in there? I glanced back at her, suddenly hopeful, but gasped at the sight of a thin trickle of red sliding from her nose.

No. There was no way. She'd had nosebleeds for weeks. I would have noticed if she wasn't my Brittany.

Wouldn't I?

"Brittany?" I whispered. "What happened?"

She brushed her hand under her nose, absentmindedly smearing red across her face.

Her eyes met mine, and a moment of clarity interrupted the endless loop of Brittany's darkest memories.

"Brittany! Him!" Hadley's—my—voice squawked through my earpiece. I saw him.

I—no, Brittany—chased a hooded figure, streaking through the crowd in a blur. He reached the alley, but I had him. With an oomph!, *I drove him into the wall. One hand gripping the man's arms behind his back, I reached back for my handcuffs.*

"Get off me, freak! I didn't do anything!" the man shouted.

"You're under arre—"

Someone was behind me. I spun in a blink, grabbing the bare wrist of the man who reached for me.

He smiled.

My knees buckled. Then, pain. I wanted to scream, but my mouth wouldn't open. I tried to reach for the hand on my neck, but I couldn't move my arm.

"You're damn lucky," the man said to Preston, fingers digging into my skin. "I thought I told you to avoid the funeral."

Preston Weiss turned, rubbing his wrists.

"I told you the telepath would be on your ass if you got too close. Do you know what could have happened if I hadn't been here?"

Preston glanced down at me, his face scrunched in confusion. Then, it went slack. He blinked, looking back at the dark-haired man as if nothing had happened.

"I was going to follow her," Preston responded.

"No," the other man said. "I've got the distraction in place. Just lay low. The Agency is going to forget all about you soon."

"That's what you said after the first bomb, then the second! You stabbed that guy and nothing changed! Those freaks are still watching me!" Preston snapped.

Navin? He *killed* Navin? I'd kill him! I'd—why couldn't I move?

"You're the one who decided to test a telepath!" the man barked. "If your ego hadn't gotten in the way, we'd be fine!"

"You said you could take care of her!" Preston snapped back.

"Just don't do anything! You've already messed this up enough!" the man commanded. "I told you to trust me. I had to make it convincing. Give it time, and the plan will go off without a hitch. The Agency is about to get their suspects, and then they'll stop looking. They want to put this behind them; they can't afford any more bad press. They won't look at you after this."

"What about her, genius?" Preston snarled, gesturing to me. "Is she part of the plan?"

The dark-haired man glanced down at me, a smile creeping across his face. "Actually, I think she'll be useful."

I gasped, the world spinning once more as I withdrew from Brittany's mind. "The funeral," I said. "H-he got you at the funeral?"

She jerked her head in a curt nod.

"I had Preston Weiss," she said. "I didn't know Julian was in the alley."

Julian. So the monster had a name.

I reached into her mind, probing for more information, but where a name usually elicited *something*—the image of a face, the sound of someone's voice, a memory or feeling associated with the person, Brittany's mind became a yawning chasm at the mention of his. Any vestige of him was utterly absent from her mind, as if she was incapable of thinking of him.

How. The. Hell*?*

"Jesus, Brittany. I'm so sorry. I should have known," I said.

"It's not your fault."

"It's not your fault either—what happened . . . and right now. I hope you know that."

If she understood, her face didn't reflect it. Her eyes drifted past me again, her mind growing increasingly addled. I frowned, concerned, but how the hell was I supposed to know what proper mind control looked like?

No, this was more than mind control. If that monster had gotten to Brittany weeks ago . . . it didn't make sense. She'd been my Brittany the entire time. Whatever was happening to her now, it was different.

"What's he doing to you?" I whispered.

Her lips twitched as if to smile. "It's okay. It won't hurt once he's done."

"What—?"

Wind kicked up around me. I lifted my hand to shield my eyes from whipping dirt.

A man with dark skin landed on the roof just above my head—Ben. I sighed in relief.

There was a bruise on his cheek I could feel guilty about later, assuming I lived, but at least he was off my conscience. I was more than likely about to be brutally murdered—by my own friends, if I had to guess—but I'd take what comfort I could.

"You're stalling," Ben told Brittany, markedly more alert than her. "He's expecting her."

485

He looked down at me, eyes still reflecting some semblance of identity. Was it because the parahuman—Julian—had only just . . . brainwashed him? Was that what was happening?

Studying Brittany, I knew it was far more than that.

"Sorry, Hadley," Ben said somberly.

"What do they want?" I asked.

Brittany and Ben glanced at each other, confused.

"They?" Ben asked.

"He's working with the Sons of Gaia—was working with the Sons of Gaia," I said, looking at them for confirmation. "Is he still? Has he gone rogue?"

Visions of automatic rifles filled my mind. Would dying in a hail of bullets under the victorious whoops of bigots be more or less painful than whatever my own friends could do to me?

"They served their purpose," Ben said. "Julian doesn't need them anymore."

Escaped attack dog, then.

"What does he want?" I asked.

Ben cast Brittany a glance, but both remained silent.

"And if I refuse?"

"He prefers you alive for the moment," Ben said, shrugging. "But he has contingencies."

"*Prefers*," I mumbled. "You and Graham nearly tossed me out a window."

"Ryker needed motivation. Graham got a little . . . overzealous. Julian will correct him."

"The Agency has Graham."

Brittany and Ben exchanged knowing looks, and my stomach twisted.

"You can't run," Ben said, clearly lucid but most definitely not in control.

He sounded like the Ben I knew. Hell, he sounded like a willing accomplice by the confidence in his voice, but when I probed his mind, black waves crashed in his brain, his thoughts dark, like someone flipped a light switch on his consciousness. No memories played in an endless loop—not yet, if I had to guess. I wondered when he would start to feel like Brittany.

I cast a glance at her, a puppet who looked like my friend. I wasn't sure she could stand for much longer, and I wondered if that was a good thing, if that meant his influence was waning.

I could fight them.

The thought settled on me with a chilling weight. They were both weak—suffering. Their minds were reeling. Brittany looked like she could barely remain conscious. I could lash out with my telekinesis. I could flatten the building Ben was standing on.

But Brittany and Ben would die—maybe I'd go with them.

If I miraculously didn't kill myself, I couldn't expect Jo to show up in time again. I'd wake up in whatever was left of Mercy Rehab not knowing who I was or what I'd done.

I didn't want that.

I wanted my friends to live.

More than that, stopping Brittany and Ben wouldn't stop Julian or the Sons of Gaia or the APA or whoever the hell else was involved. Julian would find more puppets—maybe Mark or Lilly next. Maybe he'd use Jamie again. Maybe he'd start over in another city. Either way, Brittany and Ben didn't deserve more pain.

Julian did, and as I sat there staring at the shells of my friends, I realized I wasn't scared.

What was left to fear?

Anna might never wake up. Jo had nearly killed herself trying to get between me and danger. Mark was about to sacrifice himself for his kids.

If anything, running was the more terrifying option.

I just wanted it to be over. If I ran now, I'd only have to face this moment again later. I was so tired of waiting for the next tragedy.

"Grab her," Ben commanded.

Brittany took a step toward me, and I threw my hands up.

"I'll walk!" I said hastily. "I'll go on my own."

If I stalled, maybe Brittany could find her way back to me? She didn't look like she could fight, but maybe she could run. Maybe she could live.

She stepped back, and I breathed a sigh of relief.

I still had my phone. If Brittany was regaining her autonomy, maybe Ben was too? If I could just slow things down, maybe we could take back the upper hand. Mark and Ryker could find us, and then we could make a plan that wouldn't get anyone killed.

I recognized the mural I was sitting against: a mosaic wall of sea creatures with silver reflective tiles intermixed. It was on the way to the Coronado Bridge at the start of some abandoned properties and a train yard. We were only a few miles from the Agency. Brittany could make that run in seconds—*had* made that run in seconds.

I rose, clinging to a desperate hope, still believing I could find a way out of this that wouldn't involve bloodshed and more funerals. My friends walked ahead of me, chaperoning me like executioners on the way to the noose. My bum leg impeded my movements, and I was grateful for a natural excuse to move slowly. Brittany remained by my side, Ben observing from above. When buildings gave way to the train yard, he kept pace atop the cars. Beside me, Brittany's intermittent sniffles became wetter in sound, and her hands came away with increasingly larger smears of glistening red.

"Does it hurt when he controls you?" I asked.

"It gets worse over time," Ben replied for her. "It's what he does to keep you coming back."

"Coming back?" I asked.

"The effects wear off, so he gives you a choice," Ben said from above. "Either come back before you get your autonomy back and live a few agonizing minutes of freedom or submit to his control again and avoid an aneurysm."

"Jesus," I muttered.

Having seen how the man in the hospital parking lot died, how could I judge them for going back?

"Is that what happened to Navin and Wildfire?" I asked, remembering their autopsies. "Was he controlling them too?"

"In a way," Ben said. "He needed their abilities disabled."

"So the Sons of Gaia could kill them?"

Ben glanced at me, a look of disappointment on his face.

I was still missing something.

Beside me, Brittany's breathing became labored, a sheen of sweat glistening across her graying skin. She tripped, and I gasped as she nearly went to her knees.

She *was* getting her autonomy back, just like I hoped, but with a rush of understanding, I realized Brittany was coming up on a fatal deadline.

I was forcing her into a slow, painful death. She was letting me.

She wasn't going to escape. The only way Brittany could live was as a slave.

"It would be best if we hurried," Ben said pointedly.

We weren't going to find a way out of this. I had my friends beside me. They could get their autonomy back. They might be able to help me in their few precious moments of freedom—I knew they wanted to.

But they would die.

Memories flashed before my eyes. Madison lay in a stairwell in a puddle of blood; Alice lay on a beach as waves hissed at her bloodless feet. Navin's ashen face was stark against a black body bag, the same bags that carried Gladys, Glenn, and Tom away from a cold, desolate alley. The look in Damani's eyes as he pleaded for my help in the basement. Anna . . .

I looked into Brittany's bloodshot eyes, and the part of me that held out hope she would never hurt me died. She wouldn't . . . yet.

"I'm sorry," she whispered.

My lips quivered as I smiled at her.

I didn't know what to do. I just knew I couldn't let her die. I held my arms out to her, saying goodbye to the sliver of my friend shining through. Hers reached around me, and I buried my head into her neck, clinging to her gaunt frame.

The world vanished in an assault of frigid wind. The motion sickness wasn't as bad the second time.

Telling myself that didn't make it true. I landed on my feet and swallowed a retch.

We stood outside a brick building. It had been abandoned—likely decades before. The windows were long gone, and a door barely clung to its frame. Sunlight bleached an area around which letters once spelled a company's name, but when the letters fell, the sun nearly erased the dark profiles left behind, leaving only a few legible characters. The building had been graffitied countless times, and once, someone had cared enough to paint over it. Now, graffiti layered the building, bold purple, green, and yellow, among other colors, in stark contrast to the worn, muted brick. The Coronado Bridge was overhead, and I felt small as I looked up at the gigantic structure, the distant cars producing an audible hum as they raced across.

I paused when Brittany opened the door to the warehouse, rusty hinges groaning ominously, a clear signal that this wouldn't end well. The door opened wide, revealing a dark, desolate interior punctuated with streams of light filtered through filthy, damaged windows.

One last, fleeting thought of running crossed my mind, but I'd already done that, and the result wasn't a life I could continue living. I'd come back to fight.

Granted, I thought I'd be facing Mark and his sense of honor. I didn't know what I could do in this situation—probably die, but watching Brittany stumble and gasp for breath beside me, blood streaming from her nose, I knew my only choice was through the door.

I wondered if this was how Damani felt when he approached the door to that cursed house.

I glanced back at the empty train tracks one last time, breathing in the scents of dirt, brake fluid, and diesel. The sun had almost vanished below the horizon; the clouds were turning various hues of pink and orange.

It struck me that I hadn't taken the time to see more sunsets, but it was too late for that now.

It was too late for a lot of things.

The streets remained quiet and empty. Good. Whatever happened next, maybe Mark could still go home to his children.

The mystery of the unknown ate at me, and I wondered if I'd ever know if Anna woke up. I wondered if Jo and Mark were still searching the streets for me. A sharp pang of guilt and the regret of things unrealized coursed through me.

I stepped inside. Brittany followed behind me.

I winced as the door slammed closed, sealing us in like a tomb.

CHAPTER 23

The odors of mold, mildew, and decaying wood permeated the air. The interior of the building was much like the outside. Graffiti was thicker here, the walls so saturated I could only guess at their original color. Not even the thick cement columns that ran from floor to ceiling were spared. Clouds rose off the cold gray cement floor with every step, dirt and dust piled up in every direction and the occasional brick, shattered glass, or empty beer can dotting the soot.

He stood in the middle of the empty warehouse, eerily illuminated by a dying beam of light.

I wouldn't consider Julian physically intimidating. Whereas Preston had the physique of a wrestler, Julian didn't look like a person physically capable of restraining another human being.

Julian was short, ghostly pale, skinny to the point of looking ill, and had unwashed, shoulder-length muddy-brown hair. With a long narrow face, no prominent jawline, and a pointed, bony chin, his bone structure would have led me to believe he was younger if I hadn't known better. Dark circles rimmed bloodshot eyes. The only outward symbol of the threat he posed was a tattoo on his upper arm: a red-eyed, muscular bulldog foamed at the mouth as it tore through flesh like paper, revealing banded red muscles beneath. It was the perfect metaphor for the darkness lurking within him.

Some things became perfectly, painfully clear in that moment.

I needed the APA and the Sons of Gaia to be the bad guys. After years in my observation room listening to their reprehensible thoughts, the idea of them as victims wasn't an idea I could entertain until that moment, when Julian stood at the center of the warehouse, a smile slithering across his face as his ravening eyes glittered at the sight of me—every bit a predator closing in on its kill, every bit in control. That's when I knew.

No one was ever using Julian. No one could.

A pebble skittered across the ground, retreating away from my feet, though I never touched it. At least, not physically.

"Hadley," Brittany whimpered. "Please, run."

I jumped, not expecting her to have the strength or capacity to speak. I turned to her; meeting her eyes felt like a knife to the gut—I would know. *My* Brittany looked back at me with eyes reflecting a shattered soul, a

494

dim reflection of a person with cracks spiderwebbing across her very being.

Brittany wasn't coming out of this whole, if she came out of this at all. The mind-controlled version of her was almost better.

I took her hand, gently squeezing it. "Run to what?"

"Brittany," Julian called, his voice echoing against the walls.

Brittany's eyes darted to him, her lips quivering as she shirked away, pulling back like an animal resisting the path toward slaughter, but I held her hand tight.

"Go," I told her.

She balked, staring at me with frantic eyes. "He's going to make me—"

"Go," I repeated. "I can't watch you die. Whatever happens, it's not your fault."

Brittany took an unsteady step, eyes glassy with pain holding mine as she stumbled past. She leaned in, the sharp scent of blood filling my nose. "Goodbye, Hadley," she whispered.

"Now, Brittany!" Julian shouted. "Bring her."

Brittany bowed her head, sniffling as tears made tracks in the blood crusting her upper lip. Then, the world vanished in a *whoosh!*

When I stood upright again, I stared into brown eyes so dark they appeared black in the low light.

Seething waves crashed against my brain, churning like the wrath of the sea in a midnight storm.

"Hadley," Julian said, cruel smile never faltering. His eyes held no warmth—nothing human that I recognized.

He placed a hand on the back of Brittany's neck. I fought the urge to snatch it away.

She shuddered, gasping. Her back arched, her hands twisting into claws. She panted through whatever violation he was inflicting on her.

I didn't expect her to scream. When she did, it was feral, the sound echoing against apathetic walls.

Brittany thrashed and clawed at Julian's arm. His expression twisted, teeth gnashing and eyes wild.

He gripped her wrist, and she went to her knees, still screaming.

I felt every nerve alight in both of them as bolts of lightning struck with the force of a raging storm. Every cell felt like it would be sheared in the face of a million gnawing teeth. When the sensation reached my brain, I stumbled back, blinded by explosions of light across my vision.

Then, it was over. Silence took the place of terror, like a town after a tornado levels it.

Oh, God. I still felt her. The remaining sliver of Brittany convulsed in the background, like a deer with an arrow through its lungs.

Our ragged panting was loud in the cavernous space. I stared down at my friend, slumped in the dirt with Julian's hand still clutching her neck. My breathing grew louder as fire crept across my skin.

Death would have been gentler. How could I let him do that to her?

"Up," Julian commanded, ragged breathing betraying the toll his ability took on him.

Brittany rose to her feet. Julian wiped his fingers under her nose. He smeared her blood between his fingertips, eyes focused on me. If he was concerned by my reaction, he didn't show it.

"The biology of this one is fun. Damage occurs quicker for her, but you've probably realized that by now.

Hindsight's a bitch, isn't it?" Julian said, smirking. "You should know I'm not about to kill my cash cow—not yet. She was never in any danger." He patted Brittany's cheek in a way that turned my stomach. "But I had to have assurances you'd come. You'd never let her die, after all."

I didn't respond. My jaw clenched, hands forming fists as Julian handled my friend like livestock.

"I mean, look at this pretty face," he continued, grabbing Brittany by the chin and forcing her to look at him. "It's on every screen right now. Her own parents just eviscerated her on live television. They called her a monster in front of the whole world, and I didn't have to do a thing! I can't pay for that kind of division!"

The media—they'd figured it out. Somehow, considering the circumstances, it felt less dire than I thought it would.

Julian dropped Brittany's chin and stepped toward me. I gasped involuntarily.

I telekinetically shoved him backward—a reflex I immediately regretted. He frowned, and Brittany's head snapped to attention, her pupils narrowing like a cat about to pounce.

"Not yet!" Julian said.

Brittany blinked rapidly as if dazed.

"Let's give Hadley a chance, why don't we?" He turned his attention back to me. "I don't recommend acting out around Brittany. She won't take it well."

Damn out-of-control telekinesis!

Heart racing, I waited for his next move. Eyes narrowed, he snatched Brittany's arm. My breath hitched as she doubled over, vomiting on the floor.

"You control that, or this conversation ends prematurely. You do anything to me, any fancy dangling foot trick, any explosions—anything that could disarm me, and they pay for it. You've seen what that looks like. It's not pretty."

The heat rising in my blood cooled to ice. Had he programmed them to die if anything happened to him? Could he do that? What happened if the Agency or the National Guard stormed in and apprehended him?

My cell phone grew heavy in my pocket. I swallowed hard, staring at Brittany. Why had she done that? She had to know what would happen if we were found.

Brittany righted herself and wiped her mouth. Julian approached me, and I breathed through my fear as he laid his palm on my cheek. If he wanted me dead, I'd be dead. At least, that's what I wanted to believe.

His eyebrows knotted in frustration, and his other hand gripped my neck.

My breath hitched, my ears ringing and vision growing darker at the edges.

But nothing happened.

Julian released me with a snarl, eyes smoldering with anger. He circled me like an animal looking for an opportunity to strike.

He was trying to control me. He couldn't.

"What's this?" Julian asked as he circled behind me.

Was it messed up to feel relief as my—our—only hope of rescue left my pocket?

Julian approached Brittany and dangled my cell phone in her face. "You know better. Take it to the bridge, make a call, and drop it. That should buy us enough time to talk."

A whistle signaled Brittany's exit as Julian stood before me once again. I hoped she had taken any chance of Mark finding us with her. She returned less than a minute later, wind whistling in her wake, Ben following in behind her.

Julian beckoned Brittany and Ben forward, and I gasped at the flush of blind hatred that raced through my veins as he pressed a thumb to Ben's forehead, then Brittany's. Sweat broke out across my brow.

"Daddy, stop!" a little girl screamed as a belt connected with her exposed backside. Her cries were met with another crack!

A shot echoed, a body slumping to the ground as a young man leaped to his feet. Mouth hanging open, he turned to the man looming in the doorway, gun clenched in his fist.

"I had him under control!" Julian shouted.

"I don't need out-of-control parahumans in my unit!" the older man spat. "You keep them on their leash, or I shoot them like the damned rabid dogs they are! Fucking insanity they let your kind breathe free air!"

I squeaked as hands wrapped around my neck. Brittany had a surprisingly firm grip considering her condition.

"Daddy! Stop!"

"*Out* of my head," Julian said menacingly, biting off each word. "You're convenient—*very* convenient, but you aren't necessary. You try anything, and they've been given orders to rip you to pieces—literally. We had quite the lively discussion about it. Christine thinks she can keep blood circulating in your body long enough to keep you alive for . . . let's say an hour? Brittany thinks she'd have to take your head off long before that."

My heart sank as a fourth individual detached from the shadows, and Christine joined us. I thought she left the Agency and started a new life weeks ago. She hadn't reached out when I was in the hospital. I admit I had been hurt, and I hadn't made any attempt to contact her either.

Now, she stepped to Julian's side, and her presence slithered against me. Her mind crashed against mine like waves breaking against the shore in a storm, and I recoiled with a gasp, her warped mind all too familiar yet nothing like the girl I used to know.

Too much. They were all hate and anger. I couldn't filter it out.

I jumped as a seagull cried above, the sound of footsteps on sand crunching in my ears. I clenched my eyes closed. There was no bird. There was no beach. I was losing it.

"Is *that* enough motivation for you to keep control, or is my patience better off exercised elsewhere?" Julian said, calling my attention back.

I nodded silently, aware that Brittany's nails were digging in next to my jugular if he decided to call my bluff. Let's face it, now was not the moment my telekinesis would be brought to heel.

"What are you doing to them? That's not mind control. That's-that's something—you're doing something to them," I said, voice shaking, but it wasn't from fear. I squeezed my eyes shut, breathing shallowly as my hair stuck to my perspiring neck and my friends' raw emotions buffeted me like a hurricane.

"My army can't grow if I spend all my time controlling them. Better to rewrite their way of thinking. The person they'll become will understand joining the cause is in their own self-interest. Preston was a prodigy—a sloppy brute, but a prodigy nonetheless. He took my instructions and really transformed them into his own."

At the mention of Preston, Brittany's eyes focused, and for a brief moment, hers held mine.

Preston stood outside the apartment building, eyes hungrily sweeping from window to window.

"Which one's hers?" he asked. I—Brittany?—stepped from the shadows, eyes focused on my feet. I pursed my lips, silent, as

needles pricked my brain and my muscles cramped, desperate to respond. I clenched my fists. I wouldn't. I could fight it this time. I wouldn't let him hurt Hadley.

"Which one?" Preston snapped. He unsheathed a hunting knife from his belt and brandished it angrily.

I could fight—my muscles turned to fire, the agony of it stealing my breath. I nodded toward the bedroom window of what was supposed to be Hadley's safe house. I dropped my eyes, shame overpowering relief as my body relaxed.

"Jesus Christ," Preston muttered. "Julian said you're useful. I don't care what he thinks, either do what I say, or this goes in your chest, freak. Got it?"

I didn't react as Preston jabbed the blade in my direction. I wanted to, but I couldn't. I wanted to tell him no. I wanted to scream. I wanted to beg. I wanted to plead for him to leave her alone.

But it wasn't my body anymore.

"Get rid of her security," Preston said, turning the blade's handle toward me. He wiggled it impatiently when I didn't move. I watched, as if in the background of my own life, as my hand reached out and took the knife.

"Do it quietly," Preston said. "Do not tip off that damned telepath. That bitch has created enough loose ends for me to deal with. I need her and all of your other Agency friends off my damned back."

He turned to leave.

"No! Where are you going?" I cried, then snapped my mouth shut, shocked at the sound of my own voice.

Preston paused, glancing me up and down, then threw his hood up and turned away. "I just told you," Preston snapped. "I'm getting your friends off my back."

I tried to keep my expression neutral. It wasn't her fault, but Jesus Christ, the last thing I'd considered was that Brittany led Preston Weiss to my safe house that night. All those nights she passed out drunk on my couch . . . did she report right back to Julian and Preston? I never suspected a damn thing.

"You know, I'm surprised you came back," Julian said. "But I'm grateful. Killing your family to get to you would have been so messy, and quite frankly, it's unnecessary. For now."

"You have me. Leave them out of it," I growled, wondering if I'd see it coming if Brittany decided to break my neck. "What do you want?"

"I told you. I need you to kill Ryker and Kelley."

"I'm not . . ." I glanced at Brittany.

He'd used her to get to me. He wanted me.

"If I go with you," I whispered, heart hammering in my chest as I grasped at an opportunity. "If I do what you ask, will you let them go?"

Brittany's eyes flashed something between hope and alarm before her expression became blank again, her hand never loosening from my throat.

"No," Julian said flatly, almost amused by my request.

"The National Guard is looking for you," I continued in a rush. "You can't fight them. I'll go with you—right now. They won't find you if you have a telepath. I'll help you escape if you let them go."

Oh, God. I didn't want to. I didn't want to become this monster's plaything. I glanced at Brittany, then Ben and Christine. He couldn't do to me what he was doing to them. Whatever happened, it was better than what they were experiencing. I told myself the trade would be worth it. They were worth it.

"Those idiots have to stop their wild goose chase first," Julian muttered petulantly. "Bastards really know how to follow a false lead. I suppose it's for the best. It looks like this will be a long . . . chat."

My look of bewilderment delighted him.

"You haven't figured it out, have you?"

"Y-you know? They're bringing an army," I stammered.

"It's hardly an army," he said, his tone almost bored. "Even if they were a threat, I command the land, air, and sea. Didn't I show you what Christine can do?"

The video. The boat sinking into the harbor was Christine. I was so, *so* stupid.

I cast a glance at her, but if I wasn't looking at her . . . it was like a black hole stood where a person once was. She just . . . stared, her eyes like a dead fish. No thoughts. No emotion. No sensation. There was no one in there, just an animated body. The unnaturalness of it felt like a yawning chasm.

I stepped back, my mind rushing with the sensation of falling as I focused on her for too long. Her head cocked in my direction as if sensing me, and I shuddered when her corpse-like eyes met mine.

I focused on Ben instead. At least Ben blinked.

"I don't understand," I said, my stomach doing flips. "You said you want Ryker and Kelley. Why do all of this? Why not just kill them?"

"You're *still* missing the bigger picture," Julian said, voice dripping disappointment. "Do you know what superheroes really are? They are the biggest, flashiest parahumans the Agency can find—the fire starters, the telekinetics—all of their ancestors' worst nightmares. They aren't put on stage to be celebrated but to show the masses they're contained. They are nothing more than collared circus animals doing tricks so the Agency can show off how good they are at neutralizing the threat, how good they are at making us police and lock up our own kind. It's all one big trick. *You* are now the face of that trick. You are a symbol to us all.

"I gave the other side their martyr. As we speak, the Sons of Gaia, the APA, and all of the others speak of Preston Weiss as a messiah. Preston Weiss, the poor, beautiful boy with the perfect parents, glowing grades, and dreams of becoming a lifesaving doctor. Hell, he even had the tragic backstory with the dead cousin! I couldn't have found a better attack dog, granted it took forever for me to turn that oaf. Add in the fact that the Agency never found a shred of proof—I made sure of that. DNA was destroyed. There are no witnesses. Absolutely nothing ties that picture-perfect frat boy to those crimes, and yet the Agency and their parahumans hounded him, framed him, and when that wasn't enough, they blew him to pieces."

The reality I was so desperately quashing became undeniable. Preston hadn't been Julian's partner. They weren't working together. Preston was a victim. He was a slave, used like Brittany, Ben, and Christine.

I'd killed an innocent man.

Julian laughed at the look of anguish that crossed my face. Damn the heartless bastard, he laughed in my face!

"Don't feel bad," he teased, his fake pout mocking me. "You didn't do anything I wasn't going to do."

"You were going to kill him?" I whispered.

"Obviously, he didn't know that was part of the plan. I admit I had to improvise when you killed him ahead of schedule. It was supposed to be you of course but, oh, the opportunity you created. So much better than the original plan—you'll see. Now, you get to play your part. You will play your part, won't you, Hadley?" Julian said.

He was right. I didn't get it.

"If this is about freeing parahumans, why kill everyone? You think so highly of *our kind*," I said, using his terminology bitterly, "yet you've enslaved and killed us. You used *children*. You're no better than the Sons of Gaia or the APA."

Julian's eyes smoldered like embers.

"*I've* enslaved us?" he snarled. "I'm setting us free. We were born to be gods. You and everyone who submits to the Agency and the people like them are pathetic dogs, happy to serve your masters while your leash chokes you to death. They *hate* us, and you would be their willing slaves. Better a dead god than an enslaved draft animal!" he snapped, losing control for a moment. "They served a greater good!"

Julian stood in a tent, the sound of men's baritone voices and rumbling machinery betraying how thin the canvas was. It was hot and dry, the sun penetrating the canvas in pinpricks of glowing yellow. A man lay on a cot positioned against the canvas, a camo cap pulled over his eyes. Julian stepped forward and grabbed the man's wrist.

"He—"

A flash of fire erupted from the man's hand before he relaxed, but the heat hardly deterred his captor. Julian pulled the cap off the man's face. The supine man stared up, the whites of his eyes bulging.

"Sorry about this," Julian said. "But the captain says we need you tonight. It's best if you aren't in control."

The need to breathe snapped me back to reality. I coughed, choking, as Brittany's grip grew tighter.

"I didn't mean to," I gasped. "I'm sorry."

"You see what they make us do?" Julian hissed.

"I'm sorry," I repeated, voice raspy as Brittany refused to relax her grip, my own eyes bulging like the soldier's had. "I'm sorry for whatever happened to you, but we don't deserve to be punished for it."

505

"It's okay," Julian said. "You're going to fix it for me, and I think you're going to want to."

"I don't want to—"

His eyes met mine, and he flooded into me like a tidal wave. I gasped as a memory was forced into my mind. Others had learned to project their thoughts for me to pick up, but this wasn't projection. This was violation.

A girl leaned across the bar, her long highlighted hair flowing down her back.

"Fireball!" the girl squealed at a noticeably irate bartender, her glassy eyes and questionable balance indicating she'd already had enough. She laughed and rocked back on her heels.

Her back became rigid as he took a step toward her. He felt the telepath in his mind as warm tendrils slid across his psyche, as thin and gentle as silk from a spider's web. She turned her head, and Old Hadley's eyes locked with Julian's five years ago.

She grinned.

That wasn't possible. My abilities hadn't manifested until my car went into the ocean. I'd used them for the first time to save my life. Absolutely everyone I knew said I'd had no telepathic or telekinetic abilities until that night.

Brittany released my neck, and Julian stepped closer. His breath was hot against my face.

He leaned in, his lips brushing my ear. He whispered, "Are you sure you don't remember me? We were quite close once, you and I."

What. The. **Fuck?**

My breath quickened. Around me, pebbles skittered across the ground. My friends' ravaged minds roared like waves. Footsteps crunched in the sand. A seagull cried—

There was no fucking seagull. What was wrong with—

Oh.

Telepathy is a funny thing, especially when you have a broken brain that tries to rationalize memories it can't place.

Like how a serial killer became dreams of a screaming child in a house fire or how a psychotic parahuman felt like churning waves.

Like the same waves that almost drowned me the night a traumatic brain injury stole my life.

Julian killed people with brain bleeds.

"You tried to kill me," I whispered. "It was you."

"Oh, no," Julian whispered, leaning in. His hands gripped my arms, holding them in place as I shook. "Not that time. We were having too much fun for me to kill you. Such a shame how it came to an end. You weren't much use after that. At least, that's what I thought. Now, be a good girl for me. Kill Ryker and Kelley. You'll get everything you want. I'll tell you what happened at The Library, and maybe none of your new friends have to die. I'll even consider sparing the Tank."

A jolt shot through me at the mention of Mark's superhero alias.

"Everyone knows what Brittany—" I glanced at my friend. "Everyone knows what you made Brittany do. You said it made the national news. No one's on the parahumans' side now. You turned us into the monsters the APA and the Sons of Gaia always said we were. If I do what you ask, they'll never stop hunting us. That can't be what you want."

"Oh, the other side's going to be unwavering in their beliefs," Julian said. "But remember how the mall's surveillance system mysteriously went down? And those victims . . . I think the witness's memories might be getting a little fuzzy regarding the number of attackers and the abilities they might or might not have. Won't it be so tragic when the National Guard comes in here guns blazing and puts a bullet in your sweet, innocent friends' heads?"

His grin made me ill.

"What?" I blurted out.

"*This* goes down with or without you," Julian admitted, arms stretched out to the warehouse. "But what comes next—oh, that will be beautiful. The long-term results are so much more *impactful* if you play your part."

It dawned on me. "You're controlling the soldiers. You wanted this."

"The National Guard. The Agency's containment team. Not all of them," Julian admitted. "Just enough to get the point across. William Ryker and Marshall Kelley are so predictable in their actions; they made it easy. The spark gets lit right here. This is the day parahumans everywhere see the other side for what they are. *You* will show them what they could be, and then, when the other side comes for *them*, parahumans everywhere will realize how much stronger we are. This, right here, is our revolution."

There was no reasoning with him. There was nothing left in him but hate, his mind sick and twisted. He would never stop.

My eyes roamed the room, stomach clenching as the scene suddenly made sense. This wasn't a hiding place; this was a theater. The wide, expansive space with unobscured views left nothing to the imagination. Whatever scenario Julian had orchestrated, he wanted it to play out here. I glanced into the corners of the building, the height of which were probably a perfect vantage point for a camera. I couldn't tell if they were there or not, but if Preston's videos were any part Julian's idea . . .

I couldn't see a way out of this. Damani was wrong. It wasn't going to be okay. Mark, Brittany, Ben, Christine . . . we were all going to die. He wanted them to die. Julian would move on, and even more people would die as he pushed for . . . What did he want? The end of the Agency? Civil war?

I didn't want to die.

I wanted to watch Anna wake up. I wanted to be at her wedding.

I wanted to have movie nights with my family. I wouldn't complain if Mom accidentally gave me mint chocolate chip ice cream—she didn't mean anything by it.

I wanted to sit on the beach with Jo and watch Molly and Weasel run through the surf.

To eat pizza on the couch with Brittany and force her to watch one of the awful sci-fi movies I loved so much.

To watch Lilly grow with her abilities into a confident, capable young woman.

To meet Damani's son and tell him it was okay. What happened was a horrible accident. He needed to know he couldn't punish himself for one horrible, tragic *accident.*

An accident that wasn't his fault.

It was never my fault.

Sirens wailed in the distance, a helicopter's chuffing not far behind.

Julian's grin grew impossibly wide, his eyes glinting as his endgame came into play. "Well, Hadley?" His eyes were manic with expectation.

I looked into Brittany's eyes. She knew. Whatever cognizant part of her was left knew she was about to die.

I remembered the way Damani had felt as he begged me to be scared, promising it was going to be okay.

It wasn't going to be okay. I couldn't save Damani. I couldn't save them. I couldn't save me.

"I'll take the bullet, you sick bastard," I snarled.

Julian frowned. "How disappointing."

He stepped away, focused on the door. He paused, the corner of his mouth twitching as he watched me from the corner of his eye.

"Brittany," he called, sounding almost . . . amused.

Brittany's head snapped to attention.

"We can handle things here. The roommate is in Room 7. See if that cop is still there." He turned, meeting my eyes. "Unless, of course, Hadley would like to reconsider."

Sirens wailed in the distance, growing ever louder, but the only sound I heard in that moment was blood as it rushed to my ears. With it, clarity.

There was no escape. There was no hope. There were no memories to fear losing or people to look on with alarm and disappointment as I lost control.

No one here got a happy ending.

We all died of brain bleeds or gunshot wounds today. That was it.

So why was I still holding back?

I moved toward Julian, my footfalls in time with my raging heart.

This time, I leaned in. "You say you know me?"

Julian's eyes met mine, glinting. "Oh, I do. Better than you do."

"Then you should know something about telekinetics. Something they ingrained in us at Mercy. It's a rule that shouldn't be violated at any cost," I whispered.

"*Nothing* is more dangerous than a frightened telekinetic."

"I'm counting on it," Julian whispered back.

"Except you stole everything I have, and I'm not afraid anymore," I growled, hands clenching into fists.

Julian's smile faltered.

"I think," I drawled. "I might know one thing more dangerous than a frightened telekinetic. It's a telekinetic with nothing to lose. A telekinetic who doesn't have a reason to show restraint. A telekinetic who *fucking hates you.*"

A whistle shrilled in my ears.

"No!" I snapped, thrusting out an arm.

A collective surprise passed through the room as Brittany flailed in the air a dozen feet above us, limbs moving so fast she appeared as a blur. She shrieked, her voice echoing across the warehouse. She was impossibly difficult to hold onto, like clutching a bar of wet soap. Somehow, I did.

"Is this what you wanted?" I asked.

Julian's response was an *oomp!* as I telekinetically flung him across the warehouse. He sailed through the air as if yanked back like a marionette. He didn't stop until his body connected with a cement pillar, the impact reverberating.

"*Is this what you wanted?*" I shrieked.

His body lurched forward, then slammed into the pillar again.

"*Is this wh—?*"

I choked, clawing at my throat.

Ben.

Air tore from my lungs. I gagged, my lungs burning as they shriveled inside me. My nails raked my neck; a sensation of swelling filled my limbs as Christine ripped fluids from my insides. My legs buckled against the pain, knees hitting the ground.

Julian limped forward and knelt in front of me.

"Is that really all there is now?" Blood marred his ear, a trickle of red running down his neck to splatter the ground before me. "How disappointing. Perhaps the plan is better served without you."

Not that I heard him. I was too busy dying.

My vision faded at the edges, a black void forming in my mind that matched my darkening vision. I gasped, desperate for a breath, but there was no air to breathe. The sensation of swelling turned to stinging until something in my core exploded in fiery agony.

My mouth opened in a silent cry.

Not like this. I couldn't let him win. We couldn't all die in vain.

My heart slammed against my chest.

One beat . . .

Two beats . . .

My telekinetic blast hit. A collective scream echoed against the walls as four bodies slammed into them.

My grip on Brittany slipped, and she broke free. I lashed out telekinetically, and she slid back, grunting with exertion as she fought my attack to no avail. She slammed into the wall again, her limbs pinned as Ben raised a gust that whipped dirt into my eyes.

Not that it had much of an effect. Christine was about to burst them anyway.

I wanted to scream, but there was still no air to make a sound. Instead, an ear-shattering *crack!* broke my silence.

Pillars rumbled, and the floor splintered. Chunks of concrete lurched into the air, spinning as if in orbit.

Another blast rocked the structure.

Pillars shattered as if made of glass. Concrete flew outward, chunks exploding against the wall in deafening blasts.

Air rushed into my lungs, and I gasped, the fire in my veins ceasing.

Panting, I frantically kept my hold on the four bodies pinned to the wall.

Brittany was still screaming, and Julian . . .

Why was Julian laughing?

Ben's head hung limp, but I didn't have time to wonder if I'd killed him.

Christine's eyes met mine, as empty and unfeeling as a void.

She was definitely going to kill me.

Bam!

I jerked as a shot tore through the air. Brittany's head slumped, and she was still, her fight extinguished.

"*No!*" I shrieked.

Another shot rang out.

Christine sagged against the wall.

I sensed the soldier behind me. "No, stop!"

I lashed out, and someone yelled as a thump confirmed I'd made contact.

"Hadley, stop!" someone shouted at me.

"Don't kill them! *Please*, don't kill them!" I begged, but it was too late.

Someone dropped down beside me.

I screamed on the floor. Tears streaked my face, and my shirt was saturated with something wet. I didn't care.

They'd killed them. My outstretched arms trembled violently, but I couldn't let them go. I wouldn't let them have them. My vision pulsed in and out, a rushing sensation in my head growing too intense, threatening to let me succumb to blackness.

"No," I begged.

I couldn't forget. I had to remember. People needed to know this wasn't their fault. They weren't monsters.

Someone was shouting at me.

"Why'd you kill them?" I whispered.

"Hadley!" a voice roared in my ear. "Put them down! Ian can't reach them!"

"Why'd you kill them?" I repeated.

Dozens of boots echoed like a stampede. Men rushed past me toward the four bodies on the wall. They didn't shoot Julian. He was the only one who deserved to be shot.

"Hadley, they're alive! Damn it, put them down so we can help them!"

"What?" I whispered. Blinking, I stared hopefully at the large man squatting beside me in an AGENCY vest, his wide eyes desperate.

"They're tranquilized. Please, you have to let them down so Ian can help them. Hadley, please, before it's too late!"

"I can't," I cried, my body shaking. I couldn't let them have my friends. "He turned the soldiers. They'll kill them!"

"That's not the National Guard or the Agency. That's the FBI. Ryker sent the FBI. You understand me, Hadley? Let them down."

I shook my head.

"Hadley, we heard everything. Ryker wouldn't let the National Guard in. He wouldn't let Kelley authorize deadly force. Hadley, *let them down.*"

Four bodies slumped to the floor. FBI agents leaped on Julian. Rubber gloves extended all the way to their shoulders, blocking his touch.

Where'd they find those?

Julian snarled, hands curled into claws and swiping at them.

The click of handcuffs brought a rush of clarity. I stared, dumbfounded.

Julian was dragged away in handcuffs by gloved FBI agents, two holding him at arm's length as he fought and screamed.

EMTs knelt beside Christine, Ben, and Brittany. A flurry of movement and urgent shouts highlighted the efforts being made to save their lives. Ian kneeled over Ben, hands on either side of his head.

I couldn't stop myself; I laughed, a hysterical, desperate sound that echoed through the warehouse. Laughter turned to sobs, and I slumped on the ground, shaking.

"Are you okay?" the man asked.

"They're alive?" I sobbed.

"We hit Brittany with enough drugs to drop a horse, but she should be fine. Hadley, you don't—you don't look good. Talk to me. Are you okay?"

"How?" I asked, staring at the large man hovering beside me.

His hand reached out and stopped. Why'd he look so scared to touch me?

"He told Brittany to drop my phone. He said he turned the soldiers. They were supposed to kill us."

"Did the arrogant bastard specify what had to happen after she dropped the phone?" the agent asked. "Hadley, you're bleeding. Y-you're bleeding everywhere."

I stared at Brittany. I hadn't noticed her wet jeans.

A female EMT gently patted Brittany's chest. I gaped when she respectfully leaned forward, and my phone appeared from within Brittany's shirt. She'd hidden it in her bra. The crazy, beautiful parahuman—she found a loophole.

She hid the phone in her freaking bra!

My sobs shifted back to maniacal laughter as the EMT ended the ongoing call with a beep.

"Hadley, focus on me. *Are you okay?* Can you get up?" the agent asked.

I kept laughing, not caring that my vision was black around the edges.

"Secured!" someone shouted.

I cackled, slumping over, curling into the cool floor. The agent placed a comforting hand on my back, and I gasped, my skin screaming at his touch.

"Hadley, get up. You're not okay."

Blissful darkness was coming, promising to take the bad memories away. My laughter ceased. I relaxed on the ground, giving in. It didn't matter. My friends were safe. Julian was in custody. He couldn't hurt anyone else. It was all I needed to hear.

"Hadley, get up."

"Damani was right," I whispered. "It was okay."

"I need help over here!" the man shouted.

"Tell Mark to go home," I told the man, delirium taking me. "Tell him it's okay now."

A rush overwhelmed me as I relaxed my grip on consciousness. I hoped I'd still be me when I woke up.

"Shit! Hadley, no. I'm right here! It's Mark! Get up!"

Mark? I didn't recognize his face.

The agent—Mark?—tried to pull me to my feet, but the dark was taking me. A sensation of flying came over me as he scooped me into his arms. Startled by the light, I opened my eyes to see the moon as we crossed the threshold. Night air filled my lungs, and I smiled, realizing I would see another sunset.

We all would.

"Ian! I need paramedics!" Mark bellowed.

Ambulance lights were harsh against my eyes as Mark carried me to the nearest one and lowered me onto a stretcher.

"Hadley!" Ian exclaimed as he slid to my side, face pale.

Why was everyone so damn alarmed?

"T-There's blood everywhere," Mark stammered. "I-I don't know where it's coming from."

Oh, that sounded bad. I looked down, staring at a sheen of red that covered my exposed skin—all of it. Christine had pulled my blood through my flesh. Black and purple raised bruises dotted my arms where blood vessels had ruptured.

"I'm gonna . . . I need to go now," I whispered as my eyes rolled back in my head, the blackness finally swallowing me.

"Inflammation, now!" Mark snapped.

I blinked as Ian placed his hands on my head, vision coming back in a rush and briefly doubling before returning to normal.

"Something's bleeding," Ian said.

"No shit!" Mark snapped.

The world moved in and out as people rushed around me, doing things I couldn't keep track of. A pinch in my arm signaled an IV. Hands wiped desperately at my skin, erasing all the red.

"Alert the hospital to have an operating room and blood waiting, just in case. The bleed was in her abdominal cavity," Ian said.

"I don't like the hospital," I whined.

"Hadley," Ian said, his haggard face swimming into view. "I've given you something that will reduce the

517

swelling. I have to focus on the others right now, okay? They're taking you to the hospital, but you'll be fine. I'll see you later."

"I'll live? No memory loss?" I slurred in disbelief.

He'd administered more than just anti-inflammatories, I suspected.

"You can expect some, but nothing catastrophic," Ian said. "You'll be fine. You just need time to heal."

"The others?" I asked as the stretcher began rolling toward an awaiting ambulance.

"You'll all be fine."

"Get those cuffs off my agents! They're unconscious!" Ryker's voice boomed in the night.

I lifted my head. He hovered over Ben, and a goofy, lopsided grin tugged at my lips. Brittany's blonde hair vanished as ambulance doors closed around her. I didn't see Christine.

"Heads will roll if my agents make the news in *goddamned handcuffs!*"

As if sensing my gaze on him, Ryker turned, his eyes meeting mine. I smiled at him, tears of relief rolling down my cheeks as EMTs rolled the stretcher into the back of the ambulance. He nodded at me, unspoken words passing between us, and turned back to eating a frightened FBI agent alive.

A black SUV sat in the distance, and I lurched as my eyes found Julian's. I expected him to be raging, but he sat there, quietly staring at me, a conniving smile and knowing glint in his eyes alighting his face.

Hadley . . . Julian's mind invaded mine. *You were perfect. The next part will be fun.*

I squeezed my eyes shut against his voice. The ambulance doors slammed closed, and I said a prayer to whatever higher power had intervened, realizing we were all alive.

"Hang on!" Mark shouted from outside, banging on the ambulance doors.

One of the EMTs threw the doors open, and someone leaped inside, the determination of someone refusing to be left again filling the small space. Mark closed the doors and tapped the outside, signaling for the ambulance to leave.

"Hadley!" Jo said breathlessly, tears on her cheeks. She seated herself beside me and took my hand. "Hadley, I'm so sorry! I'm so, so sorry!"

"I think I broke my promise," I slurred.

"What?" she asked, eyes examining me up and down, face paling as she realized I wasn't wearing a red shirt.

"I broke . . . promise," I said again.

"Hadley, I—"

I squeezed her hand.

"I need you to . . . know," I said, eyelids growing heavy as drugs soothed me, chasing away the pain. "More than . . ."

Her hand was warm in mine as the world fell away.

EPILOGUE

Stumbling over a box in the living room, I nearly dropped Weasel in my rush to grab the door. My toe throbbed in protest, and I muttered a curse under my breath. Tucking Weasel under one arm, I half hopped, half limped the last stretch and flung the door open just as Anna reached it with another overpacked box. She grunted, huffing, and repositioned her hands to get a better grip.

I held the door open for her. "You don't have to get everything today. The boxes have been here for weeks. Another few days won't hurt anything. There's no rush."

Anna waddled through with a box nearly the width of the doorframe, the bottom of which was maintaining its integrity thanks to a thick layer of tape and prayers to a higher power.

Weasel wriggled in my arms, whining and thumping his tail against my side in an attempt to catch Anna's attention.

"She'll pet you!" I exclaimed to the needy dog, attempting to restrain him.

Elliott staggered out of what had once been Anna's bedroom with a seemingly heavier box. I'd told Anna not to put all her textbooks in one box . . .

"I *hate* moving," Anna whined, heading toward the parking lot. "The sooner this is over, the better!"

"Thank God it's a small apartment," Elliott said under his breath, barely avoiding Weasel and me as he navigated the box through the door. "Moving puts her in an awful mood."

"I know," I said, snickering.

"I can hear you!" Anna called in response.

Brittany appeared at the front door, ducking out of the way as Elliott finally wrestled the box through.

"I really don't mind doing that for you," Brittany insisted for what must have been the dozenth time over the past few weeks. "I can have it done in just a minute."

"No," Elliott said. "We've inconvenienced you enough. We've got this." Winded, he set the box down and took a deep breath.

"*El!*" Anna called from outside, sounding frustrated.

"Maybe," Elliott groaned before dashing toward the parking lot.

Weasel wriggled in my arms, overwhelmed by the sense of change.

"Hey, buddy!" Brittany said, scratching him behind the ears. She entered the apartment and surveyed the remaining boxes.

I could sense her relief that she would get to stop tripping over them soon. She'd been a good sport waiting for Anna and Elliott to close on their house, but even I had gotten frustrated after the closing date was pushed back twice.

The sound of nails on concrete caught my attention. Weasel launched himself from my arms, paws digging into my sternum and tail thumping me in the nose. Molly galloped in, tongue hanging out and tail wagging. She made a beeline for our "garage sale special" red couch and dove into the corner, Weasel hopping up behind her in a fit of excited yips.

"Molly!" Jo called, exasperated.

"Jo?" I asked, noting the bags in her hands curiously.

"Is this a bad time?" She leaned her head back to watch Anna and Elliott struggle to force their boxes into the back seat of Anna's much-too-small car. A playful smile tugged at her lips, and she chewed her bottom lip in an attempt to hide it.

I smiled at her, my stomach fluttering as she entered. Nothing blew up when she leaned in for a hug . . . this time. I hoped my face wasn't as red as it felt.

Brittany shot me a look and wiggled her eyebrows. I rolled my eyes, trying to smother the smile threatening to crack my face and look serious. I failed.

Jo and Molly were regular fixtures in our apartment again; pizza and board games usually accompanied them.

I wasn't ready for what she wanted—what *we* wanted, though I hadn't admitted as much to her. Not yet. I'd be ready for that conversation one day.

I think she knew it was coming; I was scared shitless of digging through her mind to find out. Part of me felt guilty for making her wait, but if Jo was frustrated, she didn't show it.

My relationship with Jo wasn't the only thing changing. Brittany had moved in as Anna and Elliott struggled to become homeowners. No one had expected her to bounce back quickly after what she'd been through, and considering I could see every thought that passed through her mind, I was admittedly more protective of her than others were. Telepathy had its drawbacks sometimes, but if Brittany minded, she never mentioned it, and Jo didn't question why we exclusively spent time here.

"Wait!" Anna called from the parking lot, slamming the car door and rushing back to the apartment. "*Wait, wait, wait!* I want to see her face when she figures it out!"

"Figures what out?" I asked.

Anna breathlessly joined Jo in the doorway, Elliott on her heels carrying . . . presents?

"Surprise!" Brittany called from behind me. I turned to see a HAPPY BIRTHDAY banner and balloons filling the area around the dining room table.

"How did you—Brittany!" I laughed, fighting my smile from taking over more of my face. "My birthday is next week."

I was bewildered as Jo stepped inside, pulling a cake from the bag. Elliott handed me two wrapped boxes and stepped back through the doorway.

"It's today," Jo said, squeezing my arm as she walked by.

The rush I felt at her touch made my head spin.

A car door slammed in the parking lot, and a teenager rushed toward me.

"Did we miss it?" Lilly asked. "Was she surprised? Dad, come on!"

A brand-new minivan heaved as Mark exited the driver's seat, another ornately wrapped box in his possession.

"Did it work?" Lilly asked breathlessly, grinning as she nearly bumped into Anna.

"You planned a surprise party?" I asked, my face expressing shock.

Oh, I had known. I had known for a while, right down to Anna and Elliott's plan of coming by to collect their boxes when they needed to keep me home. I wasn't about to ruin their fun; I'd let them believe they'd pulled one over on the mind reader.

Granted, I really had thought my birthday was next week.

"Worth the back pain," Anna said, raising her hand for a high five.

Lilly slapped it, and Anna winced.

"Sorry," Lilly said, embarrassed. "Still getting used to that."

Mark dropped another present in my arms.

"Come in so I can let go of the door," I said, laughing, barely able to see over the top of the third box.

"I'll get the rest of those boxes for you," Mark offered, noting the beige moving boxes stacked outside Anna's former bedroom door.

Anna audibly exhaled. "Bless you. I'm going to be too sore to try on wedding dresses if I have to pick up another box."

I hoped my eyes didn't widen noticeably as I made a mental note to check my calendar. Thank you, telepathic powers, for ruining my surprise party. Thank, memory problems, for almost letting me forget my best friend's big day. The irony wasn't lost on me, and there was no way in hell the maid of honor was missing dress shopping.

Tables turned, I waddled across the living room with boxes of gifts, setting them down on the table next to the cake.

Wrapping an arm around me, Jo leaned in. "Were you really surprised?" she asked under her breath, her lips inches from my ear.

Blushing, I nodded. My face would never return to its normal color.

There was a knock at the door, and Anna looked at Mark and Lilly, confused.

"I thought you were the last ones?"

I might as well have flung myself across the room when Anna opened the door, revealing Christine and Ben. Christine shifted from foot to foot nervously. Ben held a comforting hand on her shoulder.

"Oh my God!" I exclaimed, wrapping my arms around Christine without hesitation. "When did you get back?"

She tensed against me, and I squeezed her tighter.

"We're fine," I whispered into her ear.

Christine relaxed into me, sighing in relief. "A few days ago." She smiled gratefully as we parted. "I think my parents were finally sick of me."

I laughed. "I'm sure that's not true."

Christine stepped inside, and Ben tried to sneak past. I snatched him and pulled him into a hug. He might not have been much of a hugger, but his arms lingered around me nonetheless.

"Have you heard anything?" I asked under my breath.

He let go. "No. Internal Affairs is taking its sweet time," he grumbled.

"Are we singing?" Lilly asked, drawing my attention toward the dining room table.

"Oh, we're singing," Anna said.

I groaned and hid my face behind my hands in childish protest. Jo pulled me forward and gave me a nudge.

I begrudgingly dropped my hands and rolled my eyes at them. "Fine," I pouted.

Brittany lit a candle, a wax number six sitting atop an obnoxious pink confection. The cake was drowning in sprinkles. Happy 6th Birthday, Hadley! was written across the top in white letters. Obviously, the cake was intended for a child, and for a moment, I stared at it, confused. Jo grinned as it dawned on me, clearly pleased with herself.

"Oh my God!" I laughed, getting the joke. It had been six years since my twenty-first birthday, the day my car had gone into the water and I'd woken up with no memories.

I blinked back tears as they sang. I leaned in and blew out the candle. It winked out in a rush.

Anna wrapped her arms around me. "Happy birthday."

Are you going to be okay? she asked in a way only I could hear.

I let go and surveyed the table.

Brittany cut the cake, handing slices to Lilly, who passed plates around our small party. Jo took hold of Molly's collar, holding her back as she licked her lips at the sight of the cake just within reach. Weasel stood on his hind legs, already begging Christine for the cake she'd just been served.

I smiled.

"More than okay," I replied. "Give me just a minute, okay?"

She nodded, and I walked to my bedroom.

The manila folder on my desk caught my attention.

"Shoot!" I muttered, closing my door behind me.

I rushed to the table, snatching the folder off the desk and checking behind me to make sure no one was coming. I opened a drawer, and the door creaked. I jumped, and sheets of paper slid out, scattering on the floor. I dropped to my knees and scrambled to scoop them up as Weasel rushed to my side, panting excitedly.

"Shh!" I hushed the dog. "You're going to get me in trouble."

I picked up the image of a brick building. Although the CCTV image was grainy and in black and white, The Library Lounge's neon sign was still obnoxious. I noted the blonde girl pushing the door open, glancing over her shoulder with a look of obvious distress. She was pulling her keys from her purse, unaware of the man in the parking lot standing in the shadows, his attention focused on her.

"What are you doing?" Brittany whispered at the door, and I flinched.

"I left it out!" I hissed.

There was a blast of wind, and Brittany stood in front of me with a stack of papers.

Julian Knight looked up at me as I tucked the images safely back inside the folder. Another man faced him, the unknown male's face hidden from the camera. I shoved the folder inside my desk and breathed a sigh of relief.

"Your girlfriend is going to kick both of our asses if she finds out what you've been up to."

"She's not my girlfriend, and I'm not doing anything with it."

Alyse N. Steves

"Yet," she said, shooting me a skeptical look.

I wasn't sure which comment that was intended for, but I meant it. I was leaving the past in the past. It was time to move forward.

"Come get your cake," Brittany said.

I nodded as she left the room. I leaned against the desk and took a steadying breath.

Across from me, nearly a dozen pictures were tucked into the edge of my dresser's mirror. I smiled at the picture of Damani, Brittany, and me, Damani grinning like a fool over that stupid crushed can.

Beside their picture was one of Madison and me in the Agency's cafeteria. She wrapped an arm around me, smiling wide at the camera while twenty-one-year-old Hadley gave an insecure grin. The bunny ears floating above my head were the only indication Navin had snuck into the shot. Another picture showed the entire team, Mark, Navin, Ben, Christine, and me flanking one side of the Agency's outdoor sign while Madison, Alice, Tom, and Glenn stood on the other. There was even a picture of Gladys, her disapproving face captured one night as Mark attempted to sneak a picture while I napped in a diner booth.

"Hadley!" Lilly called. She burst through the door in a sugar-fueled buzz. "Presents!"

I smiled as she darted away, my eyes lingering on the picture of Damani.

"You're right," I said softly. "It's going to be okay."

DID YOU ENJOY *THE DARKEST MEMORIES?*

Please consider leaving a review on Amazon or Goodreads.

Amazon

Goodreads

ABOUT THE AUTHOR

Born to a medium in a small town named after a planet, normalcy was never an option for Alyse. Once a feral homeschooled child living with eight dogs, six cats, a house-trained chicken, plus a handful of birds, rabbits, fish, and horses, Alyse grew up with a deep love of nature and animals that has led her on adventures across four countries, twenty-nine states, and a failed attempt at becoming a veterinarian (turns out, you aren't supposed to faint when administering a vaccine).

Now a somewhat domesticated adult, Alyse's sense of adventure and creativity has resulted in a science-fiction novel, *Child of Humanity*, a fantasy children's book, *Savannah the Kind*, and a superhero serial killer thriller, *The Darkest Memories*. Her books have been read in eleven countries and have been described as "an outstanding masterpiece," "thought-provoking," and "complex" by readers. For fun, she earned a PhD in Genetics and Molecular Biology.

A Southern transplant living in California, when Alyse isn't working as a toxicologist or writing, she enjoys hiking, dragging more plants into the backyard when her partner isn't looking, and looking up her nieces' and nephew's noses during FaceTime calls ("Can you give the phone back to Mommy, honey?"). She lives with her wonderfully supportive partner, part security system/part unhinged attack dinosaur packaged in a bird's body, and a toddler inhabiting the form of the fuzziest cat in existence.

Printed in Great Britain
by Amazon

44462136R00304